RENEGADE IMPERIUM: BOOK 1

GRAND THEFT PLANET

JON FRATER & A.K. DUBOFF

GRAND THEFT PLANET
Copyright © 2025 by A.K. DuBoff & Jon Frater

The Cadicle* Universe is a registered trademark of A.K. DuBoff

www.cadicle.com

Published by Epic Realms Press
Cover Copyright © 2024 Vivid Covers

ISBN-10: 1965614043
ISBN-13: 978-1965614044

0 9 8 7 6 5 4 3 2

Produced in the United States of America

TABLE OF CONTENTS

PROLOGUE

A GLASS SHATTERED against the bar's back wall, sending fragments clattering to the ground. Cheers erupted from the table in the rear right corner.

Garvin sighed. *Add it to the tab.* The group of four university-aged boys had already worked up a sizable bill with enough drinks and food to cover a party of ten.

People from all walks of life had passed through Garvin's cozy bar over the decades, giving him a keen eye for which patrons would be trouble. Somehow, he'd underestimated this lot. His humble bar was positioned along Star City's main thoroughfare between the landing bays and transport hub leading into the city proper, which made it a perfect place for a traveler to grab a quick drink before a flight or to wait for a friend to arrive. By the whoops and laughs coming from this group for the last two hours, Garvin had thought the youths must be celebrating something. However, there was also a sadness—or, perhaps, anger—in their eyes that he couldn't quite place. It made him uneasy.

"How much more of this are you going to take?" Marnie,

his waitress, asked as she walked by with a rag and dustpan to clean up the mess.

"I'll cut them off," Garvin assured her.

He didn't normally tolerate any kind of boisterousness, but business had been slow recently; he didn't want to turn away the opportunity to bank some significant credits at the rate their drinks were flowing. But, once things started getting broken, there was no choice.

"Stay with us, sweetheart!" one of the boys crooned, reaching for Marnie as she started to walk away with the dustpan full of glass.

She swiftly side-stepped his advance with the practiced grace of someone who'd dealt with far worse. "Not tonight, doll," she told him, flashing a sweet smile.

Her expression dropped the moment she turned away, instead staring daggers at Garvin. "You've got them for the rest of the night."

Garvin pulled up the group's bill on a handheld and stormed up to their table, still littered with glasses and dinner leftovers they'd refused to let them clear. "Gentlemen! Time to take the party outside."

One of the boys, tall and lanky with a smug curl to his lips, laughed so hard he nearly choked, dropping his glass on the table. A trickle of whiskey dribbled onto his friend, which made him laugh harder.

Garvin shoved the handheld in the boy's face, which sobered him some. "Pay up and be on your way."

"You have no idea who we are, do you?" another with dark hair and calculating eyes demanded.

"Not a clue. Celebrities in your own minds?"

"We're the Mesopotamians!" the four youths sang in unison, drunkenly slurring the words.

"Gah, that's an awful name for a band."

"It's a great name, old man—not that someone uncultured like you would ever understand," the laughing boy shot back. "One day, you'll look back and remember the time you met legends! I'm Sargon, that's Gilgamesh, Hammurabi, and Ashurbanipal."

"Those sound like diseases, son."

"Names from the old Earth languages don't roll off the tongue, it's true. We go by Sar, Gil, Ham, and Ash now," Sar said.

"Good for you." Garvin tried not to show his annoyance. He'd kicked enough people out of his bar to know that playing along with drunken ravings was the best way to get someone to cooperate. Anyone talking about the lost colony of Earth was clearly out of their mind.

"Last year, we were the French Revolution," added Ham, looking at Garvin as though he should know what that was.

Gil set his glass down, wincing. "Yeah, that wasn't such a good choice. I had to answer to 'Montesquieu' for six months."

"Year before that, we were the Ottomans." Ash swirled the remaining contents in his glass. "That might actually have been worse."

"It sounded cool at the time," Sar murmured.

Ham nodded. "Then we found out the Ottoman Empire had real problems. Allying with Germany against the British in the Great War was a terrible idea."

Garvin nudged the handheld with the bill. He was used to dealing with drunks, but a collective delusion on this scale was new. Though he was a little intrigued about what in the stars they were talking about, he'd still rather them get out of his bar before they broke anything else. "Sorry, boys, I'm not sure what you mean. But about your bill—"

Sar abruptly jumped to his feet and stared Garvin squarely in his eyes, utterly serious. "Babylon, Assyria, Sumer, Akkadia. That whole fertile crescent was vastly underappreciated despite giving rise to civilizations that invented essential developments in law, mathematics, agriculture, astronomy, and writing!"

Garvin took a step back to distance himself from the clearly deranged youth. He didn't have the patience to deal with them for any longer. "Those names mean nothing, boys. The only language I speak here is credits, and you racked up quite a tab tonight."

"There's so much to learn from extinct empires," Ash said. "You're missing out."

Garvin signaled to Marnie at the front of the bar, indicating for her to be ready to call the Enforcers if the situation escalated. "I think you all need a new hobby."

"We're history buffs. We prefer the old stuff," Sar insisted. "There's so much to learn from Earth, in particular. An isolated world, playing out history on a miniature scale. What takes centuries to unfold in the Taran Empire happens on Earth in decades."

Garvin crossed his arms. "Yeah. Fascinating."

"We're like kings," Gil said.

Ham held his dinner knife over his head, like a warrior victoriously raising his sword. "Like gods!"

"Well, gods, you still need to pay your bar tab. Come on, settle up or I'm calling the Enforcers. Your choice."

Sar let out an exasperated sigh as he grabbed the handheld displaying the bill. He punched in a code and then pressed his thumb to the screen for biometric verification. "You have your money, good sir. Give us a few minutes to get things settled, and then we'll be out of your hair. Yes?"

Garvin verified that the credit transfer was valid. "Keep

your voices down and your hands to yourselves, and you can take your time. But if I hear one more glass break, I'm calling the law."

— — —

Gil breathed more easily once the old man had retreated. They *had* gotten a little out of hand, admittedly, but getting booted from the Tararian Selective Service training program wasn't any old day. He wasn't sure if they were drinking their sorrows or celebrating their newfound freedom from a life of military service in the TSS, but the day marked a significant turning point in their lives.

It's not like their careers in the TSS would have amounted to anything, though. Ash and Gil were basic comm guys, while Sar and Ham had been on the diplomacy track. They'd all been Agent trainees in the low-level Trion class with unremarkable telekinetic potential and few prospects. But they had picked up some useful knowledge during their enlistment, and they'd met each other, so it wasn't all wasted time. Their expulsion had been swift and un-ceremonial after a brief 'we're disappointed that you chose ego over duty' lecture from the Lead Agent, and then they'd been dropped off here on a world at the crossroads to nowhere.

Gil had taken the TSS' parting words to behave or spend out the rest of their days in a prison colony as a challenge to test boundaries rather than a warning. Anger had been bubbling inside him for hours, which he'd been trying to numb with the booze. The more he reflected on it, he decided that the TSS was the problem, not him. *We're just too unique for the TSS!*

It was as simple as that. Tonight was definitely a

celebration, after all. They had a whole universe of possibilities before them. The only question was, where to go from here?

He realized the conversation had gotten away from him while he'd been reflecting.

Tuning back in, Ham was talking about aliens visiting Earth. "What kind of aliens would you find running a backwater like that, anyway?"

"*Ancient* aliens," Sargon said and laughed uproariously. The other three glanced furtively at each other. Sar didn't have much of a sense of humor, and what he did have was pretty strange.

"Should we get out of here?" Gil asked.

"There's something important to discuss first." Sargon put his handheld on the table and touched a button. Instantly, a holographic star map projected over the table. "I put some resources together before Lead Agent Sights gave us the boot. Behold… New Akkadia."

"Nice. Uh… what is it?" Ham asked.

"Officially, it's known as the Orion-Cygnus junction—a stretch of galactic space on the outskirts between Orino and Bashari that's far enough from anywhere important to not get much attention. There are twelve or so colonized planets that have been going through a rough time recently, with the Bakzen kicking the TSS' ass, and all."

They all nodded. Since the unexpected disclosure last year that the Bakzen were in open war with the Taran Empire—and winning—life had taken a bit of an anxious turn. Even the civilians knew something was up, but few had any idea how badly it could go, or how quickly.

"What are we going to do? Live there?" Gil asked.

"Fok no," Sargon said. "We're going to take it over."

Gil laughed to cover his surprise, and the others followed

his lead. Sargon waited for them to stop, then swiped to a new display. This one was a close-up of the same map, but it had specific worlds highlighted, with trade routes connecting them. A list of a dozen planet names, accompanied by a summary of useful facts about each target world, scrolled down the display.

"We've been saying it privately for over a year," Sar continued. "We know the TSS is the best organization equipped to run the galaxy, but it's beholden to the worst people imaginable."

"The High Dynasties," Ham groaned, a slight flush showing through his darker complexion. "Perfectly happy to keep the TSS supplied with anything they need, so long as there's a hefty profit involved, and they never do any fighting."

Gil winced. Lead Agent Cris Sights, despite his moniker within the TSS, was actually a Sietinen Dynasty heir. He had a clear conflict of interest between his duties to the TSS and High Dynasty, which everyone else in the TSS' leadership seemed keen to ignore. How could anyone with such divided loyalty be trusted?

"Power-hungry liars, all of them," Ash grumbled.

"You'd better believe it." Sar nodded. "The Dynasties are all about personal gain, willing to use or step on anyone to further their standing. There has to be a better way—a society where everyone is acknowledged for their contributions. Do you cretins have any convictions at all, or are you all talk like the perfect people? Unlike you gits, I've been thinking long and hard about how to do something that will make a real impact."

Gil raised an eyebrow. "Is that so?"

"I have it all planned out. Worlds rife for the taking, and a strategy to turn them into our own mini-Empire, answering to no one but ourselves."

Gil had always known Sargon to be a dreamer, but this was

a little much even for him. "Come on, Sar, let's—"

"No, hear me out." His friend changed the projection on his handheld to another holographic image with various data tables. "The plan isn't as crazy as you think. Here's how it would work…"

Sar laid out his long-term vision, fielding questions and offering research citations and facts when needed. After half an hour of intense questioning—without bother from the barkeeper, fortunately—they sat back in their chairs in contemplative silence. Sar really had thought through everything. The future he'd proposed offered new aspirations for them where none had existed. He'd ignited a spark that could very well be fanned into the flames of a revolution.

"It would be magnificent," Ash whispered. "If you could make it work—"

"It *will* work," Sar insisted. "Each of us will have our role. All we need is the fortitude to make it happen. I'm not saying it'd be easy or quick—this will take decades. But think of what we can build. What we can be."

"In charge of a dozen worlds. Bomax…" Ham breathed.

"How would we even get started?" Gil asked. "You make it sound like we'll just wander off into the galaxy and come back with planets on our backs."

"Certainly not," Sar said, sitting up straight in his chair. "I've put together a war chest to get us started. We'll all undertake specific missions based on our skillsets and backgrounds. But before we go any further, I need to know, are you in?"

Ham shrugged. "Sure, why not?"

"I am," Ash agreed.

"Gil?"

"I'm thinking." Sar's vision for a new society seemed

completely out of reach at present, but his plan did have the right kind of grandiose scale that resonated with Gil's ambition. They'd spent two years studying ancient civilizations and fantasizing about what they would have done differently, themselves, at each decision point. This was their chance to turn all that talk into action. He couldn't turn down the opportunity to do something important with his life. "All right," he told his friends, "it's got to be better than getting re-assigned to Jotun Division and their one-way death march."

"That's just a rumor, man," Ham insisted.

"Crews go into that division and they never come out. People getting fed into the meat grinder of the Bakzen conflict is not a *rumor*," Gil hissed.

"Be that as it may, are you in or out?" Sargon repeated.

"I'm in," Gil allowed, "but no half-assing anything. We have to do it right, and we need to make it work."

"Way ahead of you." Sar lifted a satchel to the table and began handing out small cases from inside.

Gil opened his, finding it contained a handheld, a bag of credit chips and a library of memory cards. The others' cases had identical items. "What is this?"

"Consider it your starter kit. I had everything made special," Sar explained.

"When did you arrange all of this? And where'd you get the money?" Gil asked. It'd been less than a day since they'd been cut free from the TSS. There was no way he'd gathered all of this in a matter of hours.

"Great leaders are always ready with a contingency plan." Sar flashed a coy grin. "Let's just say I hadn't liked the direction things were going for some time now, and I wanted a soft landing for us when we inevitably got the boot. And coming from a wealthy family does have its perks."

Ham chuckled. "You devious bastard." He inspected the handheld from his kit; it looked like any other standard personal communication device. "Why these?"

"These handhelds are shielded from scanners and will only connect to each other—like they are now when we're on the same local network. The biometrics will be coded only to you."

"Why?" Ash asked.

"Privacy, Ash. If you want to keep a secret, this is how you keep it. Use the local memory instead of the wireless network and no one will ever be able to steal your data. Anything related to the mission stays on here and nowhere else." He turned to Gil. "Listen up. You have *two* jobs—shows how much faith I have in you."

"Oh, you honor me, Great Sargon," Gil said sarcastically and with a mock bow in his seat. Despite his initial excitement, the reality of the situation was setting in. He was starting to have doubts that they'd be able to pull off the bold plan.

Sar handed two data chips to Gil and lowered his voice. "Gil, how do you feel about enrolling in a university?"

Gil grimaced. "One failed academic career is all I can handle, thanks."

"This time, you'll kick ass," Sar declared. "Greengard, a sophisticated planet with a public transportation hub that's to die for. The capital, Foundation City, is basically one huge university. They have schools for every program—science, medicine, math, business, history, and a hundred others. Once you're established there, your mission is to make nice with the folks who run the shipyard on Tavden and the mining outfit on Diphous."

Gil had to look up both names with his non-secret handheld. He raised an eyebrow at the search results. "Mining? That's TalEx corporate territory. I've traveled in some fancy circles, but the Talsari Dynasty is way out of my league." Really, *any* of the six High Dynasties were out of anyone's league who wasn't already entrenched in those circles. The Sietinen heir may have decided to live with commoners by joining the TSS, but the other High Dynasty elites were in their own echelon.

"Don't mistake their wealth and status for them being more than any other mortal. They still need things, just like the rest of us," Sar said. "Food, clothing, gadgets, transport, entertainment. Who do you think gets those things for them? Prove you can be useful. Indispensable. Get in close and see how they operate. Take notes. It'll be a long game, but once you're in, we can work the angle to our advantage." He slowly twirled one of the empty glasses on the table. "Next up is Ham."

Ham set down his drink. "Yes, my king?"

"You have a job to do back home."

"What home? I haven't been back to Valdos in years."

Sar leaned in. "Time to visit your old stomping grounds. There aren't many other places like it to have openly defied the Priesthood's decree against using our Gifts. Find a teacher. Find all of us teachers. We'll need to improve our telekinetic and telepathy skills to become proficient. Build us a base of operations that can link to the networks the rest of us will create. Keep it secret. Keep it safe!"

Ham sucked in a breath and let it out slowly. "All right, I'll do my best."

"That's my boy. Ash? You're going to love your assignment."

"Then tell me already."

The data chip that Sar slid to him actually seemed to glow neon green in the dim light of the bar. "How do you feel about sinking your teeth into the Dark Net… and making it do your bidding?"

"Very funny. What do you have, really?"

Sar crossed his arms and leaned back in his chair, the light bouncing off his eyes with a lurid glow. "The galaxy runs on people who need things. Sometimes, those things are hard to get in convenience shops. We're going to need weird stuff. Parts, weapons, energy sources. People who can get things done. Starships—"

"*Starships*?" Ash cut in. "What am I, a construction yard?"

Sar continued, staring at him with dead seriousness. "You will put together a brokerage outfit that we can use to move rare items all over the sector without being traced or tracked. And you will never get caught because you're just that good. Right?"

"I guess so," Ash sighed, taking the chip. His tech-intensive youth made him the perfect person to build a persona on the Dark Net, but he'd also made it clear that he detested the kinds of people who ran their businesses in the shadows. However, Gil knew that whenever Ash committed to something, he wouldn't let personal feelings get in the way of the mission. They had that in common. "If I get caught, there won't be a sling big enough to hold all our asses," Ash added. "I'm not doing a life sentence on a penal planet for you jokers. Mark my words."

"Take your usual amount of care, do your homework, and you'll be living in a palace in no time," Sar said. "I wouldn't trust anyone else with this. It's that important. You are the guy to make it work."

Ash sat for a moment, sliding the data chip between his fingers. "I think I'll start with an online lottery. People love the chance to put down ten credits for the chance to make fifty without lifting a finger."

"See? You'll be brilliant."

"And which sweet project did you keep for yourself?" Gil asked.

Sar tapped his own handheld. "I will be pulling all the threads you boys send out into a complex and intricate web of services, businesses, and trading routes. We'll need Enforcers on our side, ships, security, and people who can be trusted to stay bought. That will be my territory." He leaned forward and lowered his voice. "Now, this is important: do not contact each other directly, ever. Not until we establish a foolproof secure comm network. We'll meet back here every few months, depending on our needs, so we can review our respective progress in person. Sound good?"

It did. There were details to iron out, but the stage was set. They had assignments, credit chips, and missions to fulfill. And, most importantly, no TSS know-it-alls to breathe down their necks. The galaxy was their playground, and they intended to play hard.

PART 1

A GRAND PLAN

1

TRIUMPH

FIRST OFFICER KARMEN Sley held her cards close to her face to hide a smile. She was terrible at bluffing, and her current Fastara hand was too good to conceal.

Across the table, her longtime friend and ship's captain, Agent Auriela Thand, threw her cards down with a huff. "Stars, Karmen! Again?"

The two other players groaned.

"What?" Karmen asked innocently.

"It doesn't take a telepath to know you're sitting on riches," Bertie, the ship's galley master, said from the seat on her left, eliciting a nod of agreement from helm officer Bensen.

The helmsman nodded as he tossed his cards down. "He's, right, Karmen. A big wide grin when you look at your hand is not the definition of subtlety."

"Are you sure you're just not latent telepaths, boys?" Karmen asked.

"There will be no mind-reading as long as I'm at the table,"

Captain Thand stated. Such a task would be easy with her Gifted abilities and advanced training as an Agent in the Tararian Selective Service, but Karmen knew she'd never violate the code of conduct—game or not.

Karmen shrugged, trying to hold back a smug smile. "Sorry, I can't seem to help winning."

Their latest TSS deployment had been particularly dull, and the nightly games of Fastara helped pass the time. Generations of spacefarers had wiled away hours in the void with the game. This particular deck's well-worn cards told stories of the ship's past crew sharing the tradition during their own deployments.

It'd been the best night of Fastara she'd had in years. There was a fair amount of skill to the game, but luck was always a factor with cards. The house rules they played with on the TSS *Triumph* favored long-term strategy, but there was no denying she'd been dealt good hands all night. Sometimes, everything in the universe aligned.

"I surrender," Bertie said, pushing back from the table. "Karmen takes the night."

"No sense fighting it," Bensen agreed. The helm officer had a bit of a superstitious streak and often commented on momentum in their card games like it was some kind of pre-ordained destiny.

"Hey, we're just getting started!" Karmen protested.

"We probably should hit the rack," Thand said. "We have to prep for our rendezvous with *Charity* bright and early."

The captain was right about that, and most of the responsibilities would fall to Karmen. Ship-to-ship cargo transfers were tricky work, especially for a ship usually tasked with 'observe and report' projects. Why they'd been relegated to ferrying supplies was beyond her, but she knew better than to question official TSS orders. Command had their reasons for everything.

The group said their good nights and parted ways from the conference room that doubled as their gaming space. Bertie and Bensen headed aft, while Karmen and Thand made their way toward the senior officers' quarters in the opposite direction.

"I can't believe you've survived for this long as an officer without learning to bluff," Thand commented as they walked.

Karmen shrugged. "Being honest with our team has always been more important."

"There are plenty of things we can't talk about straight."

"Militia work isn't the same as what you do. We're not nearly as mysterious."

Thand laughed. "I don't understand the mystique around Agents. We're still just people."

"People who can control things with your mind. To a non-Gifted person like me, that's pretty incredible."

Ahead of them in the corridor, two of the low-level Militia specialists were huddled together, speaking urgently. As they got closer, Karmen realized that the young man was consoling his female colleague.

Karmen made a point of staying out of mundane interpersonal dynamics among the crew—some drama was expected among any group living in close quarters for an extended time—but it entered her domain the moment someone was tearing up in a central corridor. Such behavior was wholly unprofessional, but she wanted to know more before jumping to a reprimand.

"Everything all right?" she asked, though clearly it wasn't.

The young woman hurriedly composed herself. "Everything is fine, ma'am."

"You're an even worse liar than Karmen. What has you so

upset?" Thand pressed.

"I got news from a friend. Caught me off-guard," the specialist confessed.

"What kind of news?"

"Deployment orders. He's been reassigned to the Jotun Division."

Karmen's heart dropped. The Jotun Division was code for the frontlines of the Bakzen War. For years, the TSS had kept the truth about the conflict a secret, cloaked in codenames and carefully segmented operations. A year ago, the entire TSS had learned the truth: they'd been at war for centuries, the conflict hidden inside a dimensional rift. But the fighting had recently been encroaching on the Outer Colonies of the Taran Empire, and it was only a matter of time before everyone knew about the conflict. For now, though, the only truth that mattered was that the TSS was the single defensive force holding back the enemy.

"That particular assignment is not an easy weight to bear," Karmen said. "But those folks are holding the line between the galaxy and destruction. You understand?"

The two young soldiers nodded grimly.

"What happens on this ship is all that matters," Thand added. "We've got a big day tomorrow. Rest up."

"Yes, ma'am!" They saluted and hurried away.

"This war is nasty business," Thand murmured as soon as they were beyond earshot.

Karmen smoothed the front of her gray uniform. "I don't blame her for worrying about her friend. She's the third one who's heard news like that in the past four months. I'm running out of platitudes. If TSS Command has a big end game in mind, I wish they'd implement it and end this bloody war already."

"That's above both our pay grades. I meant what I said about our ship. We can't worry about others."

"I know."

Thand's handheld chirped. Nearly all communications were routed through the ship's comm system, so it was odd that anything was going to the Agent's personal communication device. That meant it was something sensitive enough to be for the captain only.

Karmen looked expectantly at her friend, hoping to get a hint about the news.

Instead, Thand paled as she read whatever was on the screen. "I have to go."

"Hey, what—"

"We'll talk later." Thand practically jogged down the corridor.

Karmen watched her go, an uneasy knot in her stomach. *What was that about?*

—   —   —

Thand sat in her cabin on the TSS *Triumph*, her heart heavy as she re-read the official communique on her handheld.

>>From: Jason Banks, High Commander
To: Agent Aurelia Thand, Sacon Division
Complete supply transfer with TSS *Charity* ASAP. After delivery, report immediately to H2 for re-assignment of *Triumph* and all hands to Jotun Division.<<

And just like that, she, her ship, and all its crew were dead. They'd soon reach the rendezvous point, where the

Triumph would transfer a load of medical supplies destined for a colony world the *Charity* was patrolling. It wouldn't be long before the life she knew would be over. No more diplomatic or aid missions. Her ship was heading to the front lines of a brutal war where most never came back home.

For the last year, the war had seemed far away. She was in command of a scout ship. They had weapons and shields, of course, but nothing about the craft was designed for serious combat. Death wasn't guaranteed, of course, but the *Triumph* wouldn't make a dent against enemy forces. If they were being sent into battle, it was because the TSS was desperate for bodies to fill out the field. Just the latest sacrificial offering in a war with no end in sight.

She threw her handheld across the cabin. It bounced against the far wall and dropped to the deck, unscathed. She groaned, knowing that taking out her anger on the device wouldn't change the orders. No power in the universe could alter her crew's fate.

Thand called on every bit of her training as an Agent to try to remain objective. *We have a job to complete. A duty. The TSS is counting on us.*

The words were hollow in her mind. They couldn't put up a fight against the enemy, so what was the point? Why did they all have to die for a war where no one even knew what they were fighting about?

Her hands balled into fists. She'd been so bomaxed stoic about this very assignment in front of the crew. *This isn't right! How am I supposed to tell my crew to wrap up their affairs and pray for an easy death?*

ENTER ENKIDU

GIL HAD NEVER known real freedom before. He'd been a son, a student, a would-be soldier. But now he was his own man with a new name, forging his own destiny with more credits in his possession than he'd dreamed of amassing in a lifetime.

After partying with his friends the previous night, he'd grabbed a room at one of the hotels near the bar to sleep off his overindulgence. Feeling refreshed and inspired in the new day, he was taking the scenic route to the spaceport while planning his next move.

He'd never actually taken the time to walk around a major starship port before. It was huge—a city in space. He wondered how such things were planned and designed, then built, and decided that the subject would be his first major field of study after matriculation. But first, he had to get off-world.

After studying the transportation lines and schedules, Gil realized if he left right now, it would take at least a month to reach Greengard. *A whole month. With a TSS transport ship, it would only take a few hours.*

For the first time since his expulsion from the academy, he wished that he still had those TSS connections. The jump drives used by the TSS and other military forces didn't require the same cool-down period as civilian models, and their navigation systems could also lock on to subspace nav beacons at longer intervals. The combination cut travel time by a factor of thirty. But Gil would need to travel the old-fashioned way, hopping ships from port to port, staying a day or two at each one. If only he'd applied himself more and stayed in the TSS, he could have been the one able to cross the galaxy in a day.

He caught himself. *No! This is the right path. Stick to the mission.* Sar's vision offered them a route to success. That was what had gotten Gil's attention in the first place. He intended to see it through.

However, trying to figure out how best to reach his destination was giving him a headache. Eventually, he gave up attempting to plot it out on his own and made his way to a young female clerk who was running a travel desk.

Gil put on his best diplomacy face as he approached the kiosk. "Hi. Where can I charter a ship?"

The clerk greeted him with a cheerful smile. "Local or interstellar?"

"Long-range."

"I'd be happy to make those arrangements." She looked at her console. "Let's see, for an interstellar charter, would late next week work for you?"

"You don't have anything sooner?"

"I'm sorry, we're fully booked for the next nine days."

Gil placed a ten-credit chip on the counter. "Are you sure?"

The girl blinked, scooped the chip up, and said, "Let me talk to the owner."

All right! Now he was getting somewhere. After a moment, a silver-haired man came out. "I hear you want a charter?"

"Correct. I'm interested in getting to a particular outer colony as soon as possible. Can you help?"

"Well, we're booked solid for the next couple of weeks, and I won't put my reputation on the line by breaking an existing engagement. No amount of money will change that. Best I can offer is to put you in touch with someone who could sell you a ship. Interested?"

Gil's eyes popped wide. He had to force himself to hold in his excitement. "I am." He'd had enough flight training in the TSS to get by, but whether or not he could afford a ship that could get him where he needed to go would remain to be seen. *It's not real until you're sailing through the black.*

The owner smiled amiably when Gil dropped a twenty-credit chip onto the counter to prove he was sincere. "Go to Docking Bay 93, Section 2. The man you want is Jel Gorman." He twirled the credit chip between his fingers. "Between us, Jel can be… difficult. You'll want to inspect everything before you pay."

Gil nodded. "Thank you for the tip."

"Good luck."

—

Docking Bay 93 was a grubby, ill-used storage hangar where every surface had a patina of grime. Jel Gorman was no better—exuding the slick confidence of someone who cared about making a quick buck rather than running a quality business. Why in the stars a businessman who valued his reputation would be connected with someone so smarmy was beyond Gil's understanding.

"I'd like to actually make it to my destination alive," Gil said after hearing Jel's sales pitch for a fifth ship that should have been sold for scrap or the barest kind of salvage. He was beginning to wonder if he could go back to the charter desk and demand his bribe credits back.

"Ah, they might look rough around the edges, but they still fly just fine!" Jel insisted.

Gil raised his eyebrow at an obvious hole in the side of a transport ship as they strolled through the rows of rust-bucket vessels.

"*Most* of them are space-worthy, anyway," Jel amended.

Gil was about ready to give up and go find a cabin on a civilian passenger vessel when they passed near a small transport ship. It looked industrial—a roughly thirty-meter-long flattened cylinder with a sloped nose—but its compact design appealed to him. It was also one of the best-looking possibilities in the hangar. "How about this one?" Gil asked.

Jel sniffed. "You don't want that one."

"Why not?"

"It was an old experimental design created by someone who put travel speed over safety."

Sounds like my kind of person. Gil kept his expression neutral, not wanting to appear overly eager. "What's the issue with it? Sounds convenient."

"Sure, if you think cascade failures are convenient. They integrated a bunch of systems that are normally kept separate for a reason. Honestly, I haven't been able to sell the thing, so I was planning to break it down for parts."

"Does it still fly?"

"Sure, so long as it doesn't get overheated. It has an automated self-repair system that keeps it running, which is necessary because of the integrated components."

"Does that overheating issue extend to the jump drive?"

Jel smiled. "Actually, that was one of the experimental features. It has a sort of 'quick-cool' for the jump drive—which works great, provided there's no one around to see it vent after a jump." He leaned in. "It, uh, doesn't exactly meet regulations, if you know what I mean."

"And that quick-cool is an optional feature, so you can avoid using it when near a port?" Gil asked.

"Yes, it's manual." Jel crossed his arms, sizing Gil up. "Are you really interested in this thing?"

"If it can get me to my destination faster than conventional ships, then yes."

Jel let out a long breath through pursed lips. "I know how some of these other ships look, but I wouldn't sell you anything that I believed was going to leave you stranded. Honestly, I don't totally trust this one."

All right, maybe he's not as sleazy as I thought. Gil examined the vessel, still drawn to its unique design. He could deal with some defects if the vessel came at the right price. "Sounds like its issues are manageable with a responsible pilot."

"Yes, but I should warn you that part of the ship's speediness comes from the nav system bypassing safeguards, which allows you to skip beacons. Paired with the quick-cool for the jump drive, it can cut transit time in half. But it's all dangerous and illegal. I mean, with those hacks, you might even jump into subspace without having a lock on an exit beacon. Floating endlessly in subspace sounds like a terrible way to go. In all fairness, this ship should probably be condemned."

Fast and illegal? It's perfect! "Keep talking, Mr. Gorman."

Jel shrugged and forged on. "Aside from all the issues I've

listed, it's well-built. The hull is solid as a rock, and it's got a fully equipped medical bay. Truth be told, I never should have taken it as a trade. It's just been taking up space in here for months, so if you want to take this baby off my hands, I'll make you a good deal."

Foking right you will, old man. I can read you like a map. "Can I take a look inside?"

"Sure." Jel waved his handheld over a control panel by the airlock. The hatch opened with a clank.

Inside, the flight deck was compact but not cramped. Gil spent some time testing the controls and comparing it to the knowledge he'd gathered about TSS ships during his short time at Headquarters. The primary console seemed functional, though it wasn't without blemishes, and the seats were comfortable. Down the central corridor, four narrow but proper staterooms sat between a passenger lounge and the engineering deck. The medical bay turned out to be a self-contained medpod installed in a fifth cabin, separated from the rest of the room by a privacy curtain. Gil recognized some basic medical gear in the room, as well. The aft of the ship included a small cargo area with a rear door that could drop down into a ramp for loading and unloading. It seemed legit.

"How much do you want for it?" Gil asked once he'd completed the tour.

Jel hesitated then said, "Eighty thousand should do it."

That's an insane price for something that can't pass a basic safety inspection, but it's the cheapest price he's quoted me. Still, Gil was on a budget, and he recognized that Jel genuinely wanted this ship gone. "I'm sure it would. I'll give you fifty."

"Gah, you're killing me. Make it seventy, and I'll take care of the paperwork to get you out of here today. I'll even throw in some supplies for the ship's locker."

"Sixty, with everything you just mentioned."

"You really think I'm that dense?" Jel sighed. "Fine. Sixty thousand. Let's get you out of here before the humiliation makes me cry. You want to register a name for the ship?"

"*Enkidu*. His name is *Enkidu*," Gil said. The name was the traveling companion of Gilgamesh, his namesake. He could think of no better name to capture the spirit of the journey he was about to undertake.

They took care of the administrative details and stocked the sundries, and then Jel handed Gil the codes to unlock the security system. "Have a good trip. Hopefully, the ship won't kill you and everyone around you."

Gil laughed out loud. This old man was one to hold a grudge. Maybe he should have offered sixty-five. "If I survive, I'll send my friends back to buy ships of their own."

"You do that. Good luck!"

Gil boarded and settled in. *I have a ship. I can go anywhere, any time I want.*

He stowed his gear in the ship's locker and went through the process of setting his instruments. *Enkidu* purred as Gil engaged the drives and rode it into orbit. Once in space, he plotted his first subspace jump.

Gil smiled as he confirmed the lock with the first nav beacon. *I'm on my way!*

3

COLLISION

KARMEN STRODE DOWN the main passage of the TSS cruiser *Triumph*. None of the crew would meet her eyes as she passed.

The level of tension on the ship had multiplied exponentially throughout the day, and she had no idea how to alleviate it. Well, there was *one* way, but it wasn't entirely up to Karmen. Captain Thand's demeanor had completely changed since receiving the private communique last night. Normally a disciplined but gregarious person, she'd become avoidant and terse. There'd also been several unusual commands given to the crew first thing in the morning, and everyone was on edge. There wouldn't be any relief to the collective anxiety until Thand explained what, exactly, was going on. If anyone was in a position to get the captain to open up, it was Karmen as the second-in-command.

Fortunately, Karmen knew the captain well. She wound her way to the galley, finding Bertie prepping for the evening meal. "Bertie! No hard feelings about the game last night?"

He smiled amiably. "Of course not."

"Good. Where do you keep the ice cream?"

"You know ice cream is only for special occasions."

"Come on, Bertie. Thand has clammed up, and I need to pry her shell open before we get to the rendezvous with *Charity*. Brownies won't do it today."

He sighed. "If it's for the captain, all right. But you'd better not let anyone else catch wind, or I'll have a line of people here that I'll send straight to you."

Karmen smiled. "Our secret, I promise. Can you whip up some of that Rum Raisin?"

— — —

Gil bolted upright in the pilot's seat. He'd been enjoying the ethereal blue-green lights of subspace for the last hour, but the flight deck had illuminated with red warning lights and a blaring alarm.

What in the stars happened? He frantically looked over the still unfamiliar panels and displays to identify what was wrong. There were no less than six alerts, all marked 'critical'.

Gil hit the emergency jump sequence abort on the nav console, hoping he'd set his manual beacon locks correctly. He breathed a sigh of relief as the fog of subspace dissipated and he was once again surrounded by the inky blackness of deep space peppered with countless pinpoints of light.

The panels around the flight deck hissed and popped with burning circuits. Sparks flew across him.

Shite!

Shielding his eyes with one hand, he groped under his seat for the fire extinguisher. He found it, wasting no time to foam the entire control section. Smoke and chemical spray filled the cabin.

Coughing, he fell sideways out of his seat and crab-walked back. The alarms finally cut out.

Gil fanned the remaining smoke and fumes away from his face as the air scrubbers kicked into overdrive. Crouched on the floor staring at the disaster zone that used to be his flight deck, he wondered how big a mistake he'd made by paying sixty thousand credits to Jel Gorman.

Let's find out how screwed I am. He brought up a status report on the primary display.

The diagnostics didn't reveal a total disaster, but it wasn't great. On the positive side, his life support environment was secure, so he wasn't about to freeze to death or asphyxiate. But the integrated systems... Jel had been accurate in his warnings. Who expected *that*? It turned out that when one unit experienced an issue, the entire network went out. So, there'd been a minor issue with a sensor array that had set off this particular cascade failure, which had subsequently disabled everything related to external monitoring and communications. As promised, though, the self-repair system was already engaged and seemed to be working.

However, in the meantime, the sensors and comms were down for service—including his ship's emergency beacon. Gil shook his head with disbelief. While he was all for taking shortcuts, that was downright reckless. He added it to the mental list of modifications he'd need to make to the ship as soon as time and financial resources allowed. While he could deal with *quirks*, he had no interest in the ship becoming his tomb.

What kind of insane person designs a ship that disables the emergency beacon during sensor repairs? The only saving grace was he was in the middle of nowhere, so there was little likelihood of coming across another ship.

Beyond the other issues, the jump drive was also displaying an error. Upon further inspection, he discovered that it was actually a warning that it was too hot to proceed.

There should be something to take care of that... He searched through the controls to look for the 'quick-cool' feature Jel had told him about.

After a little digging, he found something marked as 'AUTO-PURGE' in the commands. Nothing else had seemed remotely close to the functionality Jel had described, so Gil selected it to see if there was more information.

"Auto-purge will result in reset of the jump system. Proceed?" the computer asked.

"Will that vent the heat to cool the drive?" Gil questioned.

"Affirmative."

Gil didn't know enough technical details about how jump drives operated to know what, exactly, would be purged in the process. But he was far enough from any transit route where the authorities might see the illegal system and cite him for violating whatever codes, so this seemed like as good a place as any to check out the feature. "Proceed," he confirmed.

The display screen flashed with a series of process confirmations. It settled on a schematic of the jump drive with an animation of a nearby chamber opening and venting. The heat warnings next to the jump system cleared on the display, and the system status changed to 'Ready'.

"Well, that was easy." Gil muttered to himself. Now, all he needed was for the communication system repairs to finish and he could be on his way.

He settled in to wait it out, just one man alone in the expanse.

— — —

Thand had kept the *Triumph*'s new orders to herself, and it was eating her up inside. She'd been holed up in her cabin ever since, except for a few perfunctory walks to other departments. Her first officer could handle everything else; Karmen Sley was the best right hand a captain could hope for, so at least she'd have a great person by her side in battle.

Her heart wrenched. *Stars, I need to tell Karmen before the rest of the crew.* She just needed to figure out how to broach the subject. It wasn't every day a crew was issued the equivalent of a death sentence.

The door chime pulled her out of her funk.

Thand straightened her uniform and composed her face. "Come in."

Tall and slender, Karmen stood framed in the doorway with her halo of curly hair barely contained in a ponytail, holding a small tub of ice cream in one hand and spoons in the other. "Can we talk?"

Stars, I love this woman. "Get in here!"

Karmen stepped inside and closed the door. She held the ice cream and spoons close to her chest. "You only get this if you promise to be honest with me, Aura."

"I don't suppose you have a bottle of whiskey, too?"

Her friend raised an eyebrow; drinking while on assignment went against everything in the standard TSS code of conduct. "That bad?" She immediately popped open the ice cream and handed over a spoon.

The two women sat down on the couch side-by-side. Thand took a hearty spoonful, savoring the sweet, cold treat. "I needed this." She extended her spoon for more.

Karmen blocked her. "Talk to me."

Thand's shoulders rounded. "Karmen, things are about to—"

The comm chirped for attention. "Navigation to Agent Thand."

'Sorry,' she mouthed to Karmen. "Thand here."

"Captain, we're five minutes from the rendezvous with *Charity*."

"All right, I'll be there soon." The commlink disconnected.

Thand returned her attention to her first officer. They'd served together for two years aboard *Triumph*, and Karmen was the best friend she had. As selfish as it was, she was grateful they'd be heading to the Jotun Division together. But of all the ways their careers could have gone, this wasn't a path she'd choose. "Do you ever regret joining the TSS?"

Karmen dug into the tub with her own spoon. "It's better than a lot of other things. I don't regret accepting this post, if that's what you mean. Is it?"

Thand shook her head. "No, just thinking about all those little decision points in life leading us to where we are."

"Oh boy." Karmen passed her the ice cream container.

Thand dug back in. "I got involved with a Junior Agent in the cohort ahead of mine while we were training at Headquarters. I really thought I was in love with him, but after a few months, he turned into a sandbag. Clingy, controlling. I think it was his first real romance, and he tried to treat it like an academic assignment. Eventually, I had to make a choice for my own path... and it wasn't him. A week later, he told me I'd wasted his time and to not bother staying in touch after he returned from his internship. I felt guilty for months. I'm still not sure why."

Karmen harrumphed. "He wouldn't be the first Agent trainee who thought the universe revolved around him." She stole another spoonful of ice cream.

"We never promised anything serious. And it's not like

most Agents have long-term relationships. Some people may think it looks glitzy from the outside, but this is a life of service that extends beyond us. It's not in the job description to be selfish."

"Which is precisely why what happened back then was a 'him' problem and no reflection on you," Karmen pointed out as they continued to pass the dessert back and forth. "Sounds like he had his work cut out for him to pass his internship if he was still that emotionally volatile as a Junior Agent. Not every relationship is meant to last."

"I hope our friendship will."

"Are you kidding? You're stuck with me to the end—though it'd be nice to get to boss *you* around sometime." She smiled playfully at the joke.

In the official TSS chain of command, there was no scenario when Karmen, as a Militia officer, would ever outrank Thand as an Agent, but that didn't make her friend's counsel any less valuable. Thand smiled back, despite her heavy heart. "You definitely deserve your own command."

"Is that what has you so bent out of shape? Did one of us get reassigned?"

"Not exactly—"

Time elongated and then snapped back as *Triumph* transitioned from subspace to normal space. For a moment, everything was still and quiet as the peaceful starscape filled the viewport. Then, a tremor rumbled through the deck, followed by a violent jolt that nearly tossed Thand from the couch. The deep rumble of a distant explosion vibrated through the ship's superstructure.

Thand's heart leaped into her throat. "What the fok?"

The lights in the cabin flickered and died, then came back on at emergency power half-brightness.

"That's not good," Karmen jumped to her feet.

Thand was right behind her, racing for the door. "CACI, call Command Center." The computer chirped that a commlink was open. "This is the captain. Status report?"

"The pion drive exploded!" her Navigator, Bensen, replied.

Thand's stomach twisted in a knot. Anti-matter pion drives didn't simply *explode* for no reason. "How is that possible?"

"We're trying to figure out what happened. No other vessels are showing up in the vicinity. But the immediate concern is that we have a giant hole in the back of our ship, and we're running on backup batteries. We have zero propulsion, and—"

"I'm on my way. Ship-wide alert. Plug those holes!" She ended the commlink.

In a flash, Thand realized the world was a different place. A potential future death in war was no longer her greatest concern. *We might all die here and now. But not if I can help it.*

"I'll go to Engineering—or see what's left of it," Karmen said.

"Be careful!"

The two women headed in opposite directions. Thand raced down the hall toward the Command Center positioned in the heart of the ship. Bangs reverberated through the walls; she wondered just how much of her ship's structural integrity had been compromised.

Entering the Command Center, she was greeted by the horrific sight of damage reports flashing across the front viewscreen. Alarms blared.

"Kill the audible alarms," she demanded.

Bensen immediately waved her over to his Navigator station as the alarms silenced. "We finally got some clean scan data. It appears when we dropped out of subspace, the anti-matter reactor went through its standard cycle to gather space dust for processing. But it sucked up some kind of exotic particles—no clue what or how they got there—but the moment they hit the reaction chamber, it blew the pion drive and rest of the system. Took out the PEM in the process."

Thand gripped the edges of her black overcoat to keep her hands from curling into fists. *Foking pirates!* There'd been complaints circling on the official channels about illegal jump drives dumping supercharged waste material into normal space that should only ever be vented in subspace. So far, none of those claims had been substantiated, but this might be hard evidence gathered in the worst way possible.

"Can we salvage anything?" she asked, already knowing the grim answer.

Bensen shook his head. "Everything is just... gone." He levelly met her gaze. "Ma'am, the bottom line is we have no propulsion and power reserves are failing. The ship is effectively dead. I don't know how long it's going to hold together."

Thand processed the information in a split second. The ship had all kinds of safeguards, but every system had its limit. Losing all propulsion as well as the Perpetual Energy Module—the main power core—would make for a critical failure in any vessel. "Do we have subspace comms?"

"No, not without the PEM. But *Charity* should still be en route for our rendezvous."

Thand nodded as another disastrous round of reports lit up the viewscreen. "Launch our emergency beacon. Abandon ship!"

The evacuation alarm sounded in confirmation to her order. Now, the only thing that mattered was getting her crew to safety. If that meant she'd go down with her ship, at least that would mean they couldn't send her to Bakzen space. It was looking like her first command would be her last.

Thand threw herself into action, racing through the ship. She yelled forcefully as she encountered her crew members, "We're abandoning ship. Everyone into the escape pods. That's an order. Go!" She shoved people into the self-contained life pods at intervals along the outer bulkheads. Once sealed, automated machinery sent the tiny life pods on their way. *Charity* would find them.

By the time Thand had looped back to the Command Center, the emergency display showed that the ship had been evacuated. Only she remained. She stared into the corridor outside at a life pod that had been set aside for her. An escape to safety.

Or I could just die here. It would save her the trouble of following the orders that would only prolong her death. For a long moment, she wondered what death was like…

But her will to live won out. With a growled curse, she ran to the pod.

As the lid closed over her, the pod prematurely ejected from the ship. Not yet strapped in, she was thrown against the back wall. The pod changed directions, tossing her again to a side wall and then the ceiling before she crashed down again. She reflexively squeezed her eyes closed as shrapnel pocked the pod's canopy. Interior electronics sparked, searing her skin.

Half-blinded, she managed to drag herself to the cradle in the center of the pod. With bloodied, shaking hands, she strapped in.

She barely registered the pain of the burns through her shock as she got her first look at the *Triumph* out the pod's small porthole. The back quarter of the ship was gone. And along with it, an unknown number of her friends and colleagues who'd been killed before ever making it to a pod.

Karmen, did you make it out? Her heart lurched.

Alarms flashed as the pod sped away from the crippled ship. The warnings indicated an air leak, power levels were dropping, and there was a thruster malfunction. Worse, her rescue beacon wasn't active. She'd never last long enough for *Charity* to pick her up.

Well, I did my best. Resigned to her fate, Aurelia Thand was ready to die.

UNEXPECTED ALLIANCE

GIL GAPED AT the horrific scene unfolding on his viewscreen.

A sleek starship—unmistakably a TSS design, with a silvery iridescent hull and ten times the length of *Enkidu*—had dropped out of subspace and promptly exploded. The shockwave had hurled *Enkidu* several kilometers away. The once magnificent TSS vessel was now in shambles, with jets venting in multiple sections as the ship listed like a spinning top slowly losing its equilibrium.

How did I survive that? It was the universe's own luck that his ship had been hurled away instead of caught up in the explosion. The ship had practically dropped out of subspace right on top of him, which never would have been possible if his comms and nav system weren't bypassing all the normal safeguards. But he had no clue what might have resulted in the catastrophic damage to the other ship.

Gil let out a breath he didn't know he'd been holding. *I should do something. Call someone… Or should I leave?*

Sargon would tell him that their mission came first. Whatever mess was unfolding here, it would lead to nowhere good if he got wrapped up in it. They might even blame him.

He hesitated. *Until yesterday, those were my people.*

Life pods dropped out of the ship's mid-decks. That meant the crew was escaping. Emergency beacons were probably already alerting TSS Headquarters and every other ship in range. Gil had no interest in being anywhere near here when they arrived.

A proximity alarm sounded as a speeding pod narrowly missed his ship. A quick sensor check determined that the pod was spinning out of control, and the individual on board was barely alive. Not even its rescue beacon was active.

There was no way to know when rescue might arrive. As much as Gil wanted to leave his old life in the TSS behind, a sense of duty nagged at the back of his mind. Plus, he'd be a lousy empire-builder if he didn't live up to the dimmest of good intentions.

With only the barest of plans in his mind, Gil pointed his ship toward the runaway pod and gave pursuit.

—

After matching vectors and grappling the survivor into his rear cargo bay, Gil anxiously cracked open the battered pod. An auburn-haired young woman—no more than thirty—was inside, covered in burns, bruises, and scrapes. Fragments of an exploded panel littered the pod's interior, along with a broken pair of tinted glasses. She didn't stir.

Gil tensed at the sight of her black uniform, which marked her as an Agent. That meant she was one of the officers. *Fok! Of all the people I could have brought on board.*

The pod was a wreck, so there was no way he could turn her loose without it being a death sentence. And given that she was unconscious, leaving her here unattended might not be much better. So, he gathered her in his arms and loaded her into the ship's medpod. The automated machinery got to work tending to her injuries.

Gil returned to the flight deck while he waited for the medpod to complete its treatments. Real help had arrived, in the form of a TSS vessel named *Charity*. It hadn't taken long for the ship to reach the crash site, so it must have been relatively close. The ship appeared to be in the midst of rescue efforts, picking up survivors from the other emergency pods. Gil had moved far enough away that he didn't have long-range visuals on the activity, but pod transponders kept dropping off the territorial map—presumably as each was brought on board.

I need to get her back to her people. Gil went to check on his unexpected passenger.

When he walked into the room housing the medpod, the shell had opened. The woman inside had several lines hooked up to her. She was blinking and moving her head as she tried to get her bearings.

Her ice-blue eyes focused when she noticed him; lovely eyes with a bioluminescent glow indicative of her Gifted abilities. "Where am I?" she asked.

Accompanying the question, Gil sensed a pressure in his head. He recognized it as a high-level telepathic probe. Though his own telepathic skills weren't well developed, he intuitively raised mental guards—a skill taught to all first year TSS recruits. The mental wall wouldn't hold up to direct attack, but it would prevent her from learning too much through casual gleaning. "You're on my civilian jump ship. Your escape pod was heavily damaged, so I pulled you in." He grabbed a chair and sat down next to her.

The woman tried to sit up but winced, relaxing back into the seat. "My crew—"

"The TSS *Charity* is gathering up the other pods. I can bring you to them."

To his surprise, she didn't immediately agree. Instead, she asked, "Who are you?"

"My name is Gilgamesh."

She coughed and stared at him blurrily. "Yeah, right."

"I know, it's pretentious. Call me Gil instead."

"What happened? No, wait, the crash—I remember that much. Have you seen Karmen?"

"I don't—"

"She's my first officer. You'll know her when you see her. She has this crazy hair—"

"Hey, yours was the only pod I hauled in. I can see you're a TSS Agent. What's your name?" Gil asked. He wanted to get a handle on who he'd pulled out of death's jaws.

"Agent Aurelia Thand, captain of the TSS *Triumph*." She tried to get up again, grimacing.

The foking captain, just my luck. "Agent Thand, I'll tell you everything I know, but you need to take it easy while the medpod finishes." He motioned to the lines that were feeding repair nanites and fluids into her body.

She lay back in the ergonomic seat, limiting herself to flexing her hands and feet. Her shirt had holes in it from where hot metal had burned through. Pink skin showed through where her burns and scrapes were starting to heal.

"You're lucky I was here. Your ship's in bad shape. What happened?" Gil asked.

For a moment, she was intensely focused—offering a

glimpse of the amazing mind behind those mesmerizing eyes. "You were out here?"

"Yeah, I had some mechanical issues. My systems were down for repairs—"

"Without a transponder? Are you *insane*?" she snarled.

He fought to maintain composure; he hadn't expected her to verbally assault him. "I just got the ship, and turns out it has a few more quirks than I'd realized."

Her face flushed, eyes going sharp. "Does this ship have a jump drive with a contraband cool-down purge?"

Gil's heart skipped a beat. He said nothing, but the Agent studied his face to get her answer.

She scoffed, and it turned into a sob. "Not reckless? You foking pirate scum. You killed my crew!"

Fok, did I? His heart dropped. "Hey, whoa! I'm not a pirate. What makes you say that?"

"Well, whoever the fok you are, you stupidly vented out highly unstable exotic particles into space, which got sucked up by my ship and blew it all to—" Something snapped inside her. Tears filled her eyes. She thrashed in the medical chair, unable to move but unwilling to remain still. She sobbed, her body convulsing with emotion.

Gil gaped at her, stunned by the conduct of an Agent he would have thought would be unflappable. He might not have graduated from the TSS academy, but he had been recruited as an Agent trainee. If the woman had made it to a command position, she should have been able to keep her cool even under difficult circumstances. *There's something else going on here.*

Eventually, she grew quiet, distant, even apathetic. "It doesn't matter. They're just going to die anyway."

Gil schooled his expression. "Your crew? No, the rescue ship—"

She shook her head gravely. "We had orders for a new mission, and it was a death sentence."

The Bakzen War wasn't common knowledge among civilians, but Gil had learned about the TSS' covert involvement while he was still at the academy. Her statement could only mean one thing. "You were being sent to the front lines?"

Her gaze swung to him, intent and interested. "What do you know?"

"Enough to agree that facing an enemy *that* powerful is indeed a death sentence. I wouldn't want to go, and I'd want to keep anyone I cared about far away, too."

"I don't have a choice. Orders."

"Orders for your ship? Well, sorry, but it's a goner."

She stared at the ceiling. "If I commandeer your ship, I could also take charge of the rescue—pick up as many of my crew as I can, get us all to the nearest TSS outpost. Then, we'd *still* get deployed, and probably die. Even if I refused to report, I'd get sent to prison for dereliction of duty. There's no way out of this." She groaned. "I know I shouldn't hesitate to put my life on the line to serve, but when I agreed to fight in a war, it was all hypothetical. But knowing what I know now, about the endless fighting and hopeless odds, I can't imagine facing it. It feels so… pointless."

"You wanted more out of life, Agent Thand?"

"Yeah, I wanted to make a real difference in people's lives."

"What if you could?"

She shook her head. "Oh, I'm sure my death in a faraway war will have plenty of impact on a tally sheet of death."

Gil leaned forward. "No, I mean, what if there was another path your life could take? You're already dead, right?"

"Are you threatening me, Gil? I know ten ways to kill you

without lifting a weapon. Fok, I could kill you with my *mind*."

"No! No, hear me out. Your ship is a total loss, right? And your crew is being rescued. They'll search for you, too. They need you. They want you. But if your body is never recovered, what can they do? You'd just… disappear. Presumed dead, after however long. And then you'd be free to go anywhere, or do anything… or be anyone you wanted."

She sighed wistfully. "They'd still find me. They're good at that."

"If they thought you were alive, sure. But can you tell me the last time the TSS lifted a finger to search for a *dead* Agent?"

He saw the spark in her eyes. Clearly, she hadn't thought about that. "Huh."

"Right. Listen, I'm a former TSS recruit myself. They kicked me to the curb. Honestly, I'm glad they did. I have a new mission of my own. You know, I think we could help each other. We could even be friends."

He watched her eyes checking him out, judging him. "I swore to fulfill my duty."

"And how have they repaid you? By sending you to die? Like you said, that's not what being an Agent was supposed to be."

She sat in contemplative silence. Good. He wanted her to judge him—to find him worthy. "Tell me your idea," she said.

He spent some time outlining the thinking behind New Akkadia, or what might eventually grow into it. A thriving society separate from Taran bureaucracy, the TSS, and the privileged dynasties ruling from afar. Real people making their own decisions and keeping what they produced. A skilled and experienced Agent had a place above most other people who might join that cause.

She sniffed. "That's *crazy*. It'll never work."

"Why not? Who's to stop us? The Guard and its Enforcers will turn a blind eye as long as the right people are getting a cut. The TSS is busy throwing their best and brightest players into a death pit for the war—you said so yourself. Wipe out the military and what's left? Freedom. That's what. You know I'm right."

He sat back and let her think, giving her the time to put it together on her own. He could see the thoughts bouncing through her emotions; her face reflected the conflict. All the while, her wounds continued to heal. Soon, there was barely any sign of her injuries.

She relaxed, a smile playing at the corners of her mouth. "All right, I'll go with you. If I'm dead either way, I may as well take the version where I'm alive."

Gil grinned. "That's the spirit."

"Don't get too ahead of yourself. I just don't want my crew to have died for nothing. I can't bring them back to life, but maybe I can find a way to give their deaths meaning if your idea pans out."

"*When* it pans out," he said.

"It's not real until you make it. I'll see what Greengard holds, but I'm not making any promises about sticking around."

He could work with that. "I think you'll be pleasantly surprised, Agent Thand."

"We'll see. But if we're doing this, I'm not going to be an Agent anymore. Call me Aura."

"Very well, Aura." He liked the name. And he could already tell he liked her, too.

She began disconnecting her infusion tubes. "I'll fly us there. Your recklessness already got enough people killed today."

He helped her out of the medpod. "By all means. The ship is yours."

She followed him into the central corridor leading to the flight deck. "No, it's *our* ship. Our first task will be finding a spaceport where we can find a technician willing to change the transponder and credentials for a few credits."

"I can absolutely make that happen."

"Good." She sat down in the pilot's seat on the flight deck, looking at home and comfortable with the controls. "Hey, what's your real name? No way your parents called you Gilgamesh." He told her and she smiled. "I like that much better. Maybe I will be your friend."

"Then here's to new friends."

"And New Akkadia."

PART 2

VISIONARIES

KARMEN'S EYES

25 Years Later...

THE DOCTOR SET down his instruments. "I'm sorry, Karmen, I don't see any improvement."

Karmen Sley frowned but held her hysteria at arm's length. Deep down, she knew her doctor was right. But bracing for the possibility of bad news wasn't the same as hearing it and removing all doubt.

Even though it'd been more than two decades since the accident on the *Triumph* and she'd been bracing for this inevitable news, anxiety still welled in her chest. "Are you sure? I think the color sensitivity is—"

"Karmen, failing optic nerves don't regenerate. The retinal neuropathy isn't going to go away."

Wow, great bedside manner, Doc. I've been seeing you for

twenty-two years and it hasn't improved one bit. For that matter, neither had her vision. "How long do I have until I lose my sight completely?"

"That's difficult to say. A month? Maybe two?"

"Are you asking me or telling me? You're the doctor, Doctor. Don't you know?"

"I *don't* know. We've used every therapy and procedure I have available. I'm out of ideas. Unless you're willing to reconsider synthetic implants—"

She bristled. "No. I'm a woman, not a machine." They'd been over that option numerous times over the years, and her feelings hadn't changed on the matter. Sure, many people across the Taran Empire would embrace synthetic body parts—some would even voluntarily swap out pieces of themselves for cybernetic alternatives—but that wasn't for her. If she couldn't have her biological eyes, she'd rather be blind than see the world through some computer's interpretation of reality.

Doctor Asani nodded and let out a soft sigh, unsurprised by her response. "Then, I'm sorry. There are limits to what's biologically possible." He paused, tilting his head. "Hmm."

Her heart soared as she tried to claw back the fleeting hope. "Wait, what was that? That 'hmm'?"

"My intern. He's well-connected, and there might be an experimental treatment available to you. It's not something that *I* would administer, so I can't make any guarantees."

"Fok it, I'll try just about anything if it means keeping my eyes. Unless this is some sort of crazy back-alley deal…"

"No, I never would have suggested anything like that. He's actually a Junior Agent from the TSS—been here several months for his pre-graduation internship. Very bright. He specializes in applications for innovative biotech research. His name is Lee Tuyin."

Karmen's eyebrows shot up. "Wait, as in the Tuyin Dynasty, who runs the TuMed biotech mega-corporation? 'Bringing medical innovation to you.' *Those* Tuyins?"

"The same."

"Wow, the TSS has really changed over the years. The Sietinens were trendsetters, I guess."

"Regardless of pedigree, the call to explore one's Gifted abilities are too strong for some to resist. You'd know that better than most."

She nodded. "Fair point." When she'd elected to join the TSS' Militia division more than three decades ago, she'd trained at TSS Headquarters where young, aspiring Agents were learning to tap into their latent telepathic and telekinetic abilities. When she'd eventually befriended Aurelia Thand, the Agent had given her deeper insight into those with abilities. Since so few in the Taran population had Gifts, Aura had explained that it hadn't felt right to ignore that part of herself. In time, Karmen had come to respect anyone who'd take on the social stigma of embracing the telekinetic abilities that were illegal in the rest of the civilian population. To have given up a comfortable dynastic life for that said a lot about a person's character.

"Lee is working on a new therapy, which could potentially be adapted to your needs," Doctor Asani continued. "He's out on rounds now, but I can send him to make a house call."

"I don't want any false hope, Doc."

"I wouldn't be suggesting it now if I didn't think there was merit to his approach. If you're not ready to give up your natural eyes, hear him out. There's nothing more *I* can do."

"All right, send him to the house tonight," she agreed. "I'll make pizza. I can still find my way around the kitchen." *And I want to see what Daveed and the kids think of him.*

"I'll pass on the message. I hope he's able to give you a better prognosis."

"I won't give up hope yet." *But when will I need to accept my fate?*

— — —

Lee Tuyin wasn't sure what to expect when he'd stepped through the front door of the Sley home with his medical bag, but a house filled with kinetic energy and positive emotion wasn't it. Karmen was tall and regal, precise in her actions. Her husband, Daveed, was dashing and attentive. Their four teenage children—two boys and two girls—looked on with mild interest as Daveed gave Lee a narrated tour of the house.

Daveed was beginning to launch into an explanation of the neighborhood's urban development genesis when Karmen intervened. She stood a bit taller than Lee, and he could easily imagine her in a TSS uniform. "Daveed!" She smiled softly at her husband before turning to Lee. "My apologies, he'll embarrass himself by spouting little-known facts all night, if you let him."

Her husband flashed an affable smile. "Well, who else should I embarrass?"

"Twenty-six deans across seventeen departments, and somehow I marry the one weirdo." Karmen sniffed.

"You wanted a man who would complement you," her husband said. "Frankly, I was surprised when you agreed to marry me. I didn't think a mere academic would appeal to a former soldier."

She sighed dramatically. "He has a thing for women in uniform. It's positively offensive."

Lee couldn't help smiling with amusement at their banter. The adoration in the couple's expressions when they spoke to each other was impossible to miss.

Karmen looked Lee in his eyes, her mouth twitching at his tinted glasses. They were a standard part of the TSS uniform, to conceal the natural bioluminescence of his eyes from his Gifted abilities. Usually, the glowing irises made people uncomfortable. In this case, the glasses themselves were the problem—perhaps a reminder of her fading vision, or maybe just giving the impression that he was hiding something. To set her at ease, he removed the glasses and tucked them into an inner breast pocket of his dark-blue overcoat.

Karmen gave a subtle nod of approval at the gesture. She directed him into the living room for small talk.

"So, four kids," Lee commented as they got settled on the couch. "You don't see many large families around here."

Karmen handed her guest a glass of wine. "When your husband is the Dean of Interstellar Business Studies at the largest employer on the planet…"

"And your wife is a veteran with a Commendation for Meritorious Conduct and a Combat Action Ribbon…" Daveed added.

Lee held up his hands. "No need to justify it to me! I'm a fourth child, myself."

"Seems that granted you a little more freedom," Daveed said.

"Having older siblings to ensure the family legacy does have its benefits. With the TSS, I'm glad I can focus on healing people without having to make a business case."

Karmen nodded. "Fair enough. I'll finish up dinner."

Lee did his best to be cordial, but his TSS training forced him to observe everything through the lens of a scientific investigation. Kozu was the eldest boy at nineteen, and his sister Kaia was approaching her eighteenth birthday. The next down was Seandra, who was fifteen, and the youngest boy, Elian, was thirteen and doing his best to catch up in terms of being a jerk to his siblings. Elian and Seandra were much like Daveed, but Kozu and Kaia both took after Karmen, even to the blonde streak down the middle of their dark hair. Their behaviors were like an intricate ballet, with every player doing a job and being performative about it because he was in their home; an audience of one. He got the idea that Karmen and Daveed had people over often and that the children helped out both as foils and props… and sometimes as crew to judge by how effectively they were put to work. It wasn't that different from his own childhood, but he wasn't naturally good at it like these folks were; spending an hour at the university cafeteria after work was as social as he got.

At one point, in the middle of eating pizza and salad, Kaia said, "Agent Tuyin, please talk to Seandra. She's been trying to get your attention for ten minutes."

"She's not used to having to compete for a boy's attention," Kozu ribbed.

Seandra stared dagger eyes at her older brother across the table. "I already *have* a boyfriend!"

"Kaia has a boyfriend, too," Elian sang.

"He's a friend who is a boy. Not the same thing," Kaia shot back, a flush rising on her cheeks. "We're not even on the same *planet.*"

Elian leaned toward Lee and whispered, "They message each other *constantly*. It's crazy!"

Lee smiled, thinking about how his oldest sister talked about her fiancée the same way. Both of the Sley girls looked like they wanted to crawl into a hole, so Lee moved on. "Now, Seandra, what was it you wanted to ask?"

She leaned forward, grateful for the lifeline. "I was wondering about the TSS. Is it true you Agents do battles with telekinesis?"

"Some do," he admitted. "That's not my specialty. I'm a healer."

"I dunno, that doesn't sound as fun as throwing around people with your mind."

"You might be surprised. Looking inward with our abilities can be just as important as dealing with big, external things."

The teen nodded. "I guess." She resumed eating.

Dinner continued with chatter about everyone's respective days. Karmen said little, but she managed her family with gestures and pointed glances. Lee found himself absorbed by the conversation, enjoying the family dynamic of parents and children that reminded him of good times from his own childhood. Listening to Daveed describe the machinations of his workplace, the politics and conflicts, made Lee wonder just how much of the TSS's own internal struggles he'd been spared... or if he'd simply been too absorbed in his studies to notice.

When they'd finished eating and had cleared the table, Karmen nodded to Daveed. "I should talk to Lee."

"I've got a phone call to return," Daveed said, making an obvious excuse to give them privacy. "Come on, kids, time for homework."

When the family had departed, Karmen folded her hands on the tabletop. "So, Agent Tuyin, my doctor says in two months I'll be blind in both eyes. Tell me about your miracle cure."

"Please, call me Lee."

"Okay, Lee, let's hear your pitch."

He opened his medical case, which contained a variety of

small vials. He placed his handheld on the table and activated a detailed holographic representation of Karmen's eyes. "Retinal neuropathy, resulting from exotic matter radiation exposure during an incident aboard *Triumph*."

Her body stiffened, reliving the experience after all these years. "It was a one in a million of bad luck. I've heard all of their excuses and theories about how that catastrophic failure shouldn't have been possible, yet it happened anyway. I spent years thinking about how differently my life may have turned out if I'd only gone straight to the Command Center rather than trying to get to the Engineering deck. But then I think about the people I was able to get into escape pods who never would have stood a chance without my presence. There are tradeoffs for everything. Ultimately, I'd do it again. But the bottom line is, I got a dose of the bad stuff, and the doc tells me that even our modern medical miracles can only stave off the inevitable for so long."

Lee nodded solemnly. "Eyes are tricky. Your standard medical nanites have no difficulty removing cancerous cells or heading off viruses, but maintaining optic nerve function is another matter."

"So I've been told." She sighed. "It was a slow decline at first, but my vision has been getting worse for years. The world keeps becoming darker, blurrier. They've already replaced the corneas, and they've given me new lenses. No one around here offers optic nerve regeneration. The expense of traveling to a planet that does isn't realistic for me. I've been trying to wrap my head around going blind, since I absolutely refuse to get mechanical implants."

"I can understand where you're coming from, and you're not alone. That's why we've been working on a new therapy that could be easily brought to the patient for treatment on their own terms." Lee tapped his handheld, which switched the projection to a pharmaceutical advertisement. "Which is where Octarin comes in. It's still experimental, but it's shown great promise in preliminary trials. How's your background in organic chemistry and molecular biology?"

"I haven't studied much science since I left the Militia academy," she said. "It was never my strongest subject."

"Well, I bet your tactical and strategy-building skills are up to date," he said, wanting to put her at ease. "Your house runs like a well-drilled platoon."

"We just wanted to instill a good work ethic in the kids."

"It shows. I can tell you want to see them succeed—and really be able to *see* them. So, forget about the exact science; that doesn't matter. Basically, Octarin stimulates your body's own healing processes to repair your optic nerves, to restore and preserve your vision." He showed her a brief presentation of the therapy's effects, which had been created with non-specialists in mind.

Karmen took it in with cautious interest. "It sounds too good to be true."

"There are never guarantees of results, but the therapy is sound. It's customized to your specific genetics and repair needs, which makes it a step up over other treatments. And, since it's still in trials, we can avoid the pesky issue of cost."

"As long as it's not likely to kill me, seems worth being an experimental subject."

"The most likely side effect is blindness, so…"

She smiled. "No worse than what would happen to me, anyway. What else should I know?"

"We haven't yet conducted a longitudinal study, so I can't vouch for long-term results. Subsequent treatments may be necessary."

"Understood."

"Now, the treatment may do nothing, or it could actually make your remaining eyesight worse. Alternatively, it may work part-way and merely halt further degeneration of the nerves. Or it could reverse the nerve damage and restore some of your vision loss."

She tapped her fingers, lost in thought for a minute. "Has anyone in the trials regained their original level of sight?"

"No. But several patients did report significant improvement in their vision."

"All luck of the draw with the results, I suppose."

Lee closed up his sample case. "It's not completely random. Before coming here, I ran a simulation of your genome that's on file with the hospital. I didn't see any red flags. You're a good candidate."

"It sounds like my best chance. How would we get started?"

"It's a simple infusion protocol we can do at my office. But take a few days to talk it over with your family, make sure everyone is on board. You'll need to sign some releases since this is a trial."

"That sounds fair."

"Great. I'll be in touch." He got up to head for the front door.

"One more thing. Why this?" She pointed at his dark-blue TSS clothing.

He stood there in confusion for a moment, convinced she was asking about his wardrobe. It was a standard uniform for a Junior Agent, which she had to know as former TSS, herself. Then, it sank in. "I'm a fourth-in-line Lower Dynasty brat who'd rather hang out in a lab than deal with board meetings or balance sheets. I have no interest in the pageantry of a public-facing business. With all the Tuyin family's projects in the biotech space, everything's impersonal. Faceless statistics and profit margins. My siblings have the heads for it, but I'm driven by the more direct impacts of the science. What I got to do tonight—getting to know you and your wonderful family—shows how the right product can have a huge impact on your quality of life. And *that* is a worthwhile career."

Karmen raised an eyebrow. "You're a rare breed."

He smiled. "We quiet intellectuals like to keep the Empire running behind the scenes. No need for fanfare."

"It's noble."

"Just directed curiosity. In my early studies, I started thinking that what we call medicine was actually more like a cookbook. Millions of recipes, inputs, and outcomes. Boring, predictable, but beneficial. Working for a corporation puts the focus on profit. I aspired to have broader reach with my work, with patients at the center. That was never going to happen with the family business. My siblings were never interested in exploring their Gifts, so the TSS wasn't ever on the table, but I jumped at the opportunity—especially since it meant I'd have an avenue for doing research and developing therapies that could really *help* people. I've never regretted that choice."

Karmen nodded. "The TSS does attract people who feel that way. I miss that."

"I'm sorry your time was cut short."

She shrugged. "I have a wonderful family. I wouldn't have had that if I'd stayed in."

"Very true."

"I hope you have a long, wonderful career ahead of you."

"Assuming I graduate. I have to pass this internship first. The success metrics are a lot more ambiguous than I'm used to." TSS Junior Agent internships were the last step before graduation, meant to address any remaining temperament issues that might negatively impact performance as an Agent. Lee hadn't been given specific parameters for his internship, which he suspected was the real test since he preferred order and structure. He'd vowed to do his best and help as many people as he could during his year-long assignment. Stepping outside standard procedure to help Karmen seemed like a good way to score points about being adaptive and seizing unexpected opportunities.

Karmen bobbed her head. "I'm sure you'll do just fine. I understand that need to be of service. I had ten years of Militia under my belt when the accident happened. If my health had endured, I'd still be there. But, I wouldn't trade this for anything," she said, waving her arms to indicate her home.

"The universe has a way of getting us all where we're supposed to be."

"Maybe so."

"And since our paths brought us together, I'll do everything I can to help you."

"We'll *see* about that."

He laughed. "I walked right into that one."

"Prepare yourself. I'm scared out of my mind, and terrible jokes are my coping mechanism."

"Noted." He gave her a reassuring smile. "I'll talk to you in a couple days to finalize our treatment plan."

"Thank you. Really. I… I'd started to think there was no hope."

"There's always hope, Karmen."

BETTER THAN DEATH

AURA SETTLED INTO her command chair of her old cargo ship *Redemption*, letting the darkness of the empty flight deck settle her nerves. She'd spent decades preparing for the mission that was now imminent. Her crew knew their jobs and everything was in place. She could afford a few private moments for herself on the ship that had opened a pivotal chapter in her new life after leaving the TSS.

A moment became a minute, which stretched to half an hour. *Aura, snap out of it. You're hiding again!* She needed to get herself in gear, but she was reluctant to give up her peaceful solitude, knowing what was coming.

Pounding on the outer hatch drew her attention. She hit the door controls, and it hissed open. She squinted against the sudden light.

A metallic humanoid drone entered. Its sword, sash, and a tri-cornered hat unmistakably marked it as being her first officer, Lom Mench. When his consciousness was synced with the drone, he called the contrivance 'Sergeant Meklife'. Aura could never bring herself to have any cybernetic integrations, but Lynaedans like Lom had embraced such enhancements as an extension of their Taran selves. She had to admit, it was rather handy having a modular mercenary as her second-in-command.

"Captain, they're ready for you in the War Room," Meklife said.

Aura sighed heavily, not yet ready to leave the dark serenity of her hiding place. "All right."

There was such a thing as getting too comfortable with a life. For more than twenty years, she'd been tied to that ship, the *Redemption*—and everything that came from its name as the embodiment of her post-TSS life. The life she'd built after running away rather than face a meaningless death. She'd been working for decades to justify that decision and build something meaningful. It had all stemmed from that ship and the doors it had opened—buying and selling items of every description, moving cargo from planet to planet in a never-ending cycle of activity at the outer fringes of law. Slowly, she'd become the very type of person she'd once despised as a TSS officer. But she had been idealistic and naïve back then. Now, she understood how the universe really worked. And she knew what it meant to wield true power.

Aura exited the *Redemption* with Meklife and descended the gangway to the bustling hangar deck in the belly of the *Emerald Queen*. The flurry of activity and dozens of workers reminded her that she was in a better place now—a powerful place, far exceeding her position on the TSS *Triumph* back in what felt like a lifetime ago. She'd been shackled then, and now she was free to grow. Even so, she still took comfort in the *Redemption* and had insisted on keeping the small vessel. It was now permanently berthed inside the large cargo hold of the *Emerald Queen*, preserving it as a place to recenter her thoughts and to offer a constant reminder of how far she'd come. She'd tried to fight that sentimental part of herself, but she'd realized that it fueled her drive; that made it invaluable.

Walking with Meklife on the way up to the *Emerald Queen*'s flight deck, she passed by numerous other Lynaedan drones. It felt like she was among AI androids, but she had to remind herself these were just robotic bodies that their Lynaedan controllers were operating through remote connection stations on the lower decks. It didn't bother her to interact with the synthetic forms; crew was crew. But some of the other Tarans steered clear from the Lynaedan members of the crew, even when they were in the flesh. Not everyone felt comfortable mingling freely with people who'd so thoroughly integrated cybernetics and related technology into their culture. But, as captain, Aura had to set an example for unity. On that note, she realized that hiding in her old cargo ship just before an operation was a bad look.

"Do you miss the days of running cargo?" Meklife asked. "Or do you simply enjoy being alone in the dark?"

"A little of both," she said. "The *Redemption* took me to a hundred different worlds, where I met thousands of people. I did well for myself along the way. It turns out I had a head for deal-making. Who knew?"

"Lord Gilgamesh obviously saw your potential. That's why he brought you into Lord Sargon's scheme. You worked hard to make a fortune—all so he could steal from you."

When did Gil decide he and his friends were 'lords'? I must have missed that memo. She waved off the accusation. "He didn't *steal* anything."

"I see. You *gave* it to him."

Aura shook her head. "We've had a plan, decades in the making. Buying the *Emerald Queen* and refitting it was just my latest assignment in service to a larger vision. It took money to make that happen, gained through all those cargo runs. You supervised the refit; you know these things don't come cheap."

"You should be running the whole plan, not doing anyone's bidding."

"I know you don't think highly of Gil—"

"I don't think about him *at all*, if I can help it."

She held up her hands to stop the bickering. "He saved my life. Everything I've done since has been a choice of my own volition. I believe in what we've been building. We're here, so let's do our bomaxed jobs and get on with the mission."

Meklife drew himself to attention. "I serve the Queen."

The armored compartment in the heart of the ship was known as the War Room, a central location that served as the nerve center for their operations. There was no situation Aura couldn't manage from here, no order she couldn't give. On a TSS vessel, it would have been known as the Command Center. But War Room was better—concise. Honest.

A wide holodisplay showed their location relative to their destination: the planet Greengard. They'd be there very soon. It'd been years since her last visit, well before she'd acquired her ships and resources. That early reconnaissance had shaped their strategies, and they were now prepared in every way.

The blue-green light of subspace swirled outside the viewport, an ethereal realm just beyond physical reality that would never cease to amaze her, no matter how much she traveled. The sight of it helped settle her nerves and centered her.

"Sacha, status report," Aura requested.

The Lynaedan manning the Ops position touched a stud

on the nearest console with one of her four obviously mechanical arms. "All crew stations are manned and ready. Good checks on all weapon systems. We should be dropping out of subspace in five minutes."

"Are the planetary security codes ready to transmit?" Aura asked.

This time, Meklife answered. "Affirmative. Encryption, frequency, the transmission protocols—everything is queued. Just give the order and we'll be in business."

"I hope so. Those codes cost a fortune," she admitted. A king's ransom to the right people. Low men with high ambitions who were willing to trade their planet's security for a big payday. Good for them.

Without such people, New Akkadia would have remained only a crazy dream. But they did exist, and it turned out there were a *lot* of them out there. Sargon had been right about that. What had surprised Aura, though, wasn't that every man had their price, but rather that many of those prices were so *low*.

The countdown clock ran through the last few minutes. *You were trained for this. You know exactly what to do and how to respond.*

The TSS had prepared her for this very scenario—a tactical strike designed to knock the opponent down and render them helpless so the real work could begin. But this mission was also about putting on a show; Meklife had been specific on that point. A planetary assault was a military strategy, but crime was a performance, and all of Foundation City was their stage.

The Nav officer gave a signal from his station. "Dropping out of subspace in three, two, one."

The view changed to the familiar black expanse dotted with stars. Greengard lay below them. A gentle shimmer surrounding the planet revealed the security blanket of its defense shield.

The butterflies in Aura's stomach had grown to wasps. *Stars, I've gone soft! Pull yourself together.* She shoved her anxiety aside, remembering her Agent training. "Standard orbit. Transmit our entry codes and take us in when you have approval," she ordered. She sat back and let her people do their jobs.

"Callum, how is the local traffic reacting to us?" Meklife asked one of the non-Lynaedan crew.

The sensor operator ran his fingers over the console and replied, "Negative contacts. All I see are satellites and a cargo transfer elevator. Nothing notable. As far as I can tell, they think we're just another cargo freighter."

"Excellent. Nav, plot us a course down the appropriate entry path. Gallian, do you have the comms frequency sorted yet?"

A Lynaedan with a band of solid metal winding around the back of his head nodded. "Sorted and ready to transmit."

"Very well. Transmit entry codes now."

While Gallian worked the controls, Callum reported, "It's working. We have a clear window through the shield."

"Very well. Steady as she goes," Meklife intoned.

Aura fought to control her breathing as the *Emerald Queen* lowered her bulky frame through an open section of the shield. The vessel descended over Foundation City, the capital of this world.

"Over a million people down there," Meklife said. "The ensuing chaos should be most useful."

A million sounded like a lot, but the people were mostly employed by the university. Scholars, educators, researchers, students—and the working folks who made everything possible for them. *I doubt they have ever imagined a day like we're about to show them.* "Let's get this show on the proverbial road," Aura ordered. "Launch the Cloud Punch!"

The forward torpedo tube opened and blasted out a self-guided missile. The automated planetary defenses had already been disabled by the clearance code the ship's comm array had sent, so the computers cataloged the swiftly descending object as a mere shuttle and took no action.

A self-contained package within the missile began transmitting powerful signals, which were picked up by data transmission nodes all over Foundation City. By the time the projectile landed harmlessly on the ground, it had infected thousands of computers with a faulty upgrade command that forced its host to continually reboot every few seconds, freezing the planet-wide data network Greengard relied on for everything. As the wave of reboots rippled outward, it shut down banks, power stations, public transportation hubs, and all but a few government offices and centralized databases.

The crew watched from their vantage on the ship hovering in the clouds as the planet below went dark.

Aura admired the sight from her command chair. "Prepare to attack!"

DARK CITY

KARMEN FLEXED HER arm, watching the medicine flow through a narrow tube into her wrist. For two months, she'd been subjecting herself to Lee's treatment regimen, and it was astounding how clear the world looked to her these days. Dull murkiness had transformed into sharp color. And her depth perception had fully returned. It was amazing. Magical. She couldn't imagine going back to the way things had been. The thought of a relapse terrified her. *Never again.*

Lee made an adjustment to the dispensary, facing her on a swivel stool. She appreciated that he didn't wear his tinted glasses around her, letting her better read the expression in his softly glowing brown eyes. And right now, they sparkled with delight. "Feeling better, right?"

"Is it that obvious?"

"Karmen, you're positively *glowing.* When we first met, I was lucky to ever get a smile out of you. I like the difference."

"I'm too old for you, young man."

He laughed off the comment. "I went over the most recent imaging with Doctor Asani. Not only has the degeneration stopped, but the optic nerves are actually regenerating. Not quickly or completely, but I'd say this experiment is working. The research team will be thrilled with these results."

"You have no idea," she murmured. "It was like a dark curtain had been draped over my face, layer by layer. Every day another layer, making the world a little blurrier, a little dimmer. Now, instead, those curtains are lifting. I have no words for how grateful I am. I owe you and your team big time."

"A small repayment for your TSS service," Lee said, checking the flow of medication again. There was still a significant portion of the dose to go. "How's the family?"

Karmen appreciated him helping to distract her from the treatment. "Seandra and her boyfriend broke up. It was amicable, I'm told. She also says he wasn't rich enough for her, so I wonder what she'll take away from the experience."

Lee shook his head. "Oh, boy. And she's already like this at fifteen? Good luck."

Karmen let out a long breath. "Yeah, I'm going to need it. And Kaia… I don't know what to think about that one."

"I take it that means her long-distance relationship is still going strong?"

"Seems like it. I know more about him now. He's a boy on Gallos named Colin. Apparently, they want to go into business together managing a sports team. The game is called GravX."

"I've heard of it. It's extremely violent. But exciting. They sound like an ambitious pair. Does she have a team to sell him?"

"Give her time. She's quite creative when it comes to making business decisions. She gets that from her father."

Lee touched a control panel. A medical imaging arm swept past Karmen's eyes, making her blink. "How did that long-distance romance begin, anyway?" Lee asked.

"I have no idea, but it's been going on for months now. Her tablet chimes, and when she sees who the message is from, her whole face lights up. I keep thinking they'll get bored of talking through devices and it will peter out, but they're making it work."

"Living the fantasy of someone can be more exciting than the real thing."

"I don't want her to be disappointed if they do eventually meet in person. She keeps hinting at him being someone with some clout, looking to make a name for himself beyond his family. Aside from that, I have no clue about who he is."

Lee thought for a moment. "Gallos… That's the Covrani family homeworld. They're a Lower Dynasty—less influential than we Tuyin, but they manage interstellar shipping concerns all over this arm of the galaxy. If this lover boy *is* connected to them…" He sucked his teeth. "Go, Kaia!"

Karmen sniffed. The last thing any dynastic family would accept is a scheming social climber marrying up at their expense. *Not that I would accuse her of planning a coup like that—she's not as bad as her sister.* "If there *is* any relation, I don't think she's talking to the heir. I'd bet the remainder of my eyesight on that. It's probably just someone who works for the family."

"Whatever happens, I hope she finds happiness. What about the boys?"

"Kozu wants to join the TSS Militia. I'm trying to convince him it's a bad plan, but he's latched onto the idea and won't let it go. I think I've got him ready to consider that going in with some advanced education will be a better strategy but… we'll see."

"And Elian?"

"He's thinking of going into business. He just doesn't know what kind of industry suits him. He's got plenty of time to figure it out."

"Hah! In ten years, Kaia will be managing her own sports team, and she'll hire Elian as a talent scout. Seandra will be dating one of the team's star players. Kozu will run the security firm that protects them. You watch."

Karmen felt a twinge of conflict in her chest as he spoke. On the one hand, he clearly liked her brood, and they were just as taken with him. But the tone he used when he said things like that chilled her. "My children aren't game pieces to be moved on a board."

"Sorry, I didn't mean any offense." Lee leaned in as the last of her infusion dispensed. He disconnected the tubes and sprayed a nanite-infused mist to accelerate the healing of her wrist vein. "I think I have a different perspective on that kind of thing than most people. I've been listening to my relatives tell stories like that about me and my siblings my whole life. But, the truth is, I have almost no chance of inheriting any part of my family's business. Allow me to fantasize about your kids having bright futures instead."

She softened, seeing the innocence in his softly glowing eyes. "Fair enough. Welcome to the Sley Dynasty."

"Very funny. Can you stand up?"

She did so. "Even with my eyes closed. I swear, my sense of balance has improved."

"You'd be amazed how much of our sense of balance revolves around visual acuity," Lee agreed. "Stars, *I'm* amazed, and I study this stuff for a living. Anyway, your Octarin regimen is complete."

"Hooray! How long will the effects last?"

"Time will tell. We're officially moving into the post-treatment record-keeping phase of the experiment. If you have a relapse or if your vision dims again, you need to let me know immediately."

"Yes, Doctor Lee."

"Ha! Let's sign you out of the patient tracking system and get you on your way."

The lights in the treatment room flickered, dimmed, and then resumed their normal glow.

Karmen looked at Lee. "Did I just have a stroke?"

"Not unless I had one, too. Probably just a blip in the power grid. It happens, right?"

She tensed. "Not usually."

The lights dimmed and then extinguished, throwing the building into shadow. Daylight continued to stream through a multitude of windows, but the sudden change in light levels was still disturbing. Within seconds, amber emergency lights came on around the baseboards and doorways.

Karmen strode to the nearest window and looked out at the city. Her city. All the power was out. Traffic lights, billboards, everything. Not a single building in the skyline had a light on anywhere. She couldn't view the spaceport from here, but it would have been interesting to see what was going on there. Spaceports were quasi-military installations, which had their own backup systems built in as part of their planning and construction. But if that was dark, too…

Something is definitely wrong. Karmen had to fight her natural inclination to jump to a worst-case scenario whenever something strange happened, but a citywide power outage raised legitimate cause for concern. "There's a redundant power grid in the city. I've been living here more than twenty years, and I've never seen a total blackout."

"I'm going to check in with the security desk. Stay here."
Lee dashed off.

Stay here! No foking way. Karmen pulled out her handheld
and contacted city services to find out the status of the outage.

Her jaw dropped as a vaguely mechanical voice met her
ears: "—mated message. A state of emergency is declared for
Foundation City. Do not attempt to contact Foundation City
Control at this time. Go to your home and await further
instructions. Foundation City Control is working to restore
essential services as soon as possible. All first response teams
are designated top priority for emergency response directives.
All flight-capable civilian vehicles are grounded for the
duration of the emergency. All ground vehicle operators are
instructed to pilot manually and avoid blocking emergency
transportation routes. This is an automated message. A state of
emergency is declared—"

She hung up, her heart racing. Now, knowing that the
entire city was down, getting in touch with her husband and
children was her foremost concern.

She tried to make another call and sagged in relief as
Daveed picked up. "Karmen?"

"Daveed, I'm in the medical annex on the other side of the
plaza. Where are you?"

"My office. The department is using it as an operational
hub while the rest of the campus is locked down. We have
students to locate, family members to contact… it's a mess. Do
you know how widespread the outage is?"

"No, but Lee is trying to find out more. Stay where you are.
I'll meet you there." There was no way Daveed would leave the
campus if she asked him over a call, so if she had any hope of
getting him home where it'd be safe to wait out this strange
event, she'd need to talk to him face-to-face. Fortunately, his

office was close by.

As soon as she ended the call, Karmen sent out a text message to the family group, wanting to check on her kids. They quickly responded that they were fine but were being sent home for the day.

\>>I'll be there as soon as I can,<< she assured them. >>Look after each other. Keep the refrigerator closed.<< Their school wasn't far from their family's home, so she didn't have concerns about them making the trek, even with the power outage. She'd made a point of raising capable children who could take care of themselves, and she trusted them to be responsible.

Karmen gathered her belongings in the treatment room. On her way out the door, she thumbed a quick text to Lee: >>Heading to Daveed's office. Catch me up when you can. TY<<

Her heart was beating too quickly; she would have to remember to breathe deeply to slow it down. All her old TSS physical training came back to her despite her living a sedentary life for two decades. But at least now she could *see*.

That reminded her that her eyesight would only persist as long as her Octarin did its job, and even Lee didn't know how long the effects would last. But those were concerns for future times.

Right now, her city was in trouble. She ran off to find Daveed.

8

NON-ZERO EVENT

KARMEN PAID CLOSE attention to her surroundings as she wound her way across the massive plaza to Daveed's office. Foundation University was a sprawling enterprise that covered nearly one hundred square kilometers of carefully managed space. Its pride and joy was a public transportation hub that linked every campus, building, and complex, moving thousands of students, faculty, and staff between the various locations every hour. None of it was working now.

The stillness that permeated the air made for a stark contrast to the day's beauty. It was clear, warm, and sunny—a perfect day for a picnic or team sports. Even the noise level had dropped, as traffic and the maglev skytrains came to a halt. It was as if time itself had stopped.

She'd been to the business school's campus a thousand times before, visiting her husband for work or faculty gatherings. It was always a blast, even when she didn't look forward to socializing. Usually, the communal energy permeated the environment, and she often looked forward to the social games they all played. Twenty years ago, after her early medical retirement from the TSS, the promise of a fresh start had initially attracted her to this place; the reality of a new relationship had kept her here. After the *Triumph*, she'd found that she didn't want to exist without the people and the life she'd built here.

Today, though, everyone she saw was strangely quiescent. Some were angry or distraught, but most just seemed plain annoyed by the inconvenience. Karmen felt particular sympathy for the people who'd been stalled in transit. She passed beneath a skyrail train; the cars were stationary. To her horror, each car had its doors open while crew in transit uniforms shepherded passengers along the railway back to the terminal. She hated to think what people stranded on kilometers-long skyrail tracks were going to do if they were too far from a transit stop to disembark. Thankfully, that wasn't her problem to solve.

Not everyone was upset at the situation. She walked by one student who was trying to get a lottery organized, where people would make bets on how long the power would be out. He was just about the only person she could see with a plan.

A general aura of concern had descended on the city as people tried to figure out whether this was a temporary issue or the start of something major. She couldn't blame them for being bewildered; they'd all grown up surrounded by power that came on when you touched a switch without fail. Interruptions were rare and always localized. A city-wide outage was unheard of. It was only Karmen's military background that allowed her to remain task-focused and calm. However, that would only persist if she was able to find her family.

The fact that texting and calls were still operational was a good sign; those were routed through orbital satellites connected to the long-range subspace comm relays, so whatever was happening was isolated to the surface-level infrastructure on the planet. Along the walkways, students and faculty handhelds buzzed with messages, and she overheard snippets of conversations that all classes had been canceled for the day.

Enforcers patrolling the campus reminded merchants not to gouge customers, setting an expectation to charge their normal prices for their wares during the emergency. The TSS officer in Karmen wondered how commerce would fare once the handhelds ran out of power; the recharging stations wouldn't work, either. No matter what the Enforcers said, the masses would dictate the market.

What happened next would depend entirely on the nature and scope of the problem. A computer virus could have swept through the city's infrastructure and crashed anything in its path. Or maybe there had been a critical failure with the power generation stations. There wasn't any smoke in the sky and she hadn't overheard any talk of an explosion, so it seemed like some kind of technical issue. But how widespread? She found herself considering the widest possible network: the entire planet of Greengard.

I really don't know anything right now. It's probably just the city. Find Daveed and the kids—that's all that matters right now. She picked up her pace.

Based on what she knew right now, there wasn't a reason to freak out. Some emergency systems were working despite the outage since handhelds could still make calls. That meant other services were likely still active, such as hospitals and other public services; those operations had several layers of backups.

Even so, a day without power would mean an enforced holiday for the whole population. Some people would pack their families and take them to parks, just glad to have an excuse to be off from their day jobs. Some forward-thinking merchants would empty their freezers and hand out food, especially perishable items.

If the outage extended longer than a day, they'd be facing a completely different experience. People would start to worry about jobs, about family members, about what happened when the pantry ran dry. About the water. About their paychecks. It wouldn't take long for people to start hoarding.

After a week of darkness, society would be in an all-out panic.

Gah, Karmen, listen to yourself! You've dropped into soldier mode just because the lights went out. Get a grip! She took a calming breath to center herself. Letting her imagination run wild wasn't productive. Sure, this situation was unusual, but there wasn't any reason to assume that the power wouldn't be restored within the hour.

At last, she reached the entrance to Daveed's faculty building. The worst part of the day was remembering that his office was on the sixth floor. Naturally, the elevators weren't working.

Karmen wasn't in the same shape she'd been while serving, but she managed. She envied the young ones who sped past her in the hallways. Some were less fit than others, but no one with youth on their side struggled to climb the ramps like she did.

She was met with frenetic activity as soon as she stepped out of the stairwell onto the sixth floor. As a dean, Daveed had a staff and a suite of offices to use for daily work. Today, the suite was packed with students in addition to the regular administrative workers.

Karmen half-heard a flurry of conversation snippets as she looked for him. One chat between a male and female student caught her attention.

He spoke with his hands, obviously trying to impress his friend. "This is a non-zero event. Basically, it's so unlikely that nobody ever planned for it."

The girl wasn't having it. "Power going off is unlikely. It happens on plenty of outer colonies."

"Sure, on frontier worlds, but they don't have power modules with triply redundant, multi-format security and triple backups for switching nodes."

The girl's face scrunched up. "That's… what does that even mean?" she asked.

"Look, if any one node goes out, the others around it sense the gap and re-route their own outflows to cover it. There's no centralized switch that can be hacked. It's foolproof," he explained.

"No, that just means there's a very creative fool out there somewhere," she said with a smile.

A pink-haired young woman Karmen didn't know ran up to the pair. "Hey, does anyone know what kind of ship this is?"

The boy strained to look as she pointed her handheld's screen toward him. "It's a cargo ship," he announced with the confidence of a young man who was used to thinking himself bright.

Pink-hair didn't seem to think so. "You sure? Weirdest cargo ship I've ever seen."

The boy's verbal sparring partner smirked. "How many have you seen, Tess?"

Tess rolled her eyes and said, "Plenty! We used to visit the spaceport all the time when I was a kid. We'd watch the ships take off and land. Nothing that looked like this one, though."

"Where did that image come from, anyway?" asked the boy.

"Straight from the StarNews feed. Reports are that most of the heavy transports either left orbit or were grounded. But this one showed up just before the lights went out, and it's still there hovering above us. I'm not sure what it's waiting for."

Karmen waved at Tess. "Excuse me. May I see?" The pink-haired girl presented Karmen with her handheld. To the boy's credit, he'd gotten it right: it *was* a cargo ship. "Looks like one of the big ore carriers I used to fly escort for. You see those wide pods on the sides, like wings? Those are definitely bulk storage berths. But the rest of it... hmm..." Karmen enlarged the graphic and peered intently at the grainy image. The cargo pods were obvious, but what kind of a flight deck did this vessel have? She spotted the V-shape of the jump drive's rear prongs, but what were the hatches on the lowest tier for?

"Uh, ma'am? May I have my handheld back?" Tess stammered.

"Sorry." Karmen handed the device back. "Hey, may I have a copy of these images?"

Tess tapped her handheld to Karmen's to transfer the file.

"Thank you." Karmen pocketed her device while she strode to her husband's office, considering what she'd seen. Yes, it'd begun as an ore carrier. But it had been modified into something else. A better question might be, why would an ore carrier be on this side of the planet above the city?

Reaching Daveed's door, she knocked and went in without waiting for a reply. Her husband was on his handheld, listening to a speaker on the other end of a call. She hated to intrude, but now she had a mission. "Daveed, is there a visual imaging lab in the building?"

Daveed pulled his handheld away from his ear. "Karmen,

forgive me, but I really don't have time—"

"Just tell me where it is. I'll be back."

Daveed was under stress; she could hear it in his voice. "Miss Marin," he called out, "could you please take my wife anywhere she wants to go?"

Tess appeared in the doorway. She smiled at Karmen. "Of course! Happy to help. Where to, ma'am?"

"The images you sent were a little rough. Is there a computer terminal anywhere nearby with image processing software?"

"Absolutely. Follow me."

—

By the time Karmen returned to Daveed's office, he was off the phone but looking worn out. Dealing with politics and personalities was exhausting work. She had no appetite for it now, even though she knew how to navigate those waters from her time as a commander.

"It's not like you to waste your time on frivolities during a city-wide emergency," he snapped as she entered the room.

"You know me better than that. So, it *is* the whole city?"

Daveed gave an exaggerated shrug. "It might be planet-wide, but that's above my pay grade. All I know is the Vice President of Academic Affairs wants answers, and I have none to give him."

"Seems like the answers should be flowing in the other direction."

"I had the same thought." He sighed. "I'm sorry for being terse. There's been too much lunacy too early in the day."

"I love you, too."

His eyes softened as he looked at her. "You found the lab?"

"I did. Miss Marin was very helpful. She even knew how to use the battery-powered equipment. So, not a waste."

He deflated a bit at that. "What'd you find out, anyway?"

She put her handheld on his desk and projected an enhanced holographic image of the cargo ship, now rendered in three dimensions to be viewable from all angles. "The source images were taken by news cameras, which we ran through an enhancer and compiled—"

A knock grabbed their attention. Karmen was mildly surprised to see Lee Tuyin waving his handheld at her, wearing his tinted glasses and looking the part of an authority figure, despite his young age. The students and faculty outside the office were staring at him and whispering to each other, clearly confused why a TSS Junior Agent was in their midst. "You texted you'd be here. Took me a while to find this place."

She beckoned him in and moved so he could see the display. "There's only one ship in the sky right now, and this is it. We used a dozen or so images and pictures from various sources to create this composite in an imagery lab downstairs."

"What about it?" Lee said, studying the image. "The power for the spaceport's guidance system is out. Remaining stationary is standard procedure—"

"I know that. But this ship… it doesn't belong here. Take a look and tell me if I'm crazy."

Lee did as he was asked, squinting and maneuvering the holographic composite into numerous points of view. "What am I missing?"

Karmen raised an eyebrow, surprised the Junior Agent hadn't picked up on the incongruity of it all. "Lee, what's an ore cargo transport doing above the city?"

His eyes widened with the realization. "Hold on." He rapidly typed out a message on his handheld. "I want another set of eyes on this."

A few minutes later, another young man arrived, out of breath. Lee introduced him with an imperious wave of his hand. "Karmen and Daveed Sley, this is Officer Armin Godri. He's a member of the TSS Militia stationed here at Greengard."

Karmen gave a respectful nod to her fellow servicemember.

"Armin is a specialist in electronic intelligence," Lee continued. "If anyone can tell you what these images mean, it's him."

Armin nodded to Daveed but spoke cautiously to Karmen. "At your service, First Officer Sley."

Great, more bright children for me to manage. "Twenty years ago, I was First Officer Sley. Now, I'm just Karmen. You must have run from the other side of the campus," she teased.

"Lee said it's important, so I ran. What am I looking for, specifically?"

Karmen moved aside so the young man could examine the holographic image. "This is an ore transporter, right? But it's been modified." She pointed out details with a fingertip. "These hatches, all around the lower deck. See here? Here… here…"

"Looks like they're for cargo loading," Lee said.

Armin sniffed. "I don't know. Why would you want to move cargo pods through the lower hull? At least not on a ship this size."

"Plenty of people customize ships to suit their needs."

"True," Armin said. "And they've done a lot more. You see this band integrated into the hull beneath the flight deck? That looks like a Vanam array—I think the SDK-200 series. It's a sensor suite for tracking multiple targets. Top-of-the-line tech."

Daveed blanched and dropped his voice to a whisper.

"Tracking targets… as in for combat purposes?"

"Yes, you'll find an array like this on any TSS ship equipped with weapons. They made some modifications to the design after the war, so I can tell the model on this ship is older—but that doesn't make it any less effective."

"Someone took an ore freighter, added a bunch of external hatches to it, and topped it off with a military combat targeting array?" Karmen asked.

"That is my assessment."

Daveed's brows were drawn together. "What's going on?"

The two TSS members exchanged concerned glances.

"I'm going to send this up the chain," Armin said. He began furiously typing on his handheld.

Karmen fought the urge to panic. "I want to find out, but I think we should get home to the kids. Can they do without you here?"

Daveed hesitated, looking over his desk. After a few seconds, he nodded. "Yes. I've made my calls and left all the instructions I have."

"Would you like to join us?" Karmen asked Lee and Armin.

"All my patients' appointments have been canceled, so sounds good to me," Lee said.

"The TSS has been asked to help the Enforcers with patrols, so I may as well patrol your neighborhood until I receive further orders," Armin agreed.

Lee clapped the other TSS officer on his shoulder. "There's a particular house you should keep an eye on. You're going to love their kitchen!"

9

DON'T PANIC ROOM

THE GROUP TOOK the scenic route back to the house to avoid crowds along the main streets. With the public transportation system down, everyone was following the known routes mirroring the skytrains. The good news was that the Sley home was only a few kilometers away from the campus grounds; the pleasant weather made for a comfortable afternoon walk. Karmen and Daveed joked about how it was good to get a little exercise, and Lee and Armin made a habit of jogging ahead a few blocks then waiting for the others to catch up.

"It's a bit like having a pair of private security men at our disposal," Daveed said cheerfully.

Karmen smiled. "Lee's been a tremendous help. And not just with my eyes, although I'll always be thankful for that."

"He's one of your people," Daveed said. "Don't give me that look—you know what I mean. You'll always be TSS, no matter what else you do with your life. Civilians like me can't hope to compete with that."

"It's not a competition. Really."

"If you say so."

"Not because I say so. Because it isn't," she insisted.

He nodded and smiled, but she wasn't convinced he believed her.

As they approached their block, they saw a crowd milling around in the middle of the street. Some people were raising their voices. At least two arguments were in progress at the edges of the crowd.

Elian and Seandra rushed up to them from the throng.

They were supposed to go straight inside! Karmen's brows knitted. "Why are you—"

"Missus Kotalis is going crazy!" Elian burst out before Karmen could finish her question. "You need to talk her off the ledge."

Seandra nodded vigorously.

Oh no, what now? Karmen wrapped her arm around Elian.

Hellen Kotalis, the matronly wife of a Vice President at the university, recognized Karmen and Daveed and sauntered over, breathless. "The Jovaers are leaving. Should we leave, too?"

Daveed put on his most charming work face. "I don't think so, Hellen. It's just a blip in the power grid. They'll have it back on soon."

Hellen's eyes only grew wider. "What about the banks? The hospitals? The Enforcers?"

Karmen released Elian and did her best to match her husband's reassuring demeanor. "I was just at the medical annex. The main hospital is running on backup power, don't worry. They're figuring out the rest."

"We heard there was a missile! It came from that crazy spaceship. What else are they going to do? Is it an attack? I'll bet you it's an invasion!"

Lee and Armin stepped forward, ready to intervene, but Karmen motioned for them to hang back.

She gently put her hands on Hellen's shoulders. "I've seen images of the ship. It's just an ore carrier—"

Hellen pushed against Karmen, invading her space. "What's going on?" she demanded. "You know people. Who's in charge? Are they going to declare martial law? We need to protect our neighborhood!"

Engrained tactics for managing distressed soldiers returned to Karmen. "Look at me, Hellen. Look. At. Me," she commanded, drawing her neighbor's attention with her voice. "We are in a state of emergency. The city controllers have issued warnings that people should stay at home and off the roads for a while. It's a unique event. But nobody *invades* a city or planet. The war with the Bakzen ended years ago, and they will never come back. We're all safe."

"But the power is off. Some of us have been locked out of our houses. We need *help*," Hellen wailed.

"And we'll get it. I have two men from the TSS with me," she nodded toward them, "and they will keep us apprised of any significant developments. But for now, you need to help me out by keeping these people calm. You can do that by keeping it together and showing them you have discipline. Fortitude."

"I'm not your minion to manage!" Hellen gasped.

Bomax, that's not what I said. Why are you like this, Hellen? Karmen stood firm. "No, I'd never think that of you. But you're an upstanding member of this community. People respect you. You can lead by example right now, really have a chance to shine in a way that everyone will remember. Project a sense of calm, and they'll listen to you."

Hellen drew a sharp breath through her nose, processing the words. "But if this *is* an invasion," she whispered, "we need to defend ourselves. I need a gun. Do you have a gun?"

What kind of deranged mind jumps from 'power outage' to 'invasion'? It took effort for Karmen to remain civil. "Everything is going to be fine, Hellen."

Hellen fixated on the two TSS officers. "Are we in danger?"

"There's no immediate cause for concern," Lee replied. "The authorities are investigating the situation. The best thing you can do right now is wait in your homes."

"That's right." Karmen pulled Hellen's attention back to her. "Now, Hellen, I need you to organize these folks. Make sure everyone has enough food in their pantries. Anyone who's locked out should stay with a neighbor for now." Karmen found it ridiculous that anyone wouldn't have a physical key to their home stashed somewhere for emergency situations just like this, but not everyone had her training or common sense.

Hellen let out a long breath, the flush fading from her cheeks. Now that she had orders to follow, Hellen transformed from a victim to a good soldier. With a curt nod to Karmen, she turned and then addressed the crowd, suffused with new confidence. "My friends, everything is being handled. We'll get through this together. Please step forward if you're locked out!"

Daveed bent close to his wife as they walked toward the Sley house at the end of the block. "One day, you may actually have to shoot her."

"Don't even joke about that. Come on, I'll show you my Don't Panic room."

Daveed missed a step. "Wait. We have a panic room? When have you ever panicked?"

Oh, that's a long story. I promise to tell you all about it, but not right now. "It's a Don't Panic room. It's completely safe.

This way."

Elian and Seandra ran ahead to the house. Even from a distance, Karmen could tell they were arguing about something. At least that was normal.

Their own house lock was on backup battery power, so it was no trouble getting inside. The two other children were waiting in the living room.

Kaia stood up. "Mom, Dad, what—"

"We don't know any more than you do right now, but we're all together now, so that's all that matters," Karmen stated. "Everyone, come with me."

She led her party down into the basement, which the teens had long since turned into a general entertainment center. Game consoles lay on the furniture, and a viewscreen wide enough to use as a ski jump decorated the far wall. Karmen went across the room into the walk-in closet. She moved aside a stack of plastic crates filled with old memorabilia, locating a hidden latch. Pulling a panel aside, she revealed a heavy metal door.

Daveed gaped at her. "How…?"

Karmen shrugged. "Old habits die hard."

The door creaked open to reveal a set of stairs descending into darkness.

Lee raised his brows, fighting an amused smirk.

Karmen shot him a cautionary glare to keep him quiet. "It's dark, so keep your hand on the rail." She headed into the tunnel.

Power systems sprang to life with whirs and clicks behind the walls as the group began their descent. A much heavier vault-like door stood at the bottom. Karmen entered a code into the electronic lock, and the clang of bolts reverberated in the darkness.

"This is so cool," Elian whispered from the stairs above.

Maybe the kids will stop complaining about their boring mom having no style. Karmen pulled the door open.

Recessed lights came on as she entered. The room was hemispherical, with the entrance set flush against a flat section. Lockers protruded along either side, framing a large table at the center of the space. Behind it was a semicircle of control modules, with a small pedestal to the right. Another heavy door was centered on the back wall.

Daveed twirled slowly, taking it all in. "Looks like a bit of a space station business office."

"No, it looks like a starship Command Center," Lee said. "I'll bet the TSS *Triumph* looked like this."

"The *Triumph* was far, far bigger and properly staffed," she corrected. "But there is a repurposed shuttle power module down here running everything." She took an objective look around the space. Swap out the lockers for secondary control stations, add in a couple of command chairs, and change the back door to a viewscreen… "Okay, maybe I *did* try to recreate a familiar layout."

"I'll say." Lee walked past each console and touched the screens. The room came alive with electronic vitality as he recited the console names. "Ops, nav, comms, sensors, weapons, engineering. Stars, Karmen, you really went all in on this. Are these functional?"

"Let's find out," Elian said, rushing to the weapons console. Before anyone could stop him, he'd started pushing buttons at random.

The screech of metal and the *thunk* of a door opening met their ears.

Then, Seandra called out, "Mom, what are these?"

"What are what…?" She realized what her daughter had pressed. "Oh, *bomax*! Seandra, you weren't supposed to open those. Elian, step away from that."

A heavy locker to their left had popped its lock and yawned wide like an open invitation. Seandra lost no time entering. She retrieved a crate and yanked the lid open. A piercing, girlish squeal rang out as she pulled an automatic rifle from the case. "Stars! It's a Zanoff-Boland G36K! The most amazing assault rifle ever. Where did you get them from?"

"Where *did* you get them from?" Armin asked.

"I'd like to know that, too," Daveed added.

Karmen waved the men off and concentrated on her daughter. "And how do you know what it is?" Karmen asked.

Seandra let the rifle hang at her side and rolled her eyes. "That's hardly important, Mom."

"I disagree. Put it back in the case, please."

"Yes, ma'am." She set it down. "For the record, these were the absolute best weapon in Star Patrol. See? Games *can* be educational."

Daveed knocked on the other heavy locker. "What's in this one? Grenades? A warhead?"

The disapproval in his voice brought heat to her cheeks and twisted her stomach. Some part of her wanted to defend herself, but deep down she knew she'd lost some of his trust. That wasn't a fair way to treat a partner of over two decades. *I should have told him about this sooner.*

Karmen fought back her unbidden shame and anxiety about the awkward situation. "No, that locker is for general equipment. Medical supplies, first aid, some food packs. Dry goods. A water tank. Tool kits. A coil of paracord."

"Paracord? What for?"

She wanted to reply but found herself without an explanation. *Fok, why did I put that in there?* "It seemed like a good idea at the time," she said. It sounded stupid even to her.

So much of this project's reasoning had been done unconsciously over the years. Just in case.

She activated the map table to distract herself. The device projected a contoured holographic map of the city. It included the image of the converted ore carrier hanging in the sky. Karmen couldn't look away from it. There were too many strange aspects about the ship for it to be irrelevant, but the *who* and *why* of the situation remained a mystery. "Who are you, great lady?" she murmured.

A hand on her shoulder abruptly pulled her from her thoughts. Daveed's voice whispered in her ear, "I think we need to have a talk."

Karmen's gut clenched tighter. Reflexively, she raised her voice a bit. "Family talk. Kids, let's—"

"No. Just us. Kids, play with the map, but don't touch the lockers or crates. Lee and Armin, I would appreciate it if you could get on the comm to find out more about the current situation." He nodded at the other door. "What's through there?"

"Storage," Karmen replied. "A couple of rooms with bunk beds."

"Lead the way."

They went into the bunkroom and closed the door. Daveed directed her to one of the beds then sat next to her. "Karmen, tell me what's going on."

"You *know* what's going on. The start of a planet-wide disaster. How can you not see that?"

"Because all that we know for certain right now is that there's been a power outage in the city. We *don't* know that it's planet-wide or anything that won't be resolved five minutes from now. Stars, Karmen, three hours ago, our life was perfectly normal! I was at work, the kids were at school, you were getting treated for your eyes. Now, I find out you have a secret bunker full of stolen military equipment and a safe full of guns. Not even in my house. *Beneath* my house. When were you going to share this information?"

"I just did. Ideally, I would never have had to. But I wanted to be prepared, so I could protect our family. Things went bad. They always seem to go bad, eventually." The world darkened—and not because of the lights or her eyes. The floor fell away from her. She felt unmoored, in free-fall. In a moment, her eyes were wet; she blinked furiously to clear them. She groaned. "It's always something."

He moved closer and she leaned against him. He was her rock. She would never trust anyone like she trusted him. She'd made a mess of things by not trusting him with… this.

Daveed kissed the top of her head and squeezed her hand. "You want to talk about it?"

"You know what happened to the *Triumph*."

"Just what you told me."

"That was essentially all of it. But those events set me down a path that changed my perspective. After the Lead Agent investigated and determined none of my crew was at fault, we were all re-assigned. I was sent to a base on Belvil. Small outpost, remote and very hostile environment. We lived in domes. One day, we were all fine, and then something blipped or burped and the life support fell apart. The spare hadn't been properly shielded against the environment; it burned out when we powered it on. That was still deep in wartime, and we were a small team at an unimportant post. We had to live in space suits for weeks until a repair crew could get the necessary replacement parts to us. My takeaway was that no matter how safe and secure you think you are, there's always a chance that it will go wrong. Horribly, badly wrong. And I could never bear to see our children suffer because I hadn't done *everything* in my power to give them their best chance at survival."

Daveed's eyes softened. "You don't need to carry that burden alone."

"I'm sorry I didn't share this with you. I thought I was probably just being paranoid and didn't want to worry you—"

He took her hands in his. "I will always listen to your over-planning notions and support you. You don't have to spare my feelings. I'm your partner. We'll tackle every challenge together."

How did I get so lucky with this man? She met his gaze. "We can only ever truly trust our family. You saw that crowd on the way down here. Daveed, those were our neighbors. People we know, people we've been living around for years. And they were ready to start rioting after a few hours of darkness."

"Sure, because that nitwit Hellen was riling them up."

"But that's my point. There's always a Hellen. Our life support unit on Belvil was a Hellen, too. They're interchangeable. What happens if the power stays off for a week? If the food deliveries stop? If people get *really* hungry?" She pulled her hands free and glared at the floor. "So I built this. Just in case."

They sat in silence for a while. The separating door wasn't airtight, and the conversations from the other room filtered through it. They instantly recognized a growing argument between Elian and Seandra. But the low voices of Lee and Armin were somehow more worrisome.

Eventually, Daveed said, "Go help your boys."

"They're not my—"

"I'm beginning to accept that you'll always have a connection to the TSS, no matter how much time passes. You might not even realize it, but you light up every time you talk about Lee and his work. You miss that life."

Her shoulders rounded. "I don't know."

"I do. And I hope you know I'll always support you."

"Thank you, Daveed. I do."

He stood up. "But I also know you well enough to say that you have to deal with these reemerging feelings about your past or they'll get toxic very quickly. So, put your uniform and medals back on and help those two young men fix it. I'll still be here when you're done."

She stood and faced him. "I love you."

"I love you, too." He cracked a playful smile. "Hey, can you teach me how to fire one of those assault rifles?"

She punched him in the arm. "I guess I'll have to now. First, let's see what's on the comms."

10

CALL TO ARMS

KARMEN ALLOWED DAVEED to take the lead when they emerged from the back room. He was a leader in his own right, and she wanted to make sure he felt like he had a voice in what was going on with their family.

"Gentlemen, did we find out the cause of the problem?" her husband asked the two TSS officers.

"No, but we did find this." Armin turned up the volume on a speaker.

An androgynous voice spoke tonelessly into the air, "This is an official Foundation City government broadcast. All current and former military service members should now go to Schedule R. Repeat: this is an official Foundation City government broadcast—"

Armin silenced the message. "It's an automated alert that goes out in case the city council, the mayor, deputy mayor, and the council coordinator are dead or incapacitated. All available personnel are expected to check in with the local offices and await assignment."

Daveed shook his head like he was trying to clear it of evil spirits. "They can't be dead. It's just a power outage. That's temporary."

"Dead *or* incapacitated," Lee said. "That includes being stuck in a shelter without means of communicating to the outside world. A lot of city transmitters and computer networks are probably running down their battery backups right now. If the council network goes dark, then this message would activate as a precaution."

"Have you two received your orders?" Karmen asked.

Lee shook his head. "Not yet."

"In the meantime, why don't you tell us how you got those assault rifles?" Armin said.

Seandra bounced on her toes. "Right. They're so cool."

Daveed turned to his daughter. "That's no way to talk about weapons."

Seandra frowned. "Dad, I don't know about these things just because of games. Conflicts happen, and you can read about all the tactical gear on the Net. I was curious what kind of stuff Mom worked with when she was in the service, so I did my own research since you refuse to talk about it. Stars, Kozu wants to join the Militia, but you're not asking him why he's wrong in the head!"

"She has a point," Lee offered. The girl beamed at first but lost some of her shine as he continued, "But your dad has a point, too, Seandra. Weapons aren't cool or fun, they're tools of the trade. And that trade is all about killing bad guys and breaking stuff. That's just the way it is."

"You don't think your background in medical research is biasing you just a bit, Agent Tuyin?" Kaia said.

"I'm extremely biased. It comes from studying the dizzying

array of methods that exist to blow people up. That doesn't make me wrong."

Karmen folded her arms. "To answer your question, Armin, I have a supplier. One of the downtown campuses has a shooting range, which a lot of Militia and Enforcers use to keep their skills sharp. I help out a few days each month as a safety trainer with civilians. And yes, I do some shooting, too. There are always veterans there. We talk. It's fun and it gets me out of the house."

"And when you were just having a moment with the club owner, you asked if there was a way to purchase some special equipment?" Daveed surmised.

Karmen shrugged. "It's a little more complicated than that, but—"

The comm console buzzed, displaying a flashing announcement across the screen.

>>**From:** Agent Jon Lambren, Sector Agent-in-Charge
To: Officer Armin Godri; Junior Agent Lee Tuyin; Karmen Sley, Officer (retired)

STATE OF EMERGENCY now exists on Greengard. Follow-up requested on open investigation. Officer Sley's Militia status restored to ACTIVE with all privileges and responsibilities. Report to Captain Travanti, Enforcer Command, Foundation City, Peacekeeper Plaza, ASAP.<<

"What shite is this?" Lee grumbled. "They're having us report to the *Enforcers*?"

Armin shook his head. He glanced at the kids nearby and then dropped his voice to a whisper. "I don't want to read between the lines, but…"

Karmen got something very different out of the message. "Why the fok is my name on these summons?"

Armin grimaced. "That might be my fault. When I sent in my field report about that ore carrier and the imaging you did, I named the three of us. Seems like they've decided to make us an official team."

"I never agreed to that. I'm retired," Karmen shot back.

"I'm sorry, I don't make the orders," Armin replied. "This is straight from the Agent in charge of this sector. And, apparently, whatever is going on is important enough to have all hands on deck."

This shouldn't be my fight. She was a private citizen now. She was done with it. Done with the war, done with the funerals, the Bakzen, the commands, the nonsense.

"They can't do this!" she blurted out.

"Yes, they can," Lee said. "You can retire from the service, but you never really leave. We need to report in. Now."

Karmen looked pleadingly at Lee. "You can tell them I'm not qualified. My eyesight, it's bomaxed."

"Two months ago, it was bomaxed. We tested you this afternoon and you passed with flying colors. If you're that set on dodging duty, I could give you something to purge the Octarin from your system, but you'd go right back to almost-blind. It's your call."

She scoffed. "Some call."

"Mom, you don't need to pretend," Kozu said from across the room. "We all know you couldn't stand waiting out a disaster in an underground bunker. Just look at this place… it's not who you are. You're ready for a fight. And I want to help, too. I can—"

"No, you'll stay here with me and your siblings," Daveed announced. "They're not drafting all of us." He turned to his wife. "But he's right. If you don't go, you'll hate yourself. I'll hold down the fort. We'll eat the food packs, tie knots with the paracord, sleep in the bunk beds. It'll be fine. Who knows, they may even get the power back up before you get there."

They know me too well. And in her gut, she knew they were right. She had tried to convince herself that her military life was in the past, but looking around this space and everything she'd built 'just in case', it was obvious that it was still a part of her. It always would be. "Don't let anyone else in here—and especially *do not* tell Hellen anything or indicate that I'm not here," Karmen told her husband. "If she sees me go, she'll promote herself to Supreme Commander of the whole neighborhood."

"I'll keep her in line, don't worry," Daveed assured her. "Lee, Armin, take care of her."

"Never fear," Armin said. "She can probably outfight both of us with one hand in her pocket."

"Heh. I wish." Karmen pulled open another locker and hauled out a heavy binder, which she thrust into Daveed's hands. "Instructions for every system down here. Learn it all by the time I get back. Don't let the children play with the slug throwers unattended."

Daveed winked at her. "Leave my name with your friend at the training campus and it's a deal."

—

The sun was dropping behind the skyline into an orange horizon by the time they left the house. Karmen insisted on driving. She needed to have some amount of control over the situation. Besides, she knew the best roads to take during an emergency; she'd lived here long enough to memorize several access routes without the benefit of computerized navigation tools.

Peacekeeper Plaza was one of the numerous municipal areas in Foundation City that Karmen had known about but never visited. There were administrative offices and facilities for both the Guard Enforcers and TSS, though the TSS presence was significantly smaller. Seeing the Enforcer's building now, she couldn't decide if it looked more like a fortress or a prison. In any case, besides being constructed with a wide and well-defensible kill zone, it had a unique status in the still-dark city. It was one of the few buildings that still had power.

Having the two structures share a common courtyard was about as much interaction as Karmen would have expected the TSS to have with the local Enforcers. There was a longstanding rivalry between the Guard and TSS; though they'd cooperate with each other's investigations, the two organizations usually remained separate in all functions. For them to be pooling personnel resources right now meant this wasn't a minor incident.

Other people were heading toward the buildings. Karmen didn't expect to recognize anyone, but one approaching the TSS facility jumped out at her, even from a distance.

"Bertie?"

The man turned around. "Stars! Karmen Sley?"

They ran up to each other. She startled when she got close and saw the vaguely unsettling stare of artificial eyes looking back at her.

Not him, too... She gave him a hug. "Bertie, what are you

doing here?"

The *Triumph*'s head chef grinned as he pulled out from the embrace. "Here in the plaza, or Greengard in general?"

"Both!"

"I came in three years ago to help set up a culinary school with the university. Now, I'm a program director there. I had no idea you were local, or I'd have looked you up."

"Rum raisin ice cream," she blurted out.

Bertie's face contorted as he tried to remember the reference. "Gah, that's right! I hope it worked out. Before… you know… before it obviously didn't."

"Let's not think about that right now, my friend. What did they call you in for with the Schedule R?"

"I've been asked to help set up an emergency shelter as a precautionary measure, make sure we can get everyone fed, if it comes to it."

"You're the right man for the job."

"But hey, might not be needed. I heard lights are coming back on in a few neighborhoods. That must mean we're figuring it out, right?"

"Yes, good sign." She wouldn't believe it until the power was back on at her own house.

Bertie nodded to the offices beyond. "Looks like you're heading to the Enforcers. You going in for a consult?"

"Something like that."

"Nothing like an emergency to make us play nice," her old friend said.

"Karmen." Lee bobbed his head toward the Enforcer building, clearly growing impatient.

She brought up her contact card on her handheld. "Let's connect after this?" She did intend to catch up with him when the emergency was resolved. She worked hard to keep her promises. But she also knew that life had a way of dragging you in every direction except the one you wanted to go.

Bertie exchanged info with her. "Yes, ma'am. Good to see you."

Karmen ran back to rejoin Lee and Armin, then the three of them continued across the plaza. The Enforcers at the front gate nodded at Karmen and Armin but gave Lee a wider berth; they probably didn't get too many Agents on the planet.

"Come on, guys, it's not like I'm going to telekinetically shred you if I get angry," Lee grumbled as he passed through the checkpoint.

In the building lobby, they were stopped at the front desk. The two Enforcers behind it eyed Lee's Junior Agent uniform.

"What can we do for you, sir?" one of them asked.

"The three of us received summons to meet with Captain Travanti," Lee replied. "Junior Agent Tuyin, and Officers Godri and Sley."

The Enforcer checked his computer monitor. "Ah, yes. Wait here and someone will come to escort you."

Karmen shot a look toward her Junior Agent friend as they stepped away from the desk. "How much sway will you hold in this scenario, Lee?"

"Within the TSS structure, I officially outrank both of you in Militia. But I'm reporting to this Enforcer captain, same as you. Agent Lambren is a Jotun Division veteran, so if he signed off on this command structure, he has a good reason."

The words were far from comforting, but she didn't have a say in the matter.

Another Enforcer came to lead them down numerous corridors, all decorated with muted gray and green tile work, presenting them with the antithesis of the university. Karmen had never set foot in this place before—never been tempted.

Now, she remembered why. These sorts of institutions were all
about efficiency, with a focus on the collective rather than
anything personal. In recent years, being a part of the
university culture and raising a family, she'd come to value
creativity and inquisitiveness for the simple sake of
exploration. But here, everything had a distinct purpose. Cold,
calculated objectives.

She found the difference between how her companions
handled the situation fascinating. Lee kept a few paces back, his
tinted glasses proudly displayed on his face, but otherwise he
stayed quiet and out of the way. Armin, however, came alive in
this environment, smiling and exchanging greetings with the
people they passed by in the halls. Many of them seemed to
know him.

"I didn't realize you interacted with the Enforcers,"
Karmen commented.

Armin grinned. "We Intelligence guys get around. People
like that we know things, and we like to know them," he said
as if it explained everything. To him, maybe it did.

Eventually, the Enforcer stopped at a door at the end of a
hall, motioning for them to enter. "The captain is waiting."

Stepping inside, Travanti's office looked less like a military
post and more like a civilian functionary's. Paneled walls and
thick carpet gave the place a warm, cozy appearance. But the
desk the captain sat behind was pure Guard: gunmetal and
chrome.

Captain Travanti rose as they entered. He was a tall, thin
man with a pinched expression. Karmen wondered if he was in
pain; he looked like he was always in pain. "Officer Sley, Officer
Godri, Junior Agent Tuyin. Your report caught our attention.
We are grateful for your continued help."

"Captain Travanti," the three greeted in unison.

Travanti indicated a pair of older men with rugged features and no obvious sense of humor standing along the side wall of the office. "These are Investigators Russei and Sura. They'll be assisting you as long as you're working on this particular problem."

"Is that what this situation is? A problem?" Lee asked.

Russei stepped forward. "Honestly, we don't know what it is," he said with a scratchy voice. "All we do know is that ship you identified is at the center of a planet-wide cyberattack."

Armin perked up. "Oh?"

Russei pulled out his handheld and projected a holographic schematic of the city's infrastructure, filling the center of the room. "I don't have to tell you that the whole planet revolves around a finely crafted electronic data network."

"Not gravity?" Lee snarked.

"Forgive me, Agent Tuyin, I lost my funny bone when my home went dark."

"My apologies. Please continue."

"Rumors are circulating about an orbital attack. To some extent, that happens to be true, but it's not from the ship itself. A single device was launched, and it appears to be the source of some kind of cyber-weapon."

"Have you engaged the vessel?" Lee asked.

"It's been nonresponsive to our communication attempts. We can't take military action without risking extreme civilian casualties, since it's inside the planetary shield above the city. We're hoping to get a handle on the symptoms first, and then we can deal with the cause once the grid is back up. Which brings us to the specific problem…" Russei zoomed in on the holoprojection, focusing on an object resembling a missile crashed on the ground on the outskirts of Foundation City.

"Whatever this is, it broadcast a signal on the same frequency used for emergency notifications. *Everything* is connected to that communication protocol, and we have no clue how they got access credentials. We can debate the design vulnerabilities later, but the present facts are that the attackers used this back door to deploy a cyberattack.

"Even though we've now disabled the original device, our systems are infected. The virus—if that's what it is—appears to have rewritten the startup routine of every computer it encounters, locking the machine in an endless reboot loop. The techies are dealing with it, but it will be days until all systems are restored. Until then, we're on backup power with a limited number of systems that were air-gapped from the main network."

"If not a virus, what might it be?" Armin asked.

"That's something we hope you folks can help us determine."

Lee touched Karmen's shoulder. "Welcome back to the game, Officer Sley."

11

CRIME IS A PERFORMANCE

"STATUS REPORT," CAPTAIN Aura ordered from her seat behind Lom at the center of the *Emerald Queen*'s War Room.

Lom extended nanofiber wires from the wrist of his Sergent Meklife drone, tethering him to the control console. Instantly, the ship fed him a constant stream of data. As far as he could tell, all was going according to plan. But his captain would want more granular information. She was very much a hands-on commander—one thing he particularly appreciated about her.

"The missile ejected its payload and impacted on the outskirts of the city," he announced. "With very few exceptions, Foundation City's entire data network is unresponsive. There is a government broadcast in progress, but it's sluggish. Citizens are being urged to stay in their homes for the duration of the emergency."

"Excellent. I do love a government that values its people's safety," Captain Aura said. "How are the drop flights going?"

"We'll be ready to launch the shuttles very shortly. My drone pilots are programming their landing and recovery patterns. The hospital annex and several commercial plazas will be the focus of the first two drop flight attacks. It should sufficiently divert attention from the mining and processing plant for us to collect the targeted assets."

"Good. Take personal charge of the mining drop. We'll only get one shot at that. It must work as planned," the captain insisted.

Lom pulled his wires back in and saluted. "We serve the Queen. I'll supervise each drop unit as it comes up for deployment."

Captain Aura bobbed her head as she tried to watch six displays at once. The War Room was a busy place, and this op was making it busier. "Certainly. Carry on."

Lom maneuvered his drone body past Taran crew members who gave him a wide berth. He wondered if he should be going out and about the crew in his skin more often. Lynaedans looked completely Taran for the most part. Yes, some embraced more fanciful technological upgrades than others, but they were still flesh and blood. Deep down, were they that different? He didn't think so.

However, his mission demanded efficiency. That could only be accomplished with his augmentations. This was a job, a calling. Captain Aura needed people with skills, and his drone pilots had them. Being on this ship was a chance to serve the Queen.

He wove his way through hatches and down corridors. Despite the redesign, this vessel would always resemble its roots as an ore carrier. Though there had been significant improvements to its architecture—nanofiber internal structure buffers, reactive armor plates, and reinforced bulkheads, not to mention plenty of weapons—*Emerald Queen* retained the soul of a working individual, devoted to its trade. This vessel presented his people with a fitting throne for the Queen's oversight of their larger mission.

The lift deposited Lom on the hangar deck. This section of the *Emerald Queen* was given over to housing and launching various craft and had been retrofitted with the design particulars that went with it. The main hangar housed six dropships and transport shuttles, maintenance garage crew quarters, and supply holds. The deck above it housed the Lynaedans' crew quarters as well as their drone control equipment and the QEN-1000 AI that routed commands from the pilots installed in their control pods to the machines they ran with their thoughts.

A non-Lynaedan crewmate had once asked Lom what it was like walking around while knowing that his body was in a different place, and he hadn't known how to answer the question. Both of them were him, and the Meklife drone was no less a part of him than his physical skin. He was nestled comfortably in his control pod as he experienced the full sensory experience of stepping into the massive hangar with its cool air and pervasive mechanical hum. Frankly, he couldn't imagine what it was like to be limited to one frail physical form for an entire life, beholden to the limitations of the basic Taran body.

The comm officer caught up with Lom when he paused to study the flight status board, a wide display that looked like it belonged in a public transit hub.

"Commander Mench, I'm glad I found you." Gallian's eyes flashed an intense blue that denoted the fact they were artificial.

Lom could easily trace the lattice of nanofibers wired throughout his crewman's skin, as well, which fed into the bright metal bands that ran along the back of his head just above his ears. A multispectral comm net that he never went anywhere without. Very fine work. Lom approved. "What do you need?"

"I've gone over the operational plans. Will you be piloting the mining shuttle personally?" Gallian asked.

"Negative. Captain Aura wants me to attend that flight as the unit commander."

"I see. That should be… Yes, we can move you to one of the Idolon spots on the shuttle. You don't mass nearly what they do. More room for cargo if you wanted to pursue that option."

Lom pivoted to watch the loading operation on the mining shuttle. An Idolon was a brute of a drone, wide and tall with segmented arms and thick legs. Their bulk made them slow, and they were heavy besides. But each one of them could store a ton of material inside its torso. Good transport drones. Less useful in a fight, but fighting wasn't their job.

"Not at all. Sticking to the plan will be difficult enough. That shuttle has cargo capacity only for two dozen containment boxes and their contents. I wish the Idolons weren't so cumbersome," Lom said.

"They're nearly impossible for normal Taran weapons to damage. That's the point of them."

"Agreed. What about the other two shuttles?"

"The Medical Annex will be engaged by a combination of twenty Scoutmek attack drones and five cargo drone handlers. The commercial plaza will be covered by ten assault drones and twelve Blastermeks. Lots of noise and unpleasantness while five more cargo drones collect the items we've planned for."

"Remember, no lethal weapons. We aim to create chaos, not casualties."

"I've gone over the rules of engagement with all teams. Lots of noise, fireworks, and smoke, but that's all. Any Enforcers who try to engage will be neutralized with stun-based weaponry only."

"Excellent. Send the first two shuttles on their way. We'll give them time to deploy, then launch the real attack."

"Right away." Gallian rapped on Meklife's arm with his knuckles. "Will you be using that drone?"

In his control pod, Lom took stock of the supply of ready machines at his crew's disposal. Maybe the swashbuckling rapier-wielding pirate wasn't the best choice, after all. "No, I think I'll swap out to the Command model. I'll need the added bandwidth for the encryption links."

"Very well-reasoned. Good hunting, Commander Mench."

—

Walking Meklife back to the control dock was easy. Once the rakish-looking drone hooked its connector to the recharging port, Lom broke the connection and selected his new model. The Berserker had the advantage of depth and weight, but it was nowhere near as aesthetically pleasing as Meklife. This was a Command model, heavily shielded against electromagnetic bursts and other energy sources—the sort of thing one wanted when stealing nuclear weapons. It was perfect.

The new drone gleamed as the dock prepped it for deployment. Its wide eyes glowed a bright violet. Lom engaged the camouflage skin as it stepped off the platform. A few more adjustments and the drone could pass for any Taran in the empire. Perfect.

The real treat came as Lom brought his extra comm
channels online. While he approached his drop ship, he could
watch the other two raids already in progress. The two shuttles
were descending too quickly for the planet's Enforcers to do
anything about them. In minutes, his forces would be on the
ground sowing chaos, but there was nothing to watch yet. He
minimized the comm lines for now so he could concentrate on
his task.

His drop shuttle was the largest of the three, as dictated by
the needs of the mission. Idolons stalked in a line, converging
on the cargo hatch. The drones climbed aboard one by one,
their pilots locking their charges into the flight frame inside.
They were well-practiced in the equipment's use, and there
were no complications.

Once all the Idolons were in place, Lom boarded the ship
and then signaled the shuttle pilot. The vessel lifted on its
thrusters and dropped out an open hatch in the belly of the
carrier, custom installed for that very purpose.

On his integrated feed, Lom observed as the first drop
shuttles flew over the city's commercial plaza, dropping its
compliment of drones. The assault drones were multi-legged
armored constructs and genuinely disturbing to watch move,
like great spiders but with thick legs and numerous lenses for
eyes. As they walked, they popped tiny 'bees'—self-contained
units whose only job was to hover in place and monitor the
presence of enemies. The Blastermeks resembled rolling
spheres armed with floating turrets and grenade launchers.
They shot out store windows, attacked ground vehicles, and
lobbed smoke grenades in all directions. Meanwhile, the heavy
bipedal cargo drones climbed into store fronts and seized what
they were instructed to locate, placing the stolen items in their
torso cavities.

Lom quickly checked on his own mission; his ship was traversing the planet's terminator, heading to the side where it was now night. They'd be there soon.

The assault on the medical annex was far more interesting to watch, so he switched back to that channel. Scoutmeks were sleek, narrow quadrupeds, running on all fours like big cats, snarling and screaming to subdue any passerby who might want to obstruct them. A squad of Enforcers from some local base confronted them as a group. They were bold and fearless, arriving in riot armor with blunt energy rods in hand. They demanded the machines stop, but the drone pilots weren't having it. A trio of Scoutmeks bowled over the Taran defenders, scattering them to the far edge of the operational zone. Two Enforcers got the message quickly and ran. One more tried to shoot one of the Scoutmeks at close range; he even got off several shots before the mech retaliated by swatting him with a foreleg. The Enforcer retreated. Good man; one must always save oneself in order to be alive to save others.

Lom activated a set of voice circuits to broadcast from speakers on every mech on the two raiding missions. "Citizens of Foundation City!" they bellowed. "Do not interfere. We do not wish to injure you. Please stay out of the way and no harm will come to you. Mother Carnage thanks you for your cooperation."

He ended the broadcast with a satisfied feeling. *Mother Carnage* indeed. That would give the rabble something to talk about tomorrow. Aura had a lot to learn about managing her public image. She could use the push.

Lom's drop shuttle now hovered in the courtyard of a vast industrial complex surrounded by an arid wasteland, lacking even the character to be called a proper desert. Blocky structures of concrete and fused silicate walls beckoned to be pulverized.

The Idolons dropped out the hatch and spread out, prepared to address any resistance just in case all was not as quiet as they expected.

Lom was the last one out. His command drone's metal feet hit the ground with a resounding *thunk*. He felt jarred by the impact through the somatic feedback in his link to the unit; he'd have to adjust the carriage of this drone when it returned to the ship.

Lom called up a schematic of the depot he'd compiled based on the orbital images. Seven low but wide buildings formed a perimeter, while four more structures inside the base formed a set of processing units, and the central location housed the automated refinery. But the storage section—their real target—was two kilometers from their position. Not as close as he wished, but close enough. "Shuttle pilot, meet us at these coordinates. Idolon pilots, warm up your cutting torches and follow me."

He drove his drone across the plaza's bare rock. Even at night, the temperature was beyond what most Tarans could consider tolerable.

This part of the planet bore no resemblance to the sprawling university of Foundation City. And the presence of a TalEx corporate mining operation was that much stranger. But seeing this here raised interesting questions about where the academics got all their money to build a university. How did they pay their staff? Run their power systems? Manage their wonderful transit network? Through mining operations in this vast desert, that's how.

Lord Gilgamesh had done his research, identifying this world as an integral component to their larger plans. The

Foundation City council had long ago given the Talsari Dynasty exclusive rights to mine radioactive material in Greengard's southern wasteland in order to form Talsarium mining charges. It wasn't controlled as a military resource, since Talsarium's half-life was a measly twelve hours. But that didn't mean it held no value.

Nuclear dampening storage boxes could manage the rate of decay. The boxes were self-contained and used their own internal power cores and would last for years—excellent for mining work in deep space for asteroid-cracking. The storage boxes would allow Lom's team to safely transport the material just like any other cargo. And due to the perceived low-risk nature of the Talsarium, the supply warehouse was no more guarded than a standard tridillium mine.

Furthermore, massively labor-intensive enterprises like mining used optimal workflow arrangements whenever possible to increase productivity. Thus, this TalEx mining site ran just like every other, so Lom hadn't had to pay anyone off to learn the operational protocols and security procedures. They even published their production results for review by industrial partners. Learning everything he'd needed in order to execute a heist had been childishly simple. Of course, he'd had to confirm the exact location from orbit, but that was just basic due diligence. Anyone with an imaging satellite could do that.

Lom opened a channel to his drop ship's pilot. "I need a fly-over and full radiological scan of every building. Use the highest sensitivity metric."

"Got it. Scanning now… Target located. Move clockwise four buildings. The rounds are stored in the structure located between the second and third installments in the outermost ring."

Lom maneuvered his troops accordingly.

What should have been a quick two-kilometer run turned into a time-consuming challenge. Two pilots were less practiced than their peers; they couldn't maintain their balance, and their Idolons stumbled and fell. Righting them and reforming the column put the unit behind schedule. The delay irked Lom to his core. Every second they remained on the ground invited a reprisal. Sure, the drones were nearly impossible to damage without military-grade weapons, but Enforcers could be killed easily, even accidentally. They didn't want casualties; they didn't need that kind of attention.

The target building emerged from the gloom. Lom took the lead position, extending a sensor to locate the section of the wall they needed to breach. "This area. Two units here, two more there. Cut us a doorway. Fire!"

Laser bursts rocked the night, thrown from Idolon hand weapons. In less than a minute, they'd blasted a section of wall to rubble. Fine rock dust filled the air.

"Follow me." Lom led them into the structure, adjusting his vision settings to accommodate the dark. Talsarium decayed into curium isotopes, which had distinct emission patterns. Even through the tunnels and doorways, he could pick out the right path. Just follow the radioactive trail. The signal was strongest at a room protected by a vault-like door. "This room."

Three Idolon pilots placed their drones at the entrance. They quickly found it was easier to use energy beams to cut the door out of the surrounding rock rather than to blast it open.

With the hole opened, each pilot entered, pulled two boxes from the racks, and stored them in the Idolon's chest compartment. It took time and they might well be setting off alarms, but there were no Enforcers to stop them yet. Perhaps the lessons from the first two raids had sunk in.

Lom stood by and counted the returning Idolons as they marched back into the shuttle. There were no stragglers or accidents this time, and no one was left behind. Easy.

—

As soon as the three drop ships returned to the *Emerald Queen*, Lom gave the all-clear to depart. He connected to the ship's sensor feed to confirm their getaway. The codes that had enabled their entry within the planetary shield ensured that they were able to depart, and their advanced weapon targeting array deterred the small Enforcer ships from offering any kind of pursuit. No doubt, the authorities would try to track them, but they were prepared for that contingency.

As soon as Lom felt the transition to subspace, he headed to his charging platform to switch back to the Meklife drone. His sensors came online to find Captain Aura waiting for him, hands on hips, as Meklife undocked.

"'Mother Carnage'?" she demanded.

There were moments where Lom lamented that his Meklife drone couldn't display expressions well. This was one of them. "You caught my feed!"

"Mother. *Carnage.* What were you thinking, Lom?"

"I was thinking about the future. About your future, especially."

"How does coining a threatening nickname help anything we're working to accomplish?"

Lom caught sight of the mining Idolons debarking the shuttle and lumbering toward the shielded storage bays that awaited their new warheads. All according to plan. "By establishing a reputation, Captain. Let me explain. Reputation is essential in the world of business. One can have a reputation for slovenly workmanship, or mediocre quality at inflated prices. One can have a reputation for getting the job done no matter what. Mother Carnage now has a reputation for going after property and defending herself but leaving the civilians and bystanders alone."

"You think that matters?"

"I *know* it matters. Reputation is also a shield against inquiry. The galaxy knows you as a cargo runner, a trader, a businessperson. But Mother Carnage is a stranger. The aggrieved Taran citizens will now complain to the authorities about the chaos and danger and their hurt feelings, the terror they experienced. But they have no information that can help. Even the warhead we used was composed of easily available components, and the genesis file for our cyberattack program erased itself after deploying. The more damage we cause, and the fewer casualties we incur, the more hesitant Enforcers will be to engage us. That makes our task infinitely simpler."

Lom watched her run through the implications, her facial muscles twitching as she worked her mental machinery.

"Once the civilians realize we are limiting ourselves to military and dynastic targets—the same people who nearly brought utter destruction down on their heads—they may even begin to support us. Coining a nickname that people remember gives us *power*," she mused.

"Precisely. I suggest you remember that when planning the next operation," Lom offered.

"All right. I trust you can tutor me in the best use of my new call sign?"

"It would be my great honor, Mother Carnage."

12

MAD TOYMAKERS

REPORTS OF AN attack changed the nature of the investigation in an instant. A cyberattack was one thing, but a physical assault within the city... Karmen wrestled with how to feel about her involvement. Part of her wished she was hiding in the bunker with her family, because that meant she could be there to protect them. But she also wanted to find the people responsible for the attack on Greengard and stop them. That was the only way to truly make sure her loved ones would be safe.

Investigator Russei was happy enough to drive the group to the scene of the crime. The group arrived just as darkness engulfed the hospital plaza, but Karmen could see a few lights coming on in the great building. A number of Enforcer glow globes hovered overhead, pouring down intense white light on the crime scene.

Karmen swallowed a mouthful of bile as she got out of the car and stared up at the hospital annex. *I was here only a few hours ago.*

As she took in the destruction, dark scenarios filled her mind. What if she'd stayed? She'd have had a front seat at the big event. Maybe Hellen wasn't so crazy after all… What if an invasion *had* been someone's plan all along?

She shook away the thoughts. She needed to focus.

Enforcers were already at the site. Now that lights had begun to appear, bystanders had begun to come out to comb through the damage. A trio of officers were setting up barriers to hold back civilians, but a crowd kept growing. Karmen couldn't blame them. Nothing this exciting ever happened in Foundation City.

To her eyes, it looked like a bomb had gone off in the square. A section of the annex's outer wall had been blown out, probably to grant the attackers access to the supplies within.

She carefully made her way through the gap. The interior state of the hospital surprised her; once she got past the dust and detritus, it seemed as orderly as it had that afternoon. But there were Enforcers here, too, taking statements.

One woman wearing nurse's scrubs was particularly agitated. "It was insane! I've never seen anything like it in my life. Animal shapes. Like robotic cats, but big—the size of a scooter or something. And round ones! A meter or so across, with little, I dunno… turrets poking out from the sides. And others much more humanoid but very wide and very tall. Super solid."

"What did they take?" the Enforcer questioned, taking notes on a handheld.

"Everything! The drugs, the equipment. I saw two of the big ones carry off bio-beds, like one under each arm. The little ones made so much noise, screaming with machine voices. And smoke! I may call in sick tomorrow. I've been here seven years. Never anything like this! I think I *will* call in sick. I didn't sign up for this."

Karmen held up her new ID and approached cautiously. "Excuse me, I'd like to ask a question. Miss, what drugs did they take?"

The nurse pointed down the corridor. "An entire storage room's worth. They're going over the inventory now. You can look for yourself, they pulled the lock right out of the door and walked on in."

"Thank you," Karmen said and set out to do just that.

The door was a security model that slid into the wall, fortified by an electronic lock. She saw the damage the nurse had described: the lock had been burned out by an energy weapon. A scorched, perfectly cylindrical gap in the wall proved that. The door had then been pulled into its recessed space. Shelves and racks that had presumably been full of medicine were now bare. Not even a single scrap of packaging remained.

—   —   —

Lee had hardly had a moment to himself to think since the blackout began. He'd been taking the events in stride, falling back on his training to remain calm under pressure. But seeing the medical annex in shambles, the situation had become a lot more personal.

He went to check on his lab. To his relief, the room appeared untouched. *At least there's that.*

Enough else had gone sideways that he took little comfort in seeing his research intact. The world was under assault, and no one knew why. Rather than offering any insights or directions, the Agent overseeing his Junior Agent internship had allowed Lee to be handed over to the Enforcers like he was a low-level Specialist in the Militia. But he was a Junior Agent from a reputable Lower Dynasty. Where was the respect?

Fighting his annoyance, Lee placed a vidcall to his internship proctor, a fellow Agent of the Sacon division with a permanent post on Greengard.

Agent Kalshi answered audio-only. "Lee, is there a problem with your new assignment?"

"Ah, so you signed off on that."

"You *are* my direct report until I deem you fit to graduate."

Lee was grateful for the audio format since he didn't need to keep from grimacing. "I didn't expect to be assigned as staff to Enforcers."

"What would you prefer be done about that?"

"The TSS should be running its own investigation! Karmen knows this planet, and our Militia tech specialist is *way* more knowledgeable—"

"Agents—even Junior Agents—don't take orders from anyone in Militia. We give them," Kalshi interrupted.

"I know that, sir."

"I won't mince words, Lee. We're facing a crisis here. Every second I'm playing therapist to you, I'm not working on preparations to save civilians in the event we face another attack. Do you have a team capable of conducting this investigation?"

"Yes, sir."

"Then what's the problem?"

Lee swallowed. "I'm sorry to have bothered you. I'll submit a report when we learn anything notable."

"See that you do. Good luck." Kalshi ended the call.

Well, that was a colossal mistake. Lee returned his handheld to his pocket, vowing to be more careful with his communications in the future. He wasn't a full Agent yet, but he had every intention of making it through this final test before graduation.

He re-locked his lab and resumed his search of the medical annex, looking for any clues. There was a mystery to solve. Regardless of his team or the reporting structure, he was committed to seeing the mission through to the end.

—   —   —

When Karmen returned to the plaza outside, Lee walked up to meet her. "Good news for us, they didn't touch the Octarin," he reported. "Whatever they were after, it wasn't in the research labs. Nothing's been touched in any of them, as far as anyone can tell."

"But they cleared out at least one storeroom and took bio-beds," she replied, not surprised with his findings. Unless this was a case of corporate espionage, there was no reason to go after experimental products in labs. "How much would a bio-bed go for on the black market?"

"You're assuming I deal with crooks. How should I know?" Lee shot back.

"I have complete faith in your ability to find out. Your family works in the medical space, so someone in your network has to know what holds value outside the official channels."

"I live in research land, so I don't know where to start."

"Well don't look at me! I'm just your experimental subject." Karmen held up her hands. "But seriously, there has to have been some high-value stuff here, right?"

"Depends entirely on what they stocked," Lee replied. "Even simple antibiotics can generate huge cash flows in the Outer Colonies where the environment is especially harsh and advanced tech is a luxury. But I guess if you need a benchmark, then on the legal market a hospital's stock room would probably be worth millions. Black market prices would be at least an order of magnitude higher. Potentially tens of millions to the right people."

"Stars, that's a lot of credits. It's a wonder hospitals don't get robbed more often."

"It's not easy to do. The security inside the annex is pretty tight. These people planned a lot of noise and had some kind of devices to do the heavy lifting. I asked some of the Enforcers to get us descriptions of the machines they used. That will tell us more."

"I got one story about robot animals from a nurse. She wasn't in the best state of mind, so I'd definitely like to corroborate the description."

Investigator Sura walked over to them, flipping through notes on his handheld. "Well, we have a name: Mother Carnage."

Lee tilted his head, brows raised. "You're kidding."

"I wish. Apparently, there was an announcement made during the attack. 'Mother Carnage' wanted everyone to stay out of the way. She didn't want any injuries."

"How considerate," Karmen muttered.

"All I know is what the witnesses told me. I spoke to three, they all differed on the details, but they agreed on the name and the contents of the warning."

"We have imagery!" Investigator Russei announced, grinning as he strode over to them. He produced a stream of clips and images on his handheld. "Lots of photos were taken by people who were hiding. I can't say I recognize any of this stuff. It's head and shoulders better quality than anything we have locally."

They looked through the images and made copies for Armin to send for further analysis. Ultimately, there wasn't much more to do that the locals couldn't handle.

"Why animal shapes?" Karmen wondered. "I think we're missing something here."

"Don't keep it to yourself, Karmen," Lee urged.

"Investigator Sura said there were other attacks, yes?"

"Yes, at the commercial plaza downtown. From what little I've been told, it was very similar to this. But they took a different assortment of stuff. Consumer items, mostly. Data monitors, tablets, handhelds…"

"What about toys?"

"Toys? Not that I heard. Why?" he asked.

"Toys use some very advanced circuitry. Everything you mentioned is good for one thing: cracking the cases and recycling the circuits into something new."

"Like animal-shaped robots?"

"Maybe."

Armin raced up with another find: a shiny metal object in a clear bag. "Found the jackpot. Look at this."

They looked at the ambiguous item. "What is it?" Lee asked on behalf of the group.

"This is the receptor circuit for a drone bandwidth extender. Even the TSS doesn't use anything like it. There's one source of this kind of CPU, and that's the Lynaedans. One of the drones must have gotten stuck on the way in or out of the target zone and this broke free."

Lee wasn't convinced. "All right… but we already knew the perpetrators have access to high-tech gear. The ship's comm array—"

"Yes, the comm array was military tech, but this stuff goes way beyond anything I've seen in regular circulation," Armin countered.

"If Lynaedans did this, it would explain a lot," Lee said.

Armin nodded. "It might. Those folks have forgotten more about advanced tech than the TSS ever knew. AI, drones, androids—they do everything. But they're notoriously insular, and I've never heard about them getting involved in any kind of violent conflict. But, there can be rogue operators in any culture."

Karmen tried to fit the pieces together. "Stealing medical supplies but not experimental drugs. An ore carrier with a military targeting array. And, apparently, Lynaedan drone technology. Boys... what in the stars is going on here?"

13

RADIOACTIVE

KARMEN INSISTED ON the team driving over to the commercial plaza to check out the other attack site. She wanted to see everything on the off-chance that she'd notice something that the others missed. However, the tour yielded no new insights.

Investigator Sura's handheld buzzed as they were heading back to the car; he took the call. When he hung up, he said, "You three are requested to return to the captain's office."

"Why?" Lee asked.

"The captain didn't say, and I didn't ask. But it sounds like something changed while we were here."

"You think they solved the crime without us?" Armin questioned.

Karmen shook her head. She didn't want to say it out loud, but a call like that meant things had only gotten worse, not better.

They got an unexpected reception upon returning to Peacekeeper Plaza. A trio of men in expensive suits were waiting in Captain Travanti's office. None of them wore an Agent's tinted glasses but all carried themselves with an air of authority. They were used to getting what they wanted.

One of them stepped forward. "Is this them?" he demanded.

Travanti nodded. "That's them."

"I need you three to turn over everything you've collected on this incident thus far," the leader said. "Images, recordings, data files. All of it. In addition, I need you to sign this non-disclosure agreement. You will not discuss what you've seen or heard with any person not connected to the TalEx corporation."

Karmen shared a glance with Lee. TalEx was owned and operated by the Talsari High Dynasty—one of the six most powerful families in all of Taran civilization. They held mining interests literally across the galactic empire. They could buy and sell TuMed a thousand times and not feel the pinch.

Karmen smelled a rat. And she did work for the TSS. She had an official ID and everything. In a flash, every obnoxious Militia crewmember she'd ever had to manage on the *Triumph* came back to her. She didn't know who this cretin was and didn't care. This was her party, and that was that.

"Captain Travanti, who are these people?" she asked.

"Apologies, allow me to introduce you. I present Mr. Avlin, Director of Security for the Greengard mining operation in the great desert. These are his associates. Misters—"

"You don't need to know their names," Avlin said.

Travanti shrugged helplessly. "You don't need to know their names," he mock apologized. "Director Avlin, this is Junior Agent Tuyin and Officers Godri and Sley, of the Tararian Selective Service. You may make your case to them directly. I have nothing to do with it from this point on."

"Nonsense. You're the Captain overseeing this Enforcer division, aren't you?" Avlin scoffed.

"I was until the TSS took over this investigation."

"When did that happen?"

"The TSS requested lead jurisdiction over the investigation half an hour ago, in light of new information. Due to current personnel limitations, Junior Agent Tuyin has been granted provisional command of the investigation."

"I have?" Lee said before catching himself. He rose to his full height and looked the TalEx representative squarely in the eye. "Director, I'm afraid I can't legally comply with any requests that would impede an open investigation."

Captain Travanti shrugged. "I'm sorry, Director, my hands are tied. Agent Tuyin is the person you should be working with. If he's not sufficient, I'm sure he can call your manager and they'll help us figure out an appropriate workflow."

Avlin made a show of eyeing Lee. "No, I'm sure we can come to an understanding."

"I'm glad we could establish the chain of command so quickly," Lee said.

Karmen managed to hide a smile, but Armin made no attempt to conceal his.

Lee continued, "Suppose you just tell us what you know. Something tells me there's been more than a simple robbery on Greengard."

Director Avlin looked his associates in the eyes and made a calculation. "It *was* a robbery. But there's nothing simple about it."

Karmen held out her handheld. "Discovery phase, gentlemen, send us whatever you have, and we will reciprocate."

They complied, and Karmen suddenly had a ton of data to

sort through. "Nuclear materials?" she gasped.

"It's a little trickier than that. Director, would you please tell them what you told me?" Travanti requested.

"All right, I'll summarize for your convenience. The deep desert is a veritable storehouse of valuable ores, which can be refined into a wide range of useful minerals. Including radioactives. The facility that was attacked is a TalEx refinery and storage depot. A large number of Talsarium mining rounds were stored there for export to our mining ships. They were stolen about the same time the attack on the city center was logged."

"That's a bomaxed thing to put on a planet where the primary industry is a university," Karmen said.

Avlin smirked. "With respect, Officer, the mining pays for everything the university has. If TalEx decides to drop off this world, Foundation City would be a ghost town in a few years."

"I doubt that, but I'll grant you institutions do benefit from generous benefactors," she said.

"I'm heartened to hear you recognize that. The thing about Talsarium is that it's not naturally occurring. It has a very brief half-life—twelve hours. The storage containers have integral dampening equipment that nullifies the radioactive decay. If the rounds are taken out of their containers, they become useless in short order. That's why we use them."

"Use them for what?"

"Asteroid mining. You want to reduce a big rock into many small ones, use an explosive. But our targets are huge, sometimes kilometers in diameter. Conventional explosive compounds are useless. And conventional nuclear devices are difficult to manage."

"He means easy to steal," Travanti said. "I'm sorry, Director. Continue, please."

"Those are the essentials. We were alerted when the break-in occurred, but by the time we were able to visit the site, the thieves had already left."

"What was the security at the base like?" Armin asked.

"Minimal. Remote sensors and such. The system is self-contained, powered by an independent power core. We transmitted a sequence of disarming codes aimed at the full range of containers as soon as we discovered them missing, but no matching shutdowns were confirmed by our operators."

"So, you have no idea if the containers received them?" Armin said.

"We do not."

"If they were moved to a shielded room, they're probably still active," Karmen said, "which means everything depends on the length of time between the containers disappearing and you sending those codes. I think we have to assume those rounds are live and in operating order."

"I concur," Lee said.

Armin bobbed his head, his eyes staring into the distance as he thought through the problem. He pulled out his handheld and projected a wide array of images, then selected a few and minimized the rest. The stills were those of a humanoid leader apparently guiding a group of large humanoid machines. "Do these look familiar to you two?"

Karmen pulled up an image of her own. The drones that had walked out of the hospital and commercial plaza weren't identical to the heavy bipeds, but they were close enough in their design aesthetic to suggest a link. "Lynaedans," she breathed.

Director Avlin finally lost his composure. The look on his face was one of alarm. "What about Lynaedans?"

"Just a lead, Director. We promise to keep you in the loop.

We'll need you to furnish us with full inventories of all the stolen items. Including those disarming codes," Lee said.

"Those are protected intellectual property," Avlin protested.

Karmen waved a hand, indicating all was well. "That's fine and I understand your dilemma. Agent Tuyin, you know the people who manage the Tuyin security concerns, don't you? They can confer with the Talsari security people, can't they?"

"I'll find out right now," Lee said and brought his handheld to his face.

With an exaggerated sigh of victimhood, Avlin waved his device and transferred the data. "Here. Take the codes. Use them in good health. The TSS wants to step on my feet, I'm happy to let it. All your names will figure prominently in my report to corporate."

Karmen flashed a victorious smile. "I would expect nothing less."

14

FOLLOW THE CURIUM

DIRECTOR AVLIN TOOK his men and left. When the door closed behind him, Lee shook his head with disgust. Avlin and his goons were exactly the kind of corporate smarm he joined the TSS to escape.

Armin, however, laughed out loud. "I don't think he was used to hearing 'no'."

Under other circumstances, Lee may have enjoyed putting the uptight bureaucrat in his place. But now, being the one in charge of the investigation, he wanted to project a professional front. His career in the TSS depended on it. "I apologize for all that," Lee said to Travanti.

"Why? You didn't invite him here. In fact, none of us did. If anything, I should be apologizing to all of you."

"Really, why?"

Travanti leaned back in his chair. "Well, if there's one thing I know about running with the likes of the Lord High Executioner Avlin, it's this: the one thing a bureaucrat hates and fears more than anything is another, bigger bureaucrat. Just more corporate red tape to deal with. I didn't want him here. You just happened to be available, so I dragged you into the drama. I thought you all handled yourselves admirably."

"I appreciate you saying so," Lee acknowledged. "How should we proceed?"

"Oh, no. I meant what I said—this is now a TSS matter. I wash my hands of it all. Lynaedan drones, a modified starship, theft of nuclear mining charges... Not to mention, those drones put two of my Enforcers in the hospital. They're expected to make full recoveries, fortunately. But this is all much nastier than anything our staff on Greengard is equipped to deal with. My Enforcers are used to wrangling drunken university students, not confronting combat mechs. I'm happy to let the TSS handle it. Less paperwork for me that way. Of course, my office is happy to provide any assistance you may need."

Lee did his best to keep a neutral expression as the gravity of his new assignment continued to sink in. That morning, he'd been happily conducting medical research. Sure, a TSS Agent should be ready for anything, but this was an extreme shift by any measure.

But the principles are the same, he reminded himself. Regardless of the subject, any investigation relied on a similar foundation as his own research. *Observe. Form a hypothesis. Test the hypothesis.* They had already started gathering the pieces, and all they needed to do was put the facts together until they knew enough for the bigger picture to emerge.

"I don't suppose the ship's jump path was logged by the nav beacon?" Lee asked.

The captain shook his head. "Unsurprisingly, they spoofed their transit logs. Someone at SiNavTech might be able to sort it out, but that's beyond our capabilities in this office."

That could take days. Lee wasn't sure where that left them.

Armin got a faraway look in his eyes, already thinking through possibilities. "We need a shuttle equipped with radiometers. Good ones. Sensors that can sniff out curium isotopes. With that, I think we could figure out a likely variety of courses that Mother Carnage took when she left this solar system."

"Excellent suggestion," Lee said, relieved to have such a capable technician on his team.

Travanti eyed them. "What makes you think you'll be able to use that information to figure out her destination? There are more than fifteen-hundred inhabited worlds!"

"Yes, there are plenty of places she can go… but only a narrow selection of worlds lie along a given trajectory. See, there's a funny thing that a lot of people don't think about, but a pilot will naturally orient their ship toward their destination right before initiating a jump. Whatever course they took right before reaching the jump point will help us narrow the search area. It can let us get a head start while they try to pull the ping data off the SiNavTech nav beacons. But either way, we'll find her."

"Not without this, you won't." Travanti tapped on his touch-surface desktop.

A moment later Lee's, Karmen's, and Armin's handhelds all chimed with a notification. Lee opened the message and smiled at the Enforcer captain as he saw what it contained.

"As of now," Travanti recited, "the Greengard division of the Guard Enforcers, in agreement with the TalEx corporate security division, as witnessed by all of us and with my approval, does hereby formally request TSS assistance in tracking down the dangerous space pirate operating under the moniker 'Mother Carnage'. Junior Agent Tuyin, you have been designated the lead investigator for this operation. Officer Sley, you'll be his first officer. Officer Godri, you'll serve as a technical specialist. This is a sensitive issue—planets don't get held hostage, as a rule, and the official cover story will be that there was a glitch in the power grid. To maintain that cover, TalEx, the Enforcers, and the TSS have all agreed that it would be best to go about an investigation quietly, without bringing in outside resources. No one wants to call attention to a bigger issue, or make a scene that might drive the perpetrators into hiding. So, it falls to you to keep a low profile and find them and determine what they're up to. A TSS transport ship has been set aside for you at the spaceport so you can pursue the pirate ship. I'll arrange for delivery of any sensor equipment you require to assist with your mission."

"You don't have the authority to do any of this," Lee said.

"No, but Lead Agent Alexri did. I received a message from her right before I summoned you back here. She apparently spoke with my TSS counterpart here on Greengard, an Agent Kalshi. They agreed that the three of you should take point on this, given your familiarity with the situation. She also said to pass on a message, Junior Agent Tuyin, that your internship assignment just got a little more interesting."

"Lucky me." Lee hadn't had many occasions to interact with the TSS Lead Agent, but she oversaw all Agent training at TSS Headquarters and signed off on all internship assignments. No doubt, there'd been hurried discussions behind the scenes with the Sacon division lead, as well, about modifying the parameters of Lee's final field test. *Solving blindness wasn't enough. Now I need to track down a space pirate! How did I walk into that one?*

Thinking through the day's events, his first mistake had

been following Karmen to Daveed's office. His second had been calling in Armin to consult on the surveillance images. The moment they'd filed a field report of those preliminary findings, his fate had been set. And poor Karmen had been roped into the mess along with him.

There was no backing down now. Junior Agent internships were all about getting out of one's comfort zone, and they were definitely not letting him off easy.

15

ONE DOWN, MANY TO GO

'MOTHER CARNAGE' WASN'T such a bad call sign, Aura decided. Her Dark Net messages were now answered much faster, and she rarely had to ask twice for an update from a business contact.

The *Emerald Queen* currently resided in the outer belt of the Diphous System, waiting for... what? She wasn't completely sure. Her Dark Net comm board had thrown a number of messages her way in the past two days since the raid on Greengard. One had been a set of coordinates where they'd met an unmarked cargo shuttle. They'd transferred a dozen of their stolen warheads to its crew yesterday, and they were still in orbit around the primary star. Ashurbanipal, Gil's fellow Mesopotamian, had transferred a huge amount of money into Aura's Dark Net account. He'd even thanked her for making such a prompt delivery.

You're welcome, my lord. Now kindly tell me what I'm supposed to do next in the pursuit of your New Akkadia.

Eventually, the funds would find their ways to a cargo locker in a spaceport where she'd find a carrying bag full of credit chips. It would take a while to filter the funds out to the legal businesses she had a hand in managing, but money laundering was something she often went to Lom's people for help with. They were so bomaxed clever it was frightening.

As if summoned by her thoughts, a vaguely familiar face appeared at her cabin door. The powder blue bangs across his eyes and purple ocular implants were the giveaway. "Lom?"

"Yes, Captain."

"Lom, you either need to start spending more time in your own skin or I need to make Meklife a permanent crew member."

Lom stepped into the cabin and let the door close behind him. Even in his skin he was a head taller than she. The interface ports on his wrists gleamed in the dim cabin light, and his powder-blue hair kept falling into his purple eyes. "He is me; I am him. There's no real difference. It's the same mind except we share different duties. Which is why my personal recharge dock holds five different drones."

"I understand the need for an alter ego, but the Bases among the crew don't like it."

"Using our lingo, I see. Good for you."

She found the Lynaedan slang term for unmodified Tarans vaguely offensive, but she had to admit that regular people like her without cybernetic augmentations did have limitations. "It's a convenience, nothing more. I had hoped my being among the drones would change their minds, but they resist it. I may have to make it a rule that drones are only to be brought out for mission prep and execution."

"But they have so many uses between missions," Lom said. The Lynaedan peered at the display she was examining. "I will abide by your orders, whichever way they may turn. What are you diving into now?"

"I mentioned to Comm Officer Gallian that I needed a better way to make use of the various Dark Net channels I work with. I need to send and receive instructions when dealing with the details of managing New Akkadia. This is what he created."

"He's a spookily effective lad," Lom said.

"He is," she agreed. "He coded this app directly into the ship's computer. I can't say I understand Lynaedan technology, but it makes even TSS tech look positively primitive." She looked up at Lom, her eyes wholly serious. "It's curious how so much Lynaedan technology made its way into this ship during the refit," she said.

"For the computer and related systems, yes. Everything else is salvaged—a lot of it from the TSS starships destroyed during the war. Luckily for us, there's a lot of untraceable scrap still floating around. My engineers simply used the available components, while working within our given budget and timeframe, to produce a craft capable of completing our mission objectives."

Aura stared at him for several seconds, caught off-guard by his earnest response to her off-hand comment. But she shouldn't have expected anything else from a Lynaedan. "Okay, then," she said at last. "What can I do for you, Lom?"

"Gallian received a transmission from a previously unknown starship profile. He logged a request for rendezvous, which apparently came from Lord Gilgamesh. He should be arriving shortly."

Aura absently called up a file in her display. Gil's personal yacht, *Shamhat*, was well known to their instruments. Why was he showing up in a different vessel this time? "He's getting weird," she murmured.

"I prefer not to comment, Captain."

She closed the display and turned to face him. "You know he's getting stranger. Pulling more stunts like this more often. He used to be as reliable as a pulsar. I'd get messages through the Dark Net, I'd fill orders, I'd carry out missions. I'd get paid. If he wants to visit, why doesn't he just show up?"

"I don't know him nearly as well as you, Captain. I'm sure I couldn't say."

You could absolutely say. You just won't. Too polite? Or too careful? Aura didn't have that same filter. "He was different in the beginning," she reminisced. "So much energy. So many ambitions. Crazy dreams, full of conquest and control. It didn't take long for me to understand why he'd been dismissed from the TSS. But he'd literally pulled me out of the void—saved my life—and I was grateful. I went along with things I never would have dreamed I'd do. It became the two of us against the galaxy. It was intoxicating. We grew very close, and he completely drew me into his grand vision. I admired his natural ability to figure out trade opportunities and form alliances.

"I remember in the early years, he'd throw these lavish parties, and every one ended with a new contract. He could turn anyone to his side. Stars, I'd been a loyal TSS Agent, and he managed to pull *me* in. It was like that with everyone. And it wasn't just working people, he's also had an eye for the logistics of trade. He could take a sector map, do some research, and then draw lines between the various spaceports and make notes about what to buy and where and what to sell and to whom. Absolutely brilliant. Or maybe it just seemed that way to me because I don't have that skill. But it made us a number of fortunes. And we lost some, too. It was some ride."

"What happened to break you apart?" Lom asked, sitting down on the couch near her desk.

"No, it wasn't like that. We just... matured. After a few years, it became clear we had different priorities. I wanted to keep running trade and he wanted bigger things. Implementing Sargon's plans and such. So we parted ways. He emptied the bank accounts, I took the ship, and we did our own things. But we never stopped caring about each other. I used to get a thrill whenever he sent me a note about his latest plan, his newest deal. I sent him funds to invest. I started to think that New Akkadia might actually become real. But now..." She shook her head. "Nuclear mining charges. Terrorizing university students. I don't know. I think we may have crossed a boundary."

"I know we have," Lom said, brushing his powder-blue hair away from his eyes. Looking closer, Aura realized it wasn't actually hair, but rather fine synthetic filaments. "What did you expect? 'It was a misunderstanding?' 'All is forgiven?' We're pirates, Aura. We spit in the face of laws and orders. We chart our own course. We steal property and break things. If you didn't know this to be true, why did you go through with it?"

"TSS training goes deep." She sighed.

"If we wanted loyalty and obedience, I'd still be on Lynaeda and you would still be in the TSS."

"No, I'd be dead. But I take your meaning. You're where you want to be, and so am I," she assured him.

A chime sounded from a speaker, then a voice said, "Captain to the hangar deck. Starship *Enkidu* is arriving."

What? It can't be! She bounced out of her reverie.

She raced down to the hangar, with Lom easily keeping pace but following several steps behind. They arrived to see a cylindrical vessel with a sharply sloped nose settle in a docking berth, the hangar door closing behind it.

Gil emerged from the small vessel as the gangway

extended. He was wearing a business suit—an expensive one, at that. He'd always held a confident gravitas, even when they'd first met while he was still a gangly youth, but he'd matured into a man who now fully looked the part of his earned authority. She wanted to run to him and kiss him, but she decided that this was still her ship and decorum had to count for something. She settled for a fierce hug as he met her on the deck.

"You've improved your fashion sense, Gil," Aura said.

"I have a new tailor. Do you recognize my ride?" he asked, nodding at the ship.

Of course, I do. But she knew he'd want to see her surprise and excitement, so she let the drama play out. She peered intently at his ship. "Stars, is that—?"

"Yes! I brought him out of storage just to visit. Gilgamesh and *Enkidu*, together again!"

"How did you…? I sold this heap for the down-payment on *Redemption*. Seventeen years ago!"

"You did, indeed. And as soon as you left in your cargo transport, I contacted Sargon for a loan to buy *Enkidu* back. I used him faithfully for years. Then, when I traded up to *Shamhat*, I mothballed him. But it's been almost a year since you and I last spoke face-to-face. So, I thought I'd bring him out for old time's sake."

Aura nodded as she approached the ship, stroked its hull with her fingertips. She even started humming to herself. She'd had a lot of fun with Gil on this old ship. Good memories. Not quite a marriage, but something deeper than a mere friendship. She missed this ship. Now that he was in front of her, talking to her, sharing space and air, she realized just how much she'd missed Gil, too.

"Hello, *Enkidu*," she said in a low voice. "Did you miss me?

I missed you. And this time, I actually have the technical crew to fix everything that's wrong with you."

"Don't you dare," Gil warned. "I like him the way he is."

"He's a navigational time bomb waiting to strand you in subspace every time you jump," Aura insisted. "Come on. It'll only take a few hours to correct the hacks that govern his jump drive and nav system."

"I said no."

"Then take the opportunity to watch my crew in action. While the techs are fixing the jump drive, you can come along on the next mission. You do, after all, want to make sure it succeeds. Right?" Aura said. She didn't miss his eye roll. *You really think you're doing us all a favor, don't you, Gil?*

"You and your logic. Fine, I agree. Aura, reverse the hacks if you can. But I need a fast ship. Faster than standard nav beacons allow," Gil said.

"Don't worry," she cooed, stroking his face. "Lynaedan tech is head and shoulders beyond *Enkidu*'s current structure. Lom, you'll take care of it personally, won't you?"

"I will indeed, Captain."

"Very well. You know I can't say no to you, my dear," Gil sighed. "And I might as well show you the plan for the next mission. You leave in three hours."

"Three hours? You couldn't have arrived a little later and arranged a real challenge for us?"

"Don't be snide, Aura. All the pieces are in place. We just need to play our parts," Gil said.

They headed to the War Room to go over the details.

Gil put his handheld on the central map table. A planetary map appeared as a holographic projection above the device. "Behold! The world Diphous. Home to numerous industrial refineries and extraction sites, all owned and operated by the TalEx corporation."

"We know where we are, Gil. Although the planet itself is five hundred million kilometers that way," Aura said, pointing.

"Remind me to write their CEO an aggressively worded message," Lom said. "One of the transport boxes for the Talsarium had a fault that we didn't detect until long after we left orbit around Greengard. By the time anyone thought to check on it, the demolition charge was useless."

"Shoddy workmanship is always a problem," Gil agreed. "Five levels of subcontracting for every venture, it's amazing anything works as intended. You did transfer the mining charges, didn't you?"

"Of course, we did. All twelve of them," Lom said.

"Good. At any rate, here is a map of the facility you'll be hitting today."

"Looks very much like the one on Greengard," Aura noticed.

"Of course. Economies of scale work in TalEx's favor. Every mining site and refinery is laid out the same way. But today you'll be lifting merchandise from these four buildings in the outermost ring of structures."

"What's in them?"

"Everything. Nearly one thousand tons of lanthinum, isometric crystals, endorphite, hexallon, bitanium, trimagnetite, and numerous others: all minerals that are vital to the construction of jump drives and power cores. They are already loaded in standard twenty-five-ton shipping containers. All you people have to do is lift them into your ship and jump away."

Now we're 'you people'? Nice, Gil. "That will take time," Aura murmured, while calling up a schematic of her starship's cargo hold. A commercial cargo container was about three meters high and wide, and ten meters long. She only had two shuttles big enough in the correct configuration to handle anything that size. She was ready to argue the point, but Gil wasn't done.

"I can't stress this part enough, Aura. You have a very narrow window to make this mission work."

"How narrow? And why?"

Lom leaned down to bring his nose level with Gil's. "Yes, my lord. Why?"

Aura watched with fascination as Gil hesitated then took a step back from the Lynaedan. She didn't know the details of their meeting, but Gil had introduced Lom to her back in the day. She'd needed a respectable ground attack force, and Lom came highly recommended by Sargon. *Something between them has changed. But what?*

Gil recovered quickly. "Because the dock workers who are manning the platforms where our cargo is to be picked up have been paid enough to look the other way. Those who replace them with the morning shift will be very unhappy with your appearance. Unhappy labor crews fight back. They call Enforcers. They throw heavy objects and can be very creative with industrial equipment. Have you ever seen a construction crew turn a digging platform into an offensive weapon? Trust me, it's nauseating."

Aura folded her arms. "When did you see—?"

"Never mind. My point is you need to act according to this timetable without fail."

"We'll be working in the dark again," Lom said, "and making multiple round trips with each shuttle. I take it your bribed compatriots go on shift in three hours, which is when we begin, yes?"

Gil nodded furiously. "Precisely. Everything is perfectly timed. It must go off without error."

Lom's face remained neutral. "You said that already, my lord."

"I will say it again and again until it sinks in," Gil said. "How many times do I have to say it before you hear me?"

Aura sniffed. *Oh, I hear you, Gilgamesh. Loud and clear.* "Forty containers in all. Two containers per shuttle per trip means ten round trips per shuttle. Loading and unloading each one plus flight time means ten hours for the entire consignment," she estimated.

"Closer to twelve. Those containers are heavy and most of the Idolons will be employed on the surface for loading," Lom said.

"Make it less," Gilgamesh ordered.

"How much less?" Aura asked. "I don't have shuttles or cargo lifters to spare."

Gil beamed. "You won't need them. I happen to know there will be a TalEx cargo shuttle on the launch pad when you arrive. It can hold four of those containers. All you need to supply is a pilot."

"A pilot with access to TalEx security codes," Aura reminded him.

"Bah! Child's play," Gil sneered, waving his hand dismissively.

"All right. If that arrangement holds, we can do it in half as many trips. Still, that's six hours to complete the transfers," she said.

Lom straightened and flexed. "I'll arrange the work schedule."

Aura nodded. "Thank you, Commander Lom," she said, and he set off to his station to get to work. "Well, Gil, orders have been given. I'm free for a glass of wine with dinner in my cabin."

Gil glared at her hungrily. "And then?"

"I'm free for that, as well."

— — —

Lom sighed in relief as the two Tarans left the War Room. He didn't know the intimate details of whatever arrangement Captain Aura and Gil shared, but he did know that she came back from her trysts far more relaxed and ready to work than anything else she did. That was enough for him. And them being in her cabin for a while would give him time to perform the upgrades on Gil's vessel.

Gallian and their ship's chief mechanic, a surly woman named Lula, met Lom at *Enkidu*. The comm officer didn't waste any time. "Why did you lie to Lord Gilgamesh?"

"When did I lie?" Lom asked.

"When you told him we gave a dozen Talsarium warheads to Lord Sargon, you made it seem like that was the entire stock. There were *twenty* warheads in that warehouse, and we absconded with all of them."

"Are you suggesting we shouldn't have kept some?" Lom asked. "You really want that madman and his mad friends to have all those weapons while we have nothing for ourselves?"

"I suppose not. But I don't like him one bit," Gallian said. "He's a cretinous, gluttonous, primitive."

"And his ship is disgusting," Lula added.

"I don't care for him, either, but he is important to our captain. He supports her and keeps her in fighting trim, as it were. His failings as a person are beyond the scope of our responsibility to her. And we *are* responsible to her."

"*To* her. Not *for* her," Gallian said.

Lula nodded. "He's as corrupt as the galaxy is wide. Give me ten minutes. I could make sure the next time he jumps away in this shite heap will be the last. Just from what I see standing here, it's probably difficult enough to keep it from not going awry."

Lom drew himself to his full height. "No. We are thieves, not murderers. That is final. Anyway, let's examine the heap while the Bases are otherwise occupied."

Lom was appalled at the state of Gil's starship. The vessel was in dire shape; it should have been dismantled for parts years ago. Actually, it should never have been constructed in the first place. But Aura wanted it repaired, and the crew had the means and knowledge to do so. But they had options.

"Put a tracker in his nav system," Lom instructed the chief mechanic. "Make it something that no mere functionary would think to look for. And where would the travel logs be stored on a vessel this archaic, do you think?"

The mechanic stepped back, lost in thought. But Gallian knew exactly where to look. The comm specialist pulled open a panel rooted in the machinery and pulled out a set of leads. "Dumb down your nanofiber interface to half speed and it should fit. Don't try to take the information out of memory faster than the linkage allows."

Lom followed instructions and settled his leads into the wiring. "Hmm. Antiquated data signal. Now then, *Enkidu*, tell me everything you've seen and done since meeting Lord Gilgamesh."

16

TO THE STARS

BEFORE KARMEN WAS able to fully process the implications of their assignment, she and her two TSS associates were whisked away to a squad car with Investigator Russei.

Seated in the back, Karmen drafted and deleted half a dozen versions of a text message to Daveed. She couldn't decide how many details to share. Ultimately, 'none' was the only safe answer. She settled on final wording and sent it: >>I won't be home for dinner. I love all of you and will be home with a crazy story when this is over.<< Daveed would get the inside joke and know it might be several days before she could be in touch again. The thought of leaving the planet without telling him turned her stomach, but they couldn't fully trust the security of the communications network since the cyber-attack. She couldn't risk leaking any details.

Armin was engaged with his own handheld, muttering under his breath as he paged through messages from people in his local intel network.

Lee finally craned his head to look back. "Armin, you have something you want to share with the class?"

Armin snorted. "I'm polling my intel network. It's not a terror attack. Not military. Not anything that might be a threat to planetary security. Just a crime scene," he declared without elaborating.

"I'd call the fact they used a starship a matter of 'planetary security'," Karmen said. "The TalEx raid was on the other side of the world."

Russei tried to pry some more information loose. "Officer Godri, if you've learned anything that might help out our local investigation, please share. I've worked campus security at the medical annex for nine years, and I've never seen anything remotely like what we saw today."

"Oh, come on," Armin sneered, "you guys have it easy. You deal with, what, one assault a year?"

The Enforcer scoffed. "If only it were that simple."

"I'm sure it's incredibly complicated. I still think you guys are soft."

Karmen swatted Armin. "Don't belittle them. Keep your eyes on your own work. Tell us what you found."

"The lights are coming back on," Armin sullenly reported.

"I can see that."

"The *reason* they're coming back on is the virus the attackers used is a self-reducing algorithm—meaning, the effects weren't meant to last long-term. I think it was timed specifically to blank out any system that might allow our people to coordinate a defense or resistance. Six hours seems to be the window the attackers had arranged for themselves. So, it's run its course. Everything should be coming back online now—assuming there's been no permanent damage."

"So, a grand heist of medicine, microchips, and mining

charges—but not terrorism," Lee said.

"Looks like." Armin glared at Karmen and added, "No hitting."

She met his gaze evenly. "Don't make assumptions about things you don't understand."

"I understand there are rules against striking a fellow officer."

"And you are free to bring me up on whatever charges you think will bear weight. In the meantime, do you want to hear about all the times I was brought in to help manage a criminal incident on the business school campus? There are procedures, reporting requirements, laws to uphold, and traumatized psyches to mend. I don't remember seeing you at any of those meetings."

Armin broke his stare first. "Are campuses *that* dangerous?"

"Not generally. But it's far more than one incident per year."

"I'll remember that."

"Thank you."

"And thank you for helping us out, Officer Sley," the Enforcer said. "Nice to have someone from inside the university taking a role in fixing things. Too many people from outside our office try to run things some days."

"The TSS is a good agency, Investigator," she said, wishing they could simply teleport to their destination. There were too many egos in this car for her taste.

—

Greengard's spaceport had either been unaffected by the emergency or its crews had already managed to return the facility to full working order. Lighting was bright and plentiful, and all the buildings were alive with activity.

Investigator Russei left them at the departure terminal; Lee's clothing and their various IDs allowed them to breeze through numerous security checkpoints. The checkpoints were probably new; Karmen couldn't remember seeing so many in her previous trips here. She hoped it was a temporary consideration. The last thing any university needed was to frighten new arrivals.

A flight crew met them at an exterior hangar. One grizzled veteran with a Militia patch and the apparent rank of Chief walked them to the smallest starship Karmen had ever seen. It was barely fifteen meters in length and limited to what had to be a single deck. But it did have a very advanced sensor suite bubble installed on its dorsal hull, about mid-way along its length.

"That dome's perched a little close to the rear stabilizers, isn't it Chief?" she asked.

"This little runabout only has a single hard point to mount that manner of equipment. But it'll hold. My crew know their jobs. Who's the EWAR specialist this trip?"

Armin nodded to the chief. "That would be me."

"Good. Let's get you settled in, sir. We got some awesome new toys for you to play with." The chief put his arm around the younger man and squired him through the narrow airlock.

Karmen halted, unable to take another step forward. The open airlock yawned like a black hole. Who knew what was on the other side? Maybe non-existence. The disaster aboard the *Triumph* could have happened yesterday to her mind. It could be happening right now. Her body told her an emergency was in progress and her breath caught, her abdominal muscles clenched, and her heart rate doubled. She forced herself to stand still and breathe to bring herself under control.

"Are you all right?" Lee asked in his soft tone of practiced bedside manner.

"This is all happening a little quickly," Karmen admitted, taking an unsteady breath.

"It is. Are you up for this mission?"

"Yes, I'll be fine. It's just that I haven't seen anything like this in a long time."

"Says the woman who built a functional warship Command Center in her basement," Lee chided.

The jest cut through her anxiety, and she chuckled. "I know. I'm being a silly old woman. Forgive me, I'm nervous as fok. What if I do something wrong? What if—?"

Lee settled her by putting his hands on her shoulders. He was shorter than she was and had to tilt his head to look her in the eyes, but the gesture worked. Being close to him, she could sense the natural power of his Gifted abilities. She'd spent their entire relationship thinking of him as a doctor, but the fact of the matter was that he had a lot more skills she had yet to see. "Hey, what's your Course Rank, Lee?"

"I haven't officially taken the test yet, but my potential is estimated to be 6.5."

"Nice! That's not bad for Sacon class."

"I'm very middling by Agent standards—nothing compared to what someone in Primus can do. My biggest trick at the academy was using my telekinesis to guide a knife to a target. I got pretty good at it."

"Really? How good?"

"My team had a training mannequin named Harold. One day, I put a knife in Harold's eye from fifty meters away. The trainer said once was luck, twice was skill. I moved back ten more meters and drove the same knife into Harold's other eye.

No one gave me any trouble after that."

"So, of course you went into medicine."

"Why not? You commanded a warship, then got out and married a schoolteacher."

"Ouch, you win. I'll be all right. But this ship they're loaning us… it's so small!"

"I've flown in smaller."

"I haven't. But I can get used to it for a while. Let's check out our new ride."

To her horror, the ship was even smaller on the inside. The flight deck only had three stations—two up front for nav and comms, and a third behind them on the left, which took up the entire wall of the compartment. That was the sensor suite, Karmen figured. A tiny passenger compartment followed aft, which led to two staterooms, then a washroom, and a combination kitchen and pantry the size of a walk-in closet. The good news was the pantry was stocked. The bad news was that it had been stocked with military food packs. The ship's locker might have had room to store a few extra sets of clothing besides the emergency gear already inside.

"Cozy," she commented as she settled into the comm position. "We may have to sleep in shifts."

"Armin and I will. You can at least have a stateroom to yourself," Lee said.

Armin gave no sign of hearing the conversation; he was in love with the new sensor gear. "Guys, this is the most advanced sensor suite I've ever seen. I think with this we can hear gamma ray bursts and see gravity waves."

"Radioactivity?" Lee asked.

"You bet. We can plot any particle you want with this gear."

"Good. We'll start looking for curium isotopes as soon as

we're in orbit. At least those stick around for a while," Lee said. "Does anyone have a problem with me being command pilot?"

No one did.

Lee proved to be a perfectly competent pilot, and he got them into orbit in short order. Karmen took on the task of managing comm traffic and listening to the open bands for clues as to where the strange pirate ship might have gone. Armin dove into his new position and could not keep from talking himself through every experiment he tried with his sensors.

"We'll try a geosynchronous orbit over Foundation City first," Lee said. "I figure if there's a radiation trail, that's where it will start."

"The planet has made a third of a rotation since they left," Armin pointed out. "Give us a normal equatorial flight path, then increase our orbits by ten thousand kilometers on each pass over Foundation City."

Their job was tedious but not especially difficult. Lee flew them to a set of coordinates, and Armin took a reading. Then he took another. Then Lee flew to new coordinates. Over and over, they repeated the pattern.

Karmen was about to despair about getting any useful information when Armin called out, "Ha! Got you! Bomaxed curium. Lee, come to course one-eight-three mark nineteen. One hundred thousand kilometers."

Lee made the corrections. "Done. What do you have?"

"I have a definite cloud of curium isotopes. Officer Sley, can you ping the nav computer and tell us what systems lie in this general direction?"

For once she was happy to have something to do besides listen to comm channels. "Let's see. We're traveling down the galactic arm in this direction... There are twenty-one inhabited planets of various descriptions and distances."

"And we'll check out every one of them until we find our pirate," Lee said. "I hope no one had weekend plans."

Karmen hesitated then said, "Kaia was planning on inviting her GravX boyfriend to the house at some point. I would hate to miss that."

"I'm certain she'd wait until you got back to arrange a visit."

"Who's Kaia?" Armin asked.

"Karmen's oldest girl. She's long-distance dating a Lower Dynasty GravX nerd."

"No shite?"

Karmen finally had to raise her voice. "Will you two stop it? I want to track down our target and go home. I have no stomach for artificial gravity anymore."

"Sounds like a plan," Lee said, "Let's find our ship."

17

INVISIBLE SPACE

THOUGH THE TSS vessel was able to jump at longer intervals than a civilian shuttle and didn't require cool-down time between jumps, conducting a search was still slow-going. With considerable effort, they created an effective search pattern, and then the tedious work began. Karmen hated the way time dragged between checking out each destination, but she quickly adapted to the routine. And, admittedly, there was a certain thrill to seeing so many new worlds in such a short time.

Boragin was a green and blue agricultural planet, which operated under a strict regimen of partitioning its productive land so that eighty percent of it remained fallow for up to a decade while the population intensely worked the remainder. Whatever else one might imagine, it worked: Boragin's grains and produce came at a premium on interstellar markets, and all without the consolidation of a dynastic enterprise.

Sephore was a mining world with a toxic, corrosive atmosphere. But deep in the planet's crust were rich ores and minerals beyond counting. The problem was that equipment shipped there had a bad habit of breaking down, and every attempt to automate the work had ended in failure. Even TalEx had no interest in the place, as it preferred the more predictable returns of operations run on asteroids or in habitable planetary environments.

Mahalia was the third moon of a gas giant with stupendous rings around it. It only held a small ground port; however, it featured a giant space station catering almost exclusively to entertainment. Casinos, theaters, concert halls, and sports arenas filled the station. Orbiting bright boards a kilometer square projected ads directly at space travelers. Karmen wondered if they had a GravX arena, and if so, how well attended it was. It didn't take long to discover they had a game schedule that extended to the end of the year. *All right, then. Maybe Kaia is on to something. Smart girl!*

Dragos was another industrial world, far more amenable to Taran life, but it was managed by a horrifically corrupt regime, according to Armin. How they got anything of worth accomplished at all was something Karmen couldn't figure out. On the other hand, if she needed a place to hide a pirate crew, Dragos might well be on her list.

Lastarren proved to be a resort world with only one small continent but a unique form of plant life: great underwater trees that grew toward the oceans' surface from plateaus beneath the waves. Some of these aquatic colonies were the equivalent of any tourist town Karmen had ever seen. A visit would be fascinating, to say the least, but she didn't think that a starship like the ore carrier they were pursuing would do well on that world.

Field 13 was an asteroid settlement. Settlers had long ago found a mountain in space and drilled into it, until the habitable surface of the asteroid was entirely inside the great rock. There wasn't anywhere in or around the colony capable of hiding their quarry, so they jumped on to the next target in their search list.

"Welcome to destination number seven: Diphous," Lee announced as they dropped out from subspace. "So named for the abundance of naturally occurring diphous ore, which is a vital ingredient of isometric crystalline lattice matrixes, a key component to jump drives. Tell us what we're looking at, Armin."

"We have radiation sources all over the place. But with four gas giants in the system, that's not terribly unusual... Wait, there it is. Curium!" He nearly jumped out of his seat. "A big cloud of it. But it's way out in the middle of nowhere. Hmm. Lee, try taking us in a full circle with, say, a one million kilometer radius. I want to check these bearings."

"Engaging search pattern 'Giant Circle'," Lee said.

Karmen rapped her fingers on her console with anxious nerves as they waited for the updated readings to populate.

Eventually, Armin nodded thoughtfully. "That did it. The cloud isn't on the planet it... No, that has to be wrong. There's a cloud in orbit behind us—that is, further from the primary star than we are. But there's also a trail that leads *toward* the star. Where were they going? Hmm... Karmen, could you display our position relative to the planet?"

She updated the map display overlaid on the front viewport.

"There," Armin said. "Lee, plot us an intercept to deep space. Course two-nine-one mark nine. Max speed. I'm not getting any big objects near that cloud, but it's best to be sure."

"Let's see what there is to see," the Junior Agent confirmed, updating his course.

They spent another hour trying to segment their search into smaller more manageable chunks without learning anything new from the scan data. There was a distinct Curium trail, but it was unclear why there would be multiple switchbacks along the same route.

Finally, Lee threw up his hands. "What went on here?"

Karmen had been listening to the comm chatter the whole time; finally, something caught her attention that might shine light on the strange sensor readings. She raised her hand. "Hey, head to the planet. I just heard a report of a strange starship in orbit, which matches our pirate ship. One of the ground crew is calling for instructions on an open channel. It seems that several cargo shuttles are making unscheduled pick-ups of a great many cargo pods."

Lee gave a happy shout. "That's it! Let's see what Diphous looks like up close."

—   —   —

Their shuttle dropped into orbit over Diphous far enough from the suspected pirate vessel to keep the tiny shuttle at the edge of their sensor horizon. The pirate ship was in geosynchronous orbit, as they had been during the Greengard raid. The shuttle would be safe enough in this position for a while.

"We need a solid ID match. Karmen, how are you with profiling?" Lee asked her.

Karmen spoke while her fingers danced across the console. "I used to have a team just for that back on the *Triumph*, but I think I can remember how to poll a knowledge base." By the time she finished speaking, a display had opened between them. Her heart lifted; it was definitely the ship that had been spotted on Greengard. The hatches, the bulk cargo wings, and the drive signatures all matched.

As they watched, a cargo shuttle broke the atmosphere and maneuvered toward the pirate ship, gaining access through one of the unexplained hatches in the lower tier.

"I knew those weren't for loading cargo," Karmen said.

"It was just a hunch," Armin murmured.

"How do we stop them?" Karmen asked. "Do we have any weapons on this thing?"

"Do you see a weapons panel?" Lee asked. "Because I don't."

Karmen felt an intense moment of stupidity for not noticing. "Bomax! They could have at least set us up with a couple of missiles."

"Armaments draw attention. This was meant as a recon mission," Armin said. "Besides, that ship is way too big to engage on our own. We can call it in and get reinforcements."

"It'll take time for any TSS backup to arrive," Lee said. "And we need to know what to tell them about the threat level so we can stage an appropriate response. This might be one piece of a bigger operation. We don't want to blow our chance to uncover critical information about the larger threat."

Karmen hated to agree, but he was right. Lynaedan tech suggested a much broader-scale plot than a raid on one remote academic world. If they spooked this ship, the perpetrators might scatter. Better to chase the threat back to its source while they had a warm lead. Still, she hated to watch a theft in progress and not do anything about it. Nonetheless, there were more pressing concerns.

"There's something else to consider," Karmen said. "They have radioactive charges on board. Do we really want to leave those active in the hands of people who were willing to stage a planetary assault on a peaceful university?"

Lee frowned. "Like Armin said, this is a recon mission."

"There has to be something we can do without drawing unwanted attention," Karmen insisted. "Wasn't there something about the storage containers having remote shutdown codes? What if we sent out a broadcast to disable the shielding so the charges would be rendered inert?"

"A nice thought, but wishful thinking," Armin replied. "We'd have to get really close for that to have any chance of going through."

Karmen shrugged. "Okay. So we get close."

Armin side-eyed her. "Feeling suicidal, ma'am? Because that is how that tactic ends. There's no invisibility in space, Officer Sley."

"But surely—"

"There's no invisibility in space," Armin repeated.

"We're not asking for a cloaking device, Armin—and those *do* exist."

Armin looked up, obviously annoyed. "True, but not on *this* ship. For our purposes in this vessel, there is. No. Invisibility. In. Space. You can forget about us sneaking up to them unnoticed."

Karmen looked over the scan data of the cargo transfer in progress. "Well, whatever we're going to do, it should happen fast. That raid was likely in progress for some time before that transmission was made. There's no knowing how much longer they'll be engaged in their robbery."

Lee sat calmly, taking in the information. "It's clear they're following a very precise plan. All we need to do is disrupt it."

"That's… *not* a recon mission," Armin murmured.

"What if we alter our signature so that the mother ship thinks we're one of their cargo shuttles?" Karmen mused.

"Armin, could you do that?" Lee asked.

"Sure, I can make us look like any ship we've got data about. But the timing would be crazy. The other shuttle would have to be offline during the reboot, we'd have to approach from a vector the sensor operator would recognize. We'd have to time it so we arrived when the shuttle we were spoofing was supposed to get there. But to what end?"

"If we got in close enough, could you send those mining charge container shut down codes?" Lee asked.

Armin's brows drew together. "It's possible, but I'm not sure if we could get a signal through the hull. The codes are designed to work in the same room as the storage containers. Even with a signal boost, I think we'd need to get the hangar bay door open. And there are a *lot* of hangars there, so we need to first identify the right one."

"But we do have the best sensor suite on the market," Karmen pointed out. "So, if we hitch a ride with one of those shuttles, we can get close, take our readings, send the signal. Then, we'll have all the info we need to report back about what might be going on with this pesky pirate gang."

Armin frowned. "That's a lot of risky moves. It's a mediocre plan, at best."

"You have to go with the mediocre plan you have today, not the perfect plan you'll have two weeks from now," Karmen declared. "What's the other option—let them finish this theft and then jump away again?"

Armin checked his display. "Hold on… one of those four shuttles isn't like the others. It has a TalEx transponder."

"Commandeered by the pirates?" Lee asked.

Karmen crossed her arms. "Or someone is in on it."

The three of them exchanged looks.

Lee tapped his console. "We need to get in close, take as

many scans as we can. If we're able to disarm those nuclear charges, that's a huge bonus. We can start by scoping out the scene of the crime to get readings on the cargo they're taking. Then, we can pick a shuttle to shadow up to the mothership."

"If you can manage the flying, I think I can handle the spoofing needed to get us close."

"And if you *don't* fool them?" Lee asked.

"Then we'd better hope that we're already right up on their ass. Missiles and torpedoes have minimum safe firing distances, and I'd expect most of the weapons on a ship that size to be long-range and heavy-duty. Sneaking up is a better idea than trying to blitz them. That's a GravX term, Karmen," Armin said.

"Ah. Thank you for that clarification."

"All right, then… stealth over a speedy fly-by, it is," Lee stated. "Let's do it. I'll drop us down to the deck. That's a pilot term, Armin."

Armin sighed. "Thanks."

18

TOO CLOSE TO CALL

SENSOR OFFICER CALLUM Nissin was one of the few Tarans on the *Emerald Queen* who had no problem with his Lynaedan crew mates. Yes, they had mech parts here and there; Sergeant Meklife was a particularly stubborn case on that score. Some of the drone pilots were almost never outside their drone bodies, and Callum couldn't have identified them on a dare. He didn't understand the allure of getting so far into mechanical implants that you refused to retreat to flesh and blood, but he hadn't been born on Lynaeda. At least the whole crew knew who Meklife was. Callum suspected that was the point.

The question for Callum was Sacha, the Operations Officer who occupied the workstation next to his. Sacha churned his innards in a way no woman ever had. Her eyes were an impossibly rich purple only implants could achieve, and her hair was unlike anything he'd ever seen. It changed color and style more or less at her will; he'd been keeping track. One day it was a blue braid, then the next various shades of green in double ponytails. Today, she'd shown up for her shift wearing a sleek mane in a shade of purple he had never seen before. She was simply magnificent.

The worst part for him was that Sacha had no idea who he was; no matter what manner of small-talk he tried, he couldn't get her to look at him. Granted, she wasn't supposed to look at *him*, just her instruments. Keeping his own eyes focused on his station took a staggering amount of effort. Unfortunately, he'd never seen her outside her duty hours. He had no idea when she slept or what she ate, or *if* she did either.

The job was what it was, but today their mission was boring. Callum's entire duty for this op was to be a substitute flight operations officer; he'd watch four cargo shuttles lift off from the planet, ascend to orbit, and land in the *Emerald Queen*'s hangar bay, then wait for them to unload. One, two, three, four of them. And then watch them as they descended, empty, back to the planet again. One, two, three, four. He would much rather look at Sacha.

Occasionally, he did sneak a look at her, trying not to be obvious. She was stunning. Her hair and eyes—and wearing an extra set of arms. Stars, he could only imagine her hugs…

Callum couldn't stop from glancing over every few minutes, transfixed by her unique beauty. He couldn't tell if one set of arms was natural and the other mechanical, or if all of them were mechanical. They looked perfectly natural to him. What kind of tech did she use to make it all work? And what did she do with them when she wasn't at her console?

He couldn't *not* watch her work. Each arm operated a different set of controls; she never even turned her head to look at the extra limbs. Did she have eyes in the back of her head, too? He had an urge to lift her hair to find out.

At one point, Sacha raised one of her extra arms to beckon

to someone behind her. She never stopped working, never moved her eyes from the display. But Sergeant Meklife approached and thudded to a full stop next to Callum.

"Sensors, how goes the operation?" Meklife asked.

"Regular as a digital clock, Commander." Callum didn't understand why Commander Lom Mench went by *Sergeant* Meklife as a moniker in that drone body rather than mirroring his actual rank on the ship, but it wasn't his place to ask questions.

"I'm glad to hear it," the Lynaedan replied. "Sacha here has been keeping track of your efforts. She has generally good things to say. But you lose focus now and then. Please rectify the situation. And, be warned, Callum—Sacha is quite a taskmaster. Work quickly and well."

Callum fought to maintain his composure, then blurted, "Yes, sir!" He turned his head to watch the first officer thud away to another station, then brought his attention back to his job.

Sacha leaned forward a bit, finding her own instrumentation intensely interesting.

"I wasn't trying to disturb you," Callum said. He hoped he sounded apologetic.

Sacha turned to him. He was again drawn in by her unique features. "Callum, I don't *dislike* you. But the constant staring can't continue."

"I know. I'm sorry. I'm trying not to be creepy. But you really stand out."

"It's the hair mod, isn't it? Bomax, I thought it might be too much when I integrated it. But I thought the Ops position meant I might be able to carry it off."

Wow, she has no idea what she looks like. He wasn't sure how to reply diplomatically. "Your hair is amazing, but it's the arms that are making me crazy."

Sacha turned in her seat and let all four arms make a questioning gesture while her hair shifted to glow a wild red. "*These* are what you look at?"

"I look at *everything*. But who needs four arms?"

She seemed honestly bewildered at the question. She finally pointed to four separate consoles. "Ops is complicated, and this mod lets me work four consoles at once. It's efficient."

But how do you see? Her modesty somehow made her more alluring. "Well, whatever the reason, you're impossible not to notice… in a good way. Sorry."

All four arms retreated to Sacha's lap. "Callum, either you need to learn to focus, or I need to ask Meklife to move your workstation. How about we have a talk? Like, coffee in the galley. Would that work for you?" she asked.

"Yes! Yes, it would."

"Good. In the meantime…" She used both left arms to point to his console.

Yeah, I get it: back to work. But… bomax, is she smiling just a little bit? Callum was so intoxicated with the possibility that he might have a chance with her that he nearly missed the new and unexplained blip on his display.

Callum's mind instantly snapped back to his job. "Contact, contact!" he called. "Sensors to Captain Aura."

In moments, the comm net came alive. The captain's voice was unmistakable. "This is Aura, go ahead."

"Captain, I have a new contact at bearing one-eight-one."

The display changed a bit to alert Callum that other officers were now looking at his display. Sacha was one of them. But the readings didn't make sense. The contact was barely moving, but also… accelerating? How did that make any sense?

He kept his eyes on his work, but with every passing second, he became more aware of Sacha's attention. She was glancing at him, now. Shouting across the physical space between them wouldn't fly with comm protocols. He gulped and opened a channel to her comm. "Sensors to Ops," he said.

"Ops, go ahead."

"Sacha, I need a cross-check on distance and bearing."

"Stand by…"

Something was wrong, either with the ship's fancy salvaged sensor rig or he had forgotten everything he'd ever learned about the use of the equipment. According to his readouts, the target's speed was increasing but its angle of attack was nearly zero. Nothing could do that, not without being detected by the ship's point defense computer.

Sacha's voice returned. This time, it carried a note of anger. "I don't check you, Callum."

He sighed inwardly. *Maybe I did screw it up.* "Confirm your check, please."

"I did it twice. I don't check you."

"I'm resetting my board. Stand by." A big mistake if there was genuinely something dangerous out there. But his scope read the four shuttles perfectly. While they'd been talking, the heavy model had arrived on the hangar deck to join the three smaller spacecraft.

All at once, the new contact disappeared from the display. Callum carried through with his reset, but now the screen was empty. Whatever he thought he'd seen was gone. "Wait, where did it go?"

This time, Aura was on the comm—and she was far less accommodating than Sacha. "Sensors! Do you have a contact or not?"

Now, the shuttles were departing again. One. Two. Three.

Wait for it. Wait. Wait. Four.

Callum's stomach turned as he realized he was in for a stern conversation with Meklife. Maybe the captain herself. He didn't look forward to any of it. "Negative. I must have made an error in the timing. No new contact."

Sacha glared at him from her station and pointed with her left arms. She didn't bother with the comms. "Focus!"

— — —

Lee gasped as he struggled to hold his ship in its exact location. Pion drives were not meant to maneuver spacecraft at fractions of a meter per second. "I'm not sure how long this is going to work," he admitted.

"Smart move, Lee, lifting us straight up so that we approached facing their belly," Armin said. "Now what?"

Lee set their shuttle to maintain the same distance from the much larger ship they were hiding from. From the nav chair, he could ping the forward viewer and watch the expanse of hull less than six meters away. Hiding in plain sight, like med nanites hitching a ride on blood cells. "We're close enough that they should be reading us as part of their ship. Now, let's get a good look at these hatches and figure out which one leads to the storage bay holding the nuclear charges."

"Low-power pings, please," Karmen instructed. "Don't want the battle computers on board to think we're attacking them."

"That all depends on how good their sensor operator is," Armin snarked. But he complied. After a few minutes, he straightened in his seat. "I've got a trace on the curium. Bring us forward."

Lee carefully piloted their craft along the underbelly of the massive cargo ship. Outside one painted with a massive '3', Armin nodded emphatically.

"All right, this is it. The curium signature is strongest here. The charges must be inside."

"Do you have the disarm signal ready?" Lee asked.

"All queued."

"Now, the trick is convincing the door to let us in," Karmen said. It was a job that fell to the comm station, making it her responsibility. She started cycling through access codes, a series of friendly digital handshakes. The last thing she wanted was for the pirate battleship to identify them as a threat.

—   —   —

Something was going on and Callum wasn't understanding what.

"Callum!"

He looked up to see Sacha glaring at him. "Yes. Sorry, did you say something?"

"I said the loaders are having trouble working on all four shuttles at once. The TalEx shuttle is moving to Bay 3. Just call ahead and make sure the hangar crew is ready to launch it when they've finished unloading."

"That's kind of your job."

"And I'm doing seventeen things right now. One call. That's all I need from you."

"Got it." He opened the comm link. "Hangar deck, stand by to re-task shuttle TalEx to Launch Bay 3 when unloading is complete."

A hiss and a thump connected a new voice to the comm net. "Message acknowledged. Estimated turnaround time is thirty-nine minutes."

— — —

"Come on, Karmen, how long can picking a lock take?" Armin demanded, as if goading her would make her work faster.

She flashed the same glare she used when one of her children talked back out of turn. "If you're not used to it, and your coworkers keep bugging you, it can take all day. If you think you can do better, Armin, I will gladly switch positions with you."

He leaned back in his seat. "No, ma'am. You have it, you stick with it."

Karmen felt a real urge to drop what she was doing and punch Armin in the face. She'd been throwing one command code after another at the hangar door on the assumption that she knew what the carrier's computer was likely to use. The problem was that she was years out of practice and had never been primarily a comm officer. But she'd built an algorithm that had promise. This one would scan the entire range of commercial frequencies and blast every code in the knowledge base at the hangar. If that didn't break the lock, she had no idea what would.

"Karmen, we're out of time," Lee said.

Karmen completed the coding just in time to see their sensor board light up with blips. One. Two. Three shuttles were blasting out the launch hatches above them. The fourth one couldn't be far behind. And if all four left, they'd absolutely show up on the pirate ship's sensors no matter where Armin tried to hide them.

"Now or never, Sley!" Armin yelled.

Karmen slapped the command stud on her console. "Go!"

Armin powered up his signal array and they waited, everyone tense and quiet. The algorithm ran down a second time then a third and finally screeched in success. The hangar door directly in front of their small shuttle cracked open.

To reveal a heavy TalEx shuttle lifting off its pad and coming right for them.

— — —

Alarms on Callum's console shattered forty-five minutes of peace. "Commander! I have a bearing on a new contact directly obstructing access Hatch 3 on the hangar deck."

Gallian's voice rang out. "Commander! We have an attempted infiltration on the hangar deck. I need a flight drone operator at access Hatch 3, Code Blue!"

Then Meklife answered, "No flight drones are available. Nav, use evasive maneuver 7-B. Now! Ops, arm the rear missile tubes. Callum, transfer target information to Ops."

Ha! I was right! Callum used his practiced skills to clone the target's profile and fed the data directly to the battle computer while signaling Sacha's console that they had a clear ID on their target. "Target locked and profile coded. Ops!"

"I have it, Callum. Arming torpedo for launch."

From the other side of the War Room, Captain Aura's voice rang out clearly. "Wait for it. Fire torpedo!"

"Torpedo away!"

— — —

Karmen's breath caught in her throat. She wasn't sure that *she* had opened the hatch at all. But it was open now, and they had a narrow window to act.

Armin was on it. "Sending the mining charge shutdown codes!" he shouted.

The large TalEx-marked transport ship was coming through the open bay door. Their little recon ship was totally exposed.

"Oh, shite!" Lee bellowed and turned the small craft on its short axis, then dropped them in a nosedive.

The internal gravity field never wavered, but Karmen felt thrust against her four-point harness as her stomach rose into her throat. She shut her eyes. Her heart pounding in her chest in sheer terror. Even when she'd been racing to the rear section of the failing *Triumph*, she didn't feel as helpless, as out of control, as she did right now. At least then she'd been doing something. All she could do now was hang on and try not to barf on her workstation.

"Lee, we have missile fire!" Armin yelled.

"Deal with it, mister sensors. I'm trying to avoid being shot."

Armin snarled and growled as he tried different techniques to throw the missile's guidance off the shuttle's tail. "Spoof Class 1. Fok. Spoof Class 3, gah! Range Damper Class 5. No... Multi-spectrum sensor blast. *Fok!*"

Even as the comms were useless in this situation. Karmen couldn't not watch the range finder drop as the missile closed the distance. For all of Lee's crazy flying and Armin's sensor work, the missile was well-designed and more than sufficient to turn their shuttle into scrap.

But she had an idea. "Lee! Head towards the warehouse they're emptying. Now!"

19

MOTHER CARNAGE

OH, SHITE! KARMEN held onto her chair's armrests for dear life as Lee tried to lose the missile.

Twists and turns, climbs and dives—nothing the Junior Agent did seemed to work. Karmen's suggestion to head to the warehouse was a ridiculously long shot. A chance in millions that the pirates would be more concerned about the contents of their target site than eliminating a potential enemy. If nothing else, she thought Lee might be inspired to try to pull out of their steep dive at the last moment, but the maneuver might very well be their last.

Karmen kept her eyes squeezed shut, unwilling to watch the ground racing toward her.

"Missile lock broken!" Armin called out. "Detonation!"

Karmen finally dared a peek as Lee abruptly pulled the shuttle out of the dive. He made a tight circle above the base to lose some speed and then careened around the far side of the refinery and storage facility.

"Nice flying," Karmen managed to say as her stomach resettled to its proper place.

Lee didn't break his focus out the forward viewport. "We're not out of it yet."

The great desert beyond the refinery was both rocky and sand-blasted. They were flying into the shadow of night, obscuring the finer details of the landscape. As Lee leveled out the shuttle at low elevation to make them more difficult to spot on scan, he tried to shed velocity. But the angle was wrong, and there was no way to regain what vector they'd lost.

The shuttle hit the ground hard, skipping along the rocky desert floor. Landing struts plowed deep furrows in the parched earth, throwing up detritus and shale. The shuttle spun and finally came to rest in the shadow of a butte, slamming into the vertical rock face hard enough to dislodge stone fragments from above.

Karmen flailed against her four-point harness as the hail of falling rock pelted the hull, a cloud of dust rising into the air. *Rain drops. It sounds like rain drops on a tin roof.*

Then, darkness.

When Karmen came to, she was loose in her harness. It was still dark, but enough starlight was filtering through the dirt-covered viewport for her to get her bearings. She popped the harness lock and slid out of her seat. Everything in the shuttle lay askew at a crazily tilted angle. Every cabinet and locker had exploded; the shuttle floor was awash in cargo and equipment.

Her neck and shoulders felt like they'd been lying in the scorching sun for days. She gently twisted her body, blinking to clear her eyes.

"Lights!" she yelled.

"Power is out," Armin said from the shadows in front of her. He was rooting around through the chaotic mess on the floor. "You okay?"

"Yeah, I think so." She strained to see him. Based on the dirt blocking the viewport, she wondered how far they'd been buried under sand, rock, and everything else. That might make them difficult to find by rescuers. But it might also hide them if the pirates gave pursuit, especially in the dark. Not something she wanted to think about at the moment. Let that come later.

She tested her limbs, found them in working order. She looked around for Lee and spotted him laid on the ground, unconscious. "Lee? Lee!" She scrambled over to him. "What happened?'

"I think he hit his head on the dash when we came down," Armin said. "He seems stable, but he probably has a concussion, or who knows what else. Ah! Here we go." He dragged a red medkit case out from under a pile of other gear. "Do you have any field medic training?"

"Some. But I also have four teenagers." Karmen took the case from him.

Armin stayed out of her way as she plied her skills. The diagnostic scanner told her the basics: Lee's vital signs were good, but a concussion was a definite possibility. She adjusted the nanite injector's payload and gave him a dose to speed up his recovery. They'd know how he'd fared in a short while, and that was all she knew how to do.

Karmen rocked back on her heels. "How bad is it?" She looked up at the ship's controls and then roof.

"Let's find out." Her fellow Militia officer went over to the side hatch and pounded on it with his fist. It sounded hollow on the other side. "Doesn't seem like we're fully buried, at least."

He pulled the emergency release and manually shoved the

outer door open. His reward was a face full of dust and pebbles. But the night sky and landscape showed through the open door. Thankfully, burial wasn't their fate.

Thank the stars for that. The additional illumination helped tamp her panic down into her feet where it belonged. Karmen started to suck in a breath of fresh air but sputtered when she instead got mostly dust. She pulled her shirt up to cover her nose and mouth. "We couldn't crash land on a tropical beach?"

"You're telling me." Armin poked his head outside before pulling the hatch closed all but a crack. "I don't think we're leaving for a while. Not having power means we won't show up on most kinds of scan sweeps, so I doubt the pirates have any more idea where we are than we do. Maybe we can use that to our advantage."

"You have an idea, besides waiting for our Junior Agent to regain consciousness?"

"That *was* my idea," Armin admitted.

"Just sit here and do nothing? No, we have to be able to do better than that." Karmen looked around at the equipment scattered across the deck. "Do we know what all this stuff is? We took off in a hurry, so I didn't do an inventory."

"I mostly just looked at the sensor suite," Armin admitted. "I assume we have the standard emergency gear."

Karmen pulled at a few cases experimentally, heaping them one at a time in a neat pile on the downward sloping section of the cabin. Food packs were a golden find, as was a case full of flashlights. She took one flashlight for herself and gave another to Armin.

Being able to shine light into shadowed corners and under consoles made everything simpler. She kept at it, cataloging bits and pieces and trying to remember standard operating protocols for where everything should be stored.

Armin surprised her with a laugh and a joyful shout. Karmen swung her flashlight beam to him. He was holding a torso-sized case in his arms, smiling like he'd cracked an amazing joke and brought the audience to pieces. He even raised it to his face and kissed it. "I found it!"

"Oh! What? Emergency beacon? Portable generator?" she asked, wondering what could possibly make him so happy.

Armin tilted the case so she could see inside. It contained a compact winged contraption nestled in a padded compartment with a host of supporting equipment. "This, Officer Sley is a Type XV-9 scouting drone. Battery powered with night vision cameras and a range of a few hundred kilometers. It has a receiver and a dedicated tablet. I've never had an occasion to play with one before, but they're the best in the business."

Karmen arched an eyebrow. "What kinds of weapons does it carry?"

"None. It's too small for that."

"So, it's useless—"

"Karmen, no! Far from it. With this, we can see the bad guys long before they see us. What's more valuable than that?"

Weapons? She kept the retort to herself, trying to fight off her disappointment. But Armin had a point; being able to see danger coming counted for a lot.

She looked back over at Lee. He was breathing regularly, and his external wounds were already fading. As long as they didn't try to move him while the nanites finished their work, he wouldn't suffer any additional injury.

"All right, Armin, this spy business is your wheelhouse. What do we do?"

—

The first hints of dawn were lightening the sky by the time they got everything set up. That was a mixed blessing. The drone would be able to recharge its solar cells while it flew, but it would also be easier to spot in daylight. Given all the unknowns, Karmen considered longer flight time a worthwhile tradeoff.

"This will either work or it won't." Armin sighed. "Ready on the checklist?"

Karmen opened her tablet and read from the screen. "Battery check."

"Battery is… eighty percent. That'll do. Next?"

"Um… Data connection."

"Connection is strong. Five bars. Next."

"Program primary way point."

"How about we use the shuttle for our reference? Done. Now?"

"Recording mode on. Flight mode: manual or autopilot?" she asked.

"Let's go with autopilot for now. We can plot surveillance points as we get closer to the target. Then, we'll switch to manual for a close look at the bad guys. You can tab your screen for auto-follow on the bottom, there."

Karmen familiarized herself with the commands. "All right. What will I do next?"

"I'll be flying, so you get to watch your screen and pick out anything you want me to get a closer look at." He paused. "Do you want to launch it?"

"Sure! What do I do?"

"Pick it up."

The drone was barely the size of a flying disc toy for kids—

not even half a meter in diameter, and it weighed no more than a tablet. "Stars! This little thing can do all that stuff you talked about?"

"Yeah, I told you these babies are amazing. On my mark, throw the drone straight up in the air. Ready?"

Karmen got into position and nodded.

"Now!"

She flung the drone up and barely heard the whine of the engine as it continued upward on its own. After a minute, she couldn't see it anymore. She peered over Armin's shoulder as he manipulated the flight controls. Satisfied that he had it handled, she concentrated on her own gear.

The ancillary tablet showed the surveillance data stream from the drone in real-time. The camera faced the ground, while a display in the screen's margin kept a running count of the distance it flew, its location relative to the point of origin, and the altitude.

Karmen was so enthralled with the high-resolution images that she almost dropped the tablet when the refinery came into view. "There it is!" she called.

"I see it. Let's zoom in and see what we can see."

All four of the shuttles were grounded with rear bay doors wide open. A number of the same humanoid drones they'd heard described on Greengard were engaged in the act of moving giant cargo modules into them. It seemed like a well-timed and complex operation, right back to routine despite their mini firefight. This was no mere theft. Whoever was running this operation clearly understood industrial processes. Smart and motivated people had gone through considerable trouble and expense to make this heist happen.

"I wish we could see inside those containers," Karmen griped.

"We won't have to. Those numerical codes on the sides will be indexed in TalEx's inventory logs. We can use them to confirm what was being stored inside and who was supposed to be on duty to manage them."

"What do you mean, 'supposed to'?"

"Do you see any private security? Any aircraft who've come to investigate? Something tells me the help was bought off, and you don't need a college education to figure out who did it," Armin said.

He had a point. And Karmen was beginning to realize just how sheltered a life she'd been leading as a faculty wife and mother. But she noticed a new contact when it appeared on her display. "An airborne vehicle is approaching. It might be someone coming to check out the trouble."

"I don't know. It's coming from the same bearing as the big ship, and it's coming straight down out of the stratosphere. Would an Enforcer make that approach?"

"Perhaps not," she admitted.

"Definitely not. Look at that thing—it's tiny. No search lights, no sensor pods, no weapons. I'm thinking it's an accomplice, not a soldier. Or a soldier that's being paid to assist. I know you don't like to look at the world that way, but that's reality."

The tiny, sloped-nose, cylindrical-bodied craft set down outside the work zone where the drones were actively loading, but within easy walking distance of the big TalEx shuttle. Two passengers emerged.

"Can you get a look at their faces, Armin? We can run facial recognition once we get comms back up."

"I can try, but we'll have to go lower." He made adjustments to the aerial drone's course. "One thousand meters… Five hundred."

"That's better, but not enough detail yet. Try two hundred and swing around to get a better look at their faces rather than the top of their heads."

"Two hundred meters."

"Yes, that elevation is good. Just bring it around a little more…" Karmen brought the tablet closer to her face, trying to force the pictures to resolve through force of will. The two people were arguing about something. "I don't suppose this gizmo is wired for sound?"

"Not at this distance."

"Bomax. That looks like a heated discussion to me." She watched as the loaders finished stuffing containers into the TalEx shuttle. The other three finished soon after. One of the small shuttles opened a hatch to allow the loaders entry to its interior, then dusted off, followed by the other small craft.

"Who are you people?" Karmen growled. "Armin, drop it down to one hundred meters."

"That's close enough for them to hear the engine."

"With everything going on down there? I doubt it. It looks like they're wrapping up. If we don't ID them now, we never will."

Armin shrugged and did as he was asked. On the video feed, a well-dressed man was gesticulating wildly, and his tall female companion appeared to be trying to calm him down with softer gestures. *Come on, you. Look up. Look up!*

Armin dropped the drone another twenty meters. Now, they *did* look up. Good solid photos of their faces washed over Karmen's tablet.

The man was clearly outraged over the interruption. He reached out with a hand and made a grabbing motion. Seconds later, the transmission ended in a screen full of electronic snow.

"Bomax! Well, at least that all got recorded," Armin said.

Karmen rewound the last minute of footage and positioned the recorded video so that she could see the woman's face. She zoomed in and repeated the process. Her mouth went dry as she realized she knew that face.

"Aura!" she gasped.

"Who?"

"Aurelia Thand. She's alive?" She shook her head with disbelief. "How can she be alive? Her body was never recovered, but… The *Triumph* was gutted and smashed. She—" Her stomach knotted. If she'd survived the wreck and never reported back, that had been a choice. It meant the Agent had abandoned her post. Her friend had betrayed her.

Armin's faced softened as he pieced together what Karmen was saying. He voiced the question Karmen couldn't bring herself to ask. "Why is your former TSS commander stealing ore from TalEx?"

Karmen scoffed. "I trusted her!"

"Hey, we'll figure this out," Armin soothed. "There must be an explanation—"

"And that man she was with… How did he take out our drone?" Karmen continued. "It was almost two hundred meters away!"

"He must have had a weapon."

"He *didn't* have a weapon, I'm sure of it. Both their hands were empty. He just reached out and…" Her eyes went wide. "He broke it with *telekinesis*. But no one outside the TSS should have that much control."

Armin set down the now pointless drone controls and instead gripped her shoulders. "Karmen, this is a lot to process, so let's not jump to conclusions. Come on, I'll pack this stuff up, and then we can figure out how to restore power to the shuttle. Why don't you go check on Lee?"

"Right. Lee."

"Everything is going to be all right, Officer Sley. Remember to breathe."

She took a deep, deliberate breath and let it out slowly. "I wish you'd let me be angry."

"Not productive."

"Well, you'd better not find yourself between me and her. Regs or not, I *will* punch you."

Karmen stumbled back to the shuttle and sat down hard at her comm station. She stared blankly into space, not even noticing when Lee opened his eyes and looked questioningly at her.

"Bomax. I'm dead, aren't I?" he croaked.

"Stars, Lee!" She snapped back to attention, diving from her seat to crouch down next to him. She gripped his hand and squeezed it, just like she used to do to her kids when they were sick. "No! You're going to be just fine. We got you all fixed up."

He winced, propping himself up on his elbows. "Karmen, you look like you've seen a ghost."

She looked away, out through the open hatch in the direction of the distant TalEx facility. The sun had risen above the horizon and made the minerals encrusting the desert floor glitter. It was still chilly inside the darkened shuttle, but Karmen was sweating. "I wish it was a ghost. I've just seen something much worse."

"What's that?"

"A complete stranger living in my friend's body."

20

CONNECTIONS

CALLUM SAT IN the *Emerald Queen*'s galley after his shift, tapping his coffee mug to watch the ripples bounce against the edges. One thing he could honestly say about the galley food aboard the *Emerald Queen*, it was filling. You could even go back for seconds if the kitchen staff was in a good mood. Some days, all they had to work with were sandwiches. Tonight, the stew was flavorful and satisfying enough to take his mind off the fact that he'd nearly screwed up beyond all recognition.

A clattering of dishes startled him. He looked up to see Sacha arranging two plates, a mug, and a bowl, one item in each hand. She sat down opposite him. "I'm sorry. Do you mind?" she asked.

"Not at all. I figured you had other things to do."

"Don't be obtuse. I said I'd have coffee with you, just not when. The operation is over. We're off shift. And here we are, with coffee. By the way, I like how you handled yourself in the War Room today."

"Are you kidding? I nearly wrecked the whole operation."

"It's true, you dropped the ball. But then you got right back up again and ran with it. Classic recovery play. Good for you, Sensors."

"Thank you, Ops." He pushed his own bowl and utensils to the side and watched as she went to work on her food and coffee. His eyes traced each of her hands as they did their tasks. He had so many questions. "It's awful to admit, but I wasn't sure if you ate or not. Or sleep. Because of the implants and all."

"Of course, we eat and sleep! We're not machines." As if to prove her point, she raised a shallow bowl of some gelatinous dessert to her mouth and slurped it down. She even winked as she resumed her dinner.

"Yeah, you're no machine," Callum murmured. He grinned like a fool as he watched her feed herself with all four limbs. *She's showing off. Is it for my benefit?*

When Sacha finished her meal, she belched wetly. "I can see you find me amusing."

Honey, you have no idea. "Ops, I find you so much more than that. A word like 'attractive' doesn't come close, either."

"Hmm. So, here's a question. What is it about me that has you hooked? The hair? The eyes?"

"I told you back at our consoles. It's the arms."

"But *why?* They're just my extra-duty arms," she said, waving all her hands at him. "I have an exterior back piece that has telescoping tentacles for really complex work. I call it the Octopus. Wearing these *and* that, I can run the entire War Room from my Ops panel. Not well, but I can do it."

"I would pay real credits to watch you do that," he said.

"If you'd been in the War Room the day I'd interviewed for the Ops position, you'd have seen it for free. Commander

Mench and Captain Aura were quite happy with my performance."

Bomax, I'm really punching above my weight with this girl. "Yeah, but can you do this?" He put his coffee down and did a quick hand and finger dance, the sort of thing that children did with their friends.

Sacha narrowed her eyes and executed a pattern of claps and snaps with all four of her hands that was so fast, precise, and intricate that he was stunned.

"Stars, you're sexy," he whispered.

She folded all four of her arms and sniffed. "Why do you think so?"

"Is that a serious question? Have you met you?"

"Let's say, back home I was plain as a blank screen, which makes me wonder if your standards are ridiculously low. Really, you have two arms. Why is my having four such a big deal?"

Callum had to admit it was a good question that he wasn't sure how to answer. "It's *crazy*, that's why. I suppose I should ask how you can see behind you while you're multi-tasking in the War Room."

She hesitated, examining him with her intense cybernetic gaze. Judging him. No. *Evaluating* him. "My hair is a sophisticated comm net matrix. It's a little more advanced than the one Commander Mench has. Mine feels like natural fibers. I added the variable color mod before I came on board. I can also style it without touching it. Great fun at parties." To prove her point, the strands transitioned to vibrant orange and formed into sophisticated ringlets. A moment later, it returned to her previous purple do.

Callum struggled to keep his jaw from dropping. He had to play it cool or there was no way there'd be a second coffee chat. "Is it better than what Officer Gallian has? That metal band around the back of his head—"

"Oh, no, no, no. His Comms rig has a solid-state communications net that lets him manage every intercom, remote connection, and data link on this ship."

"How? He never breaks a sweat."

"He wouldn't. His console does the heavy lifting, but he can direct all the traffic without even sitting down at his station. You ever wonder how he knows everything that goes on the second it happens? That's how. He's always plugged in."

I can't even tell if she's joking or not. Upon further consideration, he realized she wasn't. The Lynaedans were simply *that* elite. So, so out of his league. He mustered his courage. "Okay, I'll be honest here. What would it take for you to agree to a date?"

She laughed, a free and happy sound. "You think you can handle a date with me, Sensors?"

"Enough to ask you for one, you bet."

Sacha leaned in, the sparkle in her purple eyes matching her hair perfectly. "First, let me ask you something. You've been with Base girls, right?"

"Of course."

"And you got close. Really skin-to-skin close with some of them?"

"Yeah."

"And I'd guess you had a favorite. One who stood out from the rest?"

"Yes…"

Sacha put all her hands on the table and leaned in, smiling just a bit. "What would you have done if she'd pulled out her eyes and handed them to you?"

Wait, what? "Uh… "

"Think about it. Her eyes in your hands. Then her hair. Her teeth. Her skin. Heart, lungs, bones. Raw. Slimy. Bloody. Literally giving them to you as an act of selflessness. Of true love. What would you have done?"

The question stopped him in his tracks. He couldn't figure out what she was trying to tell him. "I'd... have... watched her die, I guess. A normal person can't do that and stay alive."

Sacha pulled back and sighed. "No, they can't. See? If you Bases think about anything under the skin, it kills the romance."

"I don't understand—"

"Yes, you do. You don't want *me*. You want the *fantasy* of me. The metaphors. The possibility of physical conquest and emotional connection. But in the end, we're just organs and blood and some electric current running everything. On Lynaeda, we know for a fact that parts are parts and we are interconnected. We have no problem swapping parts out to improve ourselves. We keep our sights set on the game. Not the playing pieces."

I'm in over my head here. Reluctantly, he nodded. "So, no date?"

She sighed. "Insecurity leads to a defense mechanism. I'm not even singling you out, you know. Except for the captain, nearly all the Base crew on board stay away from us. We're okay with that. Less drama that way."

"Because you're not here for them."

"Right. We serve the Queen," she said, and stood to leave. "I rather enjoyed our talk, by the way. Even on Lynaeda, sharing a meal is considered an important social dynamic. I will indeed have coffee with you again. I may even show you some other tricks, too."

Goal! "I look forward to it. When do I get to see the Octopus?"

She grinned. "Not until I can trust you with my eyes."

21

THE JOYS OF BUREAUCRACY

BY THE TIME Karmen and the others had restored the interior of the shuttle to some kind of order, it was clear that the pirates had neither the time nor the inclination to try to locate them. Armin was sure that they were no longer in orbit over the planet, offering them some breathing room to finish repairs and get underway. However, that also meant they'd lost their lead. Now there was the problem of what to do next and how to go about it.

Armin slammed a maintenance hatch closed. "Try to start her up now."

Lee tapped the controls.

A gentle rumble hummed through the deck. Karmen hadn't felt anything so wonderous in a long time. "Finally! I can't wait to get out of here."

Lee stretched in his seat, testing his limbs the way a man might after having stayed in bed for a week. "We need a bigger ship. I think we should seriously consider going back to

Greengard."

"Yeah, right. Not today," Armin scoffed.

"Why not?" Karmen asked. "A bigger ship might well help—"

"No, I mean, we're not breaking atmosphere in this rig until further notice. Too many compacted struts, not enough redundancy in the linkages. There's an open hull seam in the rear compartment I can't get to seal properly. All I did was get the power back on. We're a long way off from being space worthy."

Lee's brows shot up. "You mean we're stuck here?"

"Not exactly. This adorable little disaster can probably still fly well enough to get us to a local spaceport. We should be able to find a proper mechanic there. The kind of repairs we need can't be done out here without parts, and I don't have the know-how."

"Well, at least it didn't get smashed up as badly as the drone," Karmen said.

"About that," Lee began, turning toward Karmen, "Kindly tell me again how it is you and Mother Carnage go way back? I don't think that's ever going to get old."

"I've told you all I know."

"Try once more, just in case you left something out the first time."

"The first *two* times," Armin murmured.

"Not now, Armin."

"Come on, Lee. If not now, when?"

Karmen shook her head furiously. "No, Lee, Armin's right. None of it makes sense. Where has she been all this time?" *And why did she never once try to contact me?*

"Once more, just for funsies," Lee insisted.

"I've told you both all I remember! The service, the

mission, the collision. How I got exposed to that exotic particle nonsense while I helped evacuate the crew. How I got a medical discharge, and then the eye trouble that led me to meet you and get me dragged into this mess—"

"I just want the part about how she became a deadly space pirate," Armin pleaded.

"I'd love to know, too. Believe me. But I *don't know* how that happened, or when she turned, or why. Or who the creepy man with her was." She glared at her two TSS compatriots, frustrated that they were making light of her suffering. To them, this was a mysterious woman who'd ventured down a dark path. For Karmen, it was a close friend she'd mourned for years. "I thought my commander—my dear friend—was dead. I've lived my entire post-Militia life thinking she'd died on the *Triumph*. We had a funeral and everything. It was lovely. The entire surviving crew attended, and we thanked her for her sacrifice. Stars! Did you boys know after the funeral, the TSS was apparently so concerned about tech being lost to the void that they even recovered the *Triumph* and repaired it? Put it back into service and everything. Then Wil Sights really did destroy it. No survivors. Maybe that ship was just plain cursed."

"I knew it was on the casualty list from the war, but not the details," Lee said, now sober. "If it's any consolation, I think they retired that name. No more ships called *Triumph*."

"It doesn't change anything," Karmen said. "What happened to Aura after the accident?"

"We won't find out staying here," Lee admitted. He looked back at Armin. "You say this thing should manage a short flight?"

He shrugged and shook his head. "I'm not an engineer. All I can say with any certainty is that the ship is mostly in one piece and we're passing enough automated safety checks that the engines will turn on."

Lee grimaced. "That'll have to be good enough. Everyone strap in. I'm going to power up the flight systems and see if we can't get airborne. All we need is a destination and a flight path."

"Try this," Karmen said and transferred her course plot to Lee's console. "TalEx pretty much runs this planet. There's a supply and repair base about three thousand kilometers to the west. A big one. Looks like major commercial carriers call there regularly. If anyone can repair our flight systems and hull, it would be them."

"Karmen, you just earned your salary for the week," Armin cheered.

"Wait. I get paid to do this? Something else you never told me, Lee."

"Actually, I have no idea. That's for the TSS personnel department. I'll call them on your behalf when we land."

"Assuming we don't explode," Armin said.

"Yes," Lee agreed, "assuming we don't explode."

Karmen sighed. "This. This is why neither of you have any friends."

—   —   —

Armin shook his head as he walked up to Lee. "Yeah, no. The ship is foked. It'll take days to repair."

Lee bit back a curse of his own. "Great."

"Better call us another ride, Lee," Karmen said. "I don't like the looks we're getting around here and would rather not stick around."

Lee had been noticing those same looks, and he was equally

eager to depart. Unfortunately, the call he'd need to make to facilitate their departure felt like an admission of defeat. Nevertheless, he had two team members counting on him. Sometimes, a leader needed to ask for help.

He stepped away into an alley to call up Agent Kalshi.

His proctor answered on video this time. The older man's face filled the screen, his eyes hidden by tinted glasses. But based on the tightness around his mouth, he wasn't expecting good news. "Hi, Lee. What have you found?"

"We caught up with the pirate vessel in Diphous," he reported. "They were in the midst of another raid of a TalEx facility—though based on the lack of resistance, someone had likely been paid off to let it happen."

"What happened to the ship?"

"It jumped away."

"And did you… follow it?"

"That's where we ran into a bit of trouble," Lee hedged. "We need another ship."

"What happened to the one we already gave you?"

"It got a little too well acquainted with a rock."

The Agent stared at him uncomfortably for several excruciating seconds. "Is that your way of saying you crashed it?"

"Yes, we crashed. But in all fairness, it was to avoid being exploded by a missile."

"Lee, did I make a mistake telling TSS Command that you were up for this assignment?"

He swallowed. "No, sir. I have a very capable team with the skills and experience to be successful in this mission."

"Since you're all so skilled and capable, then I'm sure you won't have difficulty procuring another ride."

Lee could think of a dozen reasons why that wasn't true.

They didn't have a credit account to buy a ship. They weren't exactly in the center of civilization with endless options. And any other vessel they could procure wouldn't have a military-grade jump drive. To have any chance of catching up to the pirate ship, they'd need TSS resources.

"The pirate ship's captain is Agent Aurelia Thand," Lee blurted out.

Kalshi's brows shot up. He'd no doubt read Karmen's file and was familiar with the *Triumph*'s fate. "That Agent was presumed dead."

"Well, surprise! And she's traveling with a man who appears to have training in telekinesis."

"Thank you for the update, Junior Agent Tuyin. I need to run this up the chain."

"About our ship—"

"I can't send you another ship without drawing significant attention. See if you can get it repaired locally. I'll make sure you have the means for payment."

Lee nodded. "Thank you, sir."

"Find out what's going on. TSS Agents don't rise from the dead."

— — —

A busy street met Karmen as she pressed her handheld to her ear. "Yes, it's actually called Diphous Talsari Commercial Spaceport," Karmen yelled into her device. "Which is what you name things when you're one of the six biggest and wealthiest families in the galaxy. You buy property, and build ports on it, then name the ports after yourself."

"Mom, that's insane!" Kaia said. "Colin will love it!"

"When do I get to meet Colin, by the way? It's customary

for daughters to bring their future husbands to visit their family before running off to build sports arenas."

"It's not like that!" Kaia joyfully screamed. "Well, it's not *exactly* like that. I do like Colin. We talk almost every day, but I've never actually met him. And I'm only seventeen, Mom. I'm not looking to get married anytime soon."

"Well, tell him I want to meet him before he runs off with you. Be insistent. Boys who work for the dynasties need direction."

"What do you mean?"

"He works for the Covrani family, doesn't he?" The silence on the line made Karmen wonder if she'd lost the connection. Then, she started wondering if she'd made a horrible mistake. "Kaia, are you there?"

"I'm here, yes. Um, Mom, he's part of that family. He *is* a Covrani."

How did that even happen? Karmen took a moment to gather herself. "Then I absolutely insist on meeting him. Does your father know?"

"Well, he's standing right here, so he does now," her daughter muttered.

"We'll talk about this later. Right now, I need to figure out what to do about our starship."

"What's wrong with it?"

"A big rock put a hole in it."

"Colin may be able to help with that. I'll let him know." She paused. "Can I tell you something, Mom?"

"Anything, my girl."

"You sound happy. It's good to hear."

"I sound *happy*?"

"Mom, I haven't heard you this excited about anything in *years*! You're in your element, I can tell. Do you have any idea when you're coming home?"

"Not at this rate. The case has taken a disturbing and unexpected turn. But we're dealing with it."

"Be safe, then. I have to go. Talk to you soon. Bye!"

Karmen caught up with Lee and Armin in a restaurant. The boys had ordered ten slices of various types of pie and sorted the plates across the table like a game board.

Lee handed her a fork as she sat down. "Dig in, Karmen."

"Don't you two believe in food without tons of sugar?"

Armin snorted and forked pie into his mouth. "Sure we do. That's called coffee."

"How are Daveed and the kids?" Lee asked.

"Everyone's well. Things are getting back to normal on Greengard. I spoke to Kaia, and it turns out her GravX boyfriend, Colin, is actually part of the Covrani family."

"I told you that girl is going places!" Lee crowed around a mouthful of pie.

"Bonus! See if you can get him to loan us a better shuttle," Armin said.

"She did offer to talk to him. She also said that I sounded happier than I've been in years."

"Yet you look disappointed. Why is this bit of news a bad thing?" Lee asked.

"I don't know." Karmen took a plate and went to work nibbling a wedge of lemon merengue thoughtfully. "I don't generally think of myself as unhappy, but…"

"But…?"

"Maybe life as a university dean's wife was a tiny bit limiting."

"See?" Armin snarked, looking at Lee. "Told you."

"Don't tell me you two were analyzing me while I made one lousy call home?"

"My mother always told me, just eat your pie while it's on your plate," Armin said, smiling just a bit as he wiped his mouth. "I don't know you nearly well enough to comment further."

Karmen turned her gaze on Lee. "But you do. Spill it, Junior Agent."

The coffee arrived. Cups were passed out and filled. Lee drank half a cup before answering. "When I arrived at your house, you seemed subdued. Once we began your treatments, you improved in mood and confidence. And since we've entered into this crazy scavenger hunt, you've morphed into a whole new person. You must have been a formidable first officer."

"I had my days."

"And you've missed those days. I get it. Part of your heart stayed with the TSS." Armin belched and leaned back in his chair. "Stars! I needed that."

The only plate with food still on it was Karmen's.

"How long until we're back in flight?" she asked, taking her sweet time about eating.

Lee drummed his fingers on the table. "I was able to get the repair shop to commit to three days. Armin was right when he said the hull seam was exposed. The mechanic we spoke to showed us the scan he made when we pulled in. The landslide cracked the mounting beneath the sensor dome. They have to take it off and re-seal the breach then put it back on. We're grounded until then."

"It's frustrating they won't send us a replacement vessel. In a few days, Aura could be literally anywhere!" Karmen griped. "As long as we're stuck here, I insist on eating real food."

Lee patted his stomach. "You go ahead, Karmen. I'm stuffed."

"No, maybe later," she said. "We need to keep moving forward. That means locating another transport that can get us back on the trail ASAP." She pulled out her handheld and flipped through a number of screens. "I think since we're working with the TalEx corporation, they can bomaxed well get us to our next destination."

"Such language," Armin sneered.

"Not now, Armin. I have a call to make."

"Yes, ma'am."

The central switchboard was easy enough to navigate until it came time for them to find a person to speak to. Two line operators and a supervisor later, Karmen managed to locate one. At least someone who was willing to listen to her for longer than fifteen seconds.

"Unfortunately, we were forced down by the pirates and our shuttle will be unavailable for a few days. Since you'll agree time is of the essence, I'd like to know if you might have a small starship we could use," she asked.

The operator sounded positively bored. "Nothing that's available for charter work."

"This isn't a charter, sir, it's official business."

"Yes, but it's official TSS business. Not official TalEx business." He flashed an insincere smile. "I'm sure you understand."

"I understand they made off with a great deal of valuable TalEx property. Speed is how my team can get that property returned to you."

"I see. If you're right, that provides some clarity. Still, nothing showing on my screen. Let me have a quick chat with my supervisor."

The display flashed a corporate logo and Lee winced. "Don't you love the utter banality of bureaucracy?"

"That bit about '*if* you're right that TalEx was robbed blind' was unnecessary," Armin muttered. "But you get used to it after a while."

"I don't want to get used to it. I want to avoid it," Lee said. "There's nothing more depraved than a bureaucrat mired in the depths of a procedural conflict."

The display changed and the clerk returned. "Officer Sley, I've been authorized to send you a code that will gain you passage on any TalEx commercial flight anywhere you need to go. All I need is a destination."

Karmen shared a look with her colleagues. *If I had a destination in mind I could tell you, but we don't know where we're going. That's the issue.* Suddenly, an idea popped into her head. "What's the biggest SiNavTech office that's relatively close to Diphous?"

"Let's see… that would be the sector data center on Kelso. Three standard jumps from Diphous. Is that your destination?"

"Yes, it is."

"Very well. Present this code to the travel representative at your location and they will arrange your passage to Kelso." The information popped up on her handheld's screen.

"Thank you. Oh! One more thing…"

"Yes?"

"Our shuttle needs to be transported to Kelso's spaceport once it's repaired. TalEx can do that, can't it? Surely there's an empty module on a cargo ship heading that way. Yes?"

The clerk sighed heavily but said, "I'll need the ship's registration number and the name of the repair shop." Lee provided the information and the clerk completed the transaction. "TalEx will send a message to your handheld when the ship is delivered. Have a good day!"

Karmen slid her handheld back into her pocket. "Pleasant little man, wasn't he?"

Armin sniffed. "Of course, he is. He doesn't actually work in a mine all day."

"SiNavTech, huh?" Lee said, nodding thoughtfully.

"If anyone can put a trace on the pirate ship, it's them," Karmen replied. The beacon network was the only means for commercial navigation, so there'd be a record somewhere in the transit logs. It might be well disguised, but it'd be there.

"Good thinking," Armin agreed. "Hopefully, they'll be as cooperative as TalEx."

22

LOW FRIENDS IN HIGH PLACES

LOM FINISHED HIS rounds early.

The ship had taken no damage from its brief encounter with an apparent enemy at Diphous. At Aura's direction, they'd recovered their shuttles and kept the stolen TalEx cargo model, as well. Gallian had balked, but Lom straightened the Comm officer out easily enough. The shuttle crew had already been paid to look the other way; frankly, the *Emerald Queen*'s crew needed the craft more than the quadrillion-credit enterprise known as the Talsari Dynasty. Insurance would cover the loss, and the workers would claim their lives were threatened by deadly pirate queen Mother Carnage so they had no choice but to hand the craft over. Everybody won.

Lom found his captain at the top of the vessel on the observation deck, which was home to the sensor array. The space had started out as the flight deck in the cargo ship's original configuration, so it still had control stations despite the operations now centering in the midship War Room. Lom didn't mind the captain's need for solitude; he supposed this was preferable to her hiding in her darkened former cargo ship berthed in the main hangar.

A giant map table with holographic fittings was anchored at the center of the observation deck. Aura was staring at a wide display of their current location in the Tavden System when Lom came in.

She glanced up at him before returning her attention to the map. "Lom, we need some fighters. Five or six would be enough to start. Eventually, I'd like a full squadron."

Lom tapped a display and brought up a review of the hangar bay's shuttle inventory. Six cargo types, three more configured for passengers, and one that would eventually be refitted as a remote sensor and communication platform. Callum and Gallian were working on the last one as a pet project; Lom allowed it as long as it didn't interfere with their regularly scheduled duties. If it worked, it would give them a real advantage in executing raids on high-tech worlds. Like it or not, their recent activity was giving them a reputation; they'd need to be stealthier going forward.

"Could you explain why, Captain?" Lom asked.

"Because on our last raid, someone very motivated and skilled figured out how to avoid detection and got close enough to nearly land on our hangar deck. We were lucky to have intercepted them when we did. And we lost a perfectly good missile in the effort. I don't want to see that happen twice. A fighter would have fixed the issue. Even a flight drone with a short-range laser weapon would have helped. Right now, we're vulnerable if anything is too close for our primary weapons."

"We don't even know if that vessel was armed," Lom pointed out.

"That's not the point. If they were, they would have shot

the torpedo out of the air. But if they had been? They could have shot a missile of their own directly inside our hangar, and we wouldn't have been able to do a bomaxed thing about it!"

Lom sighed and folded his arms. He hated her when she got like this. And it usually happened after a visit from Gilgamesh. Gil had already departed to do whatever it was he did—setting up deals, making connections, funneling money toward one venture or another. Aura was all smiles and agreeable while Gil was around; the moment he left, she'd turn argumentative and sullen. Lom couldn't blame her; how could a person *not* feel lonely when one of their few connections in life was away? All the more reason to have an integrated neural interface where the mind was never limited by physical proximity—but she'd patently shot down that suggestion. If Aura was committed to having part of her soul ripped out every time Gil walked away, then so be it.

Regardless, Lom had a mission to manage; he needed to get her back on task. "Captain, I suggest you pay less attention to the minutiae of conquest and more carefully consider the specifics of our current task."

"I am. And I'm telling you we need a fighter squadron!"

Lom switched his displays; this one showed the personnel roster covering all the businesses they operated. "Tavden is our go-to hub for ships and parts. A production manager who oversees multiple shipyards there has done some work for us in the past. His people are loyal to him, and we make a practice of sending him funds to keep his crews energized. If they get us ships, my drone pilots will have no trouble flying them."

"I'd eventually like two squadrons, if we can find a way to fund it," Aura said.

"Funding isn't the problem, as Lord Gilgamesh is fond of saying," Lom said. "There's plenty of money coming in from all manner of ventures. Some are yours, some are his. Some are even Lord Sargon's."

"But?" Aura asked.

"But overtly offensive craft like fighters can attract attention when acquired in larger numbers from private sector production yards. A handful for private security concerns won't raise eyebrows, but building a fleet… that's the sort of thing that attracts unwanted attention from the Enforcers and TSS. We can definitely arrange delivery for a few, but not many more."

"Can we spread it around—use multiple of our businesses? There's surely more than one shipyard on Tavden."

"I'm sure the production manager can figure out something, but we should probably stagger the orders to limit our exposure. Will sixty percent of a squadron do for now?"

"It will, thank you. Is there anything else?"

Lom rested his arms on the map table, looking at the display without truly seeing it. "Why was that scout ship here? What was their goal? It doesn't make sense for a tiny, unarmed ship to come after us. If it was the authorities, you'd think they'd send an armed patrol cruiser that could shoot out our jump drive until backup could arrive to take us in."

"What are you thinking, Lom?"

That's a good question. He tapped the intercom. "Commander Mench to Sensors."

"Sensors, go ahead."

"Callum, I need you to pull the sensor logs from that event with the scout ship over at Diphous. Find out exactly what they did to us, or tried to do."

"On it. Sensors out."

"We're going to need a logistics unit that organizes a greater magnitude of commercial activity," Lom said to the captain. "We're growing quickly, which means we consume supplies more quickly, too. I don't think our quartermaster can handle it all."

"He barely handles it now. All he does is source parts and supplies when we pull into port."

"I know. You need someone who knows where the reliable black marketeers work and who they know. Someone who is used to managing long, winding supply chains."

"I'll send a message to Ashurbanipal for a list of trustworthy crooks. The black market is pretty much where he lives, considering he built the New Akkadia Dark Net."

"While you're at it, if you want these fighters quickly, the request will carry the most weight coming directly from him," Lom pointed out.

Aura nodded. "Good point."

Callum's voice sounded over the intercom. "Sensors to Commander Mench."

"Go ahead."

"Sir, they didn't use any conventional weapon, at least nothing I can identify. But they did do *something*. They beamed a very high frequency burst at our ship from their shuttle through the open hatch. It was fast and so tightly encrypted that we never saw it."

"Do you know what the transmission was for?"

"No, sir. We didn't record the burst itself, so I don't have a way of analyzing its contents. I only know it happened."

"Very well, thank you." Lom turned to Aura and said, "I think we need to evaluate every piece of equipment on this ship. There's no knowing what exactly they were after, except through a manual check. We can start from the lower decks and work our way topside. It will take time, but it's essential we know if any of our systems have been compromised."

"Agreed. Send an alert to Tavden High Port. Let them know we'll need to enter under quarantine while we check our status. Better yet, see if you can hire a team of experts to go over our systems. Pay them whatever they ask for. We can't take chances. But by all means, let's get started on placing orders with our contacts for fighters and supplies."

"Right away, Captain."

— — —

Tabor Laski was having a good day. The Winn Shipyard's part-owner, Aldous Winn, was having his yacht refurbished on Tavden, and it was Tabor's job as production manager to make it happen to specification and on time—and, of course, under budget. Tabor had been prepared for a fight with every aspect of the project, but everything had gone smoothly so far. Paperwork had been signed, a hefty deposit had been delivered to the bank, and the big man himself had been unusually congenial on their call to discuss his vision for the craft. For once, Tabor felt like the universe was working with him rather than against him.

He should have known the good news wouldn't last. The follow-up call from Aldous Winn was precisely the kind of nonsense he'd hoped to avoid. "Three days? No, the interior furnishings are set for delivery at the end of the month. Having everything ready in three days simply isn't… Yes I do have some extras on hand, but the scale of what you're asking on that timeframe— Of course, I want to keep my job! All right, I'll figure something out. Three days, yes, sir! Thank you."

He slammed his handheld down on his desk. *Why did I thank him? I have to stay late because the entitled playboy wants custom-dyed leather on every surface of his bomaxed pleasure craft! No one is paying me enough for this shite.*

His job as a production manager for the facility was cover for his real business, but it was necessary cover. It gave him connections and access to highly lucrative opportunities. But some of the people he had to deal with—

A ping sounded from his infernal handheld. Then another.

Tabor didn't want to answer text messages any more than he wanted to receive another call. It was never just a friendly chat. Someone always wanted something.

Reluctantly, Tabor tapped his handheld's screen to read the incoming messages. His mood quickly lifted when he realized he was being sent orders from the big man himself, Ash. The man who made things happen in this sector. Or one of them, anyway. Aldous Winn's name might appear on the shipyard, but it was Ash who gave the real orders for the business behind the business. *The man who lines my pockets.*

The order was vague. Six craft. Expedited. There were no notes as to which models or makes or what equipment they'd need. The simpler the ship, the easier they were to source, and lower the cost. Which meant a higher profit margin for him. But, Tabor expected that there were details waiting for him in a more secure communication.

He logged into his Dark Net account to check for new messages, finding one sent at the same time as the original text: >>6 fighters, TA-90 or better. New only. ASAP delivery. Max pay 500k pr unit. Key code required for consideration. Disaggregate orders. Payment upon delivery.<< Attached to the message was a document containing six business entities with corresponding order numbers from each.

It was written in the Dark Net's spooky kind of trade-speak. The buyer wanted six fighters, with minimum TA-90 specifications, and would pay up to half a million credits for each of them. And they didn't care where the ships came from, provided each ship was its own purchase transaction, separate from the others. They didn't even seem to care if they got genuine TA-90s or if they were knock-offs, as long as they were up to spec. Well, Tabor actually *did* have access to the TA-90 pipeline, so he could provide the genuine articles. Surely, Ash would appreciate that.

But they had to be new; that was where things got trickier. A used or refurbished ship could come from anywhere; the worse the condition of the craft, the lower the price. But there was only one source for new ships, and that was a shipyard.

Good thing Tabor was the production manager here.

It had been a long time since he'd dealt with fighter supply or the technology that went into it. The TA-90 was serviceable equipment to be sure, but it was obsolete tech. Now, the TSS IT-1... that had been a star fighter worth talking about. He'd retired from the TSS before those babies had gone into production, but he remembered how the development team had spoken about them in hushed tones, like a theoretical construct. His own engineering skills had been solid enough to earn him a place on the staff of the H2 base in the Rift, where he'd seen plenty of the top war tech at the time. But he'd always regretted that he never got to see the IT-1s go into service against the Bakzen forces. A craft like that was worth millions. Tens of millions. But that was well beyond the scope of what he was attempting to do here right now.

Stick to the assignment and pad that retirement account. His civilian life was comfortable enough, but a man could only deal with entitled pricks like Aldous Winn for so long. If he could bank enough credits to retire early somewhere warm and scenic... now that was the dream.

Tabor opened his working breakdown of every production

job across the six shipyards under his purview. There were dozens of TA-90 fighters available for delivery right now. Actual working models scheduled for delivery. The trick was choosing six that no one would miss and then routing them to the right place without raising any red flags. Go figure, there were rules against re-directing weapons to random locations.

He plied the database and, with some digging, found half a dozen fighters listed in vulnerable positions. Two were due for refits, one had to be impounded due to shoddy work on the tail assembly, and three more were being sent back for additional quality control testing and evaluation. He wasn't about to send crappy equipment to his client; that would be self-defeating, or even lethal. The trick was to swap the bad equipment for a good unit.

One by one, Tabor wiped the delivery data from a completed fighter and replaced it with the service notations for one of the recalled models. He then reassigned all six of the good units for delivery to a shipping platform on the orbital station, which was operated by a shipyard subcontractor firm, of which he was a partial owner. Finally, he turned to the damaged unit's entries and changed their situation to 'Resolved'; each unit was then marked as 'Sold' to one of the six different business entities that had been provided in the Dark Net message. And just like that, Ashurbanipal was secretly the proud owner of half a dozen brand new TA-90s.

He sent a reply through the Dark Net communication portal, providing his code and pricing. He waited with no small amount of anxiety until the reply arrived: >>Offer of 6 units accepted.<<

He sat back and grinned widely. *Yes! Three million credits. Fok that playboy and his chartreuse leather.*

His smile faltered a bit when the screen lit up with an

incoming vidcall. With the red border of urgent business, at that. There was no indication of the caller.

It could be the Enforcers looking to arrest him. But why would they contact him before…? Ah! They were looking for a bribe to make sure they got a piece of his deal. Well, fine. It might make a dent in his profits, but it was better to keep the local authorities happy while dealing with big money. They could have a cut. He was greedy but not *that* greedy.

With that, he accepted the vidcall and found himself looking at a digitized face. Not the Enforcers, after all—or even the face of a person. This was a stylized rendering of a smiling mask. "Tabor Laski," the caller stated from behind the mask.

"Yes."

"I'm sending you an encryption algorithm. Hit 'Y' to accept and continue."

"What's this about?"

"Hit 'Y' to accept and continue."

"I don't play games. Who are you?"

"Hit 'Y' to accept and continue."

The caller didn't seem like they were with the Enforcers, or TSS, or any other official entity—creepy masks weren't their style. Nor were clandestine communications. Well, not usually, at least. With an undercover investigation, all bets were off. *Fok it. If this is the TSS, they can only put me in jail for something I actually did.*

He hit the requested key. A booming voice emerged from the console.

"Tabor! My name is Ashurbanipal. Pleasure to finally meet you in real-time."

"Ash?" he gasped.

"In the flesh! Or, in the screen, as the case may be. How have you been, Tabor?"

"Fine. I think. What brings you here?"

"I have a question. Honestly, I have a few questions. You see, I sent that encrypted invitation personally. I've had my eye on you for some time."

"You're kidding. Right?"

"I never kid. I do sometimes play practical jokes on my peers, but never on my help."

"So, I'm your 'help'?"

"You are my best helper, Tabor. You've secured more loot for me than any dozen of my other contacts combined. Listen, I've been sitting at my desk here, and I just put up that request for six war machines. You know what I mean. Zoom zoom! Pew-pew!"

The TA-90 fighters. Oh no, was that just a trick to get my attention? "Yes, sir."

"You responded with a sure offer within minutes. Then, I realized you respond to every one of my offers very quickly. You don't always meet the price, but you always respond. That shows ambition. I appreciate ambition."

"I'm glad to help you out, Ash. For a fair amount of money, of course."

"Of course! I get it. I'm convinced that you get it, too. Which is why I'd like to make you a proposal. It requires travel. You'd get to see the galaxy. Meet new and interesting people. Even Lynaedans. Exciting stuff."

Tech-heads? What's going on here? "What would I be doing?"

"Exactly what you're doing now. Buying and selling. But you'd be working for a dear friend of mine instcad of Lower Dynasty snakes. And, frankly, if everything I've seen about your work history is true, you are far too smart to be wasting your time managing assembly lines. What do you think, Tabor?"

"I think I'd like to hear more."

"Mother Carnage's flagship, the *Emerald Queen,* will be sailing into Tavden High Port shortly. Her captain and first officer are looking for a systems guy—a supply manager. They're growing their business far faster than their current logistics staff can handle. They need new avenues for acquiring and managing supply lines and inventory, and I thought you would be perfect. You have reach and know how to hide things from the law. There's an interview scheduled in two days. Interested?"

"I would be for, say, double what I'm making now."

"Bah! I'll give you a signing bonus that's *triple* what you're making now. If you are amenable, you and the captain can make whatever arrangement you'd like. I'll tell you this much: that vessel is going to help turn New Akkadia into a hardcore reality. A man who knows how to source everything will be a vital part of that crew."

It sounds too good to be true... which means I'm the patsy. Tabor folded his hands on the desktop. "A question of my own, if I may. Will I still be getting my three million credits for the order you just accepted?"

"By the stars, man! You are a *gem.* Once I accept an offer, I follow through. I know I'm making the right choice in offering you this opportunity. I'll ask once more. This time, it's for keeps. Are you interested?"

I'm going insane. This is what insanity feels like. I am literally less afraid of a life of crime than I am of dealing with impossible requests from my boss. "I am. Definitely. Interested."

"Good. The *Emerald Queen*'s captain will be in touch. Welcome aboard."

221

23

SENIOR CLASS

THE NEAREST SERVICE kiosk refused to honor the code issued by TalEx to book passage to Kelso.

"You have to be kidding me," Karmen groaned.

"Let's see if we can find a real person to talk to," Lee suggested.

The young Junior Agent was certainly trying his best to act like a leader, Karmen had to give him that. But the mission was off to a rough start. Not *all* of that was their fault. They'd been given minimal instructions. Their resources were profoundly limited. And the three of them weren't, exactly, the team Karmen would have assembled. But it was personal for all of them, which made them committed. She was more committed now than ever after seeing Aura's face. Or, at least it was the face that used to belong to her friend. Mother Carnage was a stranger.

The search for face-to-face assistance led them to the terminal mezzanine, where they located a travel agency.

Lee presented the coded ticket to a bleary-eyed rep while Karmen held her breath that it would be accepted.

"Yes, sir, you're in luck. The *Diamond Dust* is moving into launch position right now. If you hurry, you can probably catch them."

"*Diamond Dust*," Armin repeated. "Say thank you for luxury liners. And thank you, TalEx."

The clerk made a face clearly wondering if Armin was stupid or merely misinformed. "No, sir. That's not what your ticket is for."

"Oh, well. Middle passage isn't so bad."

The clerk sighed. "Sir, you're booked on the *Diamond Dust* as temporary crew. It's a container ship. It leaves from Concourse B in sixty-three minutes. If you take the tram, you can just be there in time."

Foking cargo crew? Karmen gripped the fabric of her pants to keep from punching the kiosk. "Who are we supposed to report to?"

"Captain Solari. Here are your work ID cards. Please don't lose them. Enjoy your flight."

Lee audibly groaned as they headed toward the tram. "This is punishment. I don't know if the TSS is messing with me, or if it's the universe itself. I apologize for dragging both of you into this mess."

"What, and miss out on crewing an ore hauler?" Karmen replied with a crazed grin. *Why would I want to be having dinner with my family when I could be here instead?!*

Armin gently placed his hand on her forearm. "Means to an end."

"Come on, we need to hurry." Lee picked up his pace.

The *Diamond Dust* was a Mammoth-class cargo hauler, a design not that unlike Mother Carnage's ship. Long, low rectangles and oblongs were hitched together with a central bus containing numerous bays along its length, which allowed for the addition of individual cargo modules.

When they arrived at the ship's gangway, a middle-aged gentleman wearing a stylized cap was punching in codes to the departure kiosk.

"Captain Solari?" Lee asked.

"Indeed. What can I do for you?"

"I'm Junior Agent Lee Tuyin. These are TSS Officers Armin Godri and Karmen Sley."

"Is this some sort of surprise inspection? We've already received our clearance. You can take it up with dispatch. Now, if you'll excuse me, my comm transfer line is down, and I need to plug data into this blasted machine by hand."

"I can do that," Armin offered.

Solari paused. "You can? Three pages of it?"

"No sweat."

The captain thrust a tablet into Armin's hands. "It's all yours." He watched Armin work for several seconds. Satisfied, he turned to Lee. "I leave in ten minutes, Agent. Please be brief."

"Of course. We're actually your temporary crew. We'll be with you as far as Kelso."

"I see. You mean, you need passage to Kelso. No one wants to pay for it, so I get your 'labor' instead. Whose bright idea was this?"

"Someone at TalEx owed us a favor," Lee explained.

"Ah, that sounds about right. Well, that makes you cargo, not crew."

"If we fix your comms and data transfer lines, that would make us crew, wouldn't it?" Karmen asked with a nod toward Armin efficiently typing in the manual data.

Solari raised an eyebrow. "You trying to sweet talk me, Officer Karmen?"

"Yes, I am. But I specialized in Comms in the TSS Militia before getting a command as a first officer."

The captain scratched his chin, considering the offer. "All right. Fix the system and we'll call it even. You, Agent—what can you do besides squeeze my brain to a pulp if I piss you off?"

"I'm a medical researcher, first and foremost, but I'm also a decent pilot. Although, I've never flown anything this size before."

"Can you run a nav console?"

"Yes, sir!"

"All right, there are a number of deliveries to be made along the way. Show me how well you can plot a course to Kelso with all the necessary stops. If you pass muster, I'll take you on as relief pilot and first nav." He turned back to the kiosk. "Are you still plugging in those numbers?"

Armin handed the tablet back to Solari and kept on making combinations. "I finished that ages ago. Now, I'm sweet-talking the flight controller into giving us priority departure clearance so we can bypass that traffic jam on the A Concourse."

Solari nodded slowly. "If you can pull that off, you just saved me two hours."

"And… done." Armin smiled. "We'll be at the top of the queue whenever you're ready to head out."

"All right, consider yourselves crew," the captain said. "It's three days to Kelso, and there's plenty of work to do. Follow me to the flight deck, and I'll show you what's what."

—

"Boys, go get some ice cream. The older folks want to have a talk," Karmen announced as she set down her last hand of Fastara.

Armin and Lee shared a glance. "Is there—?"

"Snack bar is on Deck 2. You're part of the crew, so you have access. Don't make yourselves sick," Solari said, making it sound like an order.

Karmen made a rude noise. "I sat and watched these two scarf down nine plates of pie in the time it took me to call home. They're fine."

The young men needed no urging and left Karmen and Solari alone with the remnants of the card game fanned out across the nav console at the center of the flight deck.

"I remember having that sort of energy once," the captain said. "I came into this kind of work straight out of the Merchant Academy. The work wasn't particularly hard, and I got to say I had an advanced degree in something. You want to play another game?"

"No! I concede your superiority." Fastara was the staple game of spacefarers, and plenty of people in Militia played it during rec time.

Solari gathered the cards and began putting them back in the storage case. "If you worked at it, you'd become much better."

"That's what I mean. This is exactly the kind of game that would suck down every spare minute of my life, if I let it. Better to avoid the temptation. But it's been fun passing the time with you."

He studied her expression. "What did you want to talk to me about?"

"I have a problem," she began.

"Two of your problems are in my snack bar right now."

"Heh. They're a handful, but they're good men. Listen, I have years of experience running a TSS warship, but that was a long time ago and I was never trained for detective work. At this particular time, I need insights from someone who runs lots of cargo. Do you mind?"

"Not at all. Ask your questions."

"You've heard of Mother Carnage, by now, I expect."

"Yes, ma'am. I have to admit, I never saw that coming. Piracy is usually the sort of thing done on a very small scale— at least in this part of the galaxy. But the heists she's pulled off in the last few days… That woman has a heart of stone and a brain like a steel trap."

"You admire her, then?"

Solari looked up quizzically. "Don't you?"

"I do, in a way. And it makes me uncomfortable."

"That much, I understand. But you can admire someone and also be against them. That's how I feel. Someone like that can throw an ordered universe into a chaotic mess. That's bad for business, which is bad for profits, which makes people like me queasy. So, I think we're on the same page."

"Have you seen her ship?"

He shook his head. "I've only heard chatter about her exploits on the port comms. I expect there's been a lot of exaggeration."

"You might be surprised. The ship is insane." Karmen lifted an image from her handheld for him to look at. "Behold."

"Can you enlarge that?" he asked, and she zoomed in. "Now, that *is* interesting…"

She let him look for a while but eventually got impatient. "What do you see?"

"A number of things that don't make a ton of sense. That's a Gallant-class freighter—perfect for bulk ore jobs—but she's made some interesting modifications. That sensor array at the top, for example."

"Yes, it's military tech," Karmen said.

"That must have taken some serious connections. I've been hearing about how salvage crews have re-invented themselves post-war to be salvage brokers—financializing themselves—but I've never met anyone who actually did that."

"I'd love to hear more about that. The term is new to me."

"Well, before the war, before the Empire's citizens knew that the Bakzen existed, a salvage operation was a crew with a cargo ship, a few sensor nets and tractor beams, and a very wide comm net. They'd hear about a space battle, or get an alert from a contact, and they'd travel to the site, haul in what could be hauled, and sell it back to the owner for a fee, or to a scrap yard for raw stock. Boring, predictable, routine. Know why?"

"Because how valuable can your typical cargo ship or passenger liner be if it's a ruined hulk?" Karmen guessed.

"Correct. But after the war, the galaxy was awash in broken high-tech gear. Military tech, even. All over the place, and no one knew where all the fancy rigs were because the military didn't tell anyone. They insisted on using their own crews to recover and repair damaged and wrecked vessels because they didn't want that gear falling into the wrong hands. Well, the wrong hands figured out there was good money to be made in that space, and they reinvented themselves. Big ventures sprang up, bought up scores of private crews and set them to work. Small operations consolidated and the black marketeers bought everything. Scrapyards and junk dealers started calling themselves upgrade centers and started buying and selling every piece of fancy gear they could find. I bet you my next paycheck that Mother Carnage had a link to a major upgrade center."

"I believe it."

"Bottom line is, she's taken a hauler and turned it into a respectable warship," he said. "This was an expensive job. And these types of ships are still in service all over the place, so she had to acquire a used one somewhere."

"All of which means… what?"

"It means Mother Carnage is very rich and extremely ambitious. She clearly has the support of an interstellar cartel of some kind. You may be diving into a pool far deeper than you believe."

"That sounds like quite a pronouncement, Captain Solari."

"You may call me Sol," he said with a grin. "Perhaps I'm overstating the case. I know everything I see in that image is expensive to do and takes months to arrange. That's all I know for certain. I mean what I say, though. You're up against some big players."

It made a crazy kind of sense. It was one thing to buy a few black market shuttles and use a generic transport to raid shipping traffic in the Outer Colonies. But that wasn't what Mother Carnage was doing. "Let's say you're right. Someone that heavy-hitting doesn't pop up out of nowhere. Why haven't we been hearing about her for months? Years?"

Solari shuffled his Fastara deck and began to deal a new hand for himself. "I don't think she came into her circumstances until recently. She's only hit a couple of planetary facilities so far. The targets have been large establishments with high reward, low-risk opportunities. TalEx, for example—of which I can speak because I work for them—doesn't populate its facilities with many guards. Yes, they have security—full of electronic locks and sneaky-peepy cameras because those are cheap to buy and you can put them everywhere, so they do. But one motivated investigator could figure out who she is and what she's up to. That's you in this example, by the way."

She waved at him dismissively. "Oh, you!"

"You must have *some* ideas. I've put my cards on the table. How about you?"

Karmen bobbed her head. "Fair enough. I believe she has a military background and experience. I believe that she had help. Lots of very expensive and hard to arrange help. The machines she used to rob the hospital on Greengard, for example, aren't the sort of thing anyone just buys on the open market. Only a dedicated engineering staff could build those drones. It would take time, parts, connections, and a place to assemble them. That means friends with money. So, my idea is to figure out what her travel schedule looks like and then pick it apart."

"Not a bad idea. Is that why you're keen to get to Kelso? The SiNavTech office?"

"Among other things."

"Well, I'll just say good luck with that. That outfit is even more opaque than TalEx."

She watched him play out the solo game in front of him. "How often have you been hit while en route?" she asked.

"You mean how often am I robbed on the job? Never."

"Never? Not once? By anyone?"

He finished his hand and went back to shuffling. "I've had crew who tried to make off with equipment or break open the safe. But piracy… how should I explain? A vessel this size is objectively huge. That makes piracy difficult. One, we carry large amounts of relatively cheap goods. To make real money, you'd have to abscond with the whole shipment. Frankly, you could kill me, steal the ship, wipe the transponders, and resell it on the black market more easily than you could steal and sell my haul. Then, let's say you have a giant empty container vessel and somehow bring it alongside my vessel in normal space after disabling my jump drive. You could plug my hull full of rail gun rounds or who knows what, but *Diamond Dust* would never feel it. Not because her defenses are that tight, but because it would take hours. This vessel could absorb round after round from a rail gun and not lose enough maneuvering power to force a stop. Plenty of time for me to call for help. When help arrives, big transport carriers don't make quick getaways."

"What about if some rogue attacks you with a container ship, a squadron of fighters, and enough loaders to do the job?" she asked.

"If she had that, she might as well go into business as a competitor. The dynasties are always looking for ways to save money. Promise to do my contract for a third less money, and she'd get the contract. Easier than piracy and it's legal."

She regarded him as he dealt his next hand. "You have a theory, don't you?"

He put the cards down and looked at her directly. "You said it yourself. She picks her targets too carefully to be a random hit-and-run thief. She's acting with someone with real money and big connections. Probably a number of them. She's hitting targets *they* want hit."

"Anything else?"

"Just one thing I wonder: where is she getting her supplies? She has a big crew, and they need care and feeding. Right?"

She laughed out loud. "I hadn't even gotten to thinking about that yet."

"Think about it for a while. A ship like this, sure, I could make my whole run solo. It's not easy, but it's doable. She must have a couple of hundred people on that carrier. They must have come from somewhere. And deep down, they know what they're helping her do. In a universe that offers infinite choices of employment, they chose crime. Who are they and why are they sticking with her?"

Why indeed, Karmen thought.

24

SiNavTech

THE SiNavTech DATA center on Kelso was a literal crystal castle in the midst of a grubby industrial zone. It was a multitiered building of chrome and glass, which merely drew attention to the disparities between the building and the surrounding neighborhood. It reminded Karmen of one of the downtown campuses in Foundation City. In this case, it seemed evident that the great corporation had bought up ill-used and well-worn land and then built their data center above it without considering the optics.

It took the better part of an afternoon to locate the one person who might help them on their mission: Data Supervisor Zirin. A tall thin man who looked dressed for a business presentation instead of a functionary.

"How can I help the TSS today?" he asked.

"We have a special request," Lee stated, taking the lead in the conversation. "We are pursuing a known criminal. We need your help tracing a ghost ship on the beacon network."

"No."

"No?"

Zirin shook his head but gave them a broad, congenial smile. "I'm sorry, but those records are private."

Lee wondered if an alternate form of persuasion might have an effect. "Supervisor Zirin, why don't we level with each other. Like it or not, this is a TSS matter. The High Commander of the TSS is also the heir to the Sietinen Dynasty, which just so happens to run SiNavTech. You're not violating any rules. All you're doing—all we are asking you to do—is your job. Does that work for you?"

"My job, as you put it, doesn't involve taking orders from a Junior Agent without an official written warrant for accessing our private transit data. So, no."

Armin murmured under his breath and Karmen frowned. "So, should I contact Cris Sietinen and tell him you're perfectly happy to allow this interstellar crime wave to continue?" Lee asked.

Zirin laughed, then caught himself. It came out like a shout. "Yeah, you know what? You can tell his highness to call me directly, and maybe we'll work something out. Until then, you're not getting any information about the ships traveling on our network. That is final."

"I don't understand what the problem is," Lee huffed.

"You've never worked in a data center, have you?" Zirin asked.

"No, I haven't."

"I expect you've never really thought about what we do here. Come with me, please. I think you deserve a look at what you're actually asking me to do."

They followed Zirin down the corridor and into an elevator. He surprised Lee by selecting a button near the top of the tower. For some reason, he'd assumed anything special had to be in the basement. Served him right. Never make assumptions. And Zirin made a good point; navigation beacons, or power, or plumbing, it was all background noise until something went wrong and then people noticed the equipment that ran their lives. Like on Greengard.

The doors opened to reveal a tornado of activity. A brightly lit room resembling a sports arena contained knots of techs clustered at consoles and desks at varying points. There were tiered walkways with steps leading up and down. And, in the middle, was a gargantuan holographic display. The entire galaxy.

Zirin headed into the room. "This way. I promise, it's safe."

Lee followed their guide to a closed office away from the bustle of the action. It looked like any other office but had no windows and plenty of plush chairs.

When the visitors were settled, Zirin pulled a key card from his jacket and inserted it into a wall panel. Lee watched, fascinated, as the geometry of the room changed. A map table rose from the floor to desk-height, and a projector dropped from the ceiling.

"We call this the Tank," Zirin began. "It is the most secure room on this floor. We use it for sensitive briefings, and I expect this qualifies. Valued guests, observe…" Zirin set up a display from the console.

Instantly the galactic map repeated before them, filling the room. After a few moments, the display zoomed into a specific section of the map until they were looking at a few local constellations.

The supervisor continued, "This isn't the live real-time map, of course; that's in the main room outside. But this briefing room does pull data in real-time from the countless feeds that we manage here. So, you want to locate one ship—but you don't know *which* one—that visited Greengard ten days ago. Right? Here's what that looks like." The map traced a number of stops with blue lines connecting individual stars.

"Then they traveled from Greengard to Diphous. Here's what *that* looks like." The display grew and traced red lines.

"Then you followed them. Seven more jumps, and then you were granted passage on the *Diamond Dust* from Diphous to Kelso. And here is what that three-day trip looks like. Twenty-three individual jumps made by a total of three vessels." Now a vine-like network of green lines joined the display.

"Doesn't sound so bad to me," Armin said.

"By itself, no, it sounds fine to me, too. But those jumps happened over ten days. That's a two-hundred-fifty-hour window. You want to see what else happened within that window? I'll show you." A riot of purple points joined the data set; now, it was nearly impossible to pick out which lines belonged to what destinations. The whole thing looked like a mess of purple to Lee's eyes.

"Gah. Each of those dots is a starship?" Armin asked.

"Certainly not. Each dot represents *ten* jump-capable vessels," Zirin said.

"Oh, no," Karmen groaned.

"Exactly! Let me say it as plainly as I can. More than seventy thousand individual jumps into or out of subspace were recorded by SiNavTech's beacon network in that ten-day period along these two travel routes. But we live in a galaxy with over fifteen-hundred inhabited worlds, and jump-capable ships are as common as dirt. Last year our network recorded more than forty-five million vessels spending more than eleven billion hours in flight, and traveled a total of two-point-two *trillion* collective light-years. Trying to track down a ship ghosting the nav network would require intensive manual data analysis with a team of specialists. Could we find the ship? Perhaps. But I'm not about to dedicate the kind of resources that would be necessary for that task unless I receive specific orders to do so from someone with sufficient authority. So, get yourselves an official decree, and then we can talk."

Lee had to admit the man's case was compelling. When he considered the matter from Zirin's point of view, the three of them did sound like a minor inconvenience. In the grand scheme of things, it might even be true. "Tell you what. Are you willing to copy the logs from the beacons in those sectors and download the data points so *we* can crunch the numbers and arrive at a solution on our own?"

"Would you have the ability to work with that? Those files are huge."

"The TSS does, and we have their attention."

Zirin's eyes narrowed slightly as he considered the appeal. "I still need a written request from a full Agent. As I said, the client information is confidential, and I need to know it will be secure."

"I can arrange that in short order," Lee confirmed. Agent Kalshi had been less than helpful in many regards, but Lee had no doubt he'd support this aspect of the investigation.

"Will agreeing to this get you out of my office for the foreseeable future?" Zirin pressed.

"Absolutely," Lee said.

"Then, you have my cooperation. I can furnish you with the logs for the relevant four sectors of space where you've seen your ghost ship. But I must warn you, that includes something like six thousand beacons. Once I get the written request, I'll make sure you have the logs by the end of business today. Will that be sufficient?"

"Yes, Supervisor. We can work with that."

TAKING STOCK

SUPERVISOR ZIRIN WAS good to his word. After an official TSS decree was sent over requesting SiNavTech's transit logs as part of a high-priority investigation, within the hour, a data core was delivered to Karmen's team by SiNavTech data specialists; a copy of the records were also sent via secure subspace data transfer to the TSS Militia station on Greengard.

"Lee, do you think there's any chance we can locate a ship of our own to get back home?" Karmen asked. The past week seemed like an unending family road trip, but with a family she hadn't seen in decades. She was exhausted. The sterile surroundings of the SiNavTech office building were making her homesick. She would even pay real money for a recording of Elian and Seandra's bickering.

"We're not ready to head back to Greengard yet," Lee told her. "And it turns out that the TalEx people have already loaded our Greengard shuttle. It'll be arriving tomorrow. We'll pick it up at the spaceport, as arranged. It's not fancy, but it'll get us to our next port of call, once we figure out where that is."

"Forget about fancy rides. I'm kind of in love with the sensor suite on that thing," Armin said.

"You were ready to ditch it three days ago."

"And then I rode around in an ore hauler and got some perspective."

"There's no getting around that the ship is defenseless, and it is also now known to our targets. If we're going to continue onward, I still say we need something new and more formidable. We took a big chance those pirates didn't decide to come looking for us," Karmen pointed out.

"A chance that paid off, however," Lee countered. "Either way, we're spending a night in town here. The good news is that there's a hotel a few blocks away, and rooms are available. We each get our own tonight. Courtesy of a TSS spending account."

"I love you," Karmen cooed.

Lee made a show of looking at his feet. "D'awwwwww…"

"No offense, but I love a comfortable bed more. Where's the hotel?"

They swapped the room reservations and entry data between their handhelds.

Karmen found herself desperate for a good night's sleep and real food in a proper restaurant that didn't include pie. "Lee, Armin? Can I count on you two to make sure that data gets back to the TSS data nerds? I need to lie down."

"Consider it done," Lee said.

"Well, I'm exhausted." Karmen stood up. "I want to see my family, even on a tiny screen. You know where I'll be. Come by or message me with any new discoveries."

Armin saluted. "The computers will be crunching that data a thousand different ways before you know it. We'll need speed on our side."

"Speed tomorrow. Tonight, sleep." Karmen waved them good night.

"Yes, ma'am," Armin saluted her as she headed off to find her bed.

—

The hotel had both a full-service restaurant and a take-away counter. Karmen made use of the latter to order a selection of sandwiches and three bottles of water. She brought the whole loot crate to her room and messaged Lee to alert him that food was available if they wanted it.

She collapsed on the bed and lay there, marveling at how tired she was. She didn't remember being this tired on the *Triumph*. But that was ages ago. Four kids and a marriage later, she was a different person. A wiser, tired person.

She pulled a sandwich out of the container and wolfed it down without tasting it, then chased it with a few sips of water. A deeply dark feeling fell over her—a pit of loneliness that mere food wouldn't fill. She grabbed her handheld and opened a vidcall to Daveed.

She held her breath until his image appeared on her screen. "Daveed! How are you?"

He rubbed his eyes. The camera was close to his face against a backdrop of pillows. "I'm fine for a man jolted awake in the wee hours. Is everything okay?"

The sound of his voice pushed her already strained endurance into free fall. She pushed ahead, refusing to cry. "I'm starting to think I'm in way over my head here," she choked.

His brows pinched with concern. "Hey, are you all right?"

"Physically, I'm fine. I think I'm cracking mentally."

"That's not the woman I married. What's the pressure point? The mission? The crew?"

"It's the target," she confessed. "I thought I knew Aura Thand so well. Now, I find out she's not only alive, but she's taking out civilian targets all over the galaxy. How am I supposed to deal with that?"

Daveed was silent for several seconds. "Karmen, what are you saying?"

She sniffed back sudden tears stinging her eyes. "Aura is Mother Carnage."

Her husband sucked in a shocked breath. "What? How…?

"I don't know, Daveed. I thought I was chasing a hardened criminal who'd exhausted every other option in life. But Aura… As near as I can tell right now, she chose to disappear after the *Triumph* rather than face what had happened. I've spent all these years thinking that she was the strongest, bravest person I'd ever known in the TSS. But it was a front. She's a coward. A selfish, thieving coward."

"Hmm." Daveed took on his reflective, academic tone. "I've never come up against a situation remotely like that. But it seems like one of those things that makes you relive every conversation from the past knowing what you know now. It'd be like finding out Hellen, or one of our other neighbors, was a war criminal."

Karmen scoffed. "In Hellen's case, that would actually be less surprising than this situation with Aura."

"Maybe that's a bad example."

"No, it works. It's the same deal, where you *think* you know someone, let them into your heart and home, but it turns out that they were deceiving you about who they were. You'd believed their lies about what was in their heart, and so you unwittingly trusted a monster hiding in plain sight as a friend.

I feel… betrayed. It's new for me. I've never felt that way about anyone, ever. Was she always like this and I missed it? I mean, she must have been, deep down. A person doesn't just flip allegiance in a day."

"That doesn't mean everything about your friendship was a lie. And you don't know what happened to her in the final moments on the *Triumph* or what happened afterward. Do you know for certain that she's a willing participant in all this?" he asked in the same tone he used in class on particularly obtuse students.

Karmen thought back to the brief conversation she'd overseen on the spy drone. Aura *had* been arguing with that man. That didn't count for much, but it wasn't nothing. "Maybe you're right. Or maybe hoping that you're right is just wishful thinking because I can't reconcile my memories of the good person she was when I knew her with the Mother Carnage figure of today."

"I know you'll get your answers eventually, but try to focus on the present and what you need for your mission. Build a profile of Mother Carnage based on the observable facts. Concentrate on what you know best: violence and its many uses to achieve a goal."

"I'm not a violent person."

"I didn't say you were. But you *understand* violence as a tool. So does Mother Carnage—she inflicted violence without death. A maestro of violent chaos. I know you can find a way to read that symphony and use it to gain the upper hand."

"I appreciate your vote of confidence in my skills."

"Oh, very. I sleep quite soundly at night knowing that you're trained in ten different ways of killing an intruder with a kitchen knife."

She sniffed but laughed loudly. Too loudly. "Sorry, that

shouldn't be funny. I'm just so very tired," she admitted. "I miss you and the kids. I want to make dinner in my own kitchen over my own stove—and without threat of anyone getting stabbed. I know it sounds horribly domestic, but it's how I feel."

"Believe me, you are missed just as much. And not merely because Seandra has ruined three pots making pasta this week."

"No! Maybe we can sign her up for classes with the culinary program. I forgot to mention it with everything else going on, but I found out the day of the blackout that my old *Triumph* chef, Bertie, runs that program now."

"There's a solid idea."

"I wish this investigation had an equally straightforward solution."

"Maybe you just need to look at it from a different angle. What do you know so far?"

She put the handheld on projection mode so she could talk to him while lying on her back. "Okay. Let's see. She has powerful, wealthy friends. She's made common cause with a crew of Lynaedan soldiers. She's picking her targets very carefully—attacking soft targets like the Foundation City hospital annex. And mining sites, too. She's hit two of those so far."

"Mining sites. That means going up against TalEx. That's no small thing. There's no way she'd do that if she didn't know she could stand a good chance of getting away with it. That tracks with maintaining powerful friends. What else?"

"She's got shuttles, and possibly other transportation assets we haven't seen yet. She never hit the same target twice. But that might be because she's only been doing this for a short time."

"All right. So... what is she doing with all this stuff?"

"What do you mean?"

"I mean, think about it. You have a big truck. You drive from town to town and steal everything that's not nailed down. Now your truck is full of stolen goods. What do you do next?"

"Well, I'd pull the truck up to a warehouse nobody knew about and... no. I'd *sell* it, wouldn't I?"

"Go to the top of the class," Daveed answered. "You need to keep expanding your operation, and you need money to do that. So, you sell the loot any way you can."

"Which means the black market." Karmen groaned. That was a corner of society she'd rather forget existed, let alone something she wanted to investigate.

"Not necessarily. Nearly everyone who needs a rare item buys from a friend who has a friend who can get those things. When there's risk, you want to be able to trust someone to keep your secrets, so people naturally want to work with others who run in the same circles."

Karmen nodded. "That's a good point. You can't look up an illegal arms dealer in the public directory."

"Precisely. The trick with any illicit dealing is hiding your activity. And that means not just knowing one person, but having a network. Crime is a team effort. You can't sell ten thousand tons of ore to one merchant who only deals in hundred-ton lots because it would raise all kinds of flags. But you *can* sell one hundred tons of that ore to one hundred different merchants, and no one will raise any questions," Daveed said.

"I know. How does any of that help us track down these particular criminals?"

"Karmen, you need to stop thinking like a soldier."

She sat up and glared at him. "Meaning what, exactly?"

"Meaning, you're preoccupied with analyzing the enemy's strategy and tactics, and orders and chains of command. Mother Carnage isn't running a *military* operation. Yes, she's using military assets, but those are only tools to get what she really wants, which is capital—money she can use to expand her operation. Ultimately, she's running a *business.*"

"That's not how Aura thinks."

"You said yourself, you don't know this Mother Carnage person."

The words cut deep, prompting Karmen to look away from the screen. She may have spoken the words, but she hadn't yet accepted that someone who'd once meant so much to her was now running a large-scale interstellar piracy operation. *How does someone go from an honorable TSS Agent to... that?*

Daveed's expression softened on the screen, picking up on her hurt. "You haven't spoken to her in decades. There's no telling what may have transpired in the intervening years to change her perspective. You can't apply the same reasoning patterns and motivations from back when you served together. Be objective. How would you approach any other criminal ring?"

She rolled onto her side and let her head fall back into the pillow. "It sounds like I need to do some reading on interstellar commerce."

"I can send you some materials, but get the boys to help. They need to gather financial reporting from all over the sector, and neighboring sectors. Tell them you need to find a forensic accountant—those are people who track down lost or stolen money. That'll be your key to figuring out her next move."

Karmen touched the holoprojection of his face with a finger. It wasn't the same. Images had no substance. She missed his presence. His voice. His smell. "Thank you, my love."

"I'm glad I could help. This old man never thought he'd see the day when you'd want to discuss trade theory!"

She smiled at him. "You're not so old I can't do things to you when I get home."

"I look forward to it."

—

When Karmen finished presenting the gist of her talk with her husband over breakfast in the hotel's restaurant, Lee saluted her with his coffee cup.

"Tell Daveed he wins a free car," he said.

"With a TSS decal on the dash, I'm sure." Karmen took a bite of eggs, bacon, and waffles in a perfect forkful. A hearty meal and full stomach made all the difference to her attitude. Hope did better on a full stomach.

Armin had opted for muffins over waffles. "His idea about handing the core to a forensic accountant was spot on. We got the report from one of our guys on Greengard just before you came down this morning. You wouldn't believe what the data show," he said.

"That sounds like an advertisement," she said.

Lee swiped one of Armin's muffins and scarfed it in a single bite. "It's too crazy to be an ad. It's almost too crazy for me to believe."

Armin pulled his plate closer and placed one arm around it like a fortress wall. "Yeah, our guy had to call two people to check him on it, but it's genuine. One wild ride."

Karmen found herself wishing they'd cut to the chase—but to them, this *was* the chase. She decided to concentrate on listening.

"The pirate ship is officially the *Emerald Queen*, and she has a storied history," Lee began. "She was seriously damaged, then sat in a spacedock for years. No owner came forward, or any crew. Not mothballed, really—just an aging hulk racking up docking fees. A local court listed her as abandoned, and she was slated for scrapping. Then this guy shows up. He goes by the name of Gilgamesh."

"That sounds like a disease," Karmen noted.

Lee nodded and shrugged. "There's a comment in the report from a history nerd at Foundation U. It's apparently the name of an ancient warrior-king from Earth lore. What do I know? Anyway, three years ago, Gilgamesh took ownership of the old ore carrier and paid for it in credit chips. As far as we can tell, he pays for *everything* in physical credits. And he paid a fortune to have the vessel towed to a spacedock on Tavden. The ship stayed moored there for months until a crew did finally show up, employed by a guy named Lom Mench. A Lynaedan. And he didn't hire a local crew. He brought his own people all the way from Lynaeda. For months, they lived on that ship, working, cleaning, fixing, just buffing the shite out of that beat-up hulk."

"The laundry list of vendors they used for supplies would fill a tablet," Armin said.

"Everyone needs a network," Karmen mused to herself. *Daveed really was on the money.*

"Lots of people are willing to work off the books if the pay is right," Armin continued, "especially merchants in Middle and Outer Worlds who don't necessarily do a lot of business—"

"But who *do* occasionally come across a big score," Lee cut in. "Which usually means something in the back room got discovered and someone made a killing."

"A shop owner who earns his yearly profit in one sale isn't

going to complain too loudly," Karmen surmised.

Lee nodded. "Correct."

"Such as staying quiet when they're asked to install TSS gear salvaged from who knows where?" she asked.

"Also correct. The Bakzen War wrecked a lot of warships. The recovered hardware is in salvage yards all over the galaxy, just waiting for resourceful individuals to recognize their value."

"What else do we know about the Lynaedans?" she asked.

"Frankly, except for Lom Mench, not a lot. Lom, however, has a following. An entire social network dedicated to the pursuit of crime. He started off writing about crime as part of the Lynaedan's local security force. And then, well, he started stealing things himself."

"Artwork from private galleries, then rare artifacts from museums," Armin explained. "Finally, he figured out how to tap into government databases on Lynaeda and emptied an astounding number of bank accounts. Where he stashed it all, no one seems to know."

"Away from Lynaeda, no doubt," Karmen said. "Then, he probably used it to buy legitimate businesses that could get him what he wanted."

"Very likely," Armin agreed.

Karmen leaned back in her chair. "Where is this all going?"

"Mench and Gilgamesh have a history," Lee revealed with an excited smile.

"They've been at it for a while, building a little empire for themselves," Armin continued. "It appears to be the sort of arrangement you might read about in a children's fantasy adventure, where the king fronts a reward for a rare item and the thief steals it. They fence it with private collectors who are linked by very exclusive auction houses and brokerages in the

Inner Worlds. This has been going on for years. But then this lady shows up…"

Karmen's face flushed. "Aurelia Thand, former TSS Agent."

Armin held up a hand. "Except now she's known as Aura Corriden, a cargo trader who's spent two decades running trade routes for various employers, including as a speculator on her own. Rare ores and so on. Her ship is an I-40R Free Trader and is registered as the *Redemption*."

"Registered where?"

"Gallos." Armin exchanged a worried look with Lee.

Eventually, the Junior Agent said, "You're either going to love this or hate it. She's registered as a merchant in the Covrani Dynasty shipping business."

"Wait, the whole thing with Kaia and Colin isn't—"

Lee shook his head. "No, nothing like that. As far as we can tell, that business license is the only link between Aura and anyone on Gallos. Kaia is fine. Her boyfriend, too."

Karmen pulled her arms in and hugged herself. "Stars, I hope so. This is getting too close to home."

Lee nodded. "It's not all that surprising, though. The Covrani Dynasty has a widely varied income stream made of subsidies, leases, and outright sales to thousands of traders in this corner of the galaxy. For them, it's all about cashflow. Seventy percent of the family's income comes from leases, fees, and profit shares. That's how they became a Dynasty."

"Fair enough. Where does all that leave us?" Karmen asked.

"It forces us to make a choice," Lee said. "Gilgamesh has put together a network of diverse businesses that's incredibly resilient. If we stamp out five fronts, ten more will take their place. Either we try to starve his revenue by putting a stop to all the under-the-table dealing he relies on, or we concentrate on taking out the *Emerald Queen* herself."

"Ethically, I'd rather go for the first option," Karmen said.

"I agree it's the better, more permanent solution. It would also take years to implement and probably not work very well. We'd have to rely on individual Enforcer and Militia units all doing their job to textbook efficiency and honesty. I think we know the universe just doesn't work like that. If these folks are as organized as they seem to be, they'll always be able to find a way to stay ahead of us. A paid-off official to tip them off about an upcoming raid. Or a slip of the tongue by a drunk in a bar that gives up a secret. We're merely tourists in their world. This is their livelihood, and they're just plain better at playing the game than we are."

"Which means we have to play the player, not the board," Karmen said thoughtfully.

"Excuse me?"

"Aura had one very serious flaw when I worked with her," Karmen began. "When she got bad news she didn't want to deal with, she had a habit of retreating. She'd go into her cabin and stay there for hours. Sometimes a day or more. The whole ship knew when it was bad news because their captain would simply disappear. She'd force me to come find her and break her out of her shell, and then we'd deal with it together."

"It was her cry for help. Except you knew how to listen for it," Lee observed.

"Very much so. I'm willing to bet that she hasn't changed so much that she's adopted a whole new set of habits. I wonder who she has bailing her out now?"

"Not Gilgamesh—he's not around her often enough. It might well be Lom, the Lynaedan. After all this time, he might be better at managing her than you were back in the day."

Karmen drained her cup and pushed it away. "There's one way to find out. Armin, do we still have those Talsarium nuclear mining charge shutdown codes?"

"Yes, we do. Why?"

"Can we get the nice folks at VComm to make a public broadcast of them?"

He eyed her. "Probably. But why would we do that…?"

"Because *we* know that the blast charges have been disarmed, but I'd wager that Aura and the rest of the *Emerald Queen* crew do not yet. So, let's call attention to it—give Aura a crisis to send her into her hole."

Lee's brows pinched together. "Sorry, I'm not tracking."

Armin smiled. "I am. Sending out a wide-range transmission of the codes wouldn't do anything to disarm the charges deep in the shielded belly of the ship, but it's the kind of move someone with sway would try on the chance they might get lucky. The *Emerald Queen*'s Lynaedan tech people will explain that the transmission is harmless, but they'll check the charges anyway… and find that they've already been disabled."

"Cue Aura's panic when she realizes her fancy weapons that she crippled a planet to acquire are discovered to now be utterly useless," Karmen finished. "What do you think?"

Armin shrugged, then nodded. "I think that if Lee flashes his TSS colors at the right people at VComm, we could make sure those codes go everywhere within that corporation's influence. And that will include wherever the *Emerald Queen* might presently be berthed."

"All right, let's go ruin Mother Carnage's day and force her back into her shell," Karmen declared. "Then we'll see how good a first officer Lom Mench really is."

26

THE ENTOURAGE AND THE HELP

As SOON AS the *Emerald Queen* pulled into Tavden High Port, they found a high-tech firm that was willing to scour the ship from bow to stern and analyze every system for foreign influences. After two days in Tavden High Port, Aura's crew on the *Emerald Queen* was now in a strange way. Anxious, but not bored. Busy, but not productive. Aura felt it through her comm net, and she knew she wasn't the only one.

The technical teams Gallian had hired had gone through the entire ship, obeying no boundaries, and subjecting every crew member to a battery of questions and concerns. The crew was tired of it. Lom had personally received their report and sent the techs on their way, flush with credit chips.

Now, Lom stood in Aura's ready room and dropped the tablet on her desk. It clattered loudly as it hit the hard surface. "The good news," Lom said, "is that we got a clean bill of health from the techies. No viruses, no bugs, plants, or unauthorized additions to any of the ship's systems."

Aura was huddled into herself behind the desk. Her face was drawn and her skin pale. She hadn't eaten much in days. "What's the bad news?"

"It's easier if I show you."

Aura followed him with a growing feeling of despair in her gut. This was bad. Had it been anything but truly awful, he'd have simply told her. No matter how she directed her life, it seemed she was a magnet for awful news.

They arrived at the shielded weapons storage area. It still held eight of the dampener containers containing the mining charges they'd kept from the raid on Greengard. "Mining charges. So what?" she asked.

"So… this." Lom strode to one container and yanked the cover open, then pulled out the charge. Before she could stop him or truly understand what he was doing, he'd twisted the cone off and pulled out the radioactive core.

"Are you *insane*?" she screamed.

"Hardly," he assured her. "But there is no danger. See? Decayed to lead." He pressed his thumbs into the core to show her his thumb print. "The half-lives are spent, and the core is almost entirely lead now. There isn't enough radioactivity in this to fry an egg. Nor in these others. All decayed nearly to lead."

Now, she noticed the problem. The lights that indicated the cores' utility had changed from green to black. The power lights were all on, so what…? She peered at the open container closely and saw the discrepancy. "Disarmed. All of them?"

"Every one."

"But… how?"

"I'm not sure. The chief engineer, Maesy, reported their status as operable before we made port. It might have been something that escaped scout ship beamed at us."

"That scout ship… or someone else. Might we have picked up a computer virus at some point?"

"Unclear. But it pays to ask an expert. Lom to Gallian."

"This is Gallian."

"Comms, might we have integrated a computer virus when we docked at this station?"

"Let me check the logs. Stand by… There it is. Commander, we *did* receive a transmission on the open channel just after we docked. The contents don't make any sense, though. No executable files, but—"

Aura broke into the conversation. "What were the contents?"

"A series of hexadecimal numbers. They don't correspond to any piece of equipment installed aboard the ship."

Lom shook his head. "Thank you. Lom out." He ended the commlink. "It might be that the TalEx corporation is more clever about securing their equipment than we'd given them credit for. Using a general broadcast to nullify stolen explosives is just plain devious. At any rate, we are out eight million credits worth of explosives."

"No!" She groaned. "We can't raid another TalEx facility so soon after the last job, and we don't have the materials or expertise to craft more radioactive material ourselves. Fok!"

Lom gave her another few moments to wallow in her self-pity, then asked, "How would you like to proceed?"

I don't know! "I'm going to the *Redemption*. I need to think. When is the interview with the new quartermaster?"

"He's due to arrive first thing in the morning."

"Fine. That's fine. No calls for a while," she murmured. Before Lom could bombard her with any other bad news, she retreated to the *Redemption*.

The tension started to go out from her shoulders as soon

as she stepped into the Command Center. It was dark, as always, and she settled into the command chair. But it was lumpy. Weird… and moving!

Aura screamed and flung herself out of the seat.

A skinny stranger was already sitting in it. "Gah! Bomax, woman, you scared the shite out of me!"

"Who are you? What are you doing on my ship?" she demanded.

"I'm supposed to interview with you about a position tomorrow morning."

"*You're* the new quartermaster?" she demanded.

"Yeah. Well. Okay, let's start from square one. My name is Tabor Laski. I sell weapons. And everything else."

Aura located the light controls and switched them on. They sized each other up. Laski was no work of art: tall, lanky, sandy haired and loud with sharp edges to his face. All arms and elbows and knees.

"Mr. Laski, I'm not in a mood for conversation right now. Get out, go ashore, and kindly don't return until your appointment tomorrow."

He recoiled from Aura. "Stars! No offense, Captain, but you look awful. What happened? I get the impression you might not want to wait until tomorrow for my assistance."

Why not tell him? Let's see what he comes up with. "We had eight functional Talsarium nuclear mining charges in storage. The dampener boxes failed, so all of them are now useless."

"All eight? Well, that is a shame. What did it cost you?"

"All the planning and labor expended in a very complex raid on Greengard. We were going to sell the mining charges for a million each."

"Okay, not good. But trust me, that's the least of your problems."

"What does that mean?"

Laski took a seat at the sensors station and stretched out. "From the beginning, then. Our mutual friend, Ashurbanipal, told me to get over here ASAP for a meeting with you... I assume you make the hiring decisions?"

"I asked Ash for help with supplies. So... yes."

"Good. I got here last night, and your crew were coming and going on a steady flow of foot traffic. Shore leave, I guess."

"Not exactly, but close enough. We've had a technical team going over the ship for the past few days."

"Of course! Everyone's uniforms are woefully drab and no one was checking IDs. So, I took a few photos with my handheld, sent them to a tailor I know not far from here, and two hours and a few credit chips later, I had a solid copy of one of your uniforms. Then, I just walked right aboard. I've been here since your morning shift started."

"Doing what?"

"Looking around, talking to the crew, making connections. I even had lunch in the officer's mess. The food there is actually quite good."

Aura gaped at him. "And no one stopped you?"

Laski made a show of holding in a gout of laughter. "Stopped me? Captain, not only was I not challenged at any time, but I think I have a date with your chief engineer tomorrow night. Maesy, right? Pink hair, fake eyes, kind of a husky voice. Sensors in her hands."

"That's her. How did you manage that? Maesy is barely verbal, even for a Lynaedan."

"Well, it's not a *date* date. We're watching old movies in a fly-hole on the hangar deck. Something like twenty people are supposed to show up. I was told there would be snacks. I figured that meant popcorn or kissing in the dark. Either way,

I'm there."

"Answer my question, Tabor."

"Ah. Yes. Maesy hates *people.* She tolerates the crew. But she loves the peach pudding in the cafeteria. I was sitting at her table, trying to make conversation, and she was grunting yes and no answers. Then, she dug into her pudding, and it was like… I don't know, like the sun coming out after a long, rainy afternoon. When she finished her dessert, the clouds came back. Well, I know a signal when I see one, so I went back to the cooling case and brought her a few extra. Her face changed. She saw me for the first time. Not really love—probably not even lust—but I have an invite to movie night. Game, set and match: Laski."

What a strange fellow. Aura studied him. "How does any of this relate to me hiring you?"

"It doesn't. It relates to your management of this ship. I hate to be blunt like this, but it's a real problem."

Aura pulled open a maintenance kit and extracted a spanner. "Answer my question, or I'm going to beat you to death with this."

"Yes, ma'am. It's about character and motivation. Let's take Maesy as an example. Engineers operate under a set of assumptions. All crew members do. They're motivated by their duties, by their responsibilities. By their loyalty to their officers and their captain. Maesy is probably a brilliant engineer. But it never occurred to her to just walk over and take what she wanted. No kitchen staff wants to start a fight over an extra helping of pudding. What kind of pirate sits and waits to be served? What kind of officer refuses to ask for seconds?"

One who follows instructions, which is how I like my crew. She stared at him levelly. "I made that rule. It's called conservation of resources."

"Okay, *conserve.* But don't starve your chief engineer of the one thing she may truly look forward to at lunch!" He sat back and folded his arms. "And 'Mother Carnage'? Bah! Who came up with that? It wasn't you."

"That was Lom."

"Yeah, that tracks. Lom Mench, grand theft everything. Anyway, your shipboard security is awful. That's the first thing around here we need to re-think."

Aura lost what little patience she had. She rammed the spanner into Laski's face and squeezed his nose. "You've raided my supplies, broken into my vessel, and insulted both me and my people. For the last time: why should I want to keep you around?"

Tabor's face grew red, but he never lost his composure. His eyes never wavered from her own. "See? *There's* the pirate queen. That's a woman I could follow into battle for glory and loot. We both know you're giving me the job. Sure, I was pointing out a security flaw, but I saw how your eyes lit up when you realized I knew how to work people. That's what this job is really about, isn't it? Getting things for people before they even know they need them. It doesn't matter what we call the job. Chief Logistics Officer, or something. Whatever the title, I need to have authority over all supply procedures. Your current quartermaster lacks nerve and imagination, as well as a coherent execution strategy. I have all three."

She pulled the spanner back. "How do you know he lacks nerve?"

"Because I spoke to him. He's stressed out. He is at his limit. But he can see things for what they are, and he knows he's not up to the task. He's terrified of asking you or Mench for help. I am happy to be that help. I also have a list of personal requirements. I'll send it to you after our interview."

"I could put out feelers and wait for other prospects to come in," she said, trying to regain control of the conversation.

"Yes, you could. That would take time. I come straight from Ash's contact sheet, and I'm sitting in front of you—already in uniform, even. If that's not enough, I can't imagine anyone else would be a better bet. Let me be straight: I run a conglomeration of half a dozen shipyards on the planet we are now orbiting. Over the past nine years, I have embezzled an insane amount of credits, and not only do my supervisors not see it, they keep giving me bonuses for excellent work and improving profits." He smiled. "By the way, you'll be receiving six brand new TA-90 fighters by the end of tomorrow. You're welcome."

It was over. The strange, thin man was in. All she had to do was give the order and Lom would make it official.

Part of her resented him for showing up, and resented herself for giving in. But… he reminded her of Gil, too. Not Gil as he was now—arrogant, presumptuous, and inflexible—but as he was long ago. Just as arrogant and presumptuous, but also creative and driven. She found the way Tabor ran the room reassuring. And he had a way of looking at things that could only complement her own perspective.

She sighed. "You're not what I expected when I asked for help."

"Captain Carnage, you want boom stuff? I sell boom stuff and everything besides. I can't think of any reason in the galaxy you should entrust your process to anyone else. Can you?"

— — —

Gil lay on his bed and watched the stars through a transparent dome above him. His yacht, *Shamhat,* had room for all manner of indulgences; this was one of his favorites. "Play message," he ordered.

As he relaxed, he watched Aura's face and shoulders in the hologram above him. He tightened the sash of his bathrobe and gave her his full attention.

"So, Captain's progress report. To Gilgamesh. From Mother Carnage. Tavden High Port.

"Hello, Gil. Forgive me for not being in touch more often, but we've been busy jumping around. We're finally sitting at Tavden for a while to resupply. I expect we'll be here for at least a week. The ship needs some work, resupply and so on. The crew needs a breather before we begin the next leg of the mission. I have your target list right here," Aura said, patting her shirt pocket.

"I have a new logistics officer: Tabor Laski. Ash sent him over to help grow our supply chains. He's obnoxious as the day is long and never shuts up, but he's a gifted manager. He has a knack for organization and execution that is frankly a little arousing. Don't worry, though. You're still number one in my heart."

Number one in her heart. Great. How about number one in my bed, Aura? Don't think I don't notice you refuse most of my invitations. There had to be a way of getting her back. Restoring what they used to have.

Deep down, he knew she was right. They weren't youngsters anymore; they'd worked hard to build their respective dreams into reality. They were two circles, overlapping but never occluding each other. That was why they worked. Messing with that pattern would disturb everything else.

There was more to the message, business plans and such. He found himself zoning out after a while. But a familiar name brought him back to reality.

"Oh! We finished fixing *Enkidu*. He's just as fast as before but now he'll get you to your destination without risking death. I'll hang on to him until you come by next. Talk to you soon, my love. Have a good night."

Heh. She fixed him, she can keep him. Part of the reason he'd ferried the old starship to Aura was to store it with someone he trusted. Where better than a hangar deck of a battleship? Gil missed *Enkidu*, but he preferred his yacht. *Shamhat* was a transport for a man to fly across the galaxy in style.

"Anyway, how does she know what kind of night I'm having?" he griped.

"Surely, every night is a good night," a sultry voice answered.

Bits of coherent light came together in moments, and then she was standing next to the bed. *Shamhat*'s AI. A raven-haired, dark-eyed beauty draped in layers of finery concocted by a programmer who had only the vaguest concept of what an ancient Babylonian priestess might have looked like. Gil doubted it had any link to the real thing. He didn't doubt the Lynaedan programmers had done an excellent job. She was magnificent. There was a matching android in a charging dock on the lower deck in case she needed a physical form, but the hologram worked for most things.

"Why don't we take your appearance down a notch or two?" he asked.

"Standard concierge uniform then," she said and instantly changed into a form-fitting outfit that might have suited an exotic dancer better than a flight attendant. "Would you care to eat something?"

"I'm not hungry." *Not for food, anyway.*

"Would you like me to bathe you?"

Now, there's an idea. But… no. "I really am good, thank you. Don't think I don't appreciate the offer, though. If you'd appeared a little earlier…"

"I'm always here. You could have called. Just speak my name."

"Thank you, Shamhat. That will be all."

"My pleasure."

"Oh, there is one more thing. Do you think Aura is tired of me?"

"I couldn't say. Have you asked her?"

"I have. She keeps insisting she's not. But I wonder."

"Perhaps that's your answer, then. Why not take her words at face value?"

Because she might be lying. Everyone lies about everything. "It's not that simple."

"Let me ask you this, then. Do you think it's better to be loved, or respected?"

That's easy. "Respected, of course."

"If you have the self-awareness to understand why you chose that way, you will have answered your own question. Will you be needing anything else?"

"Show me the plan for New Akkadia," he ordered. The star map appeared over the bed. "Leave me be now," he requested. "I'm going to watch the stars a bit longer, then make a few calls and go to sleep."

"As you wish. Good night, Lord Gilgamesh."

Why doesn't she just dispense with the nonsense and call me 'Gil'? he wondered as her image vanished.

He turned his attention to the star map. The AI noted the location of his pupils and responded by shifting the holoprojection. She was a little too efficient sometimes; if he looked at one planet or coordinate for too long, the AI assumed he wanted to exclude everything else and zoomed in on his target while minimizing the rest. That was great when he was actually paying attention, but sometimes his mind wandered. He found if he closed his eyes for five or ten seconds, it reset the display. Still, Lynaedan tech had given him this ship and its accompanying AI, so he couldn't complain too loudly.

The comm line beeped. Gil assumed it was Aura calling back. But he answered the line to see Sargon's head glaring down at him. "Gil!"

"Sar! It's been a minute. What's on your mind?"

"The TSS has an operation geared at dealing with your space thief. You need to pay attention."

"That's ridiculous. I've got my hands on her every move." Gil snorted a laugh as he realized the pun.

Sargon merely glared for a moment, then sighed. "Gil, I know you have a thing for your pirate queen, but you need to remember she's a means to an end. You're the entourage, she's the help."

"Don't patronize, me, Sar. Just say your piece so I can go to sleep."

"All right. I already heard from Ham and Ash. We're building up our fleet assets. Armed shuttles and warships, lots of transports. Some troops. One day, the *Emerald Queen* will be a resource sink. The ROI will collapse. We do better with a variety of assets. I need to know you'll be willing to cut her loose if she becomes a liability."

And there's the Sargon we all know so well: dividing the universe into the entourage and the help and guess who is at the top? "I remember a conversation in a bar twenty-something years ago when you said that abandoning the help was what the Dynasties did."

"I remember that day well. Especially the part where we agreed *we* were going to be in charge."

It was all your idea. The rest of us have just been along for the ride. "The point was that we were going to be better than the Dynasties."

"Sometimes, being better means making hard choices. I need to know I can count on you to do right by New Akkadia, Gil."

"Or what?"

Sar rolled his eyes. "Come on, man, don't make it like that."

But it is like that. It's always like that with you. "Or. What?"

"Or I'll find another Mesopotamian. I don't want to do that. I think we've done well for ourselves. For each other. Let's not throw all that away."

For a moment, throwing it all away sounded like the only smart move. He'd allowed Sar to direct him and use him for two decades. Maybe he deserved the abuse. Certainly, Aura deserved the chance to be free of all the nonsense. He could find a pirate captain anywhere... though no other had been with him through so much, or knew him so well, or had such lovely eyes. He knew what he had to do. "All right. New Akkadia to the end."

"That's my boy. Now, put on your pants and do something about your space pirate!"

27

PUTTING FACES TO NAMES

G IL SPENT THE night in a combination of fitful rage and despair. He raged at Aura for not being more amenable to his needs and at Sargon for being, well, Sargon. He raged at himself, too, for a long string of real and imagined failures.

At one point, he woke to utter darkness; where the starry display had once offered hope and serenity, it now seemed like a lifeless void, offering all the space in the universe and nothing of value.

Eventually, he realized that sleep wouldn't return. Instead, he set about making plans. Whatever was going on with Aura, she would need someone there to provide whatever help she might require. If there really were TSS Agents closing in, then he refused to give her up without a fight. And he had friends of his own.

He studied star maps and lists of contacts, then made several choices. Local Enforcers and poorly armed transports were no match for the TSS, but then the TSS had grown fat and lazy and had allowed the galaxy to run wild for years. The *Emerald Queen* was easily a match for any regional power who might try to stand in his way. He still had the advantage.

"Shamhat, wake up."

The AI's flight attendant image flicked into being. "How may I be of service?"

"Tell Sargon, Hammurabi, and Ashurbanipal that I'm activating War Plan Cedar Forest. The rendezvous point will be at Tavden High Port. Hammurabi should still be on Valdos; tell him to bring a few of his Scorpions to the meeting. We will meet aboard the *Emerald Queen*. Plot us a direct course to Tavden. We have to reinforce the *Emerald Queen*, and I must have a long talk with her captain."

"Right away, Lord Gilgamesh."

He headed for the flight deck. *I might not mean as much to her as I once did, but no one is going to take her away from me!*

—   —   —

"Now, *this* is a sight for sore eyes!" Armin said as they approached the gangway to their refurbished TSS shuttle. "Come to Armin, you beautiful creature."

The repair shop crew had done excellent work. The sensor bubble sat higher now, for better aerodynamics during atmospheric flight, and Karmen could see how they'd reinforced the surrounding frame, too.

Karmen and Lee followed Armin through the airlock. The ship was subtly different now, and not just because the repair shop had repacked all the loose gear into its proper places and improved the latches on the storage compartments. The ship also seemed brighter inside.

"Did they fix the lighting, too?" Karmen asked.

"It's this lighting panel," Lee said, pointing to a fixture in the ceiling. "I swear that was dark when we pulled out of Greengard. Not going to complain about more light."

"Neither will I. Low light ruins your eyes," Karmen said and laughed wildly.

"Where are we going, oh, mission commander?" Armin snarked as he settled into the sensor station.

"Tavden," Lee said. "At least, that's where the SiNavTech data is pointing us. Once we arrive in orbit, we can poll the berthing lists and see if a ship matching the *Emerald Queen*'s description is still in port, and if so, which one. Then, we figure out a next step."

"Assuming she's still in-system. If not, we'll be placing a lot of calls to Supervisor Zirin. We'll run his patience down to zero in no time." Karmen inhaled deeply and let it out. "I do believe they gave our ride a deep cleaning. Doesn't feel so grimy now."

"And there are a couple of extra food packs in the ship's locker," Lee said. "Sorry, Armin, they didn't replace your dead drone."

"It's just as well. Flying a drone inside a space station is frowned upon in most places. They get stuck in ventilation shafts, they appear on flight control sensors. It did its job. Let it rest in peace. The drone is dead. Long live the drone," Armin intoned.

Karmen and Lee shared a glance and raised their arms in a salute. "Long live the drone!"

Karmen threw her take-away food into the cooling unit and settled into her comm chair next to Lee's nav position. She felt surprisingly fresh. The gloom from last night was gone. She was looking forward to catching up to her quarry. She wasn't sure what they'd do when they found Aura, but they'd think of something. If nothing else, they'd shown each other that they were good at that.

After their previous slow ride on the TalEx ore hauler, the quick hop to Tavden reminded Karmen how much she'd missed the speed of TSS jump drives. When they arrived at Taven High Port, Karmen found it surprisingly simple to poll the station's log of arrivals and departures.

"There she is. I've found you, great lady!" Karmen called out. "Gallant-class, modified structure. She's currently docked in Section 19, Berth 385. The ship is logged under the name *Skidder*, but this has gotta be the *Emerald Queen*."

"Where the stars is that berth? Never mind, I'll find it." Armin threw a scanning beam onto the station and stopped when an alarm sounded. "Bah! station protocols won't let us do interior scans? Who came up with that rule?"

"Probably the station managers. These visitors and tourists and all the business types like their privacy," Lee said. "Karmen, a positional code would be nice."

"I have it. There's an open space ten or eleven positions down that row of berths. I'm accessing the queue now. And… we're in! Lee, the landing zone is on your board."

"I see it. This is your pilot speaking. Strap in, folks, because we're going down."

"There's no down in space," Armin argued. "There's no up, no down, no—"

Lee played with the controls, producing a swaying motion on the approach. "Quiet, please. I'm only a lowly Junior Agent who studied medicine more than flying. I wouldn't want to smear my passengers all over the landing deck."

The ploy worked; Armin shut up.

Being a small shuttle, they pulled inside a hangar rather than docking with an exterior grapple and entering the station via a gangway, like the larger ships. They emerged from the shuttle into the hangar to see a veritable canyon of metal surfaces. An information kiosk sat a few meters from the ship, offering them maps of the station that could be ported to their handhelds. Karmen experimented with the settings until she was satisfied she could find both the converted pirate ship and her own shuttle. "The *Emerald Queen* is that way. Even better, she's not scheduled to depart for four more days."

"In which case, we can take it slow. Let's get a room near the pirate ship if we can find one. We'll want to observe the targets before we strike. And, no offense, but I think a laundry run might be a solid goal, too."

"Yuck. You're right. The stuff we're wearing should be burned," Karmen said. "And I need a hat and ridiculous sunglasses. Last thing I want is my old CO recognizing my face if we get close."

"In the meantime, I smell spiced meat sticks," Lee said, following his nose to a local vendor.

—

"You know, I could learn to enjoy being a tourist," Karmen said.

"It does have its advantages over close quarters hand-to-hand combat," Armin agreed.

"Sure, you two are having a blast. All I get to do is pay for stuff," Lee griped as he shifted bags from one hand to the other.

Karmen had insisted on going shopping and further insisted the two men accompany her. There were plenty of shops to choose from; if they were going to blend in, this would be the way to do it. Truth be told, the sheer variety of local color, costumes, and styles on display within the station almost guaranteed that no one from the *Emerald Queen* would be drawn to them. On the other hand, they were tired of not having several changes of clothes. Even Lee was willing to ditch his dark-blue Junior Agent garb in favor of something both sporty and practical, but he insisted on tinted glasses to replace his normal TSS pair.

"Trust me, my friend, you will have the opportunity to blast something into telekinetic bits before we're done here."

"From your mouth to the universe's ears," Lee said.

They'd even gotten lucky in the location of their rented room: a mere hundred meters from the berth that held the pirate ship. Karmen stood at the window and couldn't help but be awed at the converted freighter's bulk and design. The images they'd collected from the news channels couldn't do the great ship any justice at all. "I'll say this for Aura, she traded up to something truly stupendous."

"How about we not stand so close to the window for a while," Armin suggested as he tore open his own purchases: a high-definition camera and a tripod, complete with a wireless distributor that let him network with the database aboard their shuttle and view all the data on his handheld.

"We're on the third floor. They'll never see me," she countered.

"Let's not make assumptions. Yes, we can see the gangway clearly from here, but you don't know who might be looking back. If I'd just pulled off two major heists, I'd be keeping close watch for who might be watching me. So, kindly step away from the window, Officer Sley."

"Yes, sir, Officer Intel Guy," she said, letting the curtains drop back into place.

"Is that all you're doing this trip?" Lee asked. "Taking photos of them?"

Armin adjusted the focus on his camera. "Not *only* that,

but it's a good start. I want to get positive IDs on as many of their crew as possible. That way, we'll get a more complete understanding of who they recruit and how. Whatever is going on is bigger than this ship, and we need to gather all the information we can to trace that web as far as it goes."

"If they're here for a few days, they're probably screening new arrivals and meeting old supporters," Karmen guessed. "I'd want to give the crew some shore leave while they had the chance."

"It's a fair bet there are high-level meetings going on right now," Armin agreed. "But I want to know who the players are, and so will the TSS and Enforcer officials back on Greengard. Nothing says 'I got you' like knowing exactly who ripped your hometown off."

Staying inside and out of sight, Armin and Lee took turns using the camera and polling knowledge bases while Karmen did research on the history of Aura's alias.

"It turns out she's got more than one fake ID," Karmen announced on their second day of surveillance. "I've got an entire crew manifest for the *Redemption* here. "Navigator Penni Kohl, comm officer Bin Delphine, engineer Keldi Percet."

"How do you know they're not all different people who merely traveled with her over the years?" Armin asked.

"Their paperwork. Aura's face is used for all of them, and I can vouch for the fact she isn't triplets," she said, flipping the tablet toward them to show the visuals.

"Did she specialize in anything in particular cargo-wise?" the other Militia officer asked.

"No, it looks like she was moving anything she could find a market for. Bulk items, commercial goods and appliances, and weapons, every now and then. There were even some building materials and the odd vehicle or two. She did everything."

"Salvaged TSS scrap, too?" Lee asked.

"I wouldn't doubt it. If Gilgamesh had a source and a buyer lined up, she made the transfer. It seems like a pretty successful partnership."

"You think that's what they are?" Lee asked. "Partners? I mean in the personal sense."

Karmen wondered about that herself. "Maybe. Aura clearly didn't have the urge to settle down, but having the odd fling with her sponsor now and then? I could see that."

"I got them. Success!" Armin called out. "Karmen, take a look at this dude and tell me if you recognize him." He pointed the camera downward, toward the street in front of the hotel, and began filming continuously, not even taking his eyes from the eyepiece.

The images were relayed to Karmen's tablet almost immediately. She swiped repeatedly at the figure Armin had filmed, finally finding a good view of his face. "He's that same man Aura came off that shuttle with on Diphous," she declared.

"Yes, he is. You want to make a bet that's Gilgamesh?"

"No bet. Although, I'd love to know why he goes by that name."

"I could tell you, but that would make it even weirder," Lee said in a low voice.

Karmen looked over to the Junior Agent. He was huddled into himself, clearly expending considerable energy in concentration. "What do you mean?"

Lee relaxed and unwound his body. "He's got mental guards. As in training. Not TSS-quality skills, but competent as anything," Lee groaned.

"Aura was a Sacon Division Agent, you know," Karmen offered.

Lee backed away from the window and thought quickly. "Even so, that's not something she taught him on the fly. He had a good teacher. It would explain how he was able to rip our spy drone out of the sky with such precision."

"Where might he have learned those skills?" Karmen asked.

"The TSS doesn't like to admit it, but there are teachers around," Lee replied. "Sure, telekinesis is illegal for anyone outside the TSS to use, but it's not like that stops everyone."

"There's also Valdos III," Armin said. "They've openly defied the anti-telekinesis decree and have been getting away with it for as long as anyone can remember."

Karmen frowned. "Is there any reason to believe there's a connection to that planet?"

"Yes, because those five folks who just met up with him are wearing Valdan spirit robes," Armin said, his voice rising in pitch. "I don't think those emblems are mere decoration."

The robes didn't seem remotely noteworthy to Karmen, just a generic tan tone with a flame-like symbol embroidered in a slightly lighter shade of beige on the back. However, when Karmen pulled up more data sheets and read the files, she could see what Armin was talking about. "You're right, that symbol is used by the Scorpion group—a known crime family. Makes you wonder who else they know..." Karmen ran searches on the newcomers' faces but only came up with a hit on one. "Hammurabi," she announced. "A known associate of Gilgamesh. There are two more in the file: one called Sargon and another that I can't even pronounce. Ash something. Ash-ur-ban-i-pal. Say that ten times fast and win a prize."

"They're all from ancient Earth lore," Lee said. "The names

of powerful leaders from the same era."

Karmen glanced at him, not liking the implications about the personality traits of individuals who'd pick such names. "How would anyone even know that? Earth is way outside normal Taran cultural references."

"But it's the backyard of TSS Headquarters. And we already know one person who's an ex-TSS Agent," Lee replied. His face dropped. "Oh, no."

"What?"

"I just had an awful thought. Armin, can you put their faces through the TSS recognition algorithms?"

"I can." He made the entry. "Shite, there he is! Gilgamesh's real name is Dal Horani. Recruited as a Trion division Agent trainee."

"An Agent?" Karmen gasped.

"No, he never graduated. Dismissed after two years as an Initiate for insubordination and 'grand, fanciful ideation'— whatever that means. Looks like he was expelled along with three fellow recruits, Holden Dolhri, Rylen Ontaro, and Kaja Akanis. They all flunked the program and were released at the same time. If they've joined forces on this project, I'd say they learned the wrong lessons."

The figures all walked up the gangway into the pirate ship, disappearing from view.

Armin finally stepped back from his camera. "I think this whole affair just got bumped up to a new level." He studied Lee for a moment, apparently considering his options. "You think the TSS will send help if you call for backup?"

"I asked for backup when we had to send the shuttle to the shop for repairs," Lee said glumly. "The TSS is insistent we try to handle the situation ourselves. They don't want to spook anyone until we know how far this crime ring reaches. They think sending anyone else would call attention to the investigation. Especially any full Agents."

Armin shook his head. "Typical."

On a whim, Karmen pulled out her handheld and quickly typed a message to Kaia. >>Hey, were you ever able to talk with Colin about arranging transportation for us? A ship with a big gun would be great. Things are getting a little tense now that we're on Tavden. NOTHING IS WRONG. JUST ASKING.<<

A few moments later, a response appeared: >>WHAT IS GOING ON???<<

Karmen couldn't explain the details of their investigation, so she ignored her daughter's message. She continued paging through the data, trying to impress the faces of their opponents on her memory. There were a lot of them. Two local warlords, one of whom brought thuggish friends with advanced telekinesis training, and whatever Aura already had on board her pirate ship. They were quickly getting deeper into very murky water.

"Oooooooh!" Armin exclaimed.

Lee groaned. "Use words!"

"A new group just came on to the dock from the pirate ship. Looks like a shore leave party. Trouble is, there's people everywhere. I can't get clean video of them all. Wait… Look at this!" He threw his feed onto the tablet.

Karmen watched as the scene unfolded in real-time. Two of the crew—a pink-haired woman and a sandy-haired, lanky man—were scanning the crowd. For what became evident quickly as the man pointed out one passerby. The woman nodded, and they converged on their victim from opposite sides of the street. She ran into him, apologizing, while the man came up and emptied the mark's pocket of… something.

"Wow, the stones on those two," Armin murmured. "Not

off the ship two minutes, and they're already at work picking pockets. That's a solid work ethic right there."

"What did he just grab?" Karmen asked.

"Couldn't see. Wallet or handheld or something... No, wait... It's an oxy inhaler. Simple drug snatch. What losers."

"Not everyone can grab a bagful of credit chips every time," Lee said. "You got your images?"

"No, they're faced away from me. Looking for an escape route. Amateurs for sure. The pros plan their escape before they go to work. Shite, they're coming this way."

"Images? Yes or no, Armin?" Lee pushed.

"No! No, still no clear line of sight. Fok, they're coming inside."

"Inside here?"

"Yep. They're in the lobby. Stars! What now? I can't get close to them with this thing in my arms," he said, cradling the tripod.

Karmen sighed. "I have an idea. A horrible, very bad idea. But I think those are the only ideas we have left."

Lee gave her a side eye. "What are you thinking, Karmen?"

"I'm thinking I need a snack from the vendor in front of this building. Armin?"

"I'm good, thanks. This is a gold mine here, I'm staying until they all move out of range. Lee, you should go with her."

Lee stretched and put his tourist jacket and glasses back on. "My thoughts exactly. Let's drive our prey to a neutral area and zap the shite out of them."

28

A CHEAP SCORE

TABOR RAISED THE inhaler to the light and shook it a few times. "Proto-Oxy 9. A cheap mix. But a score nonetheless." He pocketed the stolen item and raised his eyes to the top of the building in front of them. "Let's go up to the roof and take a few hits."

"You really can't focus on anything for more than five minutes, can you?" Maesy asked, inwardly questioning why she'd agreed to go out with him at all. Normally, she'd spent port time in her cabin, enjoying the quiet of the ship while everyone was out on shore leave.

"Come on, Maesy, let loose a little! The *Emerald Queen* won't leave without us."

"Heh. You don't know Commander Lom very well."

"Fine, they might leave without me, but definitely not without you. In any case, free time is still free. It's not like we can do this stuff on board the ship."

"Do you really consider doing stolen drugs a good time?"

"Would you rather pay for something you can get for free?"

She rolled her eyes and sighed. "Whatever. Lead the way."

The truth was, drugs didn't excite her in any way. But Tabor had grown on her. At movie night, they'd watched an old classic horror about colonists trying to form a new town on a world with weird monster things—not the most romantic backdrop. Tabor had made his intentions clear, though; they'd wound up holding hands and done some groping in the dark, but that was it. She appreciated his attention, and especially that he'd respected her boundaries to take it slow.

Heading out into the large spaceport with Tabor probably wasn't the best idea, but he had a way of convincing her to step outside her comfort zone. Going to a rooftop to get high was definitely *not* what she'd had planned for the day.

Getting to the roof meant stairs—lots and lots of stairs. She hated to admit it, but her legs were like rubber by the time they finally reached the roof. 'Roof' was relative, of course, being in an orbital structure. A massive dome curved thirty meters overhead to encompass the habitable area of the concourse, ringed by starship berths holding craft ranging from small transports to colossal cargo haulers. The *Emerald Queen* stood out from all others, both for its size and unique design thanks to all its modifications. Within the habitation dome, buildings lined the concourse much like structures along a street in planetside cities. Were it not for the too-close starscape overhead, it would almost be possible to forget one was on a stardock.

Tabor walked to the edge of the tower and sat down letting his legs dangle over the side. Maesy hung back, appalled by his lack of personal safety sense. She elected to sit down inside the low barrier, with her back to the dock, and relaxed as she took in the view of the station. So many lights and colors, with billboards advertising everything imaginable. The colors flowed together into a brightly colored riot of activity. Views like this almost made her miss Lynaeda.

Tabor took a hit from the stolen inhaler and exhaled in a rush, sighing contentedly as the drugs took effect. After a moment, Maesy felt his hand bumping her shoulder, and she craned her head to see him offering the tube to her.

"That won't do anything for me. My bio-system and lungs are meant to keep me alive in a total vacuum."

"This is an oxy inhaler," he explained. "Pure oxygen mixed with a bronchodilator. You'll be fine."

"I'm not convinced," she sang, but took the inhaler and activated it as she inhaled deeply. She held her breath and marveled at the rush she got, like the world became wider and brighter, the sudden influx of oxygen making her dizzy. She let her breath out and sat there until the effect was gone. "All right, I'm impressed. Not that it was so great, but that it worked at all," she admitted.

"Tourists know how to have a good time."

As if on cue, the stairwell door banged open and two people exited noisily, a man and a woman. The woman immediately began squealing and squawking at the view. The man seemed merely bored and tired.

Maesy handed the inhaler back. "Tabor, we should go."

He turned around and saw the newcomers, snorting loudly as he took another hit. "What, you're afraid of a couple of early drunks?"

Maesy shook her head but stayed still. The woman had amazing curly hair, but something was off. Maybe Maesy was being paranoid, maybe she just didn't have much experience around Bases, but the newcomers seemed wrong. Why were they here? The view was impressive, but not something to fall into a rapture over.

Well, whatever. She and Tabor *had* only arrived a few minutes ago. And her dizziness from the Oxy hadn't passed yet.

The woman darted from one section of the roof to the other, oohing and aahing. Maesy watched her wander perilously close to herself and Tabor. Maesy was about to get up and pull Tabor away when the woman's handheld blared loudly.

The 'drunk' pulled out her handheld and answered. Maesy winced at the shrieking quality of her voice. "Kaia! Hi, honey, it's Mommy. Yes! No, we're still on our little trip. I'll tell you about it when I see you. Yeah, so we were wondering if Colin might have a ship that we could borrow?" The drunk woman stepped too close to the edge of the roof and her shin connected with the safety barrier. She stumbled and flailed. "Oops—gah!"

Maesy, terrified she was about to witness a suicide by idiocy, bounded to her feet and raced the distance between them in seconds, aided by her newly oxygenated blood. She lunged and grabbed the stupid woman's wrist, only to hear a wail of horror as she dropped her handheld... right over the side of the building.

The woman was neither grateful nor apologetic; just hysterical. She screamed and sobbed, lamenting the loss of her device as her male companion staggered over. "Oh, no! She'll think I fell to my death! I love my daughter so much, but she's a very high-strung girl. This is the first vacation we've taken in forever, she's not used to being alone," she moaned.

Maesy sighed and put her hand on the woman's shoulder, squeezing a little too hard and pulling her away from the building's edge. "I'm sure she knows you're fine. There are public kiosks for making calls every few hundred meters on the dock. That will work for you, won't it?"

"I suppose it will have to," the woman said. "I'm so sorry to trouble you with this. I'm really not so dull when I'm at home."

"It's quite all right. We have to get back, anyway," Maesy said, gesturing vaguely to the *Emerald Queen*.

"Is that *your* ship?" the male tourist asked.

"I don't own it. I'm the chief engineer."

The stupid woman squealed. "You? The chief engineer? On that giant starship? That's *magnificent!*"

Wow, she recovered from that tragedy quickly. Was the whole galaxy filled with people like her? No wonder so many Lynaedans never left their home system.

"Yeah, she wears it well," Tabor said, brushing hair out of his eyes. "We have to be going now."

"Right. Sorry to have gotten in your way." Maesy nodded and hustled to keep up with Tabor. He was much taller than she was, and his long legs were a distinct advantage as he practically flew down the stairs. He apparently didn't share her assessment of the incident, merely muttering something about tourists being everywhere.

She waited until they emerged from the building's lobby then absently looked around for anything that might resemble a handheld. She saw nothing. But then she wouldn't have, would she? A device like that would have shattered after that high a fall, wouldn't it? With so many people milling around, wouldn't someone have been injured? But there was no medical drone, no Enforcer, no injured tourist holding their head in pain…

Tabor was completely over the incident. "Come on. You said you wanted to go shopping, right? Commercial plaza is this way," he said, pointing the way.

It was true, a visit to the commercial plaza had been why they'd left the ship... but the weird quality of their encounter refused to leave her alone. "Didn't that seem strange to you?"

"Strange how?"

"I mean, out of place."

"I... I don't know. Maybe? But crazy people always show up at the worst time, that's just life. I know a story about one guy who went into a strange shop to buy a ship and walked out without his kidneys."

"Maybe. Maybe not." She tapped her comm and opened a channel to the *Emerald Queen*'s War Room. "Maesy to Comms."

Gallian's weary voice answered instantly. "Comms, go ahead."

"Gallian, put Commander Mench on the line. I think Tabor and I have someone tailing us."

—   —   —

Lee waited until the two people from the *Emerald Queen* had gone, then said, "What did you hope to accomplish with that exchange?"

Karmen held up her handheld. "These face captures. I'm sending them to Armin now so he can run them through the database. I think we've earned some fried leeca. Let's go back down."

"You palmed your own handheld? How did you...?"

"I've been using that trick on my kids for ages. If you flail your arms and look like you've thrown something, then everyone's eyes follow the trajectory. Most folks will remember seeing something fall."

Lee shook his head gravely. "You're an evil woman, Karmen Sley. Shouldn't you call Kaia back? She *is* high-strung and probably thinks you're dead," he joked.

"She knows I'm fine. I'll call her tonight."

—   —   —

Aura was bored to tears.

Usually, meetings between the self-styled Mesopotamians were done outside her purview. Today, they couldn't exactly refuse her participation because this was her ship and they were guests. That had earned her a seat at their planning session. Unfortunately, by two hours into the meeting, she was regretting ever wanting to attend.

Gil and Ham were here in the flesh with Sar and Ash attending remotely. The expectation was that the latter two were nearby, but no one had checked and with instant transmission via the stations network; nobody seemed to care. The meeting, which she'd been looking forward to, had turned out to be the most boring event of Aura's entire life. The men spoke about cash flows. About crew rosters and recruitment. About recent business purchases and sales. About which of the four owned what local politicians and who controlled interests in the various businesses in the sector.

Eventually, she realized something. *It's a measuring contest. They're measuring themselves and comparing to each other. That's all New Akkadia is.* It had nothing to do with freedom from the TSS or the High Dynasty oligarchs. Just personal ego waxing.

She was beginning to think that she was either the biggest dupe in the galaxy or an utterly awful judge of character when the intercom chirped for her attention. "First officer to captain."

"Excuse me, gentlemen. Aura here. What is it, Lom?"

"Captain, we've had a call from Maesy. She believes she and Tabor are being followed."

"Followed? By whom?" Aura asked, noticing the men around the table tense.

"She's not sure, but she worries it's the TSS. She gave us a detailed description of the individuals in question."

Aura swore silently to herself. "But no images?"

"Sadly not. However, we know their location: the hotel on the dock front opposite our berth."

Well that changes a few things, doesn't it? Aura had spent more than twenty years trying to hide from the TSS, but now was the time to stand up for herself. No more kidding, and certainly no more playing nice. "Acknowledged. Thank you, Lom."

Sargon's image made a rude gesture. "You see? It's started. From this point forward, the pushback is only going to get worse."

Gil bristled at his friend's tone. "I've got too much invested in this project to back down, Sar. Mother Carnage has a lot of fight left in her."

Aura raised an eyebrow at him speaking for her while she was still in the room.

"I am aware," Sargon continued. "By all means, keep hitting planets and making raids. While the Enforcers and TSS are looking for you and this ship, we can consolidate our operations elsewhere. If we don't start pulling the threads together into a rope now, we never will."

A rope you can use to strangle the galaxy, hey, Sar? "I agree," Aura said, gaining a satisfied wink from Gil. "My lords, it will take some time to gather my crew back to the ship. We have four days until departure, and requesting an emergency departure this close to a TSS ploy is sure to raise more issues than it solves. We also haven't taken delivery of our new TA-90 fighters yet."

Ash's image spoke up, "Tabor insists those will be arriving tonight. He's pretty good with his scheduling."

"Very well. Lord Hammurabi, once we leave Tavden, do you think Valdos can host us for a while? We'll need security people, and you have them. Plus, I think even the TSS would hesitate to follow us to a world filled with telekinetics."

Ham nodded slowly as he thought through the logistics. "I can do that. Plenty of teachers and acolytes to choose from, too. If you put together a list of how many you need and the required skill sets, I'll make it happen."

"You honor me, sir." Aura beamed, and Gil's smile lost some of its shine. "In the meantime, we need to identify Maesy's tail. I want to know if there are more Agents here. Incidentally, I have a couple of potential spies who've been itching to get off this ship for days." She tapped the intercom again. "This is the captain. Sacha and Callum, report to my office at once. I have a job for you two."

—   —   —

Karmen followed the enticing aroma of fried dough to an unassuming cart. The leeca vendor was a middle-aged man with a stentorian baritone and an endless well of apparent good humor. He welcomed Karmen and Lee with a huge grin and pointed out his menu. Without any hesitation, they each bought two trays of the fried treat.

Lee's eyes rolled as he bit into his snack. "Wow, that is *good*!"

The vendor winked at him. "I'm glad you appreciate it. I

get my stock straight from Tararia."

"Are you kidding? You'll be a sector-wide empire in no time," Lee said.

"I wish. My mother had a leeca cart on Aldria Station for years and years. When she decided she'd had enough, I bought the business from her and figured out how to expand it to enterprising merchants all over the sector. But they don't get their stock from the homeworld. Just me."

"You sneaky little genius," Karmen said.

The vendor laughed. "Madame, you do me proud. Here, have a jamba stick on the house. What the hey, your husband can have one, too," he said, brimming with joy as he handed the dessert sticks to each of them.

Lee sighed and accepted the gift and then placed a few extra credit chips on the side. "I grew up in fortunate circumstances. I know you aren't out here for your health. But I appreciate the offer."

The vendor bobbed his head and pocketed the money. "If I had more customers like you, I'd retire early."

"And rob travelers of this amazing food? I shudder to think of it," Karmen said around a mouthful.

The vendor gestured toward the *Emerald Queen*. "I wish the crew from that cargo ship felt that way," he said.

Lee and Karmen shared a brief glance. "That big old thing? Why? What have they done?" Karmen asked.

The vendor stared longingly at the *Emerald Queen*. "Nothing. That's the problem. I don't know if tech-heads just don't eat or merely don't eat from my cart, but they haven't spent a single credit here. They've been here for days, too. Some people just don't know what they're missing."

"Tech-heads, as in Lynaedans?" Lee asked.

"Oh, yes. We don't see a lot of their kind out here, and

there are a *lot* of them on that ship. You can tell by the eyes. They love their fancy implants. Believe me, that stands out."

"They're not giving you any trouble, I hope?" Lee said.

"Nah. They just keep to themselves. They'd rather not deal with us primitives. But they still need to eat, just not here."

Something sturdy abruptly collided with Karmen, sending her stumbling several steps. She spun around to see a woman with purple hair, matching ocular implants, and four arms. A subdued man sheepishly sidled up beside her.

"Excuse me, sir," the woman said, rounding on the vendor. "I overheard what you said about Lynaedans, and I take the greatest possible offense!"

The vendor backed up a step, his face awash with surprise. "Excuse me, ma'am. I didn't mean—"

"And my friend is offended too. Aren't you, Callum?"

Callum nodded vigorously, but his heart didn't seem to be invested like hers was. "Absolutely!"

The woman refused to let up. "And you're completely correct in your assessment. We think you are a bunch of racist, classist goons! Don't we, Callum?"

"We do!"

"And we would never stoop to paying you for cheap swill on a stick—"

The vendor recovered from the barrage of insults quickly. It was one thing to insult him, but insulting his wares was another matter entirely. "But have you ever *tried* leeca, miss?"

"Never!"

"You really should," Lee said. "This stuff is amazing."

The shouting woman fixed her glare on Lee. "Don't interfere in my business!"

Callum put his hand on her shoulder. "Come now, Sacha. Maybe we should give the nice man the benefit of the doubt. I mean, we haven't had lunch yet, have we?"

"Fine!" Sacha screeched. "But I'm certain it's awful."

Callum passed two credit chips to the vendor as he took one leeca for himself and passed another to his friend. They both devoured their snacks in seconds. "Wow, that actually was amazing," Callum said.

"It was," the woman agreed, and she scanned the menu. "What are jamba sticks?"

"They're delicious, is what they are," Karmen urged. "Very popular at Foundation University," she said.

Sacha froze for the barest second then said in a low voice, "Two jamba sticks please." Another trade of credit chips was made, and the food was devoured just as quickly. "All right, that *was* excellent," she admitted. "I apologize for my rudeness. And I will let my Lynaedan friends know that your food is delicious."

"Much obliged," said the vendor. "Have a wonderful day."

"You as well." She turned and made eye contact with Karmen, bobbing her head and blinking several times. "Excuse us," she said, and dragged her friend away.

Karmen watched the two Lynaedans go. There'd been something in their expressions that didn't sit right with her.

"Was that a random encounter?" she whispered to Lee, hoping he'd been able to glean more with his telepathic abilities. She knew that TSS Agents were forbidden from outright reading people's minds, but they were permitted to skim surface-level thoughts.

The Junior Agent glanced after the two Lynaedans, pointedly not looking directly at them. "Definitely here to scope us out."

Karmen sighed. "Well, this is about to get interesting."

— — —

Aura left the Mesopotamians meeting and double-timed it to the War Room. To her surprise, Gil tagged along. Upon entering the War Room, she flagged Gallian, but the Lynaedan comm officer was well ahead of her.

"Sacha just uploaded these images. What do you think?" he asked as two well defined facial images appeared on his display.

Aura suddenly found it hard to breathe. *After two decades they finally found me.*

She forced herself to calm down. Panic was the real enemy. "I don't know the man, but sunglasses indoors probably means an Agent. The woman is Militia Officer Karmen Sley, formerly of the warship *Triumph*."

"Wait, you *know* her?" Gil said.

"I do. I served with her for two years. She was an amazing first officer and friend." Her stomach lurched unexpectedly. *Karmen, what are you doing here?*

Gil waited for something to happen. When Aura made no further explanation, he finally said, "Are you all right? I need to get back to the meeting."

Aura nodded absently. "Go ahead, I have this. Listen, I think it's a good idea for you boys to stay aboard until I can deal with this. In here, I can protect you all. Out there, you take some very big chances."

"With Ham's Scorpions hanging around? Not a chance," Gil boasted.

Aura caught his hand as he turned to go. "I mean it, Gil. Do not leave this ship without my say so. All right?"

He rolled his eyes and squeezed her hand, then smiled. "Whatever you say, Mother Carnage."

Some days, Gil, you really make me wonder why I bother.

Aura turned back to Gallian. "Is Sacha still listening?"

"Yes, ma'am."

"Then have her relay this message, word for word…"

—   —   —

Karmen and Lee looked after the couple as they walked off.

After a few moments of deliberation, Lee thanked the vendor for his time and tossed another credit chip his way. "Now, what do we do next, my lovely 'wife'?" he asked as they left the food cart.

She probably took our photos with those mechanical eyes. We won't stay anonymous for long. Karmen grew hyper-aware of her surroundings, looking for others who might be keeping watch. It was amazing how after twenty-plus years, those instincts were still alive and well. "I think we've been made. No, that's not the right way to put it. I think we've been challenged to a duel," Karmen surmised.

"That's my feeling, too. All we can do from here is dance around them while they do the same to us. I think it might be time to pull the gloves off and provoke a confrontation."

"I'm not sure how I feel about that." Karmen sighed. "Actually, I do know. I don't like that idea. That whole crew will be running our images through facial recognition software any time now."

"If you have a better plan, I'm listening."

There didn't seem to be many options. They could follow Lee's instincts, or they could go back to Greengard. "Shite."

"I thought so. Let's pick up the pace before we lose those two in the crowd."

29

AMBUSH

THE PIRATES WANDERED down the docks, weaving through the crowd like they wanted to disappear.

Karmen kicked herself for thinking of Callum and Sacha in those terms. They weren't *pirates*, for stars' sake—they weren't even suspects, really. Karmen hadn't even seen them emerge from the *Emerald Queen*. At this stage, they were a couple of people who'd intersected herself and Lee and nearly posed a problem for the leeca vendor. It wasn't fair to consider them pirates, or criminals... not without evidence. But, at the same time, Karmen recognized a random encounter scope-out when she saw one. She'd pulled that move on others in the crew, and now they were playing it right back with this pair.

Even knowing that, she couldn't help but wonder what their story was. Were they an actual couple? Were they coworkers? Most of all, how did their captain feel about the relationship? To her memory, Aura Thand hadn't been particular about the *Triumph*'s crewmembers getting together on their off-duty hours. TSS rules allowed a range of behaviors. The only hard and fast rule she'd ever encountered was a practical one: leave any relationship issues in your cabins; there was no room for them at duty stations.

Sacha's purple hair stood out even if the rest of her didn't. She and Callum had gotten well ahead of them.

"Have you been able to get any more telepathically?" Karmen asked Lee.

He shook his head. "No more than the woman's hostility and the boyfriend's embarrassment. As much as I'd love to go deeper and get to the bottom of this, I'm not allowed to breach privacy screens unless there's an immediate danger. Two rude tourists getting in a food vendor's face don't qualify. Do any Gifted abilities run in your family?" he asked as they turned a corner.

Karmen quickened her pace. "Not that anyone has talked about. I have a knack for knowing when I'm being lied to, but that's more about training and experience than telepathy. How are you at mind reading—when the occasion calls for it?"

This time his voice was in her head, startling her for a moment, *"Not bad. I can drop thoughts into your head, but picking them up takes some concentration."* Then aloud, he said, "It comes in very handy when you have a field full of Agents and no comms to work with. But it's a close-range skill for someone at my level and experience. Now, the Primus Division elites, they can pick thoughts right out of a shielded individual's head from across a station."

Well, wouldn't that be handy. She tried to keep the thought to herself. While she respected Lee and valued his medical expertise, this assignment was quickly outpacing his scope of experience. The TSS' rationale for keeping the investigation to the three of them rather than bringing in a more senior Agent investigator seemed reckless for the potential severity of the issues. Then again, TSS Command had a reputation for playing their cards close to the chest. It was entirely possible that something else was in the works and Karmen's trio hadn't been read in on the bigger plan, so she knew it was best for them to play the role they'd been assigned.

Right now, that meant learning everything they could about the *Emerald Queen* and her crew. And these particular crewmembers weren't making it easy.

Karmen tried not to shove her way through the crowd, but it was challenging to make headway. There were so many colors and costumes and smells to distract her. As she took in all the strangers, she realized that any one of them could be an enemy poised to attack. They were already deep into a dangerous situation, and getting deeper.

"Hey, are you armed at all?" she abruptly asked Lee.

"You should already know this, Karmen. I *am* the weapon. But I also have that cool knife trick I told you about, so... You?"

"I have a Pinpoint in my pocket, which I scrounged from the shuttle's locker. It's tiny and it only fires once. But it will punch a hole through an Enforcer's heavy armor at very close range."

"Can you get to it in a pinch?"

"I think so. But let's hope I don't need it."

They stopped after rounding another corner. The way forward was an alley, of sorts—apparently serving as a loading area behind the row of commercial shops, servicing the docks. Sacha and Callum were nowhere in sight.

"Did they double back?" Karmen asked.

"If so, they did it perfectly. They aren't behind us, either." Lee took a few experimental strides down the empty alley. "There's nothing here," he declared. "They *must* have backtracked. We should—urk!"

It happened so quickly that Karmen barely had time to breathe. One moment she and Lee were talking to each other, and the next thing she knew she was off her feet, her back bent the wrong way. Her wrists were gripped by impossibly strong hands while another hand clutched her throat. With a squeeze of her windpipe, she was thrown backward against a wall. She could see Lee in a similar position on the other side of the alley, pushed up against a wall, his arm twisted behind his back, and held by… *nothing*!

For a moment, Karmen thought Aura or her mysterious companion Gilgamesh might have them pinned in a telekinetic assault, but she could feel the pressure points of individual fingers on her throat. She'd experienced the effects of telekinesis during her Militia training, and this wasn't it. "Who are you people?" Karmen gasped.

The air in front of her shimmered and flexed. Then, it melted away to reveal Sacha's hand around her throat, with two of her other limbs pinning Karmen to the wall.

Callum appeared behind Lee. He held Lee in an armlock, standing in the perfect position to snap the Junior Agent's arm at the elbow or shoulder.

Personal stealth shields. That's no small thing. Karmen decided to play it cool. "Well, this is embarrassing."

"Following strangers is very rude, Officer Sley," Sacha scolded, even using her free fourth hand to wag a finger at her.

Okay, the cards are all on the table. Maybe we can use that. "So, you know who I am."

"Of course. The great thing about a comm net is being able to plan strategy on the fly with all your remote resources at your disposal," Sacha said.

"You should know that we have images of you two, as well,

and the TSS has them by now, too. You probably shouldn't have used your real names in your little drama," Karmen said.

"Maybe not, but it wouldn't have made any difference," Sacha snarked. She tightened her grip on Karmen and used her free arm to frisk her. It didn't take long for her to find Karmen's handheld. Sacha made a show of flipping through Karmen's past calls. "Wow, you talk to Kaia a *lot*," she noted, before crushing the device to pieces in one hand.

Lee, now would be a good time to break free, Karmen thought in his general direction, hoping he'd be on alert.

Sure enough, a telepathic reply filled her mind, *"This guy has some kind of stasis field built into his armor. I could break through, but it would be messier than we want to get right now. Let's see if we can talk our way out of this instead."* Lee then added aloud, "Assaulting TSS officials is generally considered poor form. You're asking for a world of trouble if you don't let us go."

"Life getting a little too real for you outside the comfort of TSS Headquarters, hmm?" Callum asked.

"I'll admit, even the criminals operate with more decorum where I'm from in the Inner Worlds."

"Well, we don't all come from there," Callum said.

Lee turned his head to glare at Sacha. "You do. The highest tech in the known universe—or some of it, anyway. What do your fellow Lynaedans think about using your technology in this way?"

Sacha glared back at him. "That's true," she called, and then looked back at Karmen. "Back home, I was kind of a lost cause. Not that good in school, not pretty enough to stand out, and not from a wealthy enough family to buy the augments that would offset what I didn't get naturally. But, of course, I know machines. So, I could have stayed on Lynaeda and been a perfectly generic nobody, or I could leave and make myself useful to people who appreciated me. Like my shipmates. Like my captain. Now, we serve the Queen. Even a Base like Callum here serves the Queen. What do you two serve?"

"We serve the Taran people," Lee replied.

Sacha scoffed. "That's cute. You really thinking you're doing 'good work' and all that, don't you?"

"It's more complicated than that. We do what's necessary to keep the peace."

"Is that so?"

Lee's voice took on a prideful tone. "They send us in when planets start fighting—or threaten to start fighting. We're the last chance local governments have before the central authorities use punitive measures to keep the peace. A safety valve. Believe me, we're the better alternative."

"Lovely," Callum said. "That is just lovely. So, tell me Agent Safety Valve, what does the TSS do when a local dictator decides to throw half the population out of work because he gave a contract to his pals in the Inner Worlds? What do you people do when a manufacturing error in a giant assembly plant grounds a cargo fleet and stops food service delivery for an entire sector? What happens when the High Dynasties decide that people who are already struggling to make ends meet cut everyone's pay ten percent so they can build a new resort world for their family and friends? Can the TSS fix that? I'd love to hear a story like that."

For once, Karmen wished she had a pulse pistol, or even some proper telekinetic ability. All she had was her Pinpoint. Until she could find a moment to act, words were all she had to work with. "Listen, you two clearly have gripes about how things work, and I get that. I wasn't an Agent, but I was a Militia officer for years. I saw my share of stupidity, incompetence, and sheer ego, and not just from soldiers. It's one thing to recognize there are problems. It's quite another to make an effort to burn everything down."

"You mean like when the Bakzen burned down Cambion?" Callum seethed. "Four billion people just vanish in a puff of smoke one afternoon and nobody does anything. Where was the TSS then?"

"It was wartime. Not every planet could be saved," Lee said.

"And we're in a war of our own. The chaos is already here," Sacha growled. "We're just making a living."

"No, you're making a *killing*. Raiding Foundation City to hide the theft of nuclear mining charges? What was the point of that?" Karmen demanded.

"That's above our pay grade. Just like Cambion was above your pay grade," Callum said.

"I see," Karmen sneered. "You want accountability from us, but where's your own?"

"*We* aren't claiming to be heroes," Sacha insisted.

"Neither are we," Lee protested.

"I think we've established there are two incompatible worldviews here," Callum said. "Sacha, will you do the honors?"

"Gladly. Look over here, handsome," she called to Lee, who complied. "I've been instructed by my captain to give you a choice. Callum here can hand you his pack, which is filled with credit chips, if you walk away and forget all about Mother Carnage. Or, we break your bones as easily as I took those photos and sent them to my crew."

Karmen thought quickly and hoped that Lee's Agent training was up to snuff. "*I can shoot her*," she thought, hoping that he got the message.

Lee's voice filled inside her head. "*No, they'll expect that.*

I'll handle her. You shoot him. Center mass."

She could feel the shape of her Pinpoint in her pocket, and she lowered her hand ever so slowly to grab it. "A whole pack of credit chips. That must be heavy," Karmen said. "Mind if we have a look?"

"Callum. The pack, please."

Karmen slipped her fingers into her pocket and pulled the Pinpoint into her grasp. It was tiny; she doubted she'd hit Callum without grazing Lee. But her Militia training stood firm: when your Agent gives you an order, you follow it.

Callum dropped his pack to the ground, where it thudded in a vaguely metallic noise. Karmen eased the tiny weapon from her pocket, but she got distracted as Sacha used her free arm to reach behind her and pulled the pack up, her limbs somehow telescoping to extend themselves. The bag clinked again as she shook it at Karmen's face. "Walk away, Officer. And this is yours."

Karmen flicked the Pinpoint and took her best guess. "No, thanks." She pressed the trigger.

A bright flash and a male scream of surprise erupted as the Pinpoint's beam gouged the wall next to Callum. The laser did minimal damage to the building, but it did spray Callum's thigh with hot fragments from the wall.

Being hit with shrapnel broke Callum's concentration, forcing him to loosen his grasp on Lee, who finally made his move. He ducked down and spun in place, grabbing Callum's arm and slamming him into the wall face first. Then, he pulled him away and telekinetically flung him well down the alley way.

Sacha bared her teeth as she tried to make good on her threat to break Karmen into pieces, but her expression turned into one of worry then fear. Lee's telekinesis pulled her away from Karmen, who ducked down and moved away, holding her throat in pain. Sacha's feet left the ground, then all four of her arms began to twist and buckle, while Lee bent them into shapes they were not built to withstand. Finally, the Lynaedan screamed in obvious pain as Lee snapped her arms in numerous places, then threw her after Callum.

Lee rubbed his arms as he helped Karmen to her feet. "We should leave. I think we have what we came for."

Karmen found herself gasping for breath as she looked down the alley. She could hear Sacha's sobs and cries. "They need help," she murmured.

"*We* need help. We need to get back to the hotel and—"

"No! They aren't Bakzen. They need *help*. That's our job, too," she said, then turned and walked down to the place where their assailants lay.

Callum was sitting up, his hand hugging his side and his burned leg extended.

Sacha sat and sobbed, looking like a woman who'd been through war, her twisted limbs sagging and hanging all wrong. She hissed as Karmen approached. "Foking TSS! You bastards broke my arms! My *arms!*"

Karmen got her hands under Sacha's armpits and lifted her to her feet. "I know. Come, on dear, let's get you home."

"Hang on a second. Let me take care of this," Lee said to Callum. "Second degree burns. I'll bet that smarts."

"I don't need your help." Callum groaned as he tried to stand and nearly fell over.

"This won't take a minute." Lee pulled a small med-kit from his pocket and went to work. In no time, the leg wound was salved and set. Lee stood and offered a hand to Callum, who slapped it away.

"I'll walk on my own, thanks."

"Suit yourself."

Karmen and Lee walked their two attackers back to the *Emerald Queen*. It was impossible to avoid people, but Karmen was able to shield Sacha from the press of the crowd. Callum stayed close to Sacha, taking her from Karmen and protectively guiding her down the street.

Eventually, Lee asked a question. "Of all the losses during the war, why call out the attack on Cambion?"

Callum sniffed. "That was home. Family. Friends. Acquaintances. Four billion other people who I never met and would never meet in a hundred years. We just happened to be offworld that day. My father's job and such. He brought me along because I wanted to see the sights. Mom stayed behind."

"I'm sorry. You know, if you'd been there that day, you'd be dead too."

Callum let out a strangled noise that might have been a laugh. "Do you really think telling me that makes it any better? All I know is I can't ever go home again. My crew is all I have. I might just be the sensor guy, but I know everyone there has my back. And we're all just trying to make better lives for ourselves and each other. So, take that to your commanders, Agent Safety Valve."

The *Emerald Queen* loomed, and Callum maneuvered Sacha down the gangway to the vessel.

Karmen folded her arms against her chest, hugging herself as she watched them. "We could have done that better."

Lee whirled on her with an expression very close to resentment. "Kindly tell me how, Officer Sley," he demanded. "How did you *think* that was going to work out?"

Heat rose in Karmen's cheeks. Lee had been her friend and doctor, but now she felt the power in him that all Gifted possessed. She could almost feel an electrical charge to the air.

When she tried to answer, all that came out was a stammer. "I… hadn't…"

"No, you *hadn't*. Ever since we left Foundation City, it's been *Triumph* this and *Triumph* that. You want to give me pointers on how to do my job, fine. I can use the help. But if you're going to advise me then *advise* me. Don't just tell me that I screwed up after the fact. Tell me how to do better or just go back to your family. You can't have it both ways."

Karmen fought for some coherent argument, but she couldn't come up with one. Eventually, she gave up trying, wondering what she was doing here. "Let's get back before Armin falls down."

30

HELP IS ON THE WAY!

COLIN COVRANI WAS in the habit of spending his morning on the balcony. It was private—or private enough—to keep him out of his family's crosshairs whenever something unexplained happened. His fault or not, he was the one they would ask about it first.

He was in the middle of a breakfast sandwich when his handheld chirped for attention. "Colin! How are you this morning? This is Alden Warsen. Do you remember me? Your family has a number of accounts with us."

Gah, another blowhard. "Your name is synonymous with banking, sir," Colin said. "I know of you quite well."

"Good. I won't keep you long. But there is a concern that's come across my desk that I felt I had to share with you."

"Of course. What's your concern?"

"Well. Joi Coshin is no longer with our bank."

The news hit Colin in his gut. Joi was his personal account manager at that institution. She'd been with him for years. If he needed an advance for a purchase, Joi made it happen. When a bill dropped out of the sky, Joi would set up a payment plan. Joi was his banker, plain and simple. Colin didn't want to break in a newbie. Joi knew everything he needed. "What happened? When is she coming back?"

"I don't think she will be returning. She resigned rather suddenly. We will, of course, connect you with another account manager. We're honored to be of service to the Covrani family."

Uh oh. Trouble. Colin stood up from his breakfast table and began pacing the balcony. The movement would help him think through whatever dire scenario Alden was about to drop on him. "I'm sure. But that's not what you called about, is it?"

"In a way, it is. You see, as her supervisor, it fell upon me to secure her workspace. It seems there was a stack of unpaid bills with your name on them in her desk."

Oh, shite. "I don't understand."

"Neither do I. I believe Joi was trying to be protective. Whenever a payment came due and there wasn't enough in your account to cover it, Joi would take the record and put it in a private folder. She'd clearly been doing it quite a lot. The sum of those invoices became quite substantial, I'm afraid— many past due, in your name. Due to the nature of this, uh… clerical oversight, we covered them all, of course. But, that puts me in an unpleasant position."

"I see." Admittedly, Colin had never paid much attention to his finances. He'd fully deferred to Joi since that's what she'd been paid to do on his behalf. As the scion of a Dynasty, he'd had no reason to question his purchasing ability, and being frugal wasn't in the vocabulary of the highborn. Sure, he didn't have access to the full extent of the family's resources like his parents, but being in *debt*? That would never have crossed his mind as a possibility.

Alden cleared his throat. "Colin, let me be direct. For the past year, you've been making bad payments to people all over the sector. Joi covered you every time it happened. I can't guess why she didn't tell you, or me, about it, but it probably explains why she's no longer with us."

Colin's heart skipped a beat at the bank manager's choice of words. Surely they wouldn't *kill* one of their employees for trying to save a client's reputation. *Would they?*

"Here's what I'll do, Colin. You have one day to correct this *oversight*. Deposit sufficient funds to cover it all. I'll look the other way this time. If you can't, or won't manage that, I'm closing the account and sending a bill for the full amount to your mother. Am I clear?"

"Crystal clear," Colin croaked. He'd lost all his saliva. "How much do you need?"

"Three hundred thousand should cover it."

He felt wobbly. His stomach churned. He'd had no idea he was that badly overdrawn. "I'll do what I can right now."

"Good man. One day. That's all. Thank you for your time."

Colin spent the rest of the morning tearing through his financial ledgers and looked through his notes on the random investments he'd asked Joi to make over the years. Why didn't he keep better notes? There was nothing liquid enough to move with only a day's notice. Finally, he scraped up the only source of funds he could find: his separate savings account that he'd intended to cover the second half of *Decius*. He loved that ship, but he owed a quarter million on it; he'd already missed quite a few payments. But, there was more than enough money in that account to cover all the bank debts.

Gah! How could I be so careless? He was stupid; his cousins were right about him. Anyone worthy of his title would have been paying attention to their own interests and would never have found themselves so carelessly backed against a wall. He should just sell *Decius* and hope he made enough back to pay for the whole thing and the overdraft, but that would take time.

Wait… what I actually need is time. This wasn't just about finances. It was a matter of asset management, and that was a longer-term view than any number captured at a precise moment. He wasn't exactly *broke*, he just didn't have credits in the bank ready to transfer this very second. Bridging the divide between assets and expenditures was the whole point of credit and loans, right? He remembered that much from his tutors and textbooks.

A strategy started to come together in his mind. If he transferred enough to the debt account to cover all the back payments, there would be ten thousand or so remaining to carry him over until his next allowance. When that happened, he could just shunt the whole thing to the *Decius* and call it a day. The bank servicing the ship's mortgage wouldn't be happy, but fok those blood-suckers. They'd still get their money; it would just take a while longer. And, frankly, he needed to deal with the problem in his lap today. That meant covering the overdraft and avoiding his mother's wrath. There could be no separating those two events.

Even so, the plan wasn't without its risks. A repossession wasn't out of the question. However, that didn't happen all that often. It was a bad look for both parties—and no one wanted to draw the ire of a Dynasty. Still, he couldn't completely ignore the possibility. On the crazy chance it might happen, he didn't want his ship to be easily tracked. And he certainly didn't want it stored at the family spaceport. He needed somewhere to securely stash it in the meantime.

A chirp from his handheld threw him off-track. Kaia's

name came up in the ID. Her incoming calls would normally settle him, but he was filled with alarm.

Trouble. Something's wrong. He and Kaia kept up an alternating call schedule. She'd called him yesterday, which meant it was his turn to call her. And they'd kept up the pattern of exchange like clockwork for months. Something was off.

He initiated the vidcall. Kaia's eyes were red, and her brows were furrowed with worry. "Colin? Hi. I'm, uh, I'm freaking out."

Has she been crying? She had his full attention, the financial worries gone from his mind. "Wait. What's going on?"

"Umm… I got a call from my mom. She's on a project for the TSS, and she's… I think she's really in trouble."

Before he could pry any more information out of Kaia, she began wailing. He let her go on like that for a few moments, then did what he could to talk her down. "Kaia, hey, it's okay. Listen, just take a deep breath. I'm here. What can I do to help?"

Kaia took a while to orient herself. She took a deep breath, held it, and then let it out in long exhales. After several repetitions, she could talk normally. "Sorry, it's just been a lot this week."

"I understand. Now, tell me what's going on."

"Mom sent me a text asking if you could help get her a ship with a big gun. I thought she was just being funny. But when I called to ask her about it, she hung up suddenly, and she hasn't been responding to any more of my messages. I'm really worried."

A ship with a big gun in the shipping business meant a defense vessel. They were small and fast, needed small crews, and had turrets filled with weaponry as well as the ability to stay docked at a station for months. It was the sort of thing one sent with a convoy into the Outer Colonies just in case a rogue with an attitude tried something dangerous. "Believe it or not, I think I can help with that. Where was she calling from, do you know?"

"Tavdy? No, Tavden High Port."

"I know that place—it's practically a neighbor to Greengard. There's a lot of construction work going on there all the time. Do you know what kind of investigation your mom is working on?"

"She's chasing down a space pirate called Mother Carnage. Have you heard of her? She's the one who attacked Greengard, and now she's apparently on Tavden."

"Oh, wow. I didn't realize that's why she'd gone away."

"Yeah, we've been getting little bits of info over the last week. If Dad knows any more, he hasn't shared it with us."

"Parents like to think that they're protecting us when they don't tell us things, but it often doesn't work out how they plan." He smoothed his hair back, debating the best course of action. He could take *Decius*, but the transport ship wasn't armed at all. He might have to do something about that in the future, but for now, he needed another option. "I think I can get your mom a gunship. Where are you right now?"

"Me? I'm at home. Why?"

"Showing up with a gunship to surprise people who are already on edge is a great way to get into trouble. But if you're with me, your mom will believe that I'm there to help."

"Yeah, good point." She sighed. "Ugh, I wish she'd just answer my calls!"

"Well, if she did that, then you wouldn't need to come along. Are you looking for an excuse to get out of us finally meeting in person?"

Her cheeks flushed a little. "No. That would be really nice."

He smiled. "I'll be there in a day or so. Greengard isn't that far from Gallos. Can you meet me at the spaceport?"

"I… yes. Yes, I'll figure something out."

"Okay, good. I'll call you when I arrive. I guess I'll see you before long, then."

"Yeah. I'm looking forward to it."

Setting aside a wave of unexpected nerves about finally meeting face-to-face after all these months of talking remotely, Colin made some notes to himself. There were a thousand things that could go horribly wrong with any part of this plan. The whole scheme got crazier the more he thought about it.

What are you doing? You hardly know Kaia. You have enough problems just staying solvent as it is! Yes, no doubt about it, he was an idiot. The family moron. All the more reason to go through with this madness, he supposed. If he couldn't help a friend in need, what was the point? What was the point of anything?

Colin gathered his notes on his handheld and went to find his mother in her business office. Yelena Covrani was seated at her desk, a coffee in her hand while she read something on her screen.

"Mom, quick question, which server do we use to keep the files on defense ship maintenance?" he asked.

Yelena paused her reading and looked up. "On-world? Or off-world?"

"On-world."

"Server fifteen. You should know that."

"Thanks!"

He jogged to one of the open kiosks in the business center, pulled up files and schedules, and began sorting through the data.

After a while, Yelena came to find him. "Colin, what are you up to?"

"Finished your coffee already? I figured I had some more time to work on this before you arrived."

"I recognize your 'new project' energy. You work very loudly when you're grabbed by an idea, if you haven't noticed. Now, what's going on?" she asked.

Giving her the full truth was out of the question, but he could share enough to get her to let him work in peace. "I am sorting through the database to find a local SDS that I could use for a while." He located the maintenance section and looked through the queue. He spotted the perfect target. "Here we go! *Percival*. I actually know that one. Two triple turrets with lasers. Score!"

"No, *not* a score." His mother crossed her arms. "Colin, tell me what's going on, right now. Why do you want a gunship?"

"My friend Kaia has a problem. Her mother is working on a case for the TSS, and they need backup—"

"The TSS is perfectly capable of providing their own backup. It's not a good look for us to get involved with military matters."

"This is an undercover-type assignment. It's important, Mom. There's a pirate causing trouble, and that's not good for our business."

She frowned. "Even still."

"It's just one ship. No one needs to know it's in cooperation with the TSS. Just us doing our part to keep the shipping lanes safe. A system defense ship fits the bill."

"No. You are *not* flying off into nowhere with one of my Dragon-class gunships!" Yelena shouted.

Colin folded his arms and glared. "First, *Percival* is not a Dragon. He's a small model, a Wyvern-class SDB-200. Second, he's *already* in the queue for maintenance. All I'm going to do is borrow him for a few days to scare a local thug into submission. He'll go right back into the maintenance queue as soon as I get home. And by then, the TSS will owe us a favor. That'd be nice, right?"

She scoffed. "Who would even fly it? You?"

"Why not? I'm a decent pilot. My gunnery skills aren't great, but it's a TSS operation. I guarantee they won't let me near the weapons station if there's actual shooting."

"Shooting! Wonderful. Just how I want my son spending his time."

"I don't think it will *actually* come to that—"

"Don't assume. 'Never count on the TSS.' That's your grandfather's rule. If anything were to happen to you—"

"I'm not your heir, and nothing is going to happen. Look, I'll just be holding Kaia's hand while the soldiers do the real work." His mother raised an eyebrow at that. He quickly moved on. "There's really nothing to worry about. If the ship gets damaged, it's insured. You can even bill the TSS for damages! Everybody wins!"

"This concept of yours is not filling me with confidence," she said. "But it *is* making me wonder if you've gone insane. A Wyvern is designed for boarding parties and custom inspections."

He turned back to the console and pulled up a new data set. "No troops, but a lot of room to house them. That means buffer zones and a reinforced structure. It's perfect. It has just the right feel."

"I'm feeling something, all right. But I think it's rage," Yelena announced.

"Mom, I *have* to go. She's a friend. She called me for help. How can I not do something?"

Yelena pinched the bridge of her nose and took a few deep breaths of her own. "Colin, *every* woman who calls you wants something. You can't rescue all of them, and you shouldn't try. It teaches them to be dependent on you. That leads to bad outcomes. Trust me on that, I've been through it too many times with your siblings. Stars, with your *father*."

What can I tell her? The only way to make any headway would be to tell her what she wanted to hear. "Sure, I've made some questionable choices in friends in the past. This one is different, though. She's a lovely girl. Smart. Cultured."

"I'm sure she's adorable. But so what?"

That should have been enough to please any parent, but he knew his mother wouldn't be in favor of him consorting with someone who wasn't highborn, or at least from a wealthy family. Unless there were business or political connections that would benefit his family's social standing, his parents would consider the relationship irrelevant. But Kaia mattered to him, and he liked that she wasn't the sort who'd freak out because her soup was cold.

There was one more thing he could try. "Her mother's a war hero."

Finally, Yelena blinked. "She is?"

We have the ball. Run with it! "Yes! And her father runs the business school at Foundation University, on Greengard."

"He does?"

"You've been saying for a while that to expand our influence, we need pathways to the Inner Worlds. This could be an avenue for that. Think about it: 'my friend the university professor'. 'My mother-in-law, the war hero'!"

"*Mother-in-law?* You're getting well ahead of yourself, young man."

"Would that really be so terrible?"

Yelena sighed. "We are not having that conversation right now. But regardless, Greengard isn't exactly Tararia."

"Mom, do you have any idea how many graduate students from Foundation City go on to build interstellar empires? The kind of empires that *do* have direct connections to Tararia, and networks to dozens of other worlds with nearly as much sway. Why shouldn't we be taking advantage of those connections? Imagine it: a Covrani-funded annex on the Greengard campus. A Merchant Academy! People would absolutely sign up. We'd get a crop of newly graduated potential hires every semester. The talent will come to us for a change."

Yelena bobbed her head. He recognized the look in her eyes. She couldn't dismiss him out of hand without looking like an idiot, and if it actually happened… bingo. "You may be onto something with that."

"And all it will take to cement those inroads is borrowing *Percival* for a few days." He flashed his most disarming smile. "What do you say?"

"All right," she yielded. "I'll indulge you your knight in shining armor adventure just this once. I can even give you a pass with the shipyard when they call. And they *will* call. But when all this nonsense is settled, we're going to have a long, long talk about your future—or lack thereof."

"Yes, ma'am!"

"'Yes, ma'am', indeed. Go save your damsel." She turned to go, then stopped to look him over. "And, Colin… this wouldn't have anything to do with a call I got last night from our bank regarding your account being in arrears, would it?"

"No, ma'am. Nothing at all."

"I'm glad to hear that. Off with you. And please don't die. Funerals are expensive."

— — —

Callum stayed with Sacha until the moment the medical staff shooed him away from her bedside in the *Emerald Queen*'s infirmary.

The medical staff plied their craft with expert speed and precision. Callum felt more like he was watching a shipyard repair operation than a hospital. The med techs swaddled Sacha's upper body in heavy drapery that immobilized her limbs as well as her head and neck, then they hooked her up to a gadget whose purpose he couldn't guess at. But whatever it was, it worked: she calmed down and smiled sleepily at him as they folded her into a bio-bed.

Eventually, a tech sat him down and examined his burns. Her uniform's name tag identified her as Doctor Tendi. "Did you treat this?" she asked, noticing that the burns had already started to heal.

"No. The guy who did it treated it."

"That… okay." The doctor shook her head. "Anyway, it's a very good job. Just keep the dressing on overnight. You want something for the pain?"

Callum had to think very carefully about that. He tested the wound patch by pressing down on it. No pain, just a twinge. "I'm good."

"All right. If it starts swelling or oozing, don't be brave. Just come back and we'll deal with it."

"Got it." He stood up to see Sacha staring at him from the bed. Her eyes were half-closed; she seemed utterly relaxed. *How can anyone relax in a hospital bed?*

"What's happening to her?" Callum asked.

Tendi gestured to the equipment. "It's a Lynaedan quadrographic neural complex. It takes her neural impulses, modifies them, and feeds them back into her brain. She doesn't feel a thing."

He spun around, marveling at the empty status of the infirmary. Very quiet. "Seems a little lonely," he murmured.

Tendi took a moment to check Sacha's equipment. "For you and me, maybe, but not for her. That neural network they all take part in? The entire tech-head crew is in there with her right now. Like having a whole extended family surrounding her bedside. She's fine. Believe me, if anything strange happens, we'll call you."

Callum turned anxiously, unsure how to proceed. "You're not a Lynaedan, are you?"

"Nope. But I applied for a residency in a Lynaedan hospital and was kind of amazed when they accepted me. I'm fully qualified to work with cybernetics and bio-systems. That's how Commander Mench found me. He made an offer, I accepted." She nodded toward the door. "By the way, he wants to talk to you when you're done here."

"This is off-topic, but maybe you can answer a question. What's a Base?"

"I don't understand."

"When we were confronting those Agents, she called me a Base. What's that mean?"

Tendi hesitated and said, "She was just showing off. Don't worry about it."

Callum wasn't sure he believed her, but there was no point in pressing the issue. After brushing the hair from Sacha's face, he left her to rest.

Lom Mench was sitting in the waiting room. He nodded to Callum.

"Commander." Callum sat down hard next to him. "I don't understand why she's in so much pain. If it's just parts…"

Lom shrugged. "Parts which are wired into our nervous systems. If your arms were broken in multiple places, you'd be in pain, too."

"What happens now? Do you have spares for her?"

"In a manner of speaking. The problem is her arms were specially designed for her back home. It would be mentally jarring for her and unethical for us to restructure her implants without her consent. But I made a request of the captain, and she's assented. New equipment for Sacha will be waiting at our next port of call. I'm paying for it out of my own pocket, so it won't impact Lord Gilgamesh's bottom line at all."

"No, stars forbid Gil should miss a yacht payment." Callum stood up with a huff. He paced, hands stuffed into his pockets, thinking out loud. "The captain could have warned us we were going up against a telekinetic Agent."

"I don't think the captain knew who they were, nor their capabilities. You were a scouting party. Now we know what the stakes are and can tailor our response appropriately."

Callum barely heard him. "Bomaxed TSS. Not only did they abandon Cambion when they were needed the most, but when I pointed that out to him, that Agent just *crippled* Sacha and his sidekick blasted a hole in my side. Stars! I've never hated anyone so much in my life."

"You really do care for her, don't you?"

Callum nodded. "Yes, I do."

"Do you care enough to work for justice on her part? Justice for Cambion, too?"

"Absolutely. What do you think I'm here for, the paycheck?"

"Others are. Tabor certainly is."

"Not me. Not anymore. I want to hurt someone."

Lom bobbed his head and stood, putting his arm around Callum's shoulders. "Then let's talk about devising an appropriate response for their crimes against New Akkadia. You're quite good with sensor work. Have you ever thought about learning to fly drones?"

31

MISTAKES AND MISGIVINGS

STATION TIME DROPPED from afternoon to evening, and the shift in the *Emerald Queen*'s War Room turned over, but Aura remained at her post. Gallian stayed with her, plugging one request after another into the station knowledge base. The display with Karmen's face never vanished. Aura was studying it to the finest detail.

She groaned. "Karmen, what are you doing here?"

"It looks like she's following you," Gallian said.

Aura waved her hand. She'd drunk numerous cups of coffee this evening and had no patience left for sarcasm. "I know that. Tell me what I *don't* know."

"Very well. This is her service record. After the *Triumph* incident, there were a number of postings at outer world stations, and she was medically discharged a few years afterward. She gravitated to a few jobs on Greengard—"

"Greengard? Are you serious?"

"I am. That planet is a magnet for troublemakers."

Aura gave him a look of disgust, and his eyes dropped back to the display. "She got married to a teacher and had four children. They're all teenagers now. Great academic records and even a handful of awards for community service. It's a model family, by all accounts. A little nauseating, if you ask me."

"I can do without the commentary. Why is she on this station, Gallian?"

The officer swapped to a more recent file. "It appears the TSS reactivated her and paired her with these two men. That one is a Junior Agent, this one is a Militia Officer. Apparently, they were following us all the way from Diphous. At least that's what Sensors and I put together after figuring out which shuttle was theirs. And before you ask, it's the same one that spoofed us at Diphous. You can tell from that high-powered sensor dome. The profile matches."

But why her? Surely, there were other former TSS personnel to choose from. Aura couldn't figure out an answer that made sense. She'd checked her trail, and every contact she'd made had been compelled or bribed into silence. She'd spent decades building a network of crooks she knew she could trust with secrets. Had someone given her up? If so, then who and for how much? The sheer randomness of her former first officer's presence was enough to make even a former Agent extremely paranoid. "She's pacing us, learning everything she can about us and forwarding it to her TSS handlers."

"I concur."

"We need to leave. With any luck, Ham has already made arrangements to receive us on Valdos. Speed is our ally. Gallian, open a channel to Tabor."

"Right away."

"This is Tabor," he said over the comm. "What can I do for

you, Captain?"

"Those fighters I ordered. When do they arrive?"

"The first of the six should be here in a couple of hours. I just got the confirmation. With any luck, we'll have all six on the platform by morning. Then we just need to load them, and we can be on our merry way."

"Thank you. Captain out."

She relaxed a bit but couldn't bring herself to leave her post. Coincidence or not, the sooner they were able to leave this station, the better.

— — —

Karmen and Lee arrived back at the hotel room in a funk that lasted until sleep took them both.

In the morning, Armin was still at work, but now he greeted them with a cheerful grin on his face. "We got them cold. They're still in the station, and now they're taking on fighters. Looks like TA-90s. Isn't that great!"

Karmen noticed the empty coffee cups on the table and couldn't remember seeing them earlier. "Have you been up all night?" she asked.

"Of course. Someone has to get this stuff on file while you slugabeds get your beauty rest."

"Back up. How is taking on fighters great?" Lee asked.

"Lots of rules and regulations about moving combat vessels from one system to another. Do you really want to bet they aren't planning to sell those babies to the highest bidder?"

Honestly, I'm not even sure I know why I'm here. Karmen rubbed her eyes. "I want to check on our shuttle."

Lee grabbed a cup of coffee for himself. "How are you planning to get inside without your handheld?"

Karmen sighed, remembering the unfortunate fate of her device in Sacha's hands. "Well, then come with me. I think we need to talk, anyway."

"Agreed. Armin, are you all right?" Lee asked, then gulped down the coffee.

"Happy as a pig in slops. Hey, now that I think about it, there were two folks that wandered back last night and they looked really bad. Like broken bones bad. You two know anything about that?"

Lee set down his empty mug. "There was an altercation. We won."

"I see. You will be telling me all about that when you guys get back." A statement, not a question.

"You bet."

—

"I'm sorry I unloaded on you yesterday," Lee began as soon as he and Karmen were out of the room. "It was unfair and unprofessional. You were right. Those two pirates needed help. It's… just…"

"They're not pirates. They're Callum and Sacha. They're *people*," she countered.

"I know that. But… gaaah!"

She recognized the frustration. In a way, Lee wasn't that different from any of her kids. So young, and so full of expectation. And so unhappy to find that life had its own expectations and rarely delivered on plans or prayers. She knew how to handle it: keep silent and let him talk. "Yes?"

"I've spent my whole life learning how to put people back together again. So when I threw Callum down the alley and ripped Sacha's arms into scrap, I felt…"

"Guilty?"

"No. Not guilty. Not even ashamed. It was a feeling of intense satisfaction. Almost fun. I mean, I could have done anything else. I could have floated both of them off their feet and held them there until Enforcers arrived. I could have knocked them to the ground and immobilized them. I could have done *anything*, but I made a choice to fok them both up. I *assaulted* them." He shook his head. "Anyway, I looked in the mirror this morning, and couldn't figure out who was looking back at me. Is that normal?"

Oh, you poor boy. Nobody should have to learn how awful the universe is by realizing they were on the wrong side of an ethical quandary. Karmen kept her tone soft—the same one she used with her children when they admitted to a mistake. "Strangely enough, yes. It *is* normal. You've been thinking of yourself as a healer for so long you forgot that you were trained to be a soldier. You saw a side of yourself you didn't know existed. It's no wonder you're a little conflicted."

"Gaaaaah." His face contorted, and he turned away from her.

She placed a hand gently on his arm. "Lee, I didn't know what I expected when we left Greengard. I just know that boy, Callum, had a good point. What are we doing out here if we can't save the people who need saving? I don't think he and Sacha are awful, but they did some awful things. I'm not sure how to reconcile any of it."

"You think we should have just taken their bag of credits and looked the other way?"

Karmen laughed. "*No.* That wouldn't have solved anything, and would have made us complicit in an interstellar crime spree. We're supposed to be stopping that. Though that kind of extra money would sure be nice," she admitted.

"Ah, so you *were* tempted?" Lee pressed.

"No! Not seriously. But it's no small thing to be offered something like that when you don't come from a wealthy family like yours."

He nodded. "I can understand that."

"But all of that is beside the point. If you really want to implement a tactical withdrawal, I won't disagree. The fact is, they have an army and a warship. We have us: one Sacon Junior Agent and two desk jockey soldiers in a shuttle with no weapons."

"I'm thinking about it," he confessed. "Let's go check on our shuttle and file an update with Command. They'll want to know about what we've discovered."

—

The shuttle was where they left it and appeared untouched. However, the kiosk at the base of the gangway reminded them they had seven hours left on their current docking permit, and extending it would cost them more credits.

Karmen reached for her handheld and then remembered it was in pieces. "Add it to the company credit account?"

"Very funny." Lee used his TSS-issued device to pay for three more days of docking time just to be safe.

Once paid up, they went to inspect the craft. Inside, all was dark… until the heat sensors detected their presence and powered up the lights and consoles.

What a thoughtful little ship, Karmen thought. Then, she balked as she looked at the comm station.

She gasped. "Nine messages… That's Kaia's number!"

"She has the shuttle's comm info?"

"No! No, I programmed a forwarding service and linked it

to my handheld. It must have forwarded all her messages. What could she possibly want?"

"Did you ever call her back after our little episode on the roof yesterday?" Lee asked.

"Oh, *no!*"

"Right. We should listen to those messages—"

Karmen was way ahead of him, settling into the comm station. She replayed the recordings one by one. The first few were innocuous enough, asking what happened and why she wasn't answering. The seventh had Karmen almost in tears as she listened to her daughter begging her to answer. The eighth call chilled her to the bone as Kaia said, "Mom! Stay there! Help is on the way!"

"Great stars, what have I done?" Karmen moaned.

"Let's find out." Lee reached out to play the final message, sent only half an hour prior. The result surprised both of them.

"Hello, Officer Sley. My name is Colin Covrani. We've never met, but I've brought you some help. Please visit me as soon as possible. My ship is registered as *Percival* and is docked in this location…"

"That's along this concourse! Let's go see," Karmen urged. "I've been wanting to meet that boy for months!"

"It might be a trap. We've fallen into one of those already this week."

"That is true. But if this *is* a trap, it's the most fiendishly imagined one in history. It will be a joy to fall into it."

"Hmm. Let's get you a new handheld, anyway. There should be spares in the locker."

She searched their stores, located a new device, and synced its number to the shuttle's comm system as well as Lee's. "All right, ready to meet a fellow Dynasty brat?"

Lee shrugged. "Why not? His family probably already

ships my family's products all over the place. But I should report in first, in case it is a trap. Do you mind?"

Karmen shook her head and even made a show of putting her hands over her ears.

Lee put in a call to Agent Kalshi and waited while the connection went through. "Lee? Where have you been?"

"Building a case to answer your question, sir."

"Don't be cryptic. Just deliver your update," Kalshi ordered.

"Yes, sir. Agent Thand didn't rise from the dead... she created a new life, reinvented herself as a merchant. She's been trading cargo for decades, moving from one job to the next, making connections, developing a robust business network, and pairing with black marketeers who can provide her with the materials to build an empire of her own. I'm sending you all the data we have at the moment. And, sir, she's taking on fighter craft now. They're being loaded aboard her starship as we speak."

"I see. This changes things. Now that we have proof she's breaking laws, we can intervene. Where is she now?"

"At the Tavden High Port docks. We have her under surveillance. And, sir... they know we're here. We had an altercation with two of her crew last night. It's a good bet they know who we are by now."

"So much for stealth. Stay there. If we lose her now, there will be no one to blame but ourselves. I'll run this intel up the chain and get authorization to send backup mission support to you. Don't let that ship leave! Is that clear, Lee? That ship stays in-system at any cost."

"Understood." Lee cut the call and turned to Karmen. "Looks like we have a new mission..."

"I heard. Shall we go meet the boyfriend and see what kind

of help he's here to offer?"

"By all means. A guy who works for a major shipping company might have a clue on how to cripple a modified ore carrier. Because I have no idea."

"Assuming it's not a trap."

"Yes, assuming it's not a trap."

—

Percival didn't look like a warship to Karmen, even a small one. Maybe she'd been spending too much time with Lee and Armin, but its silhouette reminded her of a slice of pie with rounded edges. From a distance, she could pick out the dorsal turret, but the forward viewports reminded her of a pair of black, deep-set eyes.

Karmen had to restrain herself from rushing the last few meters down the concourse. *Calm down. He's Kaia's boyfriend, not yours.*

She tapped the entry plate and stepped back to see a young man barely her own height with jet black hair and eyes that were almost as dark. He looked to be close to Kozu's age. "Officer Sley, I presume? Of course, it's you. Kaia's got the same hair."

"That she does. I'm pleased to finally meet you, Mr. Covrani."

"Gah, no! I'm Colin. Mr. Covrani is my father, and my uncle, and most of my cousins."

"Fair enough, Colin. I must say… your arrival is timely. And quite a surprise. May I present Junior Agent Lee Tuyin."

"Pleasure. The bio-med Tuyins?"

"The same. I'm sort of a Sley household mascot," Lee jested.

"Mascot? You saved my vision!" Karmen declared. "You're family, young man, like it or not."

Colin nodded, hopping from foot to foot. "Getting here with Percy took some doing. But Kaia was worried about you. That's enough for me."

"I see. Very well. Tell me about your defense ship."

Colin passed through the open airlock and waved the two visitors around. Despite the rounded exterior design, the interior was essentially a long, wide corridor. The deck was easily twice as roomy as the entire interior of their borrowed shuttle. "This is *Percival*. He's a Wyvern-class SDB-200, which is one of the smaller models we use for convoy defense. The only reason I was able to get my hands on him at all was because he's scheduled for maintenance. His maneuverability is excellent, has an oversized power core, so it'll produce extra oomph for weapons. And this is the gold mine: a triple laser cannon mounted in dorsal and two ventral turrets with the best fire control you'll find outside the TSS."

"When do you need it back?" Lee asked.

"I can let you have it for two days."

Karmen walked around the deck, trying to impress every angle and curve onto her memory. "Lee, how many fighters did Armin count going into that ship's hangar deck?"

"Six. Oh, Colin, I forgot to tell you. I recently got the opportunity to start looking for contractors to help with delivering medical supplies for my family's biotech business," Lee said. "You guys do that sort of thing, right?"

"Yes, we do. Well, isn't that something. I guess you can hang on to *Percival* for as long as you need."

Karmen ran her hands along a wall-mounted display, which showed a detailed star map of the sector. "You came all the way from Gallos by yourself?"

"It's not that far. But I did have some help. Would you like to see the main deck?"

Uh oh. This had the feeling of a set up. Karmen glanced at Lee, who mouthed one word: trap. "What's down there?" she asked.

Colin shrugged. "Troop quarters and deployment deck, mostly. Below that is Engineering, the drives, environmental systems. A very small ten-meter passenger shuttle."

"This thing carries troops?" Lee asked.

"It's easier to show you." Colin strode to the rear of the deck, slapped his hand over an activator patch and stepped into an open lift.

Reluctantly, Karmen and Lee followed. The doors opened at the bottom, and they rounded a corner to a chorus of happy shouts and a couple of too-loud screams.

"Surprise!"

Elian, Kaia, Seandra, and Kozu were dressed in shipboard uniforms. They rushed to greet Karmen. She felt the air leave her body in a *whoosh* of surprise and no small amount of dread. Daveed stood back from the throng with folded arms, a wry grin on his face. He even gave her a perfunctory salute.

"What the fok?" Karmen gasped.

Colin waved her into the main compartment. "These are my troops," he said. "I thought I was picking up Kaia, but they all showed up at the spaceport on Greengard. And, well... more hands make a ship run more effectively. Besides, they refused to let me leave without them."

"Well, this is certainly a surprise," Lee said. His tone was impossible to read through Karmen's own shock.

"I don't know what to say," Karmen breathed. Then, her eyes locked on her husband. "Yes, I do. You. Come with me."

Karmen dragged him to a random cabin, which turned out

to be an empty billet for four soldiers. Two sets of matching bunk beds, a desk and chair and that was all.

She rounded on him as soon as the door closed. "What happened? You're supposed to be the adult in the room," she said, trying to keep her voice down.

"I still am. I made an adult decision," he said. "Look, Kaia came to me in tears after you hung up on her. She couldn't get you back, she feared the worst, and I have to say, I wasn't much better."

"You're not supposed to be ruled by a seventeen-year old girl's panic."

"I wasn't. I was ruled by my own panic," Daveed countered. "One call to say you were fine would have prevented this. So there."

"Guilty as charged." She sighed. "But that doesn't change that I'm on an official military assignment, and you can't just bring your whole family to work!"

"You getting conscripted back into active duty because of an attack on our home isn't the same thing as you going off on an official deployment."

"Daveed—"

He crossed his arms. "I made a decision, and we're here now. Kozu set Kaia straight on how rescue operations could potentially work, and the young ones refused to be left at home. I promise, we won't be completely in the way. Elian and Seandra are learning the ship's weapons, and Kaia is quite good in the comm position."

"Great, my young teenagers are learning the weapon systems! What could go wrong?" She resisted the urge to scream. "And, tell me, what are the men folk doing?"

"Kozu is practicing his command skills—he's already headed off arguments between the young ones three times since leaving port. I am learning how to read an engineering display. I need a lot more practice. But, hey, we haven't exploded yet."

She blanched. "What—"

He quickly corrected course. "I'm sorry. That was a stupid, thoughtless joke. It won't happen again."

"No. I…" Her initial surprise had morphed to anger and then to awe within a minute. They'd come running to her side the moment she'd expressed a hint of trouble. *Stars, I've missed them so much!*

Had she been an active-duty soldier over these past two decades, she may have felt differently. But the wife and mother in her was deeply moved. Emotion welled in her chest as she took her husband's hands. Then, she burst into tears.

Daveed wrapped his arms around her. "I'm here, my love."

She sniffed back tears. "It happened, and I couldn't stop it. Nobody could have stopped that stupid accident. Bad things happen. We can only deal with them and keep on flying. *Triumph* or *Percival* or Greengard, there's no real difference. What matters is being with the people you love. And I am happy you're all here. *Happy.*"

"You know, Karmen, I believe you are," her husband agreed. "I told you I would support you no matter what, and I meant it."

She cupped the side of Daveed's face. "You never cease to amaze me."

He smiled back at her, resting his hand over hers. "Now, what do we do next?"

"That's what we're going to figure out. I really don't want our children—or you—anywhere near this."

"Too late."

It *wasn't* too late. She could send them all on the first

transport ship back to Greengard right now. She should. But she also wasn't sure she had the strength to say goodbye to them after such a brief reunion.

No decision had to be made this very moment. She could enjoy their company for now—recharge before it was go-time. After her unceremonious conscription, she'd earned that much, right?

Karmen's mind began to sort through future tactics and strategies she could employ. Simple things that she had kept packed up for years. It'd been buried for a long time, but none of it had disappeared. Slowly, she was preparing for battle.

When they rejoined the others, Lee met her gaze. *"This isn't what I had envisioned,"* he said in her mind.

She nodded to him. "All right, everyone, listen up." She waited for her family to quiet down and give her their attention. "I need to make something clear. We're on an important mission here. This isn't playtime. If an adult gives you an order, you follow it without question. Lee is in charge, and his word is final. Do you understand?"

There were nods and murmurs all around.

"It's absolutely madness having children with us on a gunship," Lee protested telepathically. *"But it's your family."*

"We can't leave them here on the station knowing that Mother Carnage and her people are here," Karmen replied in her mind.

"True. Fine, they can come with us for now, but we need to drop them somewhere safe. Having them around is a distraction and a liability."

Karmen didn't disagree, but that was a problem for tomorrow. Right now, they needed to figure out their next move. As she was debating how to diplomatically tell her family that she needed to focus, she noticed a stack of crates.

"You didn't just bring yourselves, did you?," she asked.

Seandra giggled and bounced to an armored locker, then threw it open. "What, and be caught unprepared? We emptied the lockers you stocked at home."

"We have the auto-rifles!" cheered Elian.

Karmen wasn't sure whether to be proud or concerned by her children's glee.

Kozu rummaged in another locker and brought out a weapon the likes of which Karmen hadn't seen in years. "And we got a little extra. Turns out Colin knows people who buy and sell guns. Who knew?"

Karmen peered into the open locker. Sure enough, six heavy support weapons were stacked neatly in a shipping case. "Plasma rifles, Colin? Really?" Karmen asked.

The boy shrugged and scratched the back of his head. "You never know what to expect in the shipping business. I've bought and sold a few lots here and there. You locate a palette of something then find a buyer. It's like day trading," Colin explained. "I just happened to keep one case for myself. You never know."

Karmen pulled the plasma rifle from her son's grasp, checked the battery, and sighed. It did have a comforting heft to it. "I suppose that's fair. Colin, you mentioned a small shuttle down below?"

"That's right. Ten passengers plus a cargo deck but no cabins. It's just meant for surface to orbit pick-ups and drop-offs."

"Is it armed?"

"You know… I believe it has a single pulse laser mounted in the forward position. It's meant for self-defense."

"But it would give us three effective ships compared to Mother Carnage's one. The *Emerald Queen* is taking on fighters for her next engagement, and there's a good chance the big men now on board will stay there for the next jump. This thing might actually put a dent in her armor, which gives me an idea. Kaia, could you do me a favor and get Officer Armin in on a call?"

To the girl's credit, she'd already figured out the console and had the call placed in less than a minute.

"Armin here, go ahead," his voice came over the speaker.

Karmen explained what she had in mind. There were questions, which she answered, and eventually the group agreed to a plan of action.

"But before we do that," she continued, "Let's not have any illusions about what any of this means. You have no idea how thrilled I am to be with all of you again, but I'm also scared out of my mind that you're here. It's dangerous. If anything happened to any of you, I could never forgive myself. So, you're all going to stay far away from the action while Lee, Armin, and I take care of business ourselves."

There were disappointed groans all around the room. *They don't understand how serious this is. They're still thinking about it like a fun adventure.*

Karmen cast her sternest mom-gaze at her children. "I know you want to help. I appreciate that. However, it's my job to keep *you* safe, not the other way around."

"Sorry, Mom, but we had our own long talk about this before we left Greengard," Kozu said. "Mother Carnage attacked Foundation City. Our home. Maybe we're not professional soldiers, but we can stars-well help you deal with that crazy woman."

"She's not crazy," Karmen shot back. "Crazy makes mistakes. Aura Thand is many things, but she's not in the habit of screwing around. She's still a TSS Agent through and through. She's put together a coalition of professional thieves and combat engineers. She's *dangerous.*"

"Then tell us to go home, and we'll go. But you come with us," Daveed said.

"Yes!" Seandra echoed. "You did your time in the TSS. But if you think it's so bomaxed important for you to be here, then we're here with you."

"I could order you all to vacate and not come back," Lee said. "Armin and I can handle it."

"Except that's not true and you know it," Daveed said. "If you thought you could handle it alone, you'd be handling it, not dragging my wife along with you from system to system."

Armin cleared his throat on the speaker. "Listen, folks, I'm not one to interject my own garbage into people's drama, but I am absolutely opposed to civilians getting in the thick of things. Especially children—however eager and capable. You want a 'no' vote, you have it. I don't think any of you will be anything but a liability. You're not trained or experienced. Enthusiasm and a crash course in handling rifles isn't enough. That's all I'll say on this subject."

Seandra waved her arms for attention. "Okay, one vote 'no'."

"*Two* votes 'no'," Lee corrected. "Armin has the right idea here."

"But come on! The three of you just aren't enough to knock a giant starship out of the sky no matter how awesome you all are. You can't even shoot the ship's weapons and fly at the same time. You need a crew. Guess what? *We're* your crew," Seandra urged.

"Seandra, one day you're going to make an excellent lawyer," Armin sneered. "A space battle is no place for a bunch of teens."

"What space battle?" Kozu asked. "You need to keep the bad guys in-system, that means shooting out a jump drive. *Percival* has the tools for that."

"And we've been using every system on this defense ship," Kaia said. "We can carry out any order any of you might give."

"How about we let people with actual training and experience do the work? Can you follow that order?" Armin pushed.

"Armin, that's enough," Karmen said. He'd made his point. He was acerbic and annoying, but he wasn't wrong. Ultimately, though, this wasn't her command. "Lee, it's your call. You're the Agent here."

"*Junior* Agent."

"Oh, I think you've qualified as a full Agent, at least for this mission. You *are* in charge. What do you want to do?"

—   —   —

Lee had found himself at many critical decision points throughout his TSS career, but he knew this moment would be one he'd reflect on many times in years to come.

The smart decision was to send Karmen and her family away. He'd grown to care deeply for all of them during their months together, and their well-being meant as much to him as his own kin. At the same time, Karmen was a critical player when it came to facing Aura Thand. Her insights into the former TSS Agent and their prior friendship may well hold the key to finding a resolution to this conflict.

Lee met Karmen's gaze, gleaning the thoughts scattered across the surface of her mind. He sensed her joy in being reunited with her family, her fear for them, but also her admiration for their courage. She was fueled by their presence.

"I want to send them to safety, but will I lose you if I do?" he asked her.

"They attacked my home, Lee," she thought back to him. *"The only place I'll feel they're safe is if they're with me. I would have made Aura a godmother to my children, but I don't trust Mother Carnage not to kidnap them and hold them against me as leverage. They don't need to be at the battle stations. Would having them here in the crew quarters of the ship be so bad?"*

He didn't have a good counterargument to that point. Anything he could tell her would be speaking as a TSS officer, not a parent. She hadn't chosen to come on this mission, and it wasn't fair to drag someone out of retirement. But the fact was that he needed Karmen if he was going to face Mother Carnage, and having her family with her would keep her at her best. TSS Command would likely disagree with that call, but he knew Karmen better than them. He knew her family. As inconvenient and uncomfortable as it was, Karmen was a package deal with her loved ones.

Lee was acutely aware that his TSS graduation was on the line with this mission. It was risky to take on a former Agent on his own, even one who was likely out of practice. They were so close to stopping the *Emerald Queen* and bringing in Aura Thand. That success would be his path to being a full Agent.

I hope I don't regret this. Lee drew a steadying breath and let it out slowly. "You can stay on the ship—as observers," he declared.

"Actually…" A plan started to form in Karmen's mind. "There might be a way you can help."

32

SHE'S A PIRATE!

"Bet you fifty credits that Karmen's kids choke if we come under fire," Armin said from his EWAR console, making adjustments to the programs he intended to use.

Lee rolled his eyes. "Piss off."

"What? You want to risk both our lives on their awesome fighting skills?"

"Not at all. We're risking our lives on *your* ability to spoof that big ship's sensors and weapons. Are you up to that?"

Armin bristled. "Totally."

"You sure? I mean, all you've done is take photos from the hotel room and mess with databases. Are you in any shape to be my EWAR officer?"

"I know what I'm doing. You *know* I know what I'm doing," Armin said. "But do you? Have you run this crazy plan by TSS Command?"

"The highlights. If Karmen's idea about locking that pirate ship into its berth long enough for our backup to arrive works, then we won't need them to do anything but look out the windows."

"I'm well versed enough in how industrial machinery operates to think it will work. It's my programming, after all. But it's not guaranteed. Did you tell them the parts about Karmen's kids coming along and having a role if it doesn't go as planned?" Armin pressed.

"This is my mission to run, and everyone involved knows the risks. Personally, I'd rather those kids know how to operate the gun turrets in case things go sideways rather than have them cowering in a bunkroom."

"Inexperienced crew can be more dangerous than no crew at all."

"We'll all know our roles and what to do in contingencies. Just like I know that those pirates won't expect us to make a move like this. As far as I'm concerned, we're on more or less even ground."

"I'm not convinced."

Armin sat with his arms folded. He had serious doubts about all the Sleys. The oldest was training with gunnery simulation software with Karmen 'just in case', and he supposed that was all right. Maybe the boy could shoot straight. The essence of lining up shots and pulling triggers on the boost was one of timing and hand-eye coordination. Like a video game. They trained sharpshooters with simulators at the Militia Academy so at least he understood that.

"It's the young one I worry about," he continued. "Elian. The kid's got the right attitude but… he's young. He's anxious. There's a reason we don't usually have children as an integral part of our tactical plans."

"We'll get the job done," Lee insisted.

"I think he wants to show off—he's so eager to stand out

from his siblings. That can get you in trouble. It can get you killed."

"Ah. You *like* the boy," Lee intuited.

"Maybe a little," Armin admitted, though that had no bearing on his concern. "He's got a solid eye for engineering, I'll tell you that much. But he gets ahead of himself. He's a long way from understanding the hows and whys of a space station's docking system."

"He showed he can do his task. You agreed to show him the ropes because 'it was so easy a child could do it'," Lee recalled.

"That doesn't mean a child *should* do it. But I was overruled." Armin sighed as he tapped a display to check the system status. "Linkage feed is… locked. As long as he enters the codes I gave him into that docking service kiosk in the correct order, it'll work. I'll pull the trigger from here, the emergency docking clamps in her berth will lock and stay locked. She won't be able to launch without tearing the docking platform in half, and Mother Carnage won't risk her ship to do that."

"So, we're good to go?" Lee asked.

"*I'm* good to go. Just saying that I didn't sign up to be a babysitter."

"There are some worlds that have kids as young as Elian in military service. They train with small arms, they defuse bombs, they dig land mines out of fields and plant them in others. Not all of them are volunteers."

"So, find me a platoon of ten-year-olds who can lob grenades accurately, we'll have a real chance."

"You're all kinds of awesome, bud," Lee sighed.

"I know my job, Lee. I just hope the Sley kid knows his."

— — —

Elian Sley stepped outside *Percival*'s outer airlock and unfolded his scooter, a reliable battery-powered form of local transport he'd brought with him from Greengard despite Kozu's complaints. Ultimately, Colin had allowed him to stash the two-wheeled scooter in the ship's locker. That made Kaia's boyfriend as cool as anything in Elian's book.

The truth was that Elian had always wanted to know if it was possible to completely tear up the interior workings of a proper space station. He expected there were countless ways that anything as complicated as a city in space had to work properly to make life in orbit possible. He'd learned firsthand recently that even a city on a planet could collapse pretty quickly if the power went off for long enough. But how it worked was something he'd only known about through books, a few classes at school, and what tutorials he could find on the Net.

He was knowledgeable enough to understand the meaning of the term 'engineer', but he'd never tried to apply it to his own interests. To him, an engineer was someone who built things. Buildings, houses, bridges, skyrails, starships, space stations. He'd never stopped to think that the folks who destroyed all those things for a living were also steeped in the lessons of engineering. It was all math and physics, the principles of loads, stresses, and the strength of materials.

One thing Elian learned was that while he liked and respected Agent Lee, he was obsessed with Militia Officer Armin. That guy was into chaos. Blowing things up. Screwing around with the functionality of life. That was killer. Yes, Armin had no real sense of humor, but he knew how the pieces fit together and also knew how to blow them apart. That suited

Elian just fine.

But there was a trick to getting close enough to deal the damage, Armin had explained. You couldn't be obvious. You had to go about your day.

Elian had an excursion already planned. He scooted down the docks, weaving in and out of the knots in the crowd. He spent the credit chips his father had given him for that purpose. You couldn't go into a commerce area and not spend money. That looked strange. He decided the fried leeca vendor was as friendly as his mother had told him, but the leeca itself wasn't that great. The jamba sticks, however, were so good he bought three and inhaled them on the spot. He toured gadget shops whenever he found one, and there were plenty. He put down credits for trinkets, a cheap folding knife, and something that might have been a bottle stopper or a nose plug—he wasn't sure—but it was a shade of blue he fell in love with; it was only five credits. He tried to get girls to look at him in the commercial plaza, and a few obliged.

Elian noted the time and decided he'd done enough browsing. The real mission awaited, and the pirate ship could leave at any time.

He worked his way down the starship berths and spent some time looking at each of the docking kiosks. It was crazy to think that all of these controlled so much. And anyone had access to them. Even him.

He struck up conversation with crew members who made adjustments, and they were happy to trade a few words with him as long as he seemed enthusiastic about their work and their lives. He offered nothing about himself except to say his family was waiting for clearance to leave a little early.

Finally, he arrived at his target: the *Emerald Queen*. The gigantic ship easily lived up to her name. He propped his scooter up against the kiosk and began entering numbers. *There we go: sequence one, done.*

All at once, he felt someone behind him. "You shouldn't be doing that."

Elian glanced over his shoulder. A girl, a little older than he was. "Shouldn't be doing what? Checking the berthing logs?"

"You shouldn't be messing with it at all. And that's not the berthing logs. That's the docking status app."

When in doubt, distract them with questions, Armin had said. "Hey, I'm Elian. What's your name?"

"Billie. Get lost, Elian."

"You're not even old enough to be crew on this giant ship. Hey, you're not even as old as me, are you?"

"Are you serious? What are you, ten?" Billie sneered.

"I'm thirteen!" His voice cracked as he punched in more numbers. *Sequence two done!*

"Congratulations, and I'm sixteen. Get. Lost. Or I'm calling the docking master."

"You know what? Go ahead. Call the docking master. My mom is a TSS Militia officer. I would love to see how that would play out." He punched more numbers. *Sequence three, done!*

"What?"

"In fact, let's go talk to the docking crew right now," Elian lied and thumbed Armin's number on his handheld. "Hey, docking master? Yeah, listen there's this weird girl at Berth 385, and she's touching the kiosk. Do something!"

"That's not true. Stop that!"

"Get lost, Billie!"

Elian thumbed the handheld, slammed his hand on the kiosk actuator and waited a second for a confirmation chime as the new program began to run. Billie made a clumsy attempt to grab him, but he easily leapt onto his scooter, started the motor, and zoomed off.

Wow that was fun!

—   —   —

"Docking master? What was that all about?" Lee asked.

Armin pulled the handheld away from his ear and checked the status board. He didn't know how to answer Lee's question. He'd expected some weird stuff from the youngest Sley but nothing like a nonsensical call.

At the same time, he couldn't simply ignore what his console told him. "He did it! Not bad for a little goofball." He confirmed the entries on his screen. "Let's get this party started... Linkage synced. Alternate program loaded, and... boom! *Emerald Queen* is here to stay until we release her."

—   —   —

Callum jumped when Aura entered his field of vision on the observation deck. "Captain?"

She hid her satisfaction at the knowledge she could still sneak up on a crew member when she had to. "Callum, I didn't expect to find you up here. Is there an issue with your console in the War Room?"

"No, ma'am. I was finding it very distracting to work down there, with everything currently going on. I asked Commander Mench if I could relocate. He approved."

That figured. He was worried about his girlfriend. A pang of guilt wavered through her core. *I probably shouldn't have sent them against a TSS Agent without warning.* "All right, then, carry on. I suppose I should mention that I stopped in to check on Sacha."

Callum's full attention was suddenly on her. "How is she?"

"No change. Still asleep, still hooked up to that neural wave complex. I had Lom confirm that the equipment he ordered for her will be on Valdos when we arrive. She'll be well cared for. You have my word on that. How are *you* doing?"

"I came up here to concentrate on work, but I'm still angry. Confused. I understand tossing us around, but the way they snapped all of her arms like that? What was the point? Why would anyone do that?" Callum asked.

Why would a TSS Agent abandon her duty, her friends, and her career to pursue a life of crime under an assumed name? Aura draped her arms over the back of the command chair. "I expect because he could. The TSS trains its Agents to neutralize any threat in whatever way is most effective. I think he just went with ingrained habit."

"Some habit."

He was stewing. She'd seen it before on other crew and done it herself more than once. She strolled up to him and tapped the console to get his attention. When she had it, she said, "Callum, it's easy to forget when you're living in a two-hundred-meter-long tube, but what we're doing—breaking rules, stealing property, kicking in doors—it's dangerous. People get hurt. Some will die. No matter what happens, if you're going to be here, you need to be someone this crew can count on. I need to be able to count on you. Can I?"

"Of course, Captain."

"Good. Now, tell me why the docking linkage indicators are red when they should be blue."

"Yes, ma'am. Sensors to Ops."

"Ops here, go ahead." Aura saw him wince as the Operations Officer's baritone came over the intercom; this was

Sacha's shift, but with her in the infirmary, it was obviously not her voice.

"Ops, I have a red indicator on the station docking clamp linkage module. Looks like the emergency docking clamps have engaged."

"Stand by... It looks like someone manually entered an emergency reset on the docking permission kiosk in our berth. It wasn't anyone from the War Room. I doubt it was anyone on this ship. I'm trying to cancel it, but it's not taking."

"We're on this station six months for repair and redesign, nothing happens," Aura groused. "We come back for five lousy days, and it's been one problem after another." Aura's mind was already working the problem. "'Manual data entry', he said. Which means it didn't come in by way of the shared data network or its backbone. Show me the docks. The area outside the ship."

Callum complied, pulling up a number of displays to show her the various views between the *Emerald Queen*'s prow and the docks with all the buildings and shops.

"There! Zoom in on that," she ordered, indicating one of the video feeds.

Callum threw data between screens and focused on what Aura had seen. A single person moving away from the vessel. A boy on a high-speed scooter.

"Now, run it backwards," she instructed.

Callum applied the filter. Sure enough, the kid had done something to the kiosk. One of the crew had apparently tried to stop him.

"Where are you going, little boy? And what would your mother say if she knew what you'd done?" she mused. *Seriously, Karmen, what are you teaching your children?* "I think it's safe to assume the TSS is making their move right now. We need to leave immediately."

"Emergency docking clamps are not like struts we can just cut away with torches, Captain."

"Understood, but that's not what I'm thinking. Captain to Engineering."

"Engineering, this is Maesy."

"Maesy we have an issue. Our berthing kiosk was reset to engage the emergency docking clamps. We need to leave this station before TSS reinforcements arrive. What can you do?"

"Let me confer with my staff. Stand by." The wait was thankfully brief until Maesy returned with her report. "Captain, one of my crew saw what happened. Some kid messed with the kiosk, and she thinks she knows what he did. We can try to reverse engineer a solution from here."

"How long will that take?"

"I can't say. An hour. Maybe two."

Aura dug into her memory and realized there was at least one TSS base an hour's jump away. "Every minute we stay here is dangerous. What else can we try?"

"I can load a new program into the docking computer to initiate an emergency departure. When faced with damage to the station or letting the ship go, the automated system should choose the latter. I don't know if it will work, but I know how to do it quickly."

"Make it happen, Chief Engineer."

"Yes, ma'am. Setting up the code now… implementing the new instructions… and execute!"

An alarm blared as the ship's computer began a digital dance with its counterpart on the station. The two machines were disagreeing about the *Emerald Queen*'s docking status.

"We'd do better dealing with them in space, anyway," she murmured, and opened a channel to the War Room. "Gallian!

Tell all crew members they have two minutes to get their hides back to the ship or they'll be stranded here."

"Aye aye, Captain."

"Captain to Lom, how long will it take to prepare those fighters for launch?"

"At least a day. They need to be configured and the components tested. The weapons aren't loaded. And our pilots will need time to familiarize themselves with the craft."

Fair points, every one, but it still burned her sensibilities to have been prematurely forced out of the station by a tween. "Understood. Captain out." She sighed. "Well, that's just lovely." She tapped her forefinger against her arm as she waited.

"Engineering to Captain Aura!"

"Aura here."

"Captain, it's working. The emergency docking clamps are retracting. We can leave on your orders."

"Captain, all sections report crew are accounted for," Gallian reported. "Ready for departure."

"Get us out of here."

33

FORMING UP

ARMIN PULLED UP a display on his console and blanched as warnings began flashing. The linkage feed had stopped abruptly, but he was watching through a visual camera feed, as well. Sure enough, the *Emerald Queen* was closing its hatches, and the gangway was retracting. "Oh, no, no, no! Fok! I don't believe it. It was working. It was *working*!" Armin shouted.

"What's happening?" Lee demanded.

"That bomaxed pirate crew figured out what I did and came up with a workaround. They'll be back in space in minutes!"

"Fok!"

"We only have a few minutes before they'll be far enough from the station to jump."

"We'll have to give chase and disable their jump drive. There's no other choice. Our relief won't be here for an hour, at least." Lee opened a commlink to the *Percival*. "Bad news. The *Emerald Queen* found a way to override the docking lock.

Is your young spy back on board yet?"

Colin's voice came through like he was sitting in the same flight deck. "That's affirmative, Lee."

"Good man, Captain Covrani. We need to enact our contingency plan to prevent the *Emerald Queen* from jumping away."

"We're on it!"

Armin initiated the launch sequence for their shuttle. "I'm going to be really pissed if this is how I die."

— — —

"All right, everyone to your cabins!" Karmen ordered.

No one moved from their seats on the flight deck.

"Or… you can just let us do what we've been training to do," Seandra countered. "If we're on the ship, anyway, is it any more dangerous for us to be up here than—"

"It's not about that," Karmen cut in.

"Then what?" Daveed asked. "You can only do so many things at once, Karmen. Isn't having more eyes and hands what you need right now?"

"I don't have time to argue." And, admittedly, she didn't have a good counterargument. There was no way around their need for the *Percival*'s guns, and it was true that her family would be on the ship, regardless. They had a better chance of making it through the engagement if all stations were covered. "I'm going to take the shuttle out. The *Percival* is Colin's command. He can crew it how he wants." Karmen stormed off the flight deck.

Kozu ran after her. "I'm coming with you."

"No—"

"Mom, one person can't fly a shuttle and shoot effectively

at the same time. It's not a fighter. You need a gunner if that ship is going to be any use in a firefight."

"Fine," she yielded against all better judgment. "And, for the record, you're a terrible influence on your siblings."

— — —

Once in space, the flight crew needed instructions, and Aura lost no time giving them some. "Captain to Nav. Let's plot a holding orbit of ten kilometers around the station. If our visitors want to cause a scene, let's not give them far to run."

The electronic voice of Lom's Meklife drone answered from the comm. "Captain, I suggest you report to the War Room."

"Negative. I'll stay on the observation deck with Sensors. Route all communications through the shared network."

"As you wish."

"New vessels just launched from the space station," Callum said. "They're taking up positions behind us."

Thank you, Karmen, for being so bomaxed consistent. "What are they bringing?"

Callum took a moment to verify his readings. "A system defense ship, which just launched a very small auxiliary vessel. And that same surveillance shuttle we've encountered before. All three vessels are taking up positions on our rear."

Aura toggled the comm. "Captain to Nav. Lock in our jump course to Valdos III. Give us a wide avenue on our route to the jump point in case we need to evade fire."

"Nav, acknowledged."

"An escape route against *those*?" Callum scoffed. "Captain, they're toys!"

"Maybe. But Karmen Sley is skilled aboard a warship, and

that makes her dangerous. I doubt she filled that gunship's weapon turrets with popcorn and peanuts. I'm not looking to fight, but if they start one, we must finish it."

—   —   —

Lom watched the monitors from his position in the War Room and lamented the fact that Callum and Sacha were not there with him. The Ops officer on watch was competent, and Callum was on duty, but there was a lack of efficiency in play here. The routine and familiarity Callum and Sacha had spent months developing was gone. Now, it was just a matter of Lom giving orders and waiting for results.

The system defense ship irked him most of all. It wasn't much more than a long shuttle with weapons turrets, but the fact that his records identified it as a troop carrier as well filled him with a deeply unpleasant feeling. He was nervous. It had been years since he'd felt this way. Logically, he shouldn't feel nervous; he had a ship filled with weapons and crew who could double as troops in a pinch. But he couldn't know what this adversary had planned. *Have I become that predictable in my old age?*

There was one thing he could absolutely do to assuage his nerves, and he tapped the comm. "Lom to Captain. I'd like to turn out several flight drones. Just in case."

"Permission granted. Be careful—we may have to jump abruptly."

"Understood." He ended the commlink. "Gallian, maintain the neural network at full bandwidth. We're dropping drones in their path."

"Yes, sir!"

Lom made his way to the lower decks. The drone pilots

were already prepping themselves for deployment, but Lom waved them off after checking the status board. He'd be flying solo this time. "We have one flight drone ready for combat, and I'll be taking it out. Make the Idolons ready for a boarding action. I think this is going to get more interesting than we bargained for."

He stepped into his control dock without further comment. The machinery took over, placing his Meklife drone into storage and transferring his consciousness into a flight drone on the hangar deck.

Lom awoke within the tiny starfighter, flexed his control surfaces, and primed his weapons. He lit the pion drive and launched the small combat craft through the hangar force field and out the open door.

Soaring freely, he prepared to take on the gunship.

—   —   —

Lee increased the shuttle's speed just enough to begin closing the distance between it and the *Emerald Queen*. Without ordering it, the other two spacecraft were following his lead, keeping pace with him and moving into their respective firing positions. "Good job, guys," he murmured. "Armin, you ready back there?"

"I've got plenty of problems, but a lack of electronic systems ain't one," Armin confirmed.

"What's that even mean?"

"You have no sense of humor, Lee. Burst jammers, ECM modules, tracking and guidance disruptors… I also have a navigation spoofer I'm dying to try out. There's even a target painter I didn't know we had! Though I don't know what we'd use that for. Our target is *right there*."

An idea sprang into Lee's mind fully formed. "I do. After you blind their nav and targeting systems, we have a jump drive to kill." He opened up a mental link to Karmen Sley. He was getting better at sending, and she at receiving; he felt her mind open to him within seconds. *"Sync up your gunnery section with our coded frequency. We'll be painting your target for you. All Kozu has to do is fire."*

"Got it. Syncing now."

"Armin, let me know when they've—"

"Synced! I have the target area identified and locked into the tracking computer. Wow, that was fast. Kozu really must have been practicing."

"Told you. I think we may pull this off. Where is their sensor guy in the great big ship…?" Lee let his mind drift without taking his attention off his console. It was a tricky balance he needed to maintain.

But he had a specific target in mind—someone he'd met and had touched minds with before, so he could trace the mental signature. Callum, the sensor guy. He was perfect for Lee's aims now.

Conveniently, Lee found him on the observation deck—the spire at the very top of the ship. It was a relief, since Lee wasn't sure he'd be able to probe deep inside the vessel from this distance, let alone maintain a strong mental link. But the universe was kind today! He found that Callum was already plenty distracted by personal concerns. This wouldn't be as hard as he'd feared.

"Found him. Start blanketing their sensors and guidance systems," he instructed Armin. "Now!" At the same moment, Lee began his telepathic assault. *Let's give poor Callum something more intense than his job to worry about.*

Callum snorted with exasperation. "Captain, I don't get it. There are no transmissions between those three ships. But they're obviously maneuvering as a coherent group. How are they organizing themselves?"

"If I had to guess, I'd say that avionics shuttle has something to do with it. Pass their positional information to the gunnery section," Aura ordered.

A long moment passed without an answer. The displays were showing her three distinct objects in space, which were not only pacing the *Emerald Queen* but closing with her. Moving into different firing positions. "Gunnery section, power up the bay-mounted plasma cannons. We'll take them out with clean shots at close range."

"Captain, those weapons are meant for mid-range engagements against much larger vessels."

"I am aware. Follow my orders."

Another long moment passed without comment. Then, "Captain, we have red lights on the combat computer. No firing information is available."

"Reboot the system."

"It's not a problem with the computer, ma'am. The firing solution can't be calculated without an active sensor feed."

"What nonsense is that? You *have* a valid sensor feed."

"Negative, ma'am. There's no feed appearing on my console."

How did I get myself into this situation? "Sensors, adjust your feed and forward the targeting information to the gunnery section," she called out over her shoulder. Her gaze was fixed on the displays. Thirty kilometers. Then twenty. Now coming up on ten. "Sensors, what are you doing?"

She whirled and saw Callum staring into space, tears running down his face. "What the—*Sensors*! Snap out of it. Callum!" she yelled.

"She's dead!" Callum cried. "*Sacha's dead*!"

Aura tried not to scream in rage as she spun her officer around in his seat and bent close to him. "Callum, that isn't true. I saw Sacha not two hours ago, and she was fine. If she was dead, the infirmary would have contacted me and told me so. You're just—" *Just what? Hallucinating? Or under someone else's influence?*

In a snap decision, she yelled into the intercom. "Nav! Jump us to Valdos III, immediately."

"Negative! We can't jump or change course. The nav computer just spewed out a wave of nonsense data and locked. We're trying to reboot now…"

With a flash of insight, Aura understood that she'd made an awful mistake in judgment. She'd neglected to take into account the Agent working with Karmen. But there was someone else, too. A technical expert—

The displays flickered and fizzed as white noise and electronic garbage wiped out the *Emerald Queen*'s sensor array.

She sat down hard in one of the open observation couches and tried to recall trained habits across two decades of disuse. *Fok the Priesthood and their stupid rules against using Gifts.* She'd allowed her hard won mental skills to languish in the effort to blend in with the masses. She slowly let out her breath, controlled her breathing and allowed her body to relax.

Hesitantly at first, then with more confidence derived from habit, she reached out with her mind. "*Where are you, fellow Agent?*"

— — —

Kozu internalized the pattern of action very quickly. "This target painter makes it almost impossible to miss. Why didn't Armin tell us about this when we started?"

"In fairness to Armin, he might not have known about it then," Karmen replied. "Besides, you needed the full gunnery skillset when we drilled. Now it's the icing on the cake instead of having to bake one from scratch."

"We've baked cakes from scratch plenty of times," he countered as he thumbed the release on the gunnery stick. "Stars! This jump drive is huge. How do we know if we're having any effect?"

A small explosion on the inner junction where the drive met the hull appeared.

"That's one clue," his mother said. "Keep shooting. Be careful… if you overheat the laser, the system will shut down and I don't know if it will come back on its own."

"Acknowledged." He kept firing. *Shoot. Shoot. Shoot!*

— — —

Daveed Sley sat in the command chair to the rear of the *Percival*'s flight deck. The forward seats were occupied by Colin as lead pilot and Kaia, who was monitoring the comms. Seandra and Elian occupied the gunnery positions directly behind them. From his point of view, it certainly seemed as if he was running a remote-link classroom, except that classrooms didn't generally have seats with four-point harnesses keeping students from flying across the room in case of violent maneuvers.

"All positions, status report," Daveed called out. He'd

always wanted to say that, and was thankful his children couldn't see the smile on his face.

"Pilot ready."

"Comms ready."

"Top turret ready."

"Bottom turrets… not ready." Seandra groaned. "Stars! Why won't this work?"

"Did you remember to sync the tracking to the main computer?" Elian asked.

"It's more efficient if we shoot at the same target," Seandra argued.

"More efficient, but it screws up the sensor track on an old ship like this," Colin said. "Let the computer pick your targets, Seandra."

Seandra murmured something that sounded vaguely distrustful, but then called out, "Bottom turrets ready!"

Daveed sighed silently. "All right. As I understand it, we must stay close to the main target, within three kilometers. Any further and they'll be able to—"

Alarms rang as the small ship shuddered. "Plasma cannon. Near hit on the port side," Kaia reported.

"Colin, get us out of their line of fire."

"Yes, sir. Bringing us in closer…"

"Good. Top and bottom turrets, open fire. Fire when ready. Fire at will!"

Seandra and Elian brought their targeting systems to life and began peppering the massive battleship with laser blasts. It was difficult to miss at this range. The great ship filled the monitors even while Colin drove the *Percival* in a corkscrew orbit around the ore carrier's impressive bulk.

Daveed watched their orbital path on the tactical display, impressed with how the young man plotted and implemented a series of twists and turns that brought the system defense ship to barely one hundred meters distance from the hull and pulled back to a kilometer or more then repeated the pattern along a different axis around the bigger vessel. No matter how he turned the ship, Colin made a practice of turning the hull so that both gunners had plenty of opportunities to shoot at the *Emerald Queen.*

Boy has some skill in this. Good for him. I'd hate to think Kaia was getting involved with a talentless playboy.

The problem was one that Karmen had described to them earlier in the planning stage: the pirate ship was so big that it could absorb effectively unlimited blasts from the *Percival*'s laser turrets. But they weren't here to destroy anything; *Percival*'s job was to occupy their damage control teams while Karmen and Kozu eliminated the *Emerald Queen*'s ability to escape to another star system.

Another set of alarms rang as an explosion occurred on the *Emerald Queen*'s hull. Daveed swore he could hear the pings of shrapnel hitting the *Percival*'s hull. At least they'd gotten their adversary's attention.

"All turrets, maintain fire!" Daveed said. *I could get used to this.* No… he could get used to the *idea* of this. The adrenaline alone was enough to keep his pulse and respiration high. But just beneath the excitement lay a pool of anxiety that he dared not dip his toes into or it would drown him. Karmen had explained the experience of combat to him before, but he'd never truly understood her until now. Had she done this every day for ten years? How had she learned to control the fear? How was *he* going to?

"Proximity alarm… new target!" Colin yelled.

Then, the rear compartment exploded.

— — —

Lom pulled out of his steep dive, virtually brushing up against the top rear hull of the gunship. His lasers peppered the hull and tore a hole in the plating, which vented gas as the compartment explosively decompressed. *It's been too long since I've had this much fun!*

He brought his drone around for another pass. In outer space, that wasn't easily accomplished. He had to give the gunship's pilot credit. Whoever he was, he knew how to cloak his own sensor profile by keeping his craft shudderingly close to his target.

Lom's problem was that to find him, he had to ping the *Emerald Queen* with his own active array and thus make it look like he was another enemy assailant, bent on the carrier's destruction. Two plasma cannon gunners had already taken shots at him. He'd ordered the gunners to stand down without clearing it with Captain Aura. But she hadn't countermanded his orders, and he got the impression that she was busy with other aspects of command. Sometimes, you had to sit back and allow your crew to do their jobs. She was quite good at that.

It was time to set up another shooting solution. He gave himself a bit of room to work with, pulling back to a three-kilometer distance before using a visual sighting to locate the gunship again. This time, he anticipated the course and reversed his own plot to lay in wait ahead of the enemy craft.

When it came around the edge of the *Emerald Queen*'s hull, he opened fire with an array of short-range missiles, which slammed into the gunship's lower deck. Another section of hull torn apart; another explosive venting! Now, he was reminded why drone pilots so rarely left their control booths and pushed their connections to the limit. After this, reality was positively *dull*.

Another burst of the lasers and another hit, but this time he merely grazed the gunship's bow. Scorch marks but little more than that.

He peeled off, gave himself another kilometer of distance—

His side exploded in pain as the blasted gunship hit him with its top laser turret. He flipped the drone on its tail and let loose with a barrage of laser fire. In his haste, he realized he'd mistimed the shot. Laser blasts rocked the hull of the *Emerald Queen*, putting a hole in one of the exterior cargo pods.

So much for snap shots. I must be more careful. The wretched gunship crew couldn't last forever.

34

DOGFIGHT

THE HOURS OF practice with simulations had paid off: Kozu Sley was in the gunnery zone.

Confident in her son's abilities, Karmen brought up a schematic of the jump drive assembly on a standard Gallant-class ore carrier and compared it to the *Emerald Queen*. She needed to find Kozu's next target.

Numerous connections directed energy flows from the power core within the ship to its jump drive. One thing that caught her eye was that on the Gallant, ten of the twelve power conduits were external, snaking out of the ship and connecting to the jump drive's prongs in heavy armored cables. Kozu had improved his technique in shooting at the conduits for some time. Nine of them were already severed—no small help from Armin's target painter. That left just one external connection to deal with. They'd worry about the internal connection after they were done here.

"Hits! Good shooting, Kozu. A few more like that and—"

A blast of energy struck the tiny shuttle amidships, knocking Kozu's firing solution to zero. At the same time, the console lit up with warnings while an alarm pealed in the background. Karmen silenced the offending noise and raised viewing surfaces to find out what the problem was.

"We're pointing the wrong way," her son said.

"I know that. But something is shooting at us, and I think that's more important right now."

The onboard shuttle sensors were nearly useless for anything except the most basic navigation solutions, but one thing that she noticed quickly was that it had an active pulse array. Not much for stealth, it was a cross between a beacon and a much larger active sensor dome. She armed the system, waiting anxiously while the capacitor charged. She let loose with a wall of energy. It was weak, but it went everywhere in every direction and in moments she had a relatively accurate map of the surface of the *Emerald Queen*'s hull.

"There you are," she scolded.

Two of the heavy bipedal Lynaedan drones were standing on the hull, pointing energy weapons at her ship like snipers with heavy rifles. As she watched, they reset their positions and launched another volley at her shuttle. Another blast erupted against the hull, bringing the alarms back from the silenced mode.

Kozu tried to train his weapon onto the snipers, but either his aim was too hasty or the shuttle's small laser wasn't powerful enough to damage the attackers. "Mom, we can't stay here."

"I can't argue with that. See if you can get one more good shot at that last cable. If we sever it we can—"

"On it. Hang on." Kozu reset his laser and this time he zoomed in on the remaining exterior conduit and held down the trigger. Laser blasts peppered the conduit, which sparked and flashed as pieces of the cabling came apart.

Now, a new alarm came up: the one that warned of the laser's capacitor overheating.

"You're getting too hot," Karmen said.

"Don't care." Kozu let up for two seconds and then fired again. The laser gave one more short burst of power then fell dead. "Fok. Burned out. We should absolutely leave now."

"Run the auto-repair cycle first," Karmen instructed. "See if you can't get the heat sink to re-engage."

"Um… hang on one second."

Without warning, the comm channel blared a hiss of confused voices and dropped words. "Karmen, we're being attacked. It's a drone. They're really knocking the fok out of us. We could use some help." Karmen recognized the tone in Daveed's voice. He wasn't panicking, not yet. But he was flustered. Fearful.

She thought through her options quickly; there weren't many to consider. She tapped her comm. "Lee! Switch places with me."

The trick worked; Lee's voice sounded inside her head. *"Wait, Karmen? I don't understand."*

"The Percival *needs backup. We've destroyed all the external power conduits that feed the jump drive. Can you take over my position and use your telekinesis to rupture the final connection?"*

"I think so. Yes, I can do that. Where's it located? Oh, I see," Lee acknowledged. *"Heading there now. Go help your husband."*

Karmen instantly realized he'd simply reached into her mind and pulled the image out of it. Good for him. The boy learned quickly.

She turned to her son, who was making himself crazy trying out various controls. "Heat sink?" she asked. It took a lot of effort to keep her tone level.

"I think I can get one shot off. Maybe two. We won't do any real damage with it, though."

"No, but that drone driver won't know that." *Hang on, Daveed, we're coming to help!*

—   —   —

Colin was starting to sweat. Rather, he was already sweating; now, he was starting to stink. His heart rate had doubled during the battle, and he was having a hard time breathing. Concentrating on doing what needed to be done was soaking up all his mental effort.

Elian and Seandra were cursing up a storm as their shots kept missing the drone. The only thing that might turn the tide was another ship to take some of the heat off them long enough for him to reorient the *Percival*'s meager defenses.

"Daveed! We need backup!" Colin yelled. "Kaia, open a channel!"

Kaia's fingers danced across her console. "Dad, you're on!"

In seconds, Karmen's acknowledgement of their call for backup came over the comms. It relieved some of the pressure in Colin's chest to know that help was on the way. Seandra and Elian had stopped their bickering, too. Now, they merely snarled under their breath when they missed a shot. Unfortunately, they were missing more than they were hitting.

But *Percival* was still his ship, and he was still in charge of its crew.

Colin swept his hand across a bank of touchscreens and blanched at what they told him. *Percival* was in trouble. There were four hull breaches of varying sizes on the main and lower decks. The power core was struggling to maintain a steady output, and the pion drive had dropped its maximum speed three times. Bulkheads were limiting the damage to non-crew sections, but the ship was bleeding atmosphere from somewhere.

Worst of all, the lower deck's docking linkage for the emergency shuttle had been badly damaged. There was no way to dock Karmen and Kozu's ship without something tearing the hull. And if, by a miracle, they did dock and the airlock did mate properly, they wouldn't be able to launch the shuttle in the future without a shipyard to pry the two vessels apart.

The main display shifted to show the emergency shuttle approaching from their port flank. The drone pilot had indeed noticed them and was pursuing. The good news was that the shuttle was considerably more maneuverable than *Percival*. Unfortunately, the drone was, too.

The two combatants swiped and swerved past each other, loosing laser bolts as they passed. Two, three, then four more passes without either craft getting a solid hit on the other.

Finally, the drone pilot took a dare, flipped his craft end-over-end, and with a burst of velocity, rammed the shuttle. The two ships bounced off each other and inertia carried them well away from the *Percival*. But even from this distance, Colin could see the shuttle had been scarred with a large dent in the main hull.

His gut contracted as if he'd been punched. "Officer Sley!"

A hiss and stutter sounded on the comms as the signal blipped, then recovered. "We're fine. Somehow. Bulkhead closed off the flight deck. The rest of the ship is not so good. I don't think we can take another hit like that."

"And weapons are officially offline for good," Kozu added.

"Acknowledged. Pretty good for a drone driver," Colin griped. "Just my luck to have to deal with a pilot who knows what he's doing. If we run, they'll kill us. And that shuttle can't mate with our lower deck with that damage."

Kaia gave him a withering side-eye. "If you have some inspiration, now is the time to share it," she said, her voice barely above a whisper.

I have one thing left. They can't use those giant guns to shoot us if we're inside their hangar bay. "Gunners! I'm locking coordinates into your targeting arrays. When I give the order, you shoot and you keep shooting until I say stop or until your systems burn out. Hear me?"

"Got it," Seandra coughed.

"Right on!"

"All right, here we go! This is going to get bumpy."

Colin pulled his ship back from the *Emerald Queen*, searched for a particular section of the great ship, and then maneuvered back to its lowermost deck. When he was done repositioning, *Percival* was stationary relative to the carrier, less than two hundred meters from one of the shuttle launch bay doors.

He locked the door into his targeting computer and implemented the firing solution for all three turrets. "Commence firing!"

— — —

"Where are you, fellow Agent?"

The thought woke Lee from a mental stupor. It hadn't been directed at him, specifically—not exactly. More of a general wave of awareness that touched his own. *I'm right here. Why can't you find me, Mother Carnage?*

Lee was tired. He'd never used his mental Gifts as intensely as he'd been doing now, maintaining his clouding of their sensor operator's mind while keeping up communication between himself and Armin verbally, and Karmen telepathically. He wasn't spent yet, but he was tiring. That was a problem.

A bigger problem was the presence of a trained Agent somewhere in that ship. She wasn't on her best game. In fact, it felt to Lee as if she hadn't done so much as moved a bag of marbles with her Gifts for years. She was badly out of practice, rusty after neglecting her telekinetic and telepathic training for so long. But she brought a raw power to the contest that Lee couldn't hope to match. The best he could do would be to use technique and skill against her. But first, he had a very specific job to do.

The sensor operator was starting to rouse, coming out of the telepathic trance Lee had imposed on him. Events were unfolding nearby, and his senses were waking him up from Lee's influence. In the end, Lee had little choice but to disable the carrier's jump drive while he could.

He called up the schematics of the carrier that Karmen had showed him across their link. The engineering was already there—one giant conduit powered the entire assembly, now that the auxiliary cables were severed.

Lee concentrated on slipping telekinetic tendrils into the machinery. Every part rested against another part. One by one, he visualized the pieces of the whole mechanism falling apart. A feeder cable shorted out; a gasket exploded into steam; an intricate network of gears and cogs screamed incoherently and shattered as the assembly failed. The leads from the power core, which fed the drive, heated beyond all tolerances and warped and then melted. Finally, the drive assembly itself came apart under his psychic talons.

Lee beamed an image of the damage to Karmen on her shuttle. *"Mission accomplished!"*

"Well done, Agent! Now we need to deal with Aura."

—   —   —

Callum blinked to clear his head. He felt like he'd woken from a too-long nap, the kind that refreshed for a moment and then sucked even more energy from him. Concentration took effort and his reactions were sluggish. He felt as if heavy streamers were affixed to his limbs, dragging him down as he tried to move.

He looked up to see his captain in the seat next to his, deep in thought, her eyes closed.

Then, he remembered. He'd been in a room filled with crew members all sobbing over Sacha's corpse. It had seemed so bomaxed *real*. Why had he— Then he intuited the answer: Agent Safety Valve. That cretin had put a whammy on him. Some kind of mental block. Kept him from doing his job.

In a fit of rage, Callum wiped the current data feed and activated a camera that kept watch over the infirmary. Sacha was still hooked up to the neural wave feedback complex, her chest rising and falling in sleep. The monitor above her bed traced a plethora of vital signs: all blue, indicating good and stable.

Sneaky bastard!

"Captain, request permission to blow that shuttle out of the sky."

"Granted," Aura whispered. "Keep them busy. I'll crush them from here."

"Yes, ma'am!"

— — —

Armin had been busy evaluating every new signal from the *Emerald Queen*—a vessel he now firmly viewed as a battleship, despite its humble origins as a cargo hauler. The equipment and efficiency with which the vessel ran was impressive for a bunch of pirates, but then again, its commander was ex-TSS. Command track training for Agents was second to none, and it wasn't too surprising that Aura Thand would have every aspect of her operation dialed in.

While Armin managed communications and sensors, Lee was off on his own thing, pulling the wires and who knew what that connected the external jump drive prongs to their power supply. That was fine; it gave Armin more time to execute his part in the mission. He was doing well, too. Surprisingly well. Maybe a little too well.

Whenever some tech on the battleship found a hole in Armin's electronic warfare, he plugged it. The only thing he ignored for now was the target painter. Its job was done, and it had performed admirably. From now on, he'd ask for a target painter to be installed on any EWAR craft he served on.

Lee called out joyfully. "That's how it's done!"

Curious, Armin took his eyes off the board to see the power output on the *Emerald Queen*'s jump drive drop to zero. "Oh, nice!"

But when he looked back to his console, it was a different situation. Almost a different console. His pulse spiked. "Lee! We have problems. The sensor operator just woke up, and it seems like he knows what he's doing."

"Jam him, Armin, I've got bigger problems to manage here."

'I've got bigger problems here,' says the big man Agent. Armin shook his head and pushed all non-job-related thoughts from his mind.

The sensor operator had, indeed, come to his senses. Armin quickly realized a blanket screen wouldn't be enough to stop him anymore. So, new strategy. He switched the navigation spoofer to standby, since it was clear the great ship wouldn't be jumping anywhere today; one less thing to worry about gave him more energy to devote to everything else.

He locked his own status board to show him the exact electronic systems of the *Percival* and its auxiliary shuttle and threw them onto a wide display. The feeds would show him target locks any vessel had on both his fleet mates and counter them.

Sensor dampeners came first—a swath of electronic noise that dropped the *Emerald Queen*'s weapons to minimal range. Three weapons got locks on his own shuttle, and two more locked onto *Percival*. Burst jammers killed the locks on the system defense ship, but only electronic countermeasures were able to disrupt the locks on his own vessel.

An alarm screamed at him to do something as a new system grabbed his EWAR net: a missile lock, burning right through his ECM screen.

Not again. Not this time, you bomaxed pirate!

He swapped his tools and focused a trio of guidance disruptors on the missile targeting array.

He breathed more easily as the lock disappeared. *Seriously, Lee! Whatever you intend to do, you need to do it fast.*

35

BOARDING ACTION

BOARDING THEM IS crazy. Even with a ship full of marines, a boarding action would be crazy! Colin risked a glance in the mirror mounted above his head, positioned to let a pilot monitor the crew deck. Daveed Sley was set like a rock, his hands clenched into fists and his eyes squeezed shut. Elian and Seandra were far more animated, plugging the thumbs down on their turret triggers and screaming hoarsely with every successful hit. Kaia kept her eyes on her comm console, her hands twitching, left with nothing to do.

The energy poured out by the gunship's weaponry was intense. The hangar bay door glowed red, then yellow, and then white. Finally, the laws of physics worked in their favor and the door shattered and burst out of its frame. Only the force field meant to maintain atmosphere was left.

"Hang on, people, we're going in! Lee, Karmen! Meet us on their hangar deck," Colin shouted and nudged the throttle.

The *Percival* stuttered then spun as the maneuvering drive

engaged. For a second, the open hatch loomed in the viewscreen like an angry mouth swallowing them. All at once, the ship dropped onto the hangar deck, replacing their smooth ride with a screech of metal grinding against metal that reverberated through their ship.

A glance at the proximity monitor confirmed that they were about thirty meters inside the hangar bay. There was plenty of room for their backup to follow.

"Gear down! Officer Sley, we're inside," Colin announced over the comm. "We'd love to have you join us. We'll keep their heads down."

"Good job, Colin!" The joy in Karmen's voice made Colin's heart sing. "Everybody in the hole. We're on our way!"

Now, if I can just get my own mother to talk to me like that. Colin popped his flight harness.

Looking out the viewports, he realized that they were now completely exposed inside an enemy vessel. He threw several switches and held his breath until blue lights winked on. Now, the viewports were covered with armored shutters. Anyone wanting to shoot at them wouldn't have an easy time of it.

By the time he finished, Kaia was already getting up from her station next to him, and Elian and Seandra were racing to the lift to descend to the muster deck. Daveed, however, was still clenched into his self-made mental cocoon.

Colin rushed over and tried tapping the older man on the shoulder, then shook him when he didn't respond. "Dean Sley! Time to go. Karmen and Kozu are on their way. Lee, too. We need to be ready to move."

"Not until we land!"

I don't have time for this. "I'm not a celestial being. Open your eyes and get out of that chair. Help your children, old man!"

"Dad, come on!" Kaia urged.

That did it. Daveed's eyes snapped open, and he flung himself out of the seat. Colin had seen this sort of thing before. Old men who wouldn't lift a finger to help themselves, but mention their kids or their legacies, and they surged into action. "Good man. Let's get below."

The lift was already down, but the three of them only had to wait a moment for it to return. Once inside, Daveed said, "If a student ever used that tone with me, I'd flunk him from here to Tararia."

Colin had his answer ready. "If I had a professor who shut down under pressure, I'd sue to have his teaching certification revoked."

"Point taken," Daveed said. "I've never done this before. It's exciting… and dreadful!"

"This is not how I normally spend my days at the family business center," Colin allowed.

Kaia cleared her throat, a strangely ladylike sound considering the circumstances. "I'm thrilled you two understand each other. But can we please do this after the fighting ends?"

The lift opened to a hurricane named Seandra; Elian was her subordinate tornado. They'd implemented an efficient assembly line, as the sister unpacked and prepped rifles from the gun locker and her brother laid out equipment. They'd obviously made good use of their time in transit; they knew every tool in the muster bay and how to put it to use.

Seandra shoved a rifle into Colin's arms. It felt weird. Heavy. Full of moving parts he'd never imagined. He barely knew which end to point at an enemy.

She didn't wait for him to have an accident, merely pulled the weapon from his arms, and showed him the works. "This is your new best friend, Colin. It's a Zanoff-Boland G36K. One of the best small arms you will likely encounter. It's got three rates of fire, uses a caseless 5.5mm round and makes a distinctive sound when it fires—"

"Don't shoot it in here!" Colin screamed. Seandra's eyes grew wide in surprise, almost in shock. He suddenly felt a wave of envy for her childhood, devoid of frequent scoldings. He'd bet real money that none of the Sley kids had any idea how good they had it.

"*Percival* has damage enough," he explained.

She nodded vigorously and continued. "Here's a standard magazine. It goes in this feed here. Slap it, hard… then select your fire rate with this lever. Pull the bolt back like this. You're ready to go. Thirty rounds per magazine, and we have plenty."

Daveed pulled on a heavy, short sleeved garment and offered one each to Colin and Kaia. "Ballistic cloth. If you wear one of these, you can take a small caliber round at close range and not die."

"Yeah, it'll just throw you halfway across the room," Elian assured him.

"What if they have things bigger than these rifles?" Colin asked. "Shouldn't someone have the plasma guns ready?"

There was no time to answer. A high-pitched whine sounded from the intercom. "Proximity alert," Colin announced. "One ship just landed close to us. And there's another one."

"Mom! Agent Lee!" Elian cried and ran to the airlock. He slapped his hand against the pad and the heavy doors slid open.

An Idolon mech loomed in the doorway as the outer lock slid open. Elian couldn't not look up in awe.

Seandra's voice rang out, "Elian! Target the waist joints!"

The boy caught the plasma rifle that his sister hucked at

him. Colin was already using his new assault rifle to shower the Idolon with rounds, which bounced harmlessly off its metal skin.

Despite its weight and bulk, Elian knew how to use the plasma rifle. He threw himself to the ground, thumbed the discharge lever to max, aimed for the seam between the drone's torso and its crotch, and pulled the trigger.

With the whine of generators and a bright flash, the giant machine was covered from neck to waist in glowing plasma. The corrosive cocktail ate straight through the drone's skin at the weak points and began melting its interior. The pilot clearly knew he was in trouble; the machine flailed, stomping away to clear the area. It finally slammed against a cargo container on the hangar deck and fell down, immobilized.

Elian stood up and grinned. "That was so cool!"

Daveed clapped him on the shoulder. "Well done, my boy."

Colin set down his rifle. "Yeah, we should definitely take *those*," he said, pointing to the plasma weapon.

"Excellent point," Daveed agreed. "You and I will take those for squad support. Elian and Seandra, use burst-fire settings on the auto-rifles for distraction. Don't even try to hit anyone, just make them keep their heads down."

"Yes, sir!"

—   —   —

Landing inside the enemy ship hadn't been part of any of Lee's variations of their slapdash plan to stop the *Emerald Queen* from escaping, but here they were. The moment the *Percival* had gone inside, he'd had no choice but to follow.

This is the kind of mess that happens when we make rash

decisions. He would no doubt get an earful from TSS Command about this. His only hope of salvaging the situation now was to take Mother Carnage into custody.

Lee brought the TSS shuttle in behind *Percival* and landed it on the larger vessel's port side. He tapped his comm and heard Karmen announce her arrival on the emergency shuttle. A glance at the monitor showed her tiny craft settle to Lee's left.

Armin busied himself shutting down the EWAR systems, but Lee had another goal in mind. He checked the exterior camera feed; what he saw filled his heart with glee. This hangar held plenty of resources for them to use, if he could reach them from here—

"Did you see that flash on the monitor?" Armin exclaimed. "The Sleys have plasma guns. I want one. Cover me!"

Gah! Not now, Armin. "I'm busy!"

"With what?"

"With *this*," Lee growled.

On the external view, a massive cargo container slid across the hangar bay to park itself on *Percival*'s port side, forming a solid bit of cover. Lee repeated the exercise and slid two more of the empty modules across the deck. One came to a stop just meters away from *Percival*'s bow, and the other positioned itself on the starboard side. They now had significant cover positions everywhere except their rear, which gave them a fully defensible position and a clear exit route.

"How's that for cover?"

"Good job, Agent. I'm getting my plasma gun." Armin headed for the exit hatch.

"Knock yourself out. I have a date with an Agent defector."

Movement on the monitor. A platoon of the same bipedal drones that had been used in the TalEx robbery on Diphous were approaching from various directions. Like it or not, Lee's handling of the cargo modules had been good, but not so good that there weren't any gaps between them. That meant access points. But the constructs were wide and slow, and Armin's plan to use a plasma gun against them wasn't bad.

"Take charge of the group," Lee ordered. "I'll take out the rogue Agent. You have to direct the civvies to hold this ground. We lose this, we're trapped. You got me?"

"Got you."

"Good. Pop the airlock in three, two, one…"

"Go, go, go!" Armin yelled. He rushed out of the shuttle while Lee followed close behind. True to form, Armin dropped to the ground and rolled beneath the TSS shuttle, then smoothly rose to his feet and ran to the *Percival*'s auxiliary.

Karmen and Kozu met Lee outside their own craft. Both were already geared up with ballistic jackets and pulse pistols in hip holsters.

Karmen nodded to Lee. "What's our plan?"

"*My* plan is to neutralize Mother Carnage while you all hold this ground. If we can't secure this ship, we'll need an escape route, and that's your combined jobs."

"Oh, no. I'm coming with you," Karmen announced.

"Not on your life. Armin is in charge, you're his backup. You hold this ground."

Karmen's face lit up bright red. She took some deep breaths to control herself and said, "She was an upper-level Sacon Agent. She's stronger than you, Lee, and you know it. She'll kill you if she feels she has to. But she won't kill me."

Lee forced himself to weigh her words carefully. True, she knew their target far better than he did. But he was in no mood to accede to her demand. "Are you willing to gamble everyone's lives on that?"

"Do you really want to push her far enough to find out?"

Lee considered it. Agent strength scores were on an exponential scale, so even though Aura Thand's numeric rating wasn't much higher than his own estimated level, her actual power was potentially ten times greater. Even if she was out of practice, she had the raw power to crush his body like a rotten piece of fruit, and there wouldn't be much he could do about it. It was a painful reminder that the only edge he had was his well-practiced skill over his hope that her own abilities were rusty. He needed a way to distract her, and if Karmen could help… "Fine. You're on my team. But when I give you instructions, you follow them. Clear?"

"Yes, sir."

"All right. I spotted her on the topmost deck with Callum. Follow me."

— — —

Lom fought to stop the whirlwind spin caused by his impact with the tiny enemy shuttle. His sensors were intermittent, and something had broken loose in the small pion drive propelling his drone. He could 'feel' it spinning in its housing, which made control far more error-prone than he wanted to admit. The weapons still worked, but he couldn't orient the tiny craft to point them at anything worthwhile. Just about the only thing that was functioning properly was his control link to the mother ship. *Thank the Queen for small favors.*

By the time he was able to bring the drone back into a coherent orbit around the pirate ship, his captain was pinging him on her priority comm channel.

"Lom, you need to return at once. He's coming for me." He heard the distraction in her voice. She was anxious, shaken. A bad sign of what might come.

"I am a little preoccupied, Captain."

"Curse the stars, Lom! It's just one drone, and it's already taken damage. Callum was specific about that. Break your connection, put on your Meklife suit, and rally the crew. You need to keep that Agent on the hangar deck at all costs. I need time to get down there to deal with him myself."

"Very well."

Lom set the drone's meager autopilot functions to maintain the orbit he'd established and then set his remote links to return him to the drone control deck.

A timeless darkness swept him up as he waited to transfer to his booth. Normally, the transition only took a moment, but something was off this time—either with the connection or his perception of the connection.

Eventually, however, it worked. He opened his eyes and found himself in his Sergeant Meklife drone body. He off-handedly wondered if Meklife couldn't stand a bit of an upgrade as he stepped off the platform and flexed his limbs. Everything worked. But the body felt *heavy*. Something was wrong, but one went to war with the drone one had, not the drone one wanted. Besides, he didn't feel up to risking his real body if he had to repel boarders. The *Emerald Queen* was never meant to deal with a boarding party.

How did things become so chaotic so quickly? They'd been in port for days without significant incident, but the moment the fighter shipment arrived, the day had been deteriorating. *Tabor better not have crossed us.*

Despite the unexpected assault, the crew was responding with trained precision. Pilots on the drone deck were racing to their control booths on one side of the bay while on the other their Idolons were activating and stepping off their platforms.

Ordnance specialists were prepping rows of hand-held weaponry for the drones to carry into battle. At least here on the drone deck, everyone knew their jobs and carried out the tasks they'd drilled for.

"Mr. Gallian, status report!" he bellowed into his comm.

From his console in the War Room, Gallian replied, "Sixteen Idolons are reporting for duty, equipped with the new E-ARC sabers."

"Sixteen? We had more than that. What happened to them?"

Gallian sighed. "There was a lack of leadership on the ground. Five of the Idolons were destroyed by enemy fire."

Enemy fire! What's going on down there? "Very well. I'll take charge of this group. Order the rest of the crew to steer clear of the hangar deck until further notice. In fact have all crew not under my command to vacate the deck immediately. We'll clear out our visitors."

"Right away, sir."

Meklife pulled out one of the electro-arc sabers for his own use and primed it. A crackle of electricity danced along its length.

"Idolons! Follow me!" He charged toward the hangar deck.

—   —   —

Aura braced herself for the fight to come. She was ready to face it head-on, and the observation deck was no place for a fight.

"I'm going to attend to our unwanted company," she told Callum as she headed toward the lift.

"Yes, ma'am," he acknowledged without looking up from his station.

Callum had returned to himself, but Aura could feel the anger burning inside of him as he managed the electronic warfare attack brought upon them by the TSS shuttle. Even now, with the infiltrators causing chaos aboard her ship, her sensor officer was struggling to fix all the damage that had been done. Cleaning up the navigation spoofer's after-effects was taking all his attention. She needed the Queen to navigate; that was non-negotiable.

Aura hugged herself as she stepped into the lift, fully aware that there was no comfort in the gesture. She'd been able to awaken her Gifts from their decades-long stupor, but even now she understood she was operating at a fraction of what she'd been capable of in her prime. Back in the day, she'd been able to manage telepathy while moving bulkheads on *Triumph*. Today, she felt lucky if she could attend to one task at a time. It had taken far too long to locate the Agent on her own ship!

Kicking herself for the failure to stay in practice did no one any good, but it was hard not to. So cathartic. She'd had good reasons to avoid using her hard-trained skills all these years, not the least of which was staying hidden from the TSS.

But face it, Aura. They did find you in the end, didn't they? She couldn't even argue the point. The TSS had infiltrated her battleship. First Officer Karmen Sley, no less. Aura refused to rest until she figured out how that insane chain of events had unfolded.

Part of her wanted to wipe Karmen from existence, but a greater part wanted to sit with her and ask, "What happened?" But before that conversation had to come the fighting. And while she had reservations about retaliating against her old friend, she had no qualms about sweeping the Agent with her from her presence. He was currently on the hangar deck. And she could manage him. He knew his job, but he couldn't match her raw power. An obstacle, not a real threat.

Are you sure? He did put you all on the defensive... the voice of her inner doubts reminded her. Like it or not, she had to prepare for the worst. And she hated herself for going along with it, but New Akkadia was now at risk. Well, she could fix that right now.

She sent a telepathic message to Gilgamesh in the briefing room. *"We've been boarded. Take the others, get on* Shamhat, *and leave. I'll meet you on Valdos. Now!"*

She felt him acknowledge the message. The lift counter dropped to zero and the doors opened.

Aura stepped out to see Meklife's Idolons engaged in a firing line, exchanging shots with the invaders across a wall of displaced cargo modules. She could sense her Agent adversary nearby. Her first officer had done his job well. Now, she had to finish it.

Here comes Mother Carnage...

36

A TALE OF TWO AGENTS

ARMIN BROUGHT OUT an equipment case from the TSS shuttle and opened it. He shoved equipment into Elian's hands as he spoke. "Elian, you are my forward observer. You ever fly a drone before?"

"Just video games."

"Close enough. The controls are here. You fly by holding the tablet like this…"

After a brief demo, the boy was hopping from foot to foot; he eagerly took the control tablet from Armin. It took no more than a few seconds for him to pick up the feedback mechanism once it was in his hands.

At least the kid is a quick learner. We don't have time to play around. The unplanned boarding was Armin's worst fears in action. He'd wanted to keep Karmen's family well away from their activities for this very reason, but now he was going into battle alongside children. But they were the backup he had, so he'd have to make the most of the extra sets of hands.

With Elian equipped, Armin looked at the two girls, estimating their capabilities by the way they held their rifles and wore their ballistic jackets. "Seandra, you're my right-hand sniper. See that space between the cargo modules there? Set yourself up there. Kaia, you do the same thing on the left, between those modules. You hang out there. Whenever someone moves, you shoot. Now, this is important. You don't try to track or follow anyone who passes outside your line of sight. If they're moving away from you, that means they're moving into someone else's firing line. You let your squad mates worry about that. You only shoot what's in front of *you*. Hear me? Semi-auto fire only. These rifles are impossible to aim on automatic fire." He ran them through a quick comm check. "You've got this. Go!"

Once the teens were off, he pulled the men toward him. "Gentlemen, we are the support unit. It's our job to keep those robots away from our rear. Colin, you're on the right, support Seandra. Daveed, you take the left to support Kaia. Kozu and I will manage the front. Don't shoot until you have an excellent kill shot. That means your eyepiece display will turn from blue to red. If you need help, call for it. Are we good?" They nodded their understanding. "Go!"

The attack began almost immediately, with Elian using his comm to call out approaching targets for the various shooters.

After a minute of chaotic chatter, Armin cut in on the line. "Use directions, Elian! Targets are on the left, the center, or the right. Keep going, you're doing great!"

Kaia and Seandra used their rifles to good effect, scattering the few Taran crewmembers who tried to approach.

Colin used three plasma bolts to take out an approaching drone. The large mech crashed to the hangar deck and powered down.

Another drone was barreling toward them within Armin's shooting zone. He fired, but the shot didn't take the behemoth down.

Daveed picked up the slack when the drone entered his field of fire. "Down!" he declared.

"Good shot, Daveed," Armin said. *For a bunch of amateurs, they're really holding their own.*

The unfortunate problem was that there were far more drones than they could shoot. All they could do was take it one at a time.

— — —

Karmen watched the battle unfold from a distance as she followed Lee across the hangar. "I get the idea they emptied their entire armory to deal with us," Karmen griped.

"Wouldn't you do the same if your ship was being invaded?"

"Sure. But *this*?"

Lee chuckled despite the tension. "Kilogram for kilogram, we're the most overpowered fighting force on this ship. Maybe in the whole empire!"

Karmen noticed that the heavy drones had arranged themselves into a wide firing line, with electro-sabers gripped in their mechanical hands. The drones were taking fire, with the missed shots sending up sparks and shrapnel from the blasts against the cargo containers. Every now and then, a plasma blast would take out one of the drone soldiers, but two or three more would arrive to plug the hole. "Why aren't they advancing?" she wondered aloud.

"I don't know, but we're not going to get an opening to break through at this rate," Lee said.

They were pinned down in their current position, unable to get to a lift or stairwell so they could reach the observation deck.

"They're not advancing because they want to keep us bottled up here," Karmen realized. "Keep us busy. We need to figure out how to get to Aura—"

"Oh, fok. She's here!" Lee exclaimed.

The air around them grew heavy as a woman's voice came from the other side of the blockade. "Hello, Karmen! It's been a long time. I'd love to chat, but I have a schedule to keep. So, get off my ship and we'll go our separate ways."

Karmen tensed. That was the same commanding voice that had been her rally cry to duty all those years ago. It was wrong for that same woman to now be treating her as a threat. "You know I can't do that, Aura," Karmen yelled back.

"I know nothing of the kind. But I do know one thing: I have you out-positioned and out-gunned by a factor of fifty to one. I'm giving you the chance to take your family and leave unharmed. Don't be stupid. Take it."

Karmen made a gesture to Lee, an invitation to read her mind. "*Can you take her out?*"

"*Bloody right I can. Watch this.*"

—   —   —

Lee slid past the armored doors and slipped into a gap between the cargo module's edge and *Percival*'s bow. From that close range, he could sense Aura's raw power. It gave him a clear target, a beacon to home in on. The trick was to neutralize her, like *that*!

Nothing happened.

He tried another telepathic block; that failed, as well.

Finally, he threw his entire being into an attempt to fling her bodily across the bay, and she countered him again.

Maybe she's not so out-of-practice, after all—

A crippling pressure closed in against his windpipe, choking the air from his lungs. In an instant, Lee lost his ability to concentrate. Whatever she was doing, he couldn't breathe…

— — —

Lee! Karmen shouted in her mind, but he was unresponsive. The Junior Agent was staring blankly into space, gasping for breath.

Karmen's comms were still active, and she whispered her command, "Plasma gunners, come forward. Three targets, right front. Wait for my mark."

Three acknowledgments met her ears as Armin, Colin, and Kozu responded.

Karmen stepped out from behind her cover. Aura stood between a trio of the heavy drones, all of which had weapons drawn and pointed at Karmen. The other woman looked wilder now without her TSS uniform. Notably, her eyes were exposed and lacked their former glow indicating her Gifts; either she was wearing muting contacts or she'd had them surgically altered as part of her efforts to blend in. The Agent Karmen had known would have considered that an affront of the highest order.

Karmen raised her hands. "Aura! You look good! A life of crime agrees with you." In her periphery she kept an eye on Lee. He was still being held in an invisible vise, but his breathing was coming a little easier now.

"Kozu here," he acknowledged over the comm. "In position."

"Don't be daft, Karmen," her former friend replied. "Just take your friends and your spawn and get off my ship. There's far more going on here than you understand."

"It's Armin, I have the shot," the officer reported on the comm.

Karmen tilted her head, feigning interest. "Really? Want to tell me about it?"

"You'll find out soon enough," Aura said. "It'll be glorious."

"Colin here. I have a good sighting." That was the final report she needed.

"You and I used to have a much more similar idea of what 'glory' meant," Karmen said. She took a few experimental steps toward her old CO.

"That's close enough. Last chance, dear. I mean it. Leave now."

"Well, Aura… I hate to say it, but as usual, you're wrong." Karmen quickly drew her pulse pistol and fired wildly, almost blindly.

Armin fired off a shot from his covered position, smashing the left-hand Idolon squarely in the chest. Colin and Kozu followed up with shots of their own, but their aim wasn't nearly as precise. Plasma bolts flew past the Idolons, splashing the deck in front of them. Finally, the two heavy drones fell down.

Aura sprinted to the side, trying to make herself a bad target—but in the process, she lost her hold on Lee.

The Junior Agent recovered quickly, lashing out in an invisible attack. Aura went rigid, her wrists and ankles locked in place. She then went flying across the empty space of the hangar deck. Her body smashed across the bulkhead and dropped to the deck like a stone. She lay still, not moving at all.

Lee rubbed his throat and sent a telepathic message to

Karmen. *"I rifled through her mind while she was airborne. Gilgamesh is here. I know exactly where he is. We can put a stop to the whole plan if we catch him."*

"Let's go."

— — —

Gilgamesh hadn't said a word in an hour. He'd been taking copious notes on his handheld, mostly contact information for the movers and shakers that Sargon had recently recruited for the New Akkadian project. His own contact list was already prodigious, but they were mostly middlemen—not people he'd want to count on in a pinch. He was entering a new potential arms contact when Aura's voice pierced his consciousness.

"We've been boarded. Take the others, get on Shamhat, *and leave. I'll meet you on Valdos. Now!"* He sensed the urgency in her mental tone. That was enough for him. "Gentlemen! Grab your things and follow me. I've got to take you all home." He stood up and pocketed his handheld.

Sargon sniffed. "Calm down, Gil, we're not done yet—"

"Oh, yes we are. Ham, get your people together and follow me. We're leaving."

The other man slowly stood up. "What? I don't understand."

"When Aura yells at me by telepathy across the width of the *Emerald Queen*, I know better than to ask questions. We need to go, *now*! Sargon, contact us when we're on Valdos." He rushed to the door. "Pick up the pace, boys!"

Sargon's image shrugged as Ash's winked out. "I think you're being paranoid, but whatever. We'll speak again soon." The image vanished.

Ham zipped a carry bag closed and gathered his Valdan

henchmen. "What's really going on?"

"Just follow me, Ham." Gil led the group into the corridor and to the closest lift.

When the lift's doors opened, they were confronted by two complete strangers. One was a woman with striking curly hair and the other was a young man wearing tinted glasses, exuding the distinct aura of someone with TSS-trained telekinesis.

"Gilgamesh!" the man yelled, and suddenly Gil couldn't breathe. But he retained enough of his own training to blast a telepathic message to his compatriots. "*Agents! Agents in the briefing room!*"

It was unplanned, but enough. Next to him, Ham steeled himself for a telepathic duel. His henchmen were quick to respond; in moments, they broke the Agent's hold on Gilgamesh. They then forced the lift doors closed again, the metal squealing as it twisted out of its frame, sealing the two intruders inside.

"TSS!" Ham gasped. "Why didn't you say so?"

Because I was hoping it wasn't true, and I didn't want Sargon to freak out for nothing, Gil thought to himself. Aloud, he simply said, "Well, now you know."

He set off down the corridor to lead their escape. He knew the ship well, and there was a smaller lift not far down the corridor. That one proved to be unoccupied, and it swiftly brought them to Gil's private docking bay, separate from the main hangar.

Gil palmed open his ship's doors, and *Shamhat*'s beautiful avatar met them at the gangway.

"Lord, Gilgamesh. Are we leaving so soon?" she asked.

"Shamhat, prep for immediate launch. We're under attack. Take us to Valdos III!"

"At once, my lord!"

Almost before the last man's feet had stepped on the gangway, the ship powered to life while the exterior hangar door began to roll open. A glimmer at the edge of Gil's awareness signaled him. *They're out of the lift. They're coming this way!*

"Shamhat, take us out!"

"Yes, my lord." The yacht lifted above the deck and retracted its landing gear, backing away from the bulk of the giant ore carrier. The Lynaedan AI expertly engaged the navigation system and pion drive, putting space between the ships. In seconds, the viewscreen on the flight deck showed Gil the blue-green streamers of subspace.

"Well done, my girl," Gil breathed. "I owe you a serious round of redecorating when we get back."

Shamhat appeared in her flight attendant costume. "Nothing from Valdos III, I hope," the AI teased. "That planet positively invented the concept of drab."

37

ESCAPE

LEE AND KARMEN slid to a halt at the private hangar bay with a
sinking feeling. The bay was empty. They were too late.

"Now what?" Karmen asked.

Lee sent out his awareness in every direction and quickly
learned they'd stirred up a wasp nest of epic proportions. "Now
we get back to the crew. The drones are on the move, and it
sounds like they're royally pissed at what I did to their captain."

Karmen tapped her comm, evidently terrified that she'd
lost it. It merely had lost the connection with the channel used
on the TSS shuttle, which Armin had set up to be a general
relay station. Lee spun her toward the small lift and said, "Trust
me. We need to go."

"But… Aura is still down there!"

Lee plucked out the comm from his own ear and plugged
it into hers. Her eyes widened as she realized the depths of their
problem.

The radio chatter was off the charts. Reinforcements were

coming from every area of the ship; most were battle-ready Lynaedan drones. "We'll come after her another time. We're out of our league here." *Coming here was never the plan. We need real backup!*

"Fok it. Retreat. Retreat!" Karmen agreed.

"My thoughts exactly. Here, we can get back to the hangar deck this way."

The small lift dropped them at the port side edge of the hangar. From this point of view, the ship seemed nearly empty, except for the knot of activity blocking the middle bay door. A platoon of bipedal drones of the heavy and other cargo-carrying varieties all converged on the cargo modules protecting their three vessels.

Karmen tapped her comm. "Armin, pull everyone back inside the shuttles! We're leaving as soon as Lee and I get aboard."

"Acknowledged, but how will you—?"

"Never mind about us. Just get it done, Officer."

"Yes, ma'am!"

"I always figured you had the heart of a proper commanding officer," Lee snarked as they wound their way through the maze of auxiliary ships, maintenance bays, and cargo modules.

"Some things just never leave you," she said. "And I hate to say it... Bomax! I'd thought I was done with this shite! I wanted to be bored and old and surrounded by my children and grandchildren. I wanted to rely on my husband for everything."

"You *are* surrounded by your kids and husband. You remember what happened, with everyone crashing our mission? And turns out, they have a warrior's spirit just like you. Face it, Karmen, you can retire from the TSS, but you will never leave. The sooner you accept that, the happier you'll be."

The deck vibrated as another wave of heavy Idolons pounded forward.

Karmen spied movement at the nearest edge of the defensive formation. She tapped Lee and made sure he saw the same thing: a trio of the heavy bipeds were moving forward, working to cut off the family's escape. That was their target.

"Get off of my lawn!" she screamed and made a dash for an open space between two cargo modules.

Lee followed her closely, now used to using telekinetic bursts as a way to shove the heavy machines out of their path.

Karmen held her pulse pistol in both hands, stopping here and there to squeeze off shots at the nearest constructs. She missed more than she hit, but the strategy was successful for confusion if not destruction. Midway in her pass down the narrow canyon between the modules, she stood her ground and began firing indiscriminately, aiming for the spaces between the drones' shoulder blades.

When the drones halted their advance, Lee swept them off their feet. The two scurried past the struggling drones and swung around the edge of the furthest cargo container.

All the Sleys and Armin were breaking their formation and dragging the last of their equipment into their respective shuttles. Kozu stood in the airlock of the auxiliary while Armin dove for the TSS shuttle.

Lee sent out a telepathic message to the group. *"Everybody launch as soon as you're on board. We're leaving!"*

—   —   —

Karmen watched as Lee raced to join Armin. Her lungs were on fire by the time she reached her son, waiting at their little shuttle's hatch. "Buckle in, this will be a bad take off," she wheezed.

"Yeah… How, exactly, are we supposed to get away without getting blown to bits?" he asked as he sealed the hatch.

"This is what we in the military like to call an 'evolving strategy'," she said, patting his arm. "Come on."

They raced to the flight deck. Kozu slid into the gunner station and Karmen powered up the nav controls.

On the viewscreen, the hangar bay swung and twirled as Karmen pointed the tiny ship toward the force field. She accelerated them toward the opening to space.

Moments later, the comparative bulk of *Percival* joined her as Colin reversed out of the hangar, then spun the nose to match her bearing. The TSS shuttle brought up the rear.

The three ships sped out into open space. Karmen braced for a barrage of weapons fire from the *Emerald Queen*, but none came. Instead, the *Emerald Queen*'s bulk spun slowly on its long axis and activated its pion drive, flinging itself into the depth of the solar system away from Tavden High Port.

They won't be able to go far, Karmen assured herself. But her heart sank as she took in the data on her screen. The jump drive's power levels were increasing now, doubling every second.

She could only watch helplessly as the pirate ship distanced itself. Then, it disappeared in a blip of subspace. *Fok! How?*

"Should they be able to do that, after what we did?" Kozu asked.

"I know we disabled that jump drive," Karmen muttered. "Apparently, not as well as I'd thought."

"Did they fix it?"

"They must have. Those Lynaedans are quite clever, and they have a big crew." She groaned, shaking her head. "There's nothing we can do now. We found them once, and we can find them again." *Except, now they have fighter craft and who knows what else.*

She fought back the feeling that their mission had been an utter failure. But, then again, apprehending Mother Carnage wasn't their objective. The original point had been to gather information, and they'd gained plenty during their encounter.

She turned to her son. "So, you still want to join the Militia?"

"More than anything!"

Karmen smiled, heartened by his enthusiasm. "All right. I'll help you with your application whenever you're ready. They'll be lucky to have you."

38

NEXT STEPS

THE TSS BACKUP they'd requested arrived an hour after the *Emerald Queen* jumped away. The debrief was uncomfortable, but it could have been worse, considering that Karmen had brought her family in on an active TSS op. However, the Agents were understanding of the extenuating circumstances, and her retired status made it difficult for them to exert punishment. What were they going to do, kick her out of the TSS?

Karmen worried that more reprimands would fall on Lee as the mission lead, but he insisted that he'd be fine. She envied his ability to stay so measured about the situation. Maybe it was his Agent training, or perhaps it was the fact that he had a biomedical career he could fall back on if the TSS didn't work out. In either case, after seeing him in action, she hoped the TSS would agree that he'd make a fine Agent.

With no solid lead on the *Emerald Queen*'s next location, Lee and Armin took the TSS shuttle to the TSS outpost managing the sector to deliver a more thorough report and figure out next steps. They'd learned a great deal about Mother Carnage and her crew, even though they were no closer to stopping her rampage.

Karmen and her family spent another three days on Tavden High Port while the *Percival* underwent repairs. It needed substantial work done, but Colin couldn't afford much more than fixing the auxiliary shuttle well enough for it to be able to dock with the gunship again. The financial limitations were surprising, given his highborn status, but Karmen didn't want to press the issue, considering that it was her actions that had led to the ship's current state. However, she would insist on a proper interrogation of Colin in the future, should Kaia continue their correspondence.

"I really do appreciate you putting yourself in harm's way for us," Karmen told Colin as they prepared to leave. "I'm sorry again about your ship."

"Ships can be fixed. It's people we can't replace. I'd never be able to live with it if something had happened to you and I could have helped prevent it."

Questionable finances aside, she couldn't help liking the guy. "As long as you keep treating Kaia that way, we won't have any problems."

He smiled. "Absolutely. And I've got a course all mapped out to get you home. We can leave first thing in the morning."

Karmen let out a long breath. "It's about time. I'm ready to be done with this place." *But is home going to be the same once we return?*

She found Daveed to give him the news.

"Home," he said, eyeing her. "How do you feel about that?"

Bomax, this man sees right through me! The impulses to forge headlong into danger and the desire to return to the comfort of home and her family warred within her. She had come this far, yet she'd given up these kinds of bold adventures decades ago. Her family was counting on her to be their mom. She was only here now because of circumstances that were closer to conscription than reenlistment. Embarking on an extended interstellar manhunt hadn't been a choice—she'd merely been swept up in the madness. She'd been retired, and happily so.

But now, she did have a choice. Time hadn't dampened her desire to serve and fight for justice, yet that only obligated her to go so far. Where the assignment would lead from now went above the common call for duty; it was the sort of danger that one must volunteer to pursue. And standing at those crossroads, she was shocked that home wasn't the standout winner.

If it was anyone else, I could walk away. I'd go back home and never think about any of this again. But it's Aura. She met Daveed's probing gaze. "I need to find her."

He hung his head for a moment, then met her eyes again. "I will follow you anywhere."

"I can't ask you to do that. To put our kids through that. What about the University?"

"I'm due a sabbatical."

Karmen rubbed her eyes. "We shouldn't make any decisions right now. And, besides, this really isn't up to us. If the TSS tells me to leave it alone, I have to listen."

Daveed took her hands in his. "I love you, Karmen. Wherever this leads, we'll face it together."

—   —   —

Lee stood at attention before the Lead Agent and realized he'd never really expected to come to this point. Until now, graduation had been a concept—a nebulous event somewhere in the future. Now, it was a reality; he could feel himself sweating in discomfort.

Saera Alexri sat behind her desk and steepled her fingers. "Lee Tuyin, I have the paperwork here to clear you for graduation. I just need to sign it, and then you'll take the Course Rank test and be declared a full Agent, with all the privileges and responsibilities thereof."

"Yes, ma'am."

"But first, I wanted to have a conversation about your path at the TSS."

Oh stars, here it comes. Lee shifted on his feet. "Yes, ma'am."

"Will you *please* sit down? This isn't that kind of talk. Not entirely, anyway." He sat in a chair across from her, and she continued, "I confess, I'm a little conflicted about your actions during your internship. Involving civilians in a TSS investigation is bad enough, but allowing the target to escape doesn't make for a favorable report."

"With respect, ma'am, we didn't *involve* Officer Sley's family. They appeared uninvited and unannounced. We simply had no way to get them to safety before the incident occurred."

"Agreed. You did what you could with the time constraints you had. But that's only the first issue. The second is the matter of tracking Aura Thand's starship. We haven't been able to trace the vessel's movements, and our best minds can't figure out why."

"I have an idea about that. A significant part of her crew are Lynaedans. I'd bet they have developed some kind of spoofing mechanism that renders SiNavTech logs useless. If it hadn't been for the nuclear mining charges on board her ship and the Curium particles they emit, we wouldn't have managed it at all."

"That's my thinking, as well. Unfortunately, we have no relationship with Lynaeda that would enable us to acquire the means to effectively pursue these renegades. We could form a team to figure out a solution, but they'd be starting from scratch, which isn't ideal. At any rate, you remain the only Agent of any rank who has personal experience with them. I know it's a significant departure from your medical path, but I don't see a reason you shouldn't stay with this case to its resolution."

Lee nodded. "Yes, ma'am. I would like to see it through."

"Good." Saera checked a note on her touch-surface desktop. "Officer Godri expressed that he would love to keep your team in place, and I have a letter from his CO on Greengard authorizing his reassignment to your command."

"I would be thrilled to have him. Which leaves the matter of Officer Sley."

"So it does." The Agent's brows knitted. "I think she's a problem. But she's also a potential resource, so I'm conflicted about involving her again. What's your read on her situation?"

"I agree that her family's refusal to be parted from her remains an issue. I'm not sure what to recommend for that. I can't very well order them all to stay home, since they're not within the chain of command. Her personal knowledge of the target makes her the best source of intelligence we have on Mother Carnage's habits. With that in mind, I'd want Karmen on my team for this assignment."

"Ah. *Karmen.*"

"You know what I mean, ma'am."

Saera leaned back in her seat. "You aren't the first Agent to befriend a subordinate. So, here's what I can allow. Let the Sleys tag along, if that will keep Karmen focused, but keep them *away* from this mission. If you need backup, call for it well ahead of time. No more acts of desperation. I can forgive one such occurrence but not two. Am I clear?"

I did call when our shuttle crashed, and my proctor told me to buckle up and deal with it. "Crystal clear, ma'am."

"Good." She drew her fingertip across the tablet's screen and pressed her palm against the glass for a biometric signature. "Congratulations, Agent Tuyin. Go bring that rogue Agent back here."

—   —   —

The eventual trip back to Greengard carried the air of a road trip. Kaia spent the first hour working on a business-related idea of hers with her dad while her mom taught the other kids the intricacies of a card game called Fastara. Empty staterooms eventually beckoned, and everyone in her family took the opportunity to catch up on lost sleep. Only Colin showed a level of endurance Kaia hadn't imagined possible, staying on duty for the entire voyage.

After returning from a short nap, Kaia watched her friend closely from the comm station as he managed the vessel. She couldn't get over how well he'd handled himself during their recent trials. It made sense that he'd know how to pilot a ship; he was part of a family that had made its fortune in the shipping trade. But staying composed while getting shot at was a whole other kind of admirable. Even while she adored their conversations, she'd never gotten past the image of him as a playboy-in-training. A young man who'd had things done for him his whole life. Apparently not. *There's a real person in there. When I asked him for help, he came running. That's something special. That's a keeper.*

If she could keep him. She was certain he was besieged by more experienced women who were richer and prettier than herself. That was a problem for another day. There was no way of getting around the reality that they lived in two very different worlds. Still... there was a chance. And if not, well, there was always GravX.

"Ready to be back home?" Colin asked her as the *Percival* pulled into the Greengard spaceport.

"In some ways. Others, not at all," she replied.

"There's a whole big galaxy out there. Lots to explore."

"Yeah, I'm learning that."

The rest of Kaia's family emerged from their cabins, stretching and yawning.

"Ah, home at last!" her father said with a grin, his travel bag in tow. "Wasn't sure we'd make it."

"I told you I'd get you all there and back in one piece," Colin said.

"And you did, thank you."

Karmen came up behind Daveed and placed her arm on his back. "Come on, let's unload and make sure we have everything. She maneuvered him toward the airlock, flashing a small smile to Kaia.

Kaia stood awkwardly by the comm station while her family filed off the ship. Once she was alone on the flight deck with Colin, she wasn't sure what to say.

"You're a pretty good pilot," she finally blurted out.

"Yep. I have a license and everything."

"Yeah, the family business and all..."

"I really didn't have a choice in the matter. My great-grandfather was very specific in his belief that any Covrani who's planning on taking on any part of the business needed to know every aspect of its operation from the ground up. Some of his heirs balked at that. He cut them off."

"He did *what*?"

"Oh, yes. They each got a commercial starship and some spending cash, and that was it. They could go wherever they wanted, but he forbade them from running anything connected with the Covrani name. So, now we all learn to pilot, navigate, troubleshoot onboard systems, that sort of thing. My gunnery skills were never good, but at least I know how to shoot. It's the paperwork that messes me up. But we have accountants and brokers for that, so…" He shrugged. "To tell you the truth, I like how it feels being on a ship. I could be a good pilot. I could be in charge of a shuttle or starship. I know how to do that."

"What about our GravX team?" she asked.

Colin gave her side-eye. "It was a fun idea to chat about, I wouldn't know how to actually get started."

"I do. I've been working on it. A business plan, you know. I even checked it with my dad. I have it all figured out."

"Right. I open up my soul to you, and you're making fun of me." He sighed.

"No way! Here, I'll show you." She pulled out her handheld, sorted through files, and threw a data packet to his device.

He skimmed through the images. "I don't understand any of this. But it looks as professional as anything I've seen in the office. Do you mind if I show it to someone who really knows what they're doing?"

"Not at all. Just don't you dare take my name off it. That would be problematic."

His frown warped into a shy smile. "Problematic, how?"

"Like, my father has a copy, and my mother is a TSS Militia

officer, and we have a stash of automatic rifles in our basement," she said. "It'd be a bad look if you never made it back to Gallos after visiting the Sley house."

Colin's eyes grew huge as he tried to process the news and the insinuation. "You guys are ruthless," he breathed.

"That's a joke, by the way," she said, suddenly worried about clarity and liability.

He laughed. "I figured. But I'm okay with ruthless. I understand it—and that's what you need in business." He hesitated, then reached out to take her hand. "I guess you've figured out that I really like you."

A warm tingle ran through her as her fingers curled around his. "I was getting that impression. I think I really like you, too. I mean, I called you in hysterics looking for a quick pep talk about my mom being in trouble, and you showed up the next day with a gunship. We brought a trailer full of rifles and emergency gear, and you didn't even blink." Her cheeks flushed. "Whatever else is going on, you'll always be my hero for that."

"Well, then you should know that back home, I'm kind of a nobody. I do everything wrong. I'm the stupid wayward child nobody can leave unsupervised for ten minutes."

"If you make off with heavy equipment on the regular, they might have a point," she said. "But you might also be brilliant, and kind, and loyal. That's not nothing. Every time I have a long talk with you, I feel... I don't know... *elevated.*"

Her handheld beeped and she looked down to see that Elian had sent her a message. >>Mom thinks you two are 'up to something'. Her words not mine. Come down!<<

And just like that, the moment was over. "I'm being summoned. Walk me back to the terminal?"

"I'd like nothing more. Can you wait a sec while I make a

call? I assume your mom will want her gear back. Might as well arrange shipping for it now."

"Absolutely."

After the logistics were arranged, they met the rest of the Sley clan inside the terminal. Daveed and Karmen were gracious and proper, while Elian, Kozu, and Seandra were welcoming and convivial. Kaia marveled at how quickly they'd developed a real connection. Maybe danger did that to you.

She had a bit more insight into her mother's past life now. Settling down to get married and have kids had undoubtedly been a giant change for her. Maybe she couldn't just push out an old life and overwrite it with another completely different one. Maybe nobody did.

Eventually, the goodbyes concluded. The parents and siblings left to arrange a ride back to the house, but Kaia decided to stay a bit longer.

"Seriously, thank you for coming to help save the day. I'm sorry Percy got beat up in the process," she told Colin.

"It's okay. As I said earlier, he's going to the shop for repairs, anyway. And I wanted to see you. I mean *actually* see you, in real life." He paused, a spark lighting up his eyes. "Hey, do you want to come back with me? Have you ever seen a real shipyard? It's fascinating work. So many people. So much stuff going on!"

Whoa, slow down, partner. "That sounds a little too industrial for me. Don't you have a yacht or something you could invite me to instead?" she joked. *Not that my parents would ever agree to let me go.*

He chuckled. "No, Covrani don't buy those kinds of entertaining yachts. It's a family tradition, or anti-tradition, I guess. My mother always says yachts are for men with big wallets who want bigger equipment. A swimming pool in space sounds cool, but it gets boring after a few hours."

She tried not to let the relief she felt appear on her face. Kaia hadn't thought about what she'd do if he'd said yes. "Oh well."

"But I'm working on getting you invited to the family estate on Gallos. My mother wants to meet you; she was very clear on that. Do you like camping? We have a private nature preserve that's so big it would take you three days to walk across it. You'd never see a soul."

"No yacht, but a private nature preserve? That's still pretty impressive."

To his credit, Colin shifted gears easily. "But you're not into camping…" he surmised.

"I'm into GravX, and so are you. Maybe we should concentrate on that for a while. Invite me to a game and we'll see what happens."

"I can agree to those terms." He smiled. "Let me get Percy back home and smooth everything over, and then we'll figure it out. Will you be all right?"

"Of course. I'm home. But it's not going to be the same. We were comfortable and settled before, but I know my mom. She won't be able to relax knowing that Mother Carnage is still out there."

"If I can help in any way, I want to."

"I keep thinking how much easier things would be if we had our own ship and could go wherever whenever we wanted. But that's silly because ships are expensive, and… it's just not practical."

Colin got a devious gleam in his eyes. "Don't rule anything out."

"Heh, right."

He admired her for a long moment. "You know, you really

are impressive, Kaia Sley." Abruptly, he gave her a quick peck on the lips. "I'll see you again soon, I hope."

Colin slowly pulled away from her and then headed down the concourse back to his ship.

When he turned back to wave, she smiled and returned the gesture, still stunned. *What am I getting myself into with this guy?*

—   —   —

Callum held in a tired yawn after his shift as he joined a long line of visitors to the infirmary to let Captain Aura know that she was valued and missed. Whatever the intruders had done to her, it had been impressive. Even with the medical nanites running through her veins, Mother Carnage was one giant bruise. She couldn't do more than wave at her guests as they offered what comfort they could.

Callum wished Aura a quick recovery and then went to linger at Sacha's bedside. The ops officer was still immobilized, still asleep, still wired to the brain complex.

Commander Mench caught up with Callum as he stared at her. "Mr. Nissin, follow me."

Callum found the route all too familiar. They came to a halt in a room he knew very well. "What are we doing at my quarters, sir?"

"Simple. You are going to visit your hospitalized girlfriend. I will stay here to make sure you return without incident."

"But… I just did that. And I think 'girlfriend' might be overstating it a bit."

"Do you? I don't agree. She asked me to set up this meeting for you two inside the Queen's neural network. That's not a thing she would do lightly. Choose a place to rest. A bed would be safest."

Callum palmed open the door and they stepped inside. He opted for a comfy chair he'd bought from an outlet on a spaceport he could barely remember. Commander Mench opened an equipment case and extracted a pair of electrodes. He affixed them to Callum's temples. "Lynaedans share mental space. You knew that already. Now, you get to experience it for yourself. It's an immersive experience. It's easy to become lost in there if you're not used to it. I'll pull you out after ten minutes. No more, no less. Make sure you're secure—don't want your body to fall over while you're in there."

Callum reclined in the chair. "I'm good. Let's go."

"This may feel a little strange." The commander activated the device.

'Strange' didn't begin to describe it. One moment, Callum was lying in his favorite chair and the next he felt like his brain was being squeezed through a sieve, each piece of his personality breaking into pieces, and then each of the pieces breaking into a thousand more pieces, and then smashed back together.

When his mind cleared, he was sitting in a garden. A café. He sat at a table, surrounded by other tables, each one with a person or a couple, eating, drinking, talking in low voices. High above him lay a transparent dome, the likes of which he'd never imagined, and surrounding the café itself was a forest.

At the other side of the small, round table was Sacha. She grinned at him, her eyes half closed, her hands folded neatly.

"Two arms," he murmured.

She brought her hands up and flexed the fingers for him. They weren't her work arms, but they didn't look natural either. "Yes! As long as I'm in here, I can look any way I want, and it feels normal to have arms again."

"This is it? The neural net?"

"Not the all-encompassing one on Lynaeda, but this is the one we use on the *Emerald Queen*. What do you think?"

"It's a new experience for me. It feels completely real. How is that even possible?"

"We don't have much time, so full explanations will have to wait," she said. "Callum, I wanted to say something. I—"

"What's a Base?" he asked, interrupting her.

"What's a what?"

"'Even a Base like Callum here serves the Queen.' It's what you said to that Agent. What is a Base?"

"It's nothing."

"It's not *nothing.*"

"It's *embarrassing.* I was angry when I said it."

"Last chance, Sacha. I mean it."

She acquiesced with a sigh. "It means Basic. Which is a slang term we use to refer to un-modded Tarans. It's short for 'Being A Single Independent Consciousness'."

He leaned back, miffed at being the object of ridicule. "It's nice to know I matter that much to you."

"You *do* matter. I was being a jerk. But I didn't mean to be one to you."

"I'd like to believe that."

"You should believe it, because it's true," she urged. "You've gone and pulled my heart right out of my chest, Sensors. You don't need to prove a thing to me or anyone else."

Callum couldn't repress the grief he'd experienced at that Agent's directions. That had been real. He'd become insane with rage afterward. Whatever he felt for Sacha, it was obviously real, no matter how badly he reacted to her private Lynaedan jokes. "He messed with my head. Made me think you were dead. And when I came back to myself, I went a little crazy. I've never gotten that angry before. I had to do *something.*"

"I've been that angry. I understand. And it helped me make a decision."

"What did you decide?"

Sacha brought up a narrow box from her lap and placed it between them. She slid the box across the table to him. "I think you've earned these."

Callum had a sinking feeling in his gut. Pushing through it, he opened the box. He refused to recoil when he saw its contents.

A pair of ocular implants. But these looked different to him. The irises didn't glow, and the sclera was a dull white, shot with tiny veins. "You're giving me your eyes," he whispered. "I don't deserve this."

"Oh, yes you do. Those are my first implants. It was after getting them fitted that I realized the whole universe was open to me. I could see the entire spectrum of light. I could see *everything*." She reached across the table and took his hands. "I can see you."

"I can see you, too."

"Good. Listen, I'll be out of here in a couple of weeks. Lom ordered some gear for me."

"Yes, he told me that."

"Well, then. You have time to do some real deep thinking."

"About what?"

"On where to take me on our date. Make it interesting."

Callum returned to himself with a jolt, his whole body quaking with the aftereffects of the neural experience.

"I take it your chat went well?" the commander mused as he pulled the electrodes off Callum's skin.

He grinned like a fool in love. "She likes me. She *likes* me!"

"I told you. What did she say?"

"She agreed to a date. And she gave me her eyes."

"Really? You must have impressed her mightily. That's a very strange thing for a modern woman to do. It comes from an ancient fairy tale."

"With a happy ending, I hope?"

"Do any of those old stories really end well? Call it a happy beginning instead. In any case, your system has endured a shock. Stay here and rest. I'll have some food brought down from the galley. I'll see you at your duty station tomorrow morning. Good night."

"Good night." *I am so in over my head.*

— — —

Gil sat at the control console in *Shamhat*'s flight deck, looking for patterns in the streamers of subspace but seeing only chaos. How could all their plans go so wrong so quickly?

The more Gil considered what he knew, the more he came to an unpleasant realization: New Akkadia was getting away from them. The problem wasn't just that this had been a bad week—and it had been a *very* bad week. The problem, he was coming to understand, was *people*.

One person might be able to buck their genetics, to break free from education or training, to fan a spark of creativity, but most were nothing like that. They were panicky herd animals, easily startled and willing to crush their children and neighbors into a faceless, conformist mass. Even the best of them were selfish and stupid, preferring sure but small gains to the risk of even the smallest loss.

Why did he think New Akkadia would be any better than the galaxy they already lived in?

But they were here, and New Akkadia was slowly coming into being. The four Mesopotamians were unquestionably coming into a level of power they'd never have been able to realize without Sar's leadership and initiative, even if they'd somehow gotten through the TSS training program. They were collectively worth billions already. It would be so easy for him to have the others buy him out of his holdings and then retire to a tropical planet and forget about all of this. But he wouldn't; he was hooked. He was too far into the process to just let it all go.

The easy part was over. Sar had been right there, too. Now, they needed a way forward. The competition for economic power would only grow worse with time. The TSS might be late to the proverbial game, but they had caught on, and Aura was in their sights.

Aura. He felt like a creep for abandoning her the way he had, orders or not. Ham had been happy enough to comply with her instructions to leave on *Shamhat* once Gil had been able to convince him the emergency was real. But Gil would hear about this intrusion from Sar and probably Ash, too. To their minds, Aura was a liability. Gil couldn't quite convince himself they were wrong. As if having an experienced starship captain was a thing you could cast aside when she'd become inconvenient. He would never leave her, would never abandon her. But they probably had a solid point... He really should be recruiting new people. New captains with different skill sets. If the TSS was closing in, they needed people to fight.

Then there was Lom 'Crime is a Performance' Mench. What to do about that guy? In hindsight, it might have been a mistake to introduce him to Aura, but that pairing had made so much sense at the time. Aura had needed staff for the next phase of Sar's plan, and Mench was a known quantity. Yes, he had a weird sense of duty to his Queen—whatever that truly was... Gil knew it had to do with the *Emerald Queen*'s main computer, but the Lynaedans were so bomaxed opaque about everything.

The real problem with Lom was the fact that he'd come from somewhere. He had a past, he had friends, and his network reached much further into Lynaedan space than Gil could hope to duplicate. Lom had plans that didn't include New Akkadia—and possibly not Aura, either. Worse, he had backers who didn't care what Gil had accomplished. Gil still had a hold over Aura, but he had nothing over Lom. That was the worst problem Gil needed to solve. Lom could sell Gil out on a whim. How did one deal with a threat like that?

Kill him first, said a small voice in Gil's head. No! Well, not yet. The big Lynaedan was getting out of his place, and like it or not, Gil needed him for a while longer. But one day…

Like all things involved in New Akkadia's formation, Lom was growing past the original limits of their association. So was Aura, for that matter. And that was the real essence of what Gil was witnessing every day. Big personalities were growing past the plan's contours; now, they were breaking out of their shells, evolving way past the structure of the network they had collectively created.

New Akkadia was going to have some growing pains going forward, Gil could see that clearly now. And he would have to distance himself from Sar's ego to help manage that growth. Because New Akkadia would need more than pirates and billionaire tycoons to defend itself from the TSS.

New Akkadia would need a king named Gilgamesh.

THE STORY CONTINUES IN
CARNAGE AND COURAGE...

Books in the Series:
Book 1: Grand Theft Planet
Book 2: Carnage and Courage
Book 3: Homeworld for a Queen

CADICLE UNIVERSE: ADDITIONAL READING

Cadicle Space Opera Series by A.K. DuBoff
Book 1: Rumors of War (Vol. 1-3)
Book 2: Web of Truth (Vol. 4)
Book 3: Crossroads of Fate (Vol. 5)
Book 4: Path of Justice (Vol. 6)
Book 5: Scions of Change (Vol. 7)

Mindspace Series by A.K. DuBoff
Book 1: Infiltration
Book 2: Conspiracy
Book 3: Offensive
Book 4: Endgame

Verity Chronicles by T.S. Valmond & A.K. DuBoff
Book 1: Exile
Book 2: Divided Loyalties
Book 3: On the Run

Shadowed Space Series by Lucinda Pebre & A.K. DuBoff
Book 1: Shadow Behind the Stars
Book 2: Shadow Rising
Book 3: Shadow Beyond the Reach

In Darkness Dwells by James Fox & A.K. DuBoff

AUTHORS' NOTES

From Jon Frater:

Leo Tolstoy opened Anna Karenina by writing that every happy family was the same, but every unhappy family was unique in its unhappiness. Renegade Imperium is the story of two families, one happy, and one unhappy. I leave it up to the reader to figure out which is which.

The original idea for this tale was meant to be a riff on Mother Courage and her Children by Berthold Brecht. The funny thing about that play is that Brecht hated it: his audience always came away feeling bad for the main character even though she was a shameless arms merchant, selling weapons and supplies to both sides in a conflict to survive. I wondered if I could do better and decided to find out. So I thought about how every conflict ultimately starts: with two opposing and irreconcilable points of view, and went from there.

I want to thank Lara, Chuck, Robby, and Vincent as well as Chris and Craig who all gave extremely useful feedback on early versions of this story. I especially want to thank the members of the Long Island Roller Rebels for allowing me to pick their brains while I was figuring out the rules and action sequences for the GravX sports teams.

And of course I need to thank you for reading this series and this note. Without you, I'm just another guy putting words on a page. But if you're reading this, then I'm a writer! (Woo!) Big thanks!

An additional note from A.K. DuBoff:

It's great to be back in Cadicle Universe! No matter how many books I write, this will always be one of my happy places. It's an honor to not only have readers who want to experience this world, but also to have other writers want to use it as their playground.

Jon and I have known each other as casual indie author acquaintances for years, and I'm so glad we finally had the chance to work together! He's been a joy to work with throughout this entire process, bringing excellent creative ideas, asking great questions, and bringing new characters and cultures to life within this universe I love so much. I've been especially excited to further explore the Lynaedans and life in the fringe worlds away from politics on Tararia.

Many thanks to our amazing beta reader team for offering valuable feedback to elevate this story! John, Leo, David B, Eric, Kurt, David F, Gil, and Chris—you are awesome, and I so appreciate your candid feedback and ongoing support of my writing. My greatest appreciation also to Steve and Bryan for their excellent proofing eyes!

My love and thanks to Nick and my parents for their encouragement and cheerleading. I could not ask for a better family!

The rest of this series is going to be a wild ride, and I hope you'll join us on the journey.

Until next time, happy reading :-)!

ABOUT THE AUTHORS

Jon Frater

Jon Frater is an academic library director by day, a sci-fi writer by night, and an old school gamer with thirty plus years of experience, reviewing, writing, designing, and playing video games and tabletop RPGs, as well as fiction, non-fiction, articles, and blogs. He's worked as a game writer, reviewer, and developer, cranked out countless game and book reviews, and tried his hand at writing for the screen and audio. He has published short works for the Future Chronicles and Tales From the Canyon of the Damned series, and published longer works in the Legends of Legacy Fleet series by way of Desperate Measures Press. His Battle Ring Earth and Crisis of Command military fiction series are published by Aethon Books. Renegade Imperium represents his first foray into the A.K. DuBoff's Cadicle Universe.

jonfraterbooks.com

A.K. DuBoff

A.K. (Amy) DuBoff has always loved science fiction in all its forms—books, movies, shows, and games. If it involves outer space, even better! She is a Nebula Award finalist and USA Today bestselling author most known for the Starship of the Ancients series and her Cadicle Universe, but she's also written a variety of sci-fi and fantasy. Amy can frequently be found traveling the world, and when she's not writing, she enjoys wine tasting, binge-watching TV series, and playing epic strategy board games.

www.akduboff.com

Made in United States
Troutdale, OR
08/12/2025

33581821R00245